"After you're in the house, I'm sure there'll be additional shopping," **Melissa advised.**

"For what?" Edmond asked.

"Curtains, for one thing. As I recall, the blinds in that house provide privacy but they aren't decorative."

"Oh, right." While he'd considered the cost of child care, he hadn't factored in everything else. "And a cleaning service, too. Any recommendations?"

"We clean our own house, so I'm not sure. Just ask at work. You'll be inundated with suggestions." She was grinning widely.

"What's so funny?"

"You're usually on top of every situation. It's refreshing to see you out of your element."

"Refreshing?" That wasn't the word Edmond would have chosen. "Awkward, maybe. Embarrassing."

"No, it's cute." She'd never called him that before. "Human."

"As opposed to my usual robotic self?" he asked.

"In a sense," she teased. "It's fun to watch the ice melt."

The Unexpected Baby Situation

USA TODAY BESTSELLING AUTHOR

JACQUELINE DIAMOND
&
MELISSA SENATE

**Previously published as *The Surprise Triplets*
and *The Baby Switch!***

HARLEQUIN

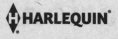

Recycling programs for this product may not exist in your area.

ISBN-13: 978-1-335-17999-9

The Unexpected Baby Situation
Copyright © 2020 by Harlequin Books S.A.

The Surprise Triplets
First published in 2014. This edition published in 2020.
Copyright © 2014 by Jackie Hyman

The Baby Switch!
First published in 2018. This edition published in 2020.
Copyright © 2018 by Melissa Senate

This edition published by arrangement with Harlequin Books S.A.

For questions and comments about the quality of this book, please contact us at CustomerService@Harlequin.com.

Harlequin Enterprises ULC
22 Adelaide St. West, 40th Floor
Toronto, Ontario M5H 4E3, Canada
www.Harlequin.com

Printed in U.S.A.

CONTENTS

Medical themes play a prominent role in many of **Jacqueline Diamond**'s one hundred published novels, including her Safe Harbor Medical miniseries for Harlequin. A former Associated Press reporter and TV columnist, Jackie lives in Orange County, California, where she's active in Romance Writers of America. You can sign up for her free newsletter at jacquelinediamond.com and say hello to Jackie on her Facebook page, Jacqueline Diamond Author. On Twitter, she's @jacquediamond.

Books by Jacqueline Diamond

Harlequin American Romance

Safe Harbor Medical

Officer Daddy
Falling for the Nanny
The Surgeon's Surprise Twins
The Detective's Accidental Baby
The Baby Dilemma
The M.D.'s Secret Daughter
The Baby Jackpot
His Baby Dream
The Surprise Holiday Dad
A Baby for the Doctor
The Surprise Triplets
The Baby Bonanza
The Doctor's Accidental Family

Visit the Author Profile page at Harlequin.com for more titles.

The Surprise Triplets

JACQUELINE DIAMOND

For Kevin and Renée Brown,
two very special friends.

Chapter 1

The man and woman sitting in front of Melissa Everhart's desk held hands as if about to jump off a cliff together. In a sense, that *was* what they were doing.

Be careful what you wish for, she wanted to caution them. But in her role as Safe Harbor Medical Center's *in vitro* fertilization and egg donor coordinator, she was already providing them with full information. Any further warning would be an unprofessional insertion of her personal concerns.

"Most people who hire a surrogate and can't provide their own eggs prefer to use a separate egg donor," she was explaining.

"Why bring in a third party?" The woman, Bev Landry, an accountant in her early forties, projected a professional image in her tailored gray suit with a rose-colored silk blouse. Only the clenched hands in her lap betrayed her nervousness as she and her husband embarked on an expensive and by-no-means-guaranteed quest to have a child via surrogacy. An ovarian cancer survivor, she had tried to adopt without success.

Bev longed for a baby with all her heart. Melissa understood that yearning because she'd shared it.

"I'm not a lawyer, but I can tell you that while surrogates—or gestational carriers, as they're termed—sign away their rights to the baby, it's still safer legally and emotionally if there's no genetic link," Melissa informed her.

"That brings up the issue of legalities…" Bev's husband, Mick, a rough-hewn building contractor, leaned forward aggressively. It was, Melissa judged, merely his way of taking control of a scary situation. "What protection do we have when we commission—if that's the right word—a child?"

"We're fortunate that California leads the world in safeguarding your rights," she said. "I have several documents here on the subject, including new laws and court decisions favoring the designated parents."

Mick glanced at the documents she handed him, then set them aside for later. "Thanks. And I'll be the biological father, after all."

"That's right. Now let's talk about how you would select your egg donor and your surrogate." Although the hospital's brochures covered all aspects of its fertility program, the information could be overwhelming. It was Melissa's job to steer clients through the process.

If she deemed it advisable, she could also refer them to the hospital's psychologist. And, starting today, she could offer them a free session with the hospital's new consulting family attorney. Who just happened to be her ex-husband.

Her throat tightened. A year ago, without explanation, her ex-husband Edmond had given up a high-paying position in Los Angeles to join a tiny law firm here in Safe Harbor. Then, a month or so ago, he'd applied for a consulting job at the hospital. Despite her reservations, when the administrator had asked Melissa whether bringing Edmond on board in a part-time position would pose problems for her, she'd said no.

His new job meant they might occasionally have to work together, but since their divorce three years ago, they'd remained on civil terms. She respected Edmond's abilities and had always found him easy to confer with.

Except on one issue. Edmond had vehemently opposed having children. Initially, Melissa hadn't wanted them, either, but she'd changed her mind during their five-year marriage. As her thirtieth birthday approached, her longing for little ones to love had intensified to the point that she could no longer ignore it.

Hesitantly, she'd brought up with her husband the possibility of having kids. Edmond hadn't taken it well, and to her shock, he'd then gone out and had a vasectomy without consulting her. Stunned by this high-handed maneuver and devastated that he thought so little of her needs, Melissa had left him.

The man she'd believed was her true love had turned out to be fatally flawed. Unfortunately, her post-divorce attempts at finding another Mr. Right had led nowhere.

Now she was going it alone, she reflected as her hand drifted to her abdomen, where it felt as if she had a watermelon strapped to her midsection. No telling how Edmond would react when he saw her condition. But then, he'd made his choice, and she'd made hers.

She trained her attention on the computer screen and angled it toward the Landrys. "We provide photographs and profiles of our surrogates, as we do with egg donors in a separate registry. You'll have your own code to sign onto our secure website from home...." As Melissa spoke, she heard a flurry of noises outside the closed door. Hers was one of four offices opening off the fertility support program's reception area on the hospital's ground floor. Judging by the scuff of footsteps and the warm tones of her colleagues, she guessed that the hospital administrator was introducing the new consultant.

Then a deep, familiar voice rumbled through her. Melissa's skin prickled. *Edmond.* If only she wasn't still so sensitized to his nearness. Maybe agreeing for him to join the staff had been a mistake. Too late to change her mind now.

"Oh, my goodness!" Bev tugged an ultrasound photo from beneath a few papers on the desk. "Is that twins? No, there's a third one. Triplets! Incredible."

Her husband craned his neck to study the image. "Somebody hit the jackpot."

Melissa's cheeks heated. "I shouldn't have left that in view."

"I'm sorry." Bev set down the image. "I didn't mean to invade anyone's privacy. That woman is so lucky!"

Is she? "Actually, it's me."

Bev's mouth flew open. "Seriously? I noticed you were pregnant but I had no idea it was triplets. How far along are you?"

"Four months down, five to go." According to Melissa's obstetrician, multiple births usually resulted in early deliveries, but she was trying to think positively.

"Your husband must be excited," Mick said.

Melissa tilted her head in a half nod and hoped he wouldn't notice her failure to respond further. "Do you have questions about what we've discussed so far?"

"Once we've chosen the surrogate, how many fertilized eggs would be implanted?" Mick said. "I mean, assuming more than one is usable."

"That can be a difficult decision," she told him. "Multiple pregnancies are risky. On the other hand, only implanting one embryo lowers the odds of success. In the U.K. and Australia, doctors are limited by law to transferring a maximum of two embryos."

He scowled. "Are there any restrictions in California?"

"No." Trying to ignore the increasingly loud chatter from the outer office, she said, "However, our doctors limit themselves to implanting a maximum of three embryos, for medical and ethical reasons."

"But the embryos won't all attach, right?" Bev asked.

"Not usually." She certainly hadn't expected them to. "Twins or singletons are much more common than triplets."

From the outer office came the squeal of the high-spirited receptionist, Caroline Carter. "I had no idea you were Melissa's ex-husband!"

Melissa winced.

Edmond replied in a low tone, something about "good terms." All the same, Melissa's face was flaming. "Sorry for the disturbance," she said to the Landrys.

"No need to apologize," said Mick. "We're the ones

who changed our appointment at the last minute." They'd been scheduled to meet with her in the afternoon.

"It didn't occur to me that this might overlap. We have a new legal consultant at the hospital." At a tap on the door, Melissa started to rise. When her abdominal muscles protested, she put a hand on the desktop for support.

"Please don't exert yourself. I'll get it." Uncoiling from his chair, Mick crossed the floor. Since he was closer, she yielded without protest.

Melissa braced for this encounter with Edmond. They'd run into each other occasionally since he'd arrived in town and they'd exchanged polite how-are-yous. He'd represented one of her housemates in a divorce, and another, briefly, on a custody issue. She'd assured her friends that he was an excellent attorney, which was true. But this was her home territory.

Just say hello and it'll be over. For now. And if she remained seated, she might be able to save her startling news until they were alone.

Mick opened the door. "Don't mind me. I'm the butler," he joked to the imposing administrator, Dr. Mark Rayburn, a large man with black hair and power eyebrows.

"Pardon the interruption," Mark said. "We have a new attorney on staff and today's his first chance to meet everybody. We'll just be a sec."

"No problem." Extending his hand, Mick introduced himself and his wife.

The slim, strong man Melissa had once loved moved past Mark, and cool brown eyes met hers from behind steel-framed glasses. It was lucky that her clients were comfortable chatting with the newcomers, because her voice got stuck in her throat.

As always, her ex-husband was impeccably groomed—even in July, he wore a jacket and tie. Being in the same room made her keenly aware of his light, spicy scent and the breadth of his chest.

And it also made her aware of how much she missed curling against him at night, missed talking over the day's events and missed his logical insights. Once, she could have tracked his reactions to people and events as easily as her own. It was disorienting, to have no idea what he was thinking right now.

What was wrong with her? It must be the emotional effect of maternal hormones. She'd long ago resolved any lingering sense that she belonged with this man.

"Good to see you, Melissa." He sounded slightly hoarse.

"You, too," she managed. She ought to rise, but if she did...

At Mark's subtle prompting, Edmond greeted the Landrys and handed them his business card. "If you have any legal questions, I'd be happy to schedule a free consultation here at the hospital. I have office hours Monday mornings and Thursday afternoons."

"Maybe later," Mick said. "We're still in the early stages."

The administrator indicated they should move on. Just when Melissa figured the encounter was over, Edmond swung toward her. "Okay if I stop by in a few minutes? There are a few matters we should discuss."

"Certainly." All very professional, although everybody in the office—plus the cheerily nosy receptionist lingering outside the door—must be aware of the undercurrents.

When he held out his hand, there was no avoiding it. Melissa stood up, big belly and all.

Edmond's jaw dropped and his body went rigid. His double take might almost have been comical, had she not felt his shock so keenly. Melissa had prepared herself for his disapproval or anger, or perhaps indifference. To her surprise, she caught a glint of pain.

His gaze went to her left hand, to her ringless third finger. But he could hardly draw conclusions from that. Pregnant women often removed their wedding rings to accommodate puffiness.

He cleared his throat. "I'll talk to you later, then. Nice to meet you, Mr. and Mrs. Landry."

As Mark ushered Edmond out, he regarded Melissa with concern. He didn't miss much, she reflected, and she smiled in an attempt to reassure him.

With a nod, the big man closed the door. She hadn't fooled him. She wasn't fooling anybody these days, except maybe herself. *Oh, quit overthinking this.*

The Landrys resumed their seats and Melissa did the same. Returning to their discussion, she said, "You might try listing the qualities that are most important to you in an egg donor and a surrogate. That will guide your choices."

Her suggestion had the desired effect of pushing the interruption from their minds. When the clients departed a quarter of an hour later, Melissa had recovered her equilibrium.

She reached for her cup of tea, to find it empty. Although an hour remained until lunch, she was starving, and she'd already finished off the crackers in her desk. These days, she found herself eating more than enough for four. Her doctor insisted her weight gain was healthy, but Melissa had trouble adjusting to her rotund body shape. At five-foot-eight, she'd always been tall and slender.

Well, she was still tall.

The slightly open door swung wider, and she forgot to breathe. Then she saw with relief that her visitor wasn't Edmond.

Karen Wiggins, the fertility program's financial counselor and occupant of the adjacent office, handed her a cup of white liquid. "It's almond milk—fifty percent more calcium than cow's milk."

"Thanks, Mom," Melissa teased. Ten years her senior, Karen was a nurturing friend as well as her landlady.

"How'd it go with the ex?" Karen lingered near the desk. This month, she'd dyed her shoulder-length hair reddish-brown, which Melissa preferred to some of her friend's more flamboyant choices.

"Smoothly. Oddly. I don't know." Staying alert for approaching footsteps, Melissa added, "He'll be back any minute."

"I'll talk fast. Did you pay attention to the guest list for Saturday?"

"No. Should I?" Melissa and three other coworkers rented rooms in Karen's large home. This weekend, one of their group, nurse Anya Meeks, was getting married there. "As long as we have enough food, who cares?"

"You don't mind that Edmond's invited?"

That was a less-than-welcome surprise. "I had no idea. I wasn't aware he knew Anya and Jack that well."

Karen shrugged. "Anya posted on her wedding website that he'd brought them together. You'll recall she hired him to arrange for Jack to waive his paternal rights after she found out she was pregnant. That set off a whole chain of events leading to…" She hummed a few bars of "Here Comes the Bride."

"Oh, that's right." Several months ago, Anya had asked about a lawyer to help her explore giving up her baby for adoption and Melissa had recommended Edmond. "That hardly qualifies him as Cupid." She sipped the milky liquid, enjoying its slight vanilla flavor.

"She led me to believe she'd already told Jack about the pregnancy." Edmond peered through the doorway, his brown eyes alight with amusement at slipping into the discussion. "I dropped off what I assumed was routine paperwork to Jack and—bam! Fireworks."

Despite an instinctive tensing at his appearance, Melissa had to smile at the image of her normally unflappable ex-husband facing Jack's outrage. "You smoothed things over."

"Not entirely. It was among the more awkward moments of my career," Edmond said. "But all's well that ends well."

"And you're coming to my house on Saturday?" Karen asked.

He gave a start. "The wedding's at your house?"

"The address is on the invitation," Karen pointed out.

"I didn't check where it was. I figured I'd GPS it." A puzzled line formed between Edmond's dark eyebrows. "By the way, why did the invitation come with nose clips?"

Both women laughed. "You'll find out," Karen said.

Aware that Edmond disliked being kept in the dark, Melissa explained, "The house is next to an estuary. The smell of decomposing vegetation and fish can get a little ripe."

"Dare I hope the wedding's indoors?" he asked. "Nose clips don't work too well with glasses."

"It is," she assured him.

"Glad to hear it."

Karen scooped up Melissa's empty mug. "Later, guys."

Then she left them alone.

Chapter 2

Edmond's ethics had prevented him from questioning fellow staffers about his ex-wife's pregnancy. Now that they were in private, though, it took all his resolve not to blurt the questions bedeviling him.

How frustrating that her condition made her glow even more than usual. That was saying a lot. The first time he'd seen Melissa, sitting with her friends at a UCLA campus coffee shop, light through a leaded glass window had bathed her in gold. Now, at the memory, her radiance hit him doubly hard.

They'd been a couple from the moment they met. He'd opened up to her, and she to him, or so he'd believed. They'd agreed that their marriage, their intimacy and their commitment would always be the center of their lives.

He'd been frank about the fact that fatherhood, on top

of his demanding profession, would bring too many pressures. Edmond did nothing halfway, and he understood how important a father was to his children—a loving, devoted father, not a man who had them just because others expected him to. He'd taken on family responsibilities too young, filling in with his younger sister for an often-absent father and an emotionally withdrawn mother. And had done a poor job with her, as things turned out.

His wife's announcement after five years of marriage that she wanted children had come out of nowhere. No warning, no hints before then that she'd changed her mind. Astonished and angry, he'd reacted strongly. Perhaps too strongly, but surely they could have saved their marriage if she was open to it. Instead, she'd walked out and cut off all communication about everything except divorce.

Despite his resentment, their deep connection had lingered in Edmond's thoughts through the years. Although her presence in Safe Harbor hadn't been his only reason for moving here, he'd looked forward to reconnecting, at least on a friendship basis. A friendship that might, in time, have grown.

No chance of that now. Not that Edmond begrudged her happiness. "Pregnancy suits you."

Melissa's eyes widened in surprise. "Nice of you to say so."

"I never pay idle compliments."

"I'm aware of that." She waved him into a chair in front of her desk. A handful of brochures and papers were stacked more or less neatly on its polished wooden surface.

"Thank you for consenting to me being hired." He'd

been pleased to learn from Dr. Rayburn that she'd raised no objection.

"You'll do a good job." Her tapered fingers started to drum the desk, then stopped. "Why do you wish to be a consultant here?"

Noting her tension, he wondered at it. If she'd fallen in love with someone new, surely she'd be indifferent to him. Also, if she loved the father of her child, why was she sharing a house with friends?

"I applied for the post for financial and professional reasons," he answered. "Until I arrived at Geoff Humphreys and Associates, the 'associates' consisted of a legal secretary and a receptionist. I'm slowly building a clientele, but it's going to take a while." He decided against mentioning that he'd also been attracted to the hospital opening because she was on staff.

"Why did you leave L.A.?" she asked. "I'm sure it paid better." He'd earned a hefty salary, plus bonuses.

"It was cutthroat." The partners at his old firm had encouraged associates to go for the jugular. The more Edmond saw of vicious divorces and custody battles, the less he appreciated that approach to family law.

Despite their pain, he and Melissa had behaved like rational adults during the divorce. That experience had been part of the reason he'd switched his focus to collaborative law and joined a smaller firm.

There'd been other reasons, as well. He'd sought to reduce his hours so he could help his parents and sister, who'd had a rough year. Then, after meeting Geoff and finding that their views dovetailed, he'd leaped at the chance to move to Safe Harbor. And possibly, to start over with Melissa.

Until today, he hadn't admitted to himself how much

he'd hoped she'd let go of her desire to have children. Once, she'd valued being with him above everything else, and as the years passed and she hadn't remarried, he'd wondered if she might be experiencing some regret.

Obviously, he'd been wrong. Regardless of who the father was, she'd made an irreversible commitment to the child inside her. This pregnancy meant he'd truly lost her.

"So the short version is, you took the hospital consulting job because you need the business," Melissa summarized.

"Harsh but accurate," Edmond conceded. "Also, the legal aspects of new medical technologies present an interesting challenge."

She crossed her arms. "I don't view my clients' legal concerns as an 'interesting challenge.' They're individuals facing real-life issues." Judging by her tone, he gathered that he'd irritated her.

"Of course they're individuals, but when they consult a lawyer, they deserve objective advice more than hand-holding." Rather than continue in this vein, Edmond added, "My job description also includes educating the staff on family law topics, such as changes regarding adoptions and surrogacy."

"I presume Tony is on board with this."

"He's the one who requested they hire a consultant." Tony Franco, the hospital's regular attorney, had his hands full dealing with liability and malpractice matters, as well as refining policies on patient privacy, patient rights and the *in vitro* program. "Geoff introduced us on the golf course a few months ago. He suggested I apply for the opening."

"Congratulations." Melissa stopped there. Whatever

she was thinking, she guarded it well. He used to consider her an open book, but then again, if that had been true, he'd have had some idea of how radically she'd altered her opinion of parenthood.

After a brief silence, he said, "Let's discuss how I can assist you with fertility patients. You're on the front lines, I understand."

"Fine. Later."

"Why not now?" He wasn't ready to cut short this meeting, not until he had a clearer picture of where she stood. How she felt. Who the damn father was.

Instead of a direct answer, she blurted, "Don't go to the wedding."

So that's what's on her mind. Edmond struggled to catch this conversational curve ball. "I already RSVP'd."

"It isn't set in concrete." A cord of tension stood out in her slender neck. "You're only attending to expand your contacts in the community, right?"

Not entirely. "There are personal as well as professional reasons. I had no idea it was at your house." Why did this bother her? She'd agreed to work with him.

"It's an informal event," Melissa said. "One person more or less won't affect anything. It's not as if Jack and Anya will be stuck paying a caterer for an uneaten meal."

Edmond had a tight schedule on Saturday, and skipping the afternoon event might ease things. But in view of his new consulting job, her friends were now his co-workers. Breaking his promise to attend would be rude. And he didn't understand her reluctance.

Was she trying to hide the circumstances of her pregnancy? Surely she didn't expect to keep him in the dark for long. Had she broken up with the father? Or was the prospect of introducing him to her ex-husband uncomfortable?

Edmond half hoped the guy was a bum with body odor. *Maybe that's the real reason for the nose clips.* At the ridiculous notion, he smiled.

"You find this funny?" she asked.

"I was just…" He shook off his reflections. "We live in the same community."

"Your choice, not mine." Her low tone bordered on a growl.

"You gave your permission," he reminded her.

"Not for you to relocate to Safe Harbor, only for this job. I've never been vindictive."

"That's true."

"Then do me a favor and…" Halting, she paled, and sucked in several quick breaths.

"Are you okay?" Edmond leaned across the desk. "Shall I call someone?"

"What I need is tea."

"I'll get it."

"Never mind."

This was ridiculous. "We aren't enemies," he said. "Melissa, tell me what I can do."

"I don't want your help." Were those tears in her eyes? "And it's just a touch of morning sickness. Gone already."

Perhaps, yet her distress troubled him. "You're sure?"

"Yes. And if I change my mind about the tea, I'll ask Caroline."

Damn, she was hardheaded. "Surely we can find common ground and give each other a break," he said. "I've been dealing with family matters… I could use your insights. And in your situation, you shouldn't be too quick to reject an offer of friendship."

He'd phrased that badly, he saw when her chin lifted defiantly. "I have plenty of friends. What do you mean by 'my situation,' anyway?"

"You haven't mentioned the father." Oh, hell, he was making matters worse. "Not that it's any of my business."

"There is no father."

She hadn't fallen in love with another man. That discovery brought some comfort, but Edmond also found it disturbing. How desperately she must want a child to undergo insemination by an anonymous donor.

She was awaiting a reaction to her statement. If she expected reassurances, he had to disappoint her. "Is that fair to the child? Fathers matter."

"I have guy friends," she told him. "Guys who think kids are precious."

"Friends aren't family." Nor did she have any other family, unfortunately. Her parents had died years ago, and her younger brother had drowned as a toddler.

"Lots of women raise children alone," Melissa flared.

Edmond was glad the color had returned to her cheeks, even though it was an angry red. "In any case, nothing I say matters. Your baby is your priority now."

"That's right."

They'd reached an impasse, and the end of this conversation. Edmond didn't offer to shake hands, which might force her to rise. "I'll see you on Saturday."

"You're determined to attend the wedding?" she asked tightly.

"As I said, I already accepted." If she could be stubborn, so could he. On the spur of the moment, he added, "I'll be bringing a plus one, by the way."

"Suit yourself." She faced her computer, dismissing him.

In the outer office, Edmond paused at Caroline Carter's desk. An attractive young woman with a smooth dark complexion and a romance novel partly visible on her lap, she regarded him brightly. "Yes, Mr. Everhart?"

"If you wouldn't mind, my... Melissa could use some tea. Her stomach's bothering her," he said.

"I'm on it," she responded. "And welcome to Safe Harbor."

"Glad to be here." He exited into the main-floor hallway, where he was engulfed by the chatter and bustle of personnel heading for the cafeteria. Despite the flat lighting and the smell of antiseptic, he liked this place. The air hummed with the enthusiasm of people dedicated to their work.

It had been a rocky meeting with his ex-wife. But they'd accomplished an important task: clarifying that they stood as far apart as ever.

Every minute closer to lunch, Melissa felt nearer to starvation, and today's cafeteria special had been posted as chicken enchiladas with guacamole, a favorite of hers. Nevertheless, her friends would spot her frayed emotional state the moment she sat at their table, and she wasn't ready to field questions.

Why was Edmond so stubborn about the wedding? And why had she overreacted? She hadn't intended to demand that he skip it.

When he'd observed that pregnancy suited her, a wall inside her had started to crumble, and his strong presence had reawakened a longing to lean on him. What an absurd idea, and yet he'd been her rock after her parents' sudden deaths in an accident, and she needed someone to talk to right now.

But when he'd pushed her away, it stung, revealing a vulnerability Melissa had believed long vanquished. How could she still have feelings for the man who'd broken her heart?

Considering his dismissive attitude toward fatherhood, he had a lot of nerve, criticizing her decision. *Is that fair to the child? Fathers matter.* As if she hadn't taken that into consideration.

In fact, she'd been reluctant to undergo artificial insemination. Melissa had questioned how she would explain to a child later that its father had no involvement, indeed no awareness of its existence.

Then a couple of *in vitro* clients to whom she'd grown close had faced a dilemma. After bearing healthy triplets, they'd been left with three unused embryos. Due to a difficult pregnancy and with three children to raise, they'd decided against another pregnancy. Instead, they'd resolved to donate the embryos.

Recalling an earlier conversation with Melissa, they'd offered the little ones to her. With her, they'd insisted, they wouldn't worry because they had confidence she'd be a wonderful mother. But they'd also been in a rush to settle the matter and told her if she didn't seize the chance immediately, they'd select another recipient.

Her physician, Dr. Zack Sargent, had noted the potential physical complications of a multiple pregnancy but, in view of her general good health, he'd given his approval. When she'd solicited the opinions of her housemates and a few dinner guests, Anya's fiancé, obstetrician Jack Ryder, had said that frozen embryo transfers at Safe Harbor had about a fifty percent success rate. That statistic reinforced Melissa's assumption that at most she'd bear twins.

She'd also received enthusiastic support from Karen. Divorced and in her early forties, her friend had no plans for children of her own but loved being around babies. Another housemate, male nurse Lucky Mendez, had advised Melissa to follow her heart instead of obsessing about everything that could go wrong. Only ultrasound technician Zora Raditch had been dubious, but then, Zora had accidentally become pregnant with twins after having breakup sex with her faithless ex-husband, so her opinion of men and maternity was understandably jaundiced.

It had felt like fate. Then all three embryos had taken. *And now here I am, hurting because the man I used to love won't accept me the way I am.* What a waste of energy.

Annoyed at her weakness, she picked up the phone and put in a call to Rose's Posies. As her wedding gift to Jack and Anya, she was providing the bouquets for the bride and for two flower girls, as well as for one of Anya's sisters, who was flying in from Colorado to serve as maid of honor.

The shop owner, Rose Nguyen, answered on the fourth ring. "I'll go check to be sure my daughter has all in order," she said after Melissa explained she was calling to confirm the arrangements. "Hold for Violet, okay?"

"Thanks." Melissa smiled at the name of Rose's daughter. Like her mother's, it was sweetly appropriate. She stretched her legs, slipped off her pumps and rested her swollen feet on a stool beneath the desk while making a mental note to buy larger shoes. Preferably before Saturday, to go with the flowing silk caftan she'd found at the Gently Used & Useful thrift shop.

Heat flooded her at the realization that, flattering as the lavender print dress might be, it emphasized her girth. She'd been rather proud of that until Edmond mentioned bringing a date.

Who was it? The legal secretary or the receptionist from his office, a friend from L.A., or a new acquaintance? She'd probably be pretty, smart and slim.

Melissa shook her head at her insecurities. *Take Lucky's advice. Stop obsessing.*

On the other end of the line, someone picked up. "Ms. Everhart?" It was Violet. "Let me review the order with you to be sure we have everything as you requested."

"Good idea."

A few minutes later, as they finished talking, Melissa's stomach quivered. No, that wasn't her stomach. She clamped her hand to her abdomen. The babies were moving. Although they'd been visibly active during a recent ultrasound, she hadn't been able to feel them.

Her tests had revealed three girls, but until now they'd remained figures on a screen. This fluttery sensation filled her with wonder. *My daughters are playing.*

Picking up the sonogram picture, she studied the tiny people until tears blurred her vision. They were helpless, utterly dependent on their lone parent. Sometimes the reality of her pregnancy and her future as a single mom to triplets was overwhelming, but she could do it.

Everyone believed in her ability to love and raise them—her friends, her coworkers and Nell and Vernon Grant, the couple who'd donated the embryos. Everyone except Edmond. Well, he was wrong, just as he'd been wrong three years ago.

As for how she'd compare on Saturday to whoever he was bringing to the wedding, why should she care? They'd spent five happy years together but, ultimately, he'd been the wrong man for her.

Still, it wouldn't hurt to stop by The Baby Bump on her way home. Perhaps the shop carried something more flattering than the billowy lavender dress.

Chapter 3

A white satin bow and a bouquet of red, white and blue balloons adorned the mailbox in front of the two-story house. Edmond didn't have to check the address as he wedged his black sedan into a space by the curb. Even had the decorations not identified this as the wedding site, it was the only residence along this stretch of Pelican Lane, bordering the salt marsh and ending half a block away at the Pacific Ocean. If there'd been other homes here in the past, they must have been bought up and removed to restore the estuary.

"Is this it?" His wedding date, her green eyes filled with uncertainty, regarded the rolling lawn and long gravel driveway packed with vehicles.

"We're here," he confirmed. As she unstrapped the belt that she'd carefully positioned to avoid wrinkling her party dress, Edmond reached for his door handle.

The ground was soft, and he'd prefer to carry her rather than risk dirtying her sparkly shoes.

Although he'd been warned, he hadn't been prepared for the pungent smell that struck his nostrils the instant he stepped out. His date noticed, too, of course. As he swung her from her seat and around to the roadway, her nose wrinkled in disgust. "Pee-yoo."

"Want to borrow those nose clips?" He'd shown them to her earlier.

She gave him a gap-toothed smile. "That might leave red marks, Uncle Eddie."

"We can't have that!"

"A fairy princess has to look perfect," she agreed.

"And so you do." Taking her hand, he led seven-year-old Dawn along the street bordering the yard. There was no sidewalk.

Behind the house and on either side stretched marshy land that, he'd read on the city's website, provided refuge for hundreds of bird species as well as wildlife from rabbits to coyotes. As for vegetation and terrain, the site had mentioned pickleweed, cattails, mudflats and tidal sloughs. No wonder the place stank.

Yet Geoff Humphreys's wife, Paula, a second-grade teacher, had declared the estuary far more interesting than the sailboat-filled marina that gave Safe Harbor its name, or the enticing stretch of sandy beach on the west side of town. Edmond supposed that the educator had a valid perspective, but he was far from impressed. The house itself appeared inviting, though, with a wide front porch and clean white paint trimmed in blue.

As he rang the bell, his niece pressed against his side. Dawn had become shy this past year, which was understandable in view of the turmoil in her family. With matters still unsettled, Edmond was doing his best to keep her spirits up.

The door flew open. Two girlish faces, both topped by curly red hair, peered out eagerly. "Hi!" declared the taller one, whom he guessed to be about twelve. "I'm Tiffany, Jack's niece. Well, he's our cousin really, but he's more like an uncle."

"I'm Amber," said the younger one, who wore a matching blue dress with red-and-white trim.

"Nice to meet you. I'm Edmond Everhart and this is Dawn." He saw no reason to explain further.

As they entered the house, Dawn indicated circlets of blue-and-white blossoms atop the girls' heads. "What pretty flowers!"

"We're the flower girls," Amber said. "See, we match!" She pointed to the blossoms festooning the banister of the nearby staircase.

Tiffany regarded Edmond speculatively. "Everhart. Are you related to Melissa?"

"Yes. Is she around?" He'd rather not provide details of his marital situation.

"She's in the kitchen."

"But the wedding's that way." Amber pointed to their right.

"Thank you both." Amused by the unconventional welcome, Edmond escorted Dawn into the high-ceilinged living room.

Curio cabinets dominated the far wall, with a striped sofa positioned beneath the front windows, no doubt shifted to provide space in the center. Several dozen chairs, half of them already filled, faced a slightly elevated dining room at the rear. Its table had been moved to accommodate a flower-covered arch, while a boom box in one corner played an instrumental version of "We've Only Just Begun."

Edmond recognized some of the guests as hospital staff. In his law practice, he'd learned to quickly commit names and faces to memory, and he was trying to place as many as possible when a small hand tugged his sleeve. "What's up, tiger?" he asked.

"Let's go see Aunt Lissa." Dawn peered across the room. "That girl said she was in the kitchen."

"It would be rude to barge through the house." Immediately regretting his phrasing, Edmond added, "I'm sure she'll join us later. We can talk to her then."

"I want to see her now." The girl's lower lip quivered. "I miss Aunt Lissa."

"How well do you remember her?" Dawn had been only four when they divorced. Edmond's sister Barbara had mentioned that Melissa had sent a birthday present for her daughter the following year, but Barb's life was chaotic, with many changes of both physical and email addresses. To the best of his knowledge, the two women hadn't stayed in touch.

"She used to read to me. Why did she leave?" Dawn glared up at him accusingly, as if it was his fault she'd lost one of her small circle of loved ones. Well, perhaps it was, in part.

"We divorced, but I'm sure she's missed you, too. I suppose we could take a peek." Melissa *had* emphasized the informality of the occasion.

"Yay!" Dawn gave a little hop, brown curls bouncing. Her Grandma Isabel, Edmond's stepmother, had done a fine job of styling the child's hair—not only for the wedding but also for an earlier, less pleasant outing this morning.

They were saved the need to intrude past the wedding bower when Melissa, blond hair shining above a pink dress, emerged into the dining room. Her gaze met his, then fixed on the little girl beside him.

"Dawn?" Her expression warming, Melissa descended the two steps from the elevated level. "My goodness, you've grown."

"Aunt Lissa!" The child flung herself forward. As her arms stretched to embrace her aunt, she halted in confusion. "You've grown, too."

Melissa laughed and hugged the child around her enlarged midsection. "I'm pregnant."

"You are?" Dawn patted the extended tummy. "He's a big baby."

"That's because…" She broke off suddenly.

"Is something wrong?" Edmond touched her elbow to steady her.

"No." She cleared her throat. "It's just that…"

"He's a she and she's coming in triplicate." A fortyish man with a short beard and black top hat joined the conversation from the side.

"You're having three babies?" Dawn asked.

"That's right," her aunt said. "All girls."

Triplets. Melissa didn't do things by half measures, Edmond thought. "Congratulations."

Dawn patted her aunt's tummy again. "What are their names?"

"I haven't decided."

"Can I pick?"

Melissa brushed a curl off the little girl's forehead. "I'm not ready to name them yet."

What else was one supposed to say under the circumstances? Edmond wondered. "When are you due?" he asked.

"December," she said. "If I can hold out that long."

That exhausted his very short repertoire of small talk on the subject. Besides, in Edmond's opinion, this was far from a light topic, since multiple pregnancies carried extra risks. "I hope this won't endanger your health."

"She's being closely monitored." The bearded man extended his hand. "I'm the groom's uncle, Rod Vintner."

"We've met before." He shook hands with the man, who then solemnly did the same with Dawn. She giggled. "At the hospital."

"Ah, that's right." The man nodded.

"Rod's an anesthesiologist," Melissa said to Dawn. "He puts patients to sleep while they're in surgery."

"And I'll soon be sleeping myself, here at Casa Wiggins," Rod announced. "I'm trading residences with the bride. She's moving into the apartment Jack and I shared, and I'm taking her old room."

"Ah."

Don't get ideas now that you're living with my wife. Where had that notion come from? Edmond had no claim on Melissa. Besides, a positive aspect occurred to him. "I'm glad she'll have an M.D. on hand."

"I don't deliver babies." Rod waggled his eyebrows. "Come to think of it, I don't make house calls, either."

"But you'll live here," Dawn pointed out.

"You're right," Melissa said. "He can serve as the house physician."

"Living together means we'll all be one big happy family, and doctors don't provide medical care to family members," the man deadpanned.

"You wouldn't help her?" Dawn demanded.

"Of course he would," Melissa assured the child. "Rod's joking."

"It's lucky his patients are asleep," Dawn replied tartly. "'Cause his jokes aren't funny."

Edmond laughed at the unexpected jab. The man in the top hat clutched his side. "Ow! A direct hit."

"I'm impressed," Melissa said. "You have a wicked wit, Dawn."

She took her aunt's hand. "Will you sit with us?"

"Of course."

"On that note, I have best man duties to attend to." Rod patted his pocket, which presumably held the ring, and went to join an older man in a suit waiting beneath the arch.

"That must be the minister," Edmond observed.

"He's from Karen's church." Melissa glanced toward the kitchen door. "I'm supposed to be helping her with the food."

"Isn't the ceremony about to start?" The invitation said 2 p.m., and it was almost that now. The seats had been filling as they spoke. "If we wait any longer, we'll be sitting on the window ledge."

"You're right." Melissa led the way down the narrow aisle to three empty seats. The folding chairs, fitted with white covers, weren't exactly comfortable, but Edmond found room to stretch his legs beneath the seat in front of him.

Being near Melissa was a treat. Just the musical sound of her voice calmed him. During their marriage, her nearness had filled the dark spaces in Edmond's soul. With her, he hadn't had to throw up protective walls. She'd understood him intuitively, which was why he'd expected her to understand that his vasectomy was a declaration of how strongly he felt about preserving their union.

She had a gift for nurturing, and he'd needed that. He still did. But she'd chosen motherhood over him.

Dawn, too, seemed to retain a bond with her. In the seat between them, the little girl hung on to her aunt as if she might disappear at any moment. In Dawn's world, people vanished too often. The therapist Edmond had hired for her said she suffered from separation anxiety.

"You look like a princess," Dawn told Melissa.

"So do you." She fingered the little girl's curls. "Who fixed your hair?"

"Grandma Isabel." Nodding at Melissa's bulge, she asked, "Who's the daddy?"

That brought a flush to his ex-wife's cheeks. "It's a long story."

"Can you make it shorter?"

"Sorry. Not now," Melissa said gently. "Another time."

Reluctantly, the little girl subsided. "Okay."

Edmond hoped his niece wouldn't demand that *he* explain. While he believed she was acquainted with the facts of procreation, artificial insemination seemed too intimate a subject for an uncle to describe.

"How's your mommy?" Melissa asked.

Oh, damn. Edmond wished he'd had a chance to bring up his sister's situation sooner. But before he could find the right words, Dawn blurted, "We visited Mommy in jail this morning. She's scared."

Nearby, several heads turned. "Barbara's in jail?" Melissa regarded Edmond with concern.

"I'll fill you in later." Surely she would have read the articles in the newspaper about the robbery. However, the reports had misstated Barb's last name as Greeley, although she and Simon had never married.

Melissa's nod conveyed her understanding, and she directed her next question to Dawn. "Who are you staying with?"

"Grandma and Grandpa."

"My father and stepmother, not Simon's," Edmond clarified. Simon's parents—an ex-convict father whose whereabouts were unknown and an alcoholic mother with half a dozen children by assorted men—had no contact with Dawn.

"I'm glad you brought her with you." Melissa reached across her niece to touch Edmond's hand. "And that you're here."

So was he. All the same, he couldn't resist teasing. "Glad I ignored your request?"

"Oh, Eddie, is it written somewhere that we're forbidden to get everything we want?" Her wistfulness curled inside him.

The discovery that she, too, had regrets, or at least doubts, warmed him. "I'm beginning to think so," he admitted.

He might have added more, but just then a handsome man in a dark suit joined Rod and the minister at the arch. Dawn stared, entranced. "Is that the groom? He could be a movie star."

"That's Jack," Melissa confirmed. "He's an obstetrician. The nurses at the hospital went into mourning when he got engaged to Anya."

Jack beamed with happiness. He and Anya hadn't had an easy relationship, Edmond knew, but overcoming obstacles had apparently bonded them all the more strongly.

Too bad it hadn't worked that way with us.

A muscular fellow knelt by the boom box to change the recording. Tattoos peeked from beneath his shirt collar. "Who's that?" Edmond asked.

"One of our housemates, Lucky Mendez, R.N."

Dawn studied the man dubiously. "He's a nurse?"

"Men can be nurses, too. He assists Dr. Cole Rattigan, the head of the men's fertility program," Melissa said, adding, "Also, he just earned a master's degree in nursing administration."

"What's he plan to do with that?" Edmond asked.

"Hopefully stay in Safe Harbor, if the men's fertility program expands, although that's up in the air." Melissa cast the fellow a sympathetic glance. "Otherwise he might have to find a position elsewhere."

"My daddy had tattoos," Dawn put in.

Melissa frowned. "Had, past tense?"

"He died about six months ago." Edmond didn't care to say anything more around his niece.

Dismay clouded Melissa's expression. "I've missed a lot."

"I've missed *you*," Dawn said, and smiled when her aunt kissed the top of her head.

The music changed to a march. Conversations among the guests died out.

From the front hall, the younger flower girl entered. Clutching a bouquet, she strode up the aisle a little too fast for the music.

"Slow down, for Pete's sake," growled a bulldog of a man sitting on the aisle.

The girl—Amber, Edmond recalled—flinched and slowed. Her sister, following, scowled at the man from outside his range of vision.

Edmond raised an eyebrow questioningly at Melissa.

Leaning close, she murmured, "That's the girls' stepfather. Vince Adams."

"The billionaire." A private equity investor, Vincent Adams was famous throughout Southern California for his business success and for his ruthlessness. He was also, Edmond had learned from the hospital administrator, considering donating millions of dollars to expand the men's fertility program.

As the girls took places by the arch, a pretty young woman in a dress matching theirs marched up the aisle. "That's Anya's sister Sarah," Melissa murmured. "Anya has a big family. They couldn't all come, but they're planning a reception in Colorado after the baby's born."

"How big a family?" Dawn whispered.

"She's one of seven kids."

"Wow."

The music shifted to "Here Comes the Bride." Anya entered from the hall on the arm of a distinguished older man, no doubt her father. Edmond wasn't up on the latest fashions in wedding gowns, but this one was suitably white with a lot of lace. It skimmed Anya's expanded midsection, a reminder that she was only a few months from delivering her own baby.

"Is *everybody* pregnant?" Dawn asked, a little too loudly. Nearby, several people chuckled. "I'm sorry."

Noting her tense expression, Edmond leaned close. "It's a fair question," he whispered.

"Yes, this house is baby central," Melissa said softly.

Dawn relaxed. The poor kid sometimes acted as if she carried the weight of the world, Edmond thought.

It was her parents' job to protect her childhood. Too bad they'd failed. Who would protect her now?

To Melissa, joy illuminated the familiar room. How

Anya glowed as her father handed her to the groom. Judging by Jack's grin, it took all his self-control not to hoist Anya in his arms and whisk her off to their secret honeymoon destination, which Melissa had discovered was Santa Catalina Island. Rod had mentioned it to Karen, who'd passed it on to Melissa. Secrets didn't stay secret long in Casa Wiggins.

Located a little over twenty miles off the California coast, the island was noted for its old-fashioned charm and for ocean-related activities in its clear waters, including snorkeling and viewing undersea life from glass-bottom boats. Jack had arranged for them to stay at a romantic Victorian bed-and-breakfast with a view of the small-boat harbor in the town of Avalon.

How wonderful that the baby, whom they planned to name after both their grandmothers, would be born to such a loving pair. She was a lucky little girl.

A fluttery sensation alerted Melissa that her as-yet-nameless babies were stirring. Whenever she tried to focus on names for them, her mind went blank. Well, what was the rush?

Beneath the arch, Jack kept peeking at his bride, tuning out the minister. Anya gave him a poke, which restored him to the proper demeanor.

How comfortable they were with each other, Melissa reflected. Edmond's and her ceremony had been more formal, although every bit as enchanting. Her father, a psychologist, and her mother, a high-school math teacher, had treated her to the wedding of her dreams. A hotel ballroom in Santa Monica, the coastal city where they'd lived, had provided a fairy-tale setting for soul mates embarking on a life together. Or so she'd believed.

She'd met Edmond in a coffee shop at UCLA, where

she'd been earning her master's degree in molecular biology and Edmond had been a law student. She'd admired his boldness in taking a seat at the table with her and her friends. He'd been a complete stranger but he'd teasingly claimed they kept running into each other. After she played along, they'd stayed to talk hours after her friends left. From then on, they'd gravitated to each other, a pair of intense high-achievers who shared many of the same political and social views. Their wedding day had been the happiest day of her life.

During her painful recovery from the divorce, friends had repeatedly advised her to throw her wedding album away, but Melissa couldn't imagine sacrificing those memories. There was an especially lovely photo of her with the maid of honor, Edmond's sister, Barbara, who'd bloomed with sixteen-year-old innocence.

Only a few months later, Barbara had run off to live with an ex-con. Despite Edmond's protests, his normally stern father had refused to call the police. Edmond himself had tried hard to reach out to his sister, calling and dropping by her place, but Barbara had refused to talk and Simon had threatened him.

Why hadn't her parents struggled harder to keep her? They could have brought charges against the man. As for Edmond, he'd taken his sister's rejection hard, as if he'd failed her. Melissa suspected the situation had reinforced his conviction that he wasn't cut out for parenthood. She'd soothed him as best she could, hoping that he'd heal. She'd learned the hard way that he hadn't.

Now, Dawn's mother was in jail. What crime had Barbara committed? How long would she be separated from her daughter?

While the minister expanded on the transformative

power of marriage, Dawn wiggled in her seat. Edmond murmured to her—Melissa caught the words *soon* and *food.*

"Okay, Uncle Eddie." Trustingly, Dawn rested her cheek on his arm.

A glaze of tears in his eyes might not seem remarkable, considering how many people cried at weddings. But to Melissa, they showed how much Edmond's usually guarded heart was aching for this little girl. Was he finally discovering a paternal instinct?

These past three years, she'd pictured him enjoying his freedom, traveling abroad the way they used to. She'd fought painful images of him finding a woman who shared his tastes and his pleasures.

Instead, here he was, still single. Evidently he'd been tied up with family issues. He'd shouldered an unusual amount of responsibilities since his teen years, with his father frequently off driving long-distance truck routes and his reticent mother intimidated by her strong-willed daughter. Edmond's efforts to help raise his sister had smashed head-on into her adolescent rebellion. No wonder he'd craved peace and quiet as an adult.

As Anya and Jack exchanged rings and said their vows, tears blurred Melissa's own gaze. She and Edmond couldn't go back to their wedding day eight years ago and make things come out differently. Yet today he was showing a different side of himself....

What an idiot she was! When she entered into this pregnancy, she'd been well aware that she couldn't expect any man to love and care for her *and* her babies. Her longing for them had overwhelmed all other considerations.

They were enough to fill up her life and her heart. They had to be.

Chapter 4

Edmond had intended to stay after the ceremony only long enough to be polite. He'd assumed his presence might be uncomfortable for Melissa.

Instead, she was friendly toward him, while Dawn eagerly joined the red-haired flower girls at the buffet table in an area connecting the kitchen and den. He was glad he'd brought her. His niece could use a change of scenery to take her mind off visiting her mom in jail.

Worse might lie ahead for Barbara. Edmond tried not to dwell on that disturbing prospect. He needed today's change of pace as much as Dawn.

"You and your housemates are wonderful cooks," he told Melissa as they waited in line. Delicious smells wafted from the array of dishes, while a separate table displayed a three-tiered white cake decked with blue and red berries and, on top, a large red heart. Plates of cookies surrounded it, presumably for those too impatient to wait for dessert.

"The food is mostly Karen's doing. I'm the baker. I can't take credit for the wedding cake, though," she added. "I'm the cookie lady."

"I'm impressed by anything people do in a kitchen, other than set fires." Growing up, Edmond had learned the basics, but rarely cooked.

"When we moved into the house, the five of us voted to take turns, each fixing dinner for a week. That didn't last," Melissa admitted. "Now we all pitch in or go our own ways."

"The kitchen must have been upgraded." From where they stood, Edmond noted gleaming new appliances.

"Karen remodeled after her mother died last year," Melissa said. "She didn't change the basic shape of the room, though. You still have to perform the limbo to get into the pantry."

"So she inherited the place. I was wondering why she bought a house here, considering the smell. Although the scenery *is* striking." Sliding glass doors offered a view across the patio and rear yard to the gray-and-green estuary. "What's the layout—any bedrooms downstairs?" While he didn't expect a tour of the place, Edmond was curious about the sleeping arrangements.

"Lucky has a small suite through there." She indicated a doorway on the far side of the den. "Karen, Zora, Anya and I have bedrooms upstairs."

"Except now Rod's taking Anya's place," he muttered, half to himself.

Melissa ducked her head. "I keep forgetting."

"Won't that be awkward, having a guy upstairs with the ladies?"

In a low tone, she confided, "He and Karen have become close. I hope that won't blow up in our faces, but she seems happy, and he's a solid guy underneath the kidding."

"Yes, I got that impression."

As Edmond filled his plate at the serving table, he recalled his intention of cultivating new acquaintances. There were a lot of people here, and he supposed he could chat them up, but he'd much rather spend the afternoon in Melissa's company.

Also, he suspected many of the guests, aside from those he'd already met, were from out-of-town. The father of the bride was busy tending to his wife, who moved stiffly with the aid of a cane. Jack was introducing his friends to a fiftyish woman dressed in knock-your-eyes-out Caribbean colors. Edmond had heard that Jack's mother lived in Haiti and raised money for charities there.

He decided to forget duty for one day. Aside from keeping an eye on Dawn, of course. She and the two older girls had gone outside to eat at the patio table. Before they closed the glass door behind them, Dawn had sent Edmond a questioning gaze. He nodded his approval. If the girls didn't mind the smell, more power to them.

"I'm glad she's found playmates," he said, following Melissa to a well-worn couch. "She tends to be shy, especially with new people. Jack's nieces seem outgoing."

"Except around their stepfather," she murmured.

Edmond didn't spot Vince Adams or his wife in the den, although they'd been at the head of the buffet line. He assumed the couple had carried their plates into the dining room, where some of Melissa's housemates had put back the dining room table and set it immediately after the ceremony. That suited him fine. No matter how important the Adamses might be as potential donors, Edmond was in no mood for apple-polishing, especially to a guy who'd publicly humiliated his stepdaughter.

"You're good with Dawn." Melissa set her plate on the coffee table.

"I try." He stared moodily at his food. "Let's hope I do better with her than I did with my sister. I wish I understood where I went wrong."

"Why do you blame yourself for her problems?" she asked.

"When we were young and Dad was on the road, Barbara used to confide in me about everything, value my advice, follow me around. But when she hit adolescence, I was commuting to college so I couldn't be there for her. She began acting out, cutting school, skipping her homework assignments."

"Many teenagers rebel to a degree," she pointed out.

"Sure, but then she ran off with Simon. I should have done more to stop her." It had been only a few months after their marriage. "She was sixteen. We could have gone to the police."

"That was your parents' decision, not yours," she reminded him. "And she did get legally emancipated after Dawn's birth."

"I can't shake the sense that I let her down. Did she mention why she'd been so eager to leave home?" While Edmond knew Simon could be charming and manipulative, surely his sister hadn't been totally blind to the man's faults.

"I sensed she was angry, but not necessarily at you. She didn't say anything specific, though." Flecks of green stood out in Melissa's hazel eyes. "I tried to talk to her after she had the baby, about planning a future for herself and Dawn, but she pushed me away. Edmond, why is she in jail? That sounds serious."

"It is." Months of holding his emotions in check, of standing strong for everyone around him, yielded to the relief of confiding in a person he trusted. "That jerk Simon talked her into driving the getaway car for a robbery."

"I can't believe she'd do something that stupid." Melissa set down her fork, giving him her full attention.

Around them, people mingled and chatted. Edmond saw Karen glance their way as if about to approach, but he shook his head. She went in another direction. He decided he liked that woman. "According to Barbara—after the fact—Simon claimed he owed money to a criminal gang and that if he didn't pay up, they'd kill him."

"Was it true?"

"I have no idea." Either way, that didn't excuse the man's crimes, nor Barb's. "During the robbery, he and a policeman traded gunfire, and Simon was fatally wounded. The officer escaped injury, mercifully."

That was fortunate both for the officer and for Barbara. Under California law, the district attorney could have charged her with murder just for being a participant in the robbery. However, perhaps doubting that a jury would convict her of murder under the circumstances, the D.A. had only charged her with robbery.

"Your sister was waiting in the getaway car?" Melissa asked.

"That's right." She hadn't witnessed the shooting, but she'd heard gunfire. "Simon staggered into the passenger seat. While she was arguing that they should go to a hospital, he died."

Melissa shook her head. "How awful."

"I can't spare any regrets for that man," Edmond said bitterly. "He ruined my sister's life—with her compliance."

"What about Dawn? Where was she during all this?"

"She'd gone to the beach with a friend's family." The shootout had occurred on a Saturday, while his niece was out of school. "The police contacted my father and stepmother, who called me. I picked her up and broke the news." He clenched his fists at the memory.

Edmond had built up to the subject gradually during the drive from the beach, telling his niece as much as he'd learned of the robbery and assuring her that her mother was unharmed but under arrest. Dawn had taken the news of Simon's death solemnly, her response hard to read.

Then, tearfully, she'd asked, "Is it because I was mad at him?"

Shocked, Edmond had assured her that Simon's death wasn't her fault. "Neither you nor I nor anyone else has magical powers," he'd told her, hoping that was the right thing to say. "This has nothing to do with you. Why were you mad at him?"

"He yelled at me for leaving my toys out."

Edmond hadn't been sure a seven-year-old understood what death meant, but later, after he'd hired a therapist, she'd insisted that Dawn did understand. Grieving was a complex process, she'd added. As Dawn entered new phases of development, she'd revisit the loss. For now, she needed to feel secure that the other people she loved weren't going to disappear from her world, too.

Unfortunately, Edmond couldn't promise that about Barbara. He could only do his best to hold Dawn's world together. Given his poor track record with his sister, he sometimes panicked over the missteps he might make.

Melissa touched his arm, a soothing gesture that brought him back to this comfortable room and cheerful gathering. "Dawn's been through a lot this past year," she said. "So have you and Barbara."

"It's been rough." He sketched the rest of the sorry tale. After Barb's arrest, a judge had granted bail, and she and Dawn had moved in with his father, Mort, and stepmother, Isabel, a retired nurse's aide. During the trial, the grandparents had helped supervise the little girl, with frequent visits from Edmond until the jury had come back with the verdict two weeks ago. The jurors had convicted his sister of robbery and related charges. "Her sentencing is Monday afternoon."

She blinked. "The day after tomorrow?"

"That's right." Edmond had already arranged to take the day off work to be there for moral support. Barb's defense attorney, Joseph Noriega, had submitted a sentencing memorandum requesting leniency. By now the judge also had a probation report and the prosecutor's recommendation. Edmond suspected they'd be less favorable.

Melissa's hand cupped his. "What kind of sentence is she facing?"

"Minimum, a year in county jail plus probation."

"And the maximum?"

Noriega had warned them to prepare for a longer term, to be served in state prison. "I'm trying not to dwell on it. Let's wait till we know for sure."

"How can the judge separate her from her little girl any longer than necessary?" Melissa asked.

"She's the one who chose to break the law." As an attorney, Edmond was a sworn officer of the court, and he understood the legal perspective. "If Simon had lived, she might have negotiated a deal based on testifying against him. But that's not possible now."

The prosecutor had had no difficulty winning a conviction. The jury had reached a verdict in three hours, which was lightning speed, considering that they'd also had to elect a foreman, fill out paperwork and review multiple counts during that time.

Melissa returned to her main concern. "You said she'll be in jail at least a year. What are the arrangements for Dawn?"

"That reminds me, I'd better check on her. I'll tell you in a minute." Before he could rise, however, Edmond observed his niece entering with the other girls, then sliding the glass door shut behind them. Tiffany shepherded the little band into the kitchen with their empty plates and glasses.

While the youngsters were out of earshot, he said, "My Dad and Isabel indicated they'd take her, with my assistance. But that's not settled."

"What do you mean?" Worry suffused Melissa's expressive face. She'd always been empathetic, and he recalled how she used to love holding Dawn on her lap and paging through picture books with the little girl.

Had that been a factor in her change of heart about having children? Later, he'd tried to figure out how she could have changed her opinions so dramatically without his awareness, and perhaps her relationship with Dawn had been a clue. But it wasn't enough to explain her sudden shift.

How ironic that he was now forced to step in as a

substitute parent of sorts. "While Barb was preparing for trial, she was afraid that if she were convicted, the authorities might put Dawn in foster care," he answered.

"That would be horrible!"

"Yes." It didn't take an expert in child psychology to understand how traumatic that would be for everyone. "Barb wanted to assign temporary guardianship to Isabel and Dad, but they were too tied up with Dad's medical issues to go to family court with her."

"Medical issues?"

"Skin cancer." He explained briefly that his father had undergone treatment and tests now showed him to be cancer-free. Then he continued, "Appointment of a guardian requires a judge's approval." Nearly hysterical with fear for her daughter's well-being as the trial date approached, Barbara had begged Edmond to take emergency guardianship himself.

"What did you do?" Melissa watched him intently.

"I agreed, even though I'm obviously not the ideal person to raise a little girl." That was an understatement for a guy who lacked paternal instincts, had failed miserably in protecting his sister, and lived in a one-bedroom apartment.

However, he refused to abandon his family. He'd promised in court to take responsibility for Dawn, and he meant it. If necessary, he'd move in with his parents for a year and commute an hour each way from their home in Norwalk, in eastern Los Angeles County. It would be uncomfortable and inconvenient, but he'd do it for Dawn and for Barbara.

"Dawn said she was staying with your parents," Melissa reminded him.

"She and Barb were already living there." He blew

out a long breath. "We all agreed it's vital that she have what her therapist calls 'continuity of care.'"

"I'm glad she has a counselor," Melissa said. "That doesn't substitute for being with her mom, though. Why couldn't Barb stay out on bail until she's sentenced?"

"She's considered a flight risk." The Mexican border was only a couple of hours' drive away.

"That's too bad." Melissa regarded him with a warmth he'd missed—a lot. "Edmond, what you're doing for Dawn, protecting her so she won't go into foster care, it's wonderful."

"I would never let her be yanked away from her family." To him, it was the only decent way to behave. He'd been blessed with many gifts, including loving if flawed parents, educational opportunities and an aptitude for the law. Surely there was a reason he'd also been given enough strength to stand tall when others needed him. Though it was a relief to express the situation openly to someone, without fear of judgment.

He'd done his best to be there for Melissa after her parents' deaths. And he'd counted on her being there for him, too.

"Did it occur to you that you might have paternal instincts after all?" she asked.

"I'm sorry?"

"You have a big heart," she said gently. "Big enough to love more than one person. You'd make a wonderful father."

He stiffened. Just when he'd believed she understood him, she was viewing his confidence through the lens of her own wishes, trying to convert him into her idea of what a man ought to be. "I'm not her father, I'm her guardian."

"I've seen how you act with her," Melissa said. "You've changed these past three years."

Not that much.

This past year had been one blow after another. Edmond had rarely had a chance to replenish his inner strength with quiet hours to read, visit museums and travel. The worst part had been enduring these crises alone. That was, in part, why he'd opened up to Melissa today. To his disappointment, her attitude reminded him that she didn't accept him for himself, only as a wish-fulfillment fantasy.

It was important to clear up that misunderstanding. "Don't interpret my actions to suit your assumptions. My views on fatherhood haven't changed."

"Are you sure you have an accurate perception of yourself?"

How insulting. "While I respect your decision to have children in whatever manner you choose, you shouldn't cast me in the role of father-knows-best simply because it's convenient."

Her mouth tightened. "That's not what I was doing."

Instinctively, he echoed her earlier words. "Are you sure *you* have an accurate perception of yourself?"

"Don't be arrogant!" As she leaned forward to pick up her plate, a startled expression crossed her face and her hand flew to her midsection.

"Is anything wrong?" Although she didn't appear distressed, Edmond hadn't forgotten the bout of nausea in her office.

Melissa shook her head, blond tendrils quivering. "They're scooting around in there."

"You can feel the babies?" She'd mentioned being due

in December, he recalled, and that was many months off. "How big are they?"

"Four or five inches apiece." A smile bloomed, and wonder touched Melissa's eyes. "They're small, but I can tell when they're active."

While the gestation and birth process *was* miraculous, Edmond couldn't pretend to share her enthusiasm. "Doesn't it feel strange, having other people living inside you?"

She chuckled. "What a funny way to put it. This is normal."

"Having triplets?"

"Not that part."

Across the room, someone clapped for the guests' attention. At the cake table, Zora Raditch, one of Melissa's housemates, waved a metal spatula. "We're doing the cut-the-cake thing now, and if either bride or groom shoves a slice in the other person's face, I will personally smash the entire remaining cake over that person's head. Fair warning!"

A ripple of laughter greeted this announcement. Edmond, however, was concerned about the baby bump visible beneath the woman's dress. Another unmarried pregnancy in the house wouldn't concern him, but he'd represented Zora in her divorce from a self-centered businessman named Andrew. Despite an agreement to negotiate fairly, the man had played games with the settlement and with signing the papers.

That had all been resolved, finally. But what about this pregnancy? "Dare I ask if Andrew's the father?" In Edmond's opinion, a child deserved better than to be born into such a mixed-up situation.

"Yes, he is, sad to say." Melissa arose gracefully considering her awkward distribution of weight. "They had break-up sex. Then he went and married his new girl-friend."

Edmond collected their plates. "He has obligations, regardless. Their child is legally entitled to parental support."

"It's children, plural. Twins." Melissa shrugged. "I'm not sure why, but I don't believe Zora's even broken the news to Andrew. She can't keep her pregnancy secret from him long, since her former mother-in-law works at the hospital."

"Please let her know I'd be happy to help." Regardless of Andrew's attitudes toward fatherhood, he had obligations to these children. And he owed his former wife his support during her pregnancy, as well. "She shouldn't have to go through this alone."

"She isn't alone," Melissa reminded him. "She has me and Karen."

"Five babies. I'd call that a full house."

"Plus Anya's having a baby. But that little girl's father gives a damn." With that, Melissa went to join the gathering around the cake table.

I'm not the father of your babies. Her unjustified anger annoyed Edmond. Well, he *was* responsible for his niece, and no one could accuse him of not giving a damn about her.

On Monday, he'd find out exactly how big a responsibility he'd undertaken. Hopefully, this would prove to be an unpleasant but limited blip in his sister's troubled life, and Dawn could resume living with her. Pushing aside his worries, Edmond carried the dirty dishes to the kitchen.

Chapter 5

The savory scent hit Melissa's senses the moment she opened the oven door. Orange and lemon zest, balsamic vinegar, olive oil and a touch of sweetness—it transported her instantly to a cozy hotel in Sorrento she and Edmond had used as a base for exploring southern Italy during one of their favorite trips.

She'd discovered this unusual muffin recipe on a website. After her roommates tasted it, the muffins had become an instant hit.

With the aroma, perhaps because she'd encountered her ex-husband yesterday, memories flooded in. As she set the hot tin on the stovetop and began transferring the muffins to a wire cooling rack, Melissa recalled the view from their hilltop hotel over the deep blue Gulf of Naples.

She and Edmond had spent days exploring the partially restored ruins of Pompeii and Herculaneum, which had been buried in the eruption of Mount Vesuvius in 79 A.D. Images of her husband remained etched in her memory: sweat darkening his shirt as he led the way along a narrow, ancient street; his grin shining from his sun-darkened face as they shared a glass of red wine over lunch; his boyish enthusiasm for the voluptuous frescoes decorating two-thousand-year-old palatial homes. They'd hated to leave Sorrento, even though they were continuing on to Rome, Florence and Venice.

If only she could live two lives, Melissa reflected wistfully as she fetched a box of powdered sugar from the cupboard. In the other life, she and Edmond would continue to travel together and, when at home, spend cozy Sunday mornings nestled on the couch, sharing the newspaper. There'd be no risk of provoking his rejection, because she wouldn't long for babies.

But she would never give up this reality. Inside her, as if to reassert their presence, the little ones squirmed. Melissa smiled, imagining her daughters' rambunctious play. She'd read that multiples interacted in the womb. Was one of them already bossy? Was another learning to assert herself in response?

"Ooh, Italian muffins!" Zora bounced into the kitchen, although how anyone five months pregnant with twins could bounce was beyond Melissa. Her housemate's hand shot toward the cooling rack.

"Stop!" Melissa cried. "They'll burn you. Besides, they aren't powdered yet."

"Can I help?" Without waiting, Zora plucked the box from her hands. Since Melissa had pried the spout partway open, soft sugar floated out, touching Zora's ginger-colored hair with white and speckling the floor. "Oh, sorry. I'll clean up."

"No, you won't." Melissa removed the sugar from her grasp before any more escaped. "Neither you nor I ought to be kneeling on the floor."

"We aren't invalids." Zora rarely requested assistance or complained about her pregnancy-related ills, except perhaps to Anya. The two had shared an apartment before moving into this house, and initially their pregnancies had drawn them closer. But Anya was on her honeymoon now, and had already packed most of her possessions to move in with Jack.

"We may not be invalids but we should be sensible," Melissa told her.

"Don't lecture me. I get more than enough of that already." Zora flinched as a heavy tread crossing the den announced Lucky's approach. "Speak of the devil."

"Behave," Melissa cautioned her friend. "He's a prince of a guy."

"You mean a royal pain?"

Melissa chuckled. "Lucky can be that, too."

"Do I hear someone taking my name in vain?" The male nurse appeared in the doorway, his dark eyes sweeping to Zora. Melissa wondered if either of them noticed how he always focused on her first, no matter who else was around.

Although Lucky wasn't Melissa's type, she appreciated his macho appeal, from his cropped hair to his colorful tattoos of a dragon and a sword-wielding woman in skimpy armor. These were revealed today, along with his sculpted muscles, by a sleeveless black T-shirt. New acquaintances often reacted with surprise on learning he was a nurse and a vegetarian, as if those aspects were incompatible with rough-hewn virility.

"No more than usual," Zora said.

"I'm not sure how to interpret that, so I'll ignore it."

Melissa was glad Lucky didn't respond with a jab. He and Zora could pick at each other no end, and Sunday mornings ought to be restful.

When he moved into the kitchen, Melissa halted him with an upraised hand. "Don't step there." She pointed to the spilled sugar. "If you would please clean that up, I'll finish sifting this on the muffins."

"Sure thing. Since you're baking, it's the least I can do." Cheerfully, Lucky went to fetch cleaning supplies. He really was a good housemate.

"I'll brew coffee." Zora took out the canister, although neither she nor Melissa had a taste for it these days. Still, Karen would be down soon, and she didn't function well till she'd had her first cup.

"I should have put some on earlier," Melissa reflected.

"Why should you? I just want to look busy. And thanks for not telling him I spilled it," Zora said in a low voice. "He expects everyone to be perfect."

"Not everyone. Just you." For some reason, Lucky was harder on Zora than on anyone else.

Zora measured the coffee, careful to avoid any further spillage. "It's none of his business whether I inform Andrew about the babies. If I go after my ex for support, he'll jerk me around, maybe sue for custody just so he feels like he's on top. He always has to win."

"What about Betsy?" Andrew's mother, Betsy Raditch, was the hospital's director of nursing. Since Zora worked as an ultrasound tech, she wasn't directly under Betsy's supervision, but they'd remained on friendly terms after Zora had split with Andrew. "She must have noticed."

"She hasn't asked who the father is, and I haven't told her. No sense putting her in the middle." Zora broke off as Lucky returned. He wiped the floor without comment.

Melissa finished sugaring the muffins and put them on a platter. After setting one aside for herself and giving Zora another, she set the plate on the table.

"May I eat now, Mommy?" Lucky joked. "I did my chores."

"Good boy," Melissa said. "Dig in."

Soon the three of them were lounging around the table with the newspaper, silent except for the occasional chuckle at a comic strip or wry comment about a news story. Melissa was grateful for the company. Before moving into the house last spring, she'd lived alone in an efficiency apartment, missing married life and yearning for a baby.

She wished she could have found the right man. But her desire for motherhood had become too powerful to resist, and being surrounded by friends provided all the support she could ask for. Most of the time, anyway.

Zora departed first. Waiting until they heard the shower running upstairs, Lucky caught Melissa's eye and said, "Since you're on positive terms with your ex, you should talk to him about Zora. As her divorce attorney, he's the best person to explain about Andrew's legal obligations."

"Zora's well aware that he owes her support," Melissa answered. "She has her reasons for keeping mum. And it isn't my business to intervene with her attorney."

"Well, she does a rotten job of taking care of herself. Her mom and stepfather live out of state, and we're the only family she has around here." Lucky set aside the sports section. "She ought to put her life in order before the twins are born."

"You think involving Andrew will put things in order?" Although Melissa didn't disagree with Lucky's premise, she also understood Zora's side. "It's a messy situation no matter what she does."

"She must love messy situations, because she's always in one." Morning light through the glass door played across his smooth olive skin. "First she had an affair with Andrew while he was married to his first wife, then, after he cheated on her, too…well, what kind of bonehead has break-up sex with a guy like that?"

"She doesn't always show the best judgment." Melissa left it at that. She didn't want to run down her friend.

"That's putting it mildly," Lucky grumbled. "Someone has to keep after her."

"Be careful about imposing your values." Melissa didn't understand why he insisted on stirring things up, unless it was a desire for control. "It's been said that you expect people to be perfect."

"I expect people to learn from their mistakes, that's all."

Through the kitchen doorway, she glimpsed Karen beelining for the coffee. Her voice drifted out. "Is he on Zora's case again?"

"If there's one thing I've learned, it's that I can't win against a houseful of women." Lucky arose with the comics section and his coffee. "I'll be in my room."

"Enjoy." Since he had the downstairs suite, with a private bath and a small enclosed sunroom, Melissa had no compunctions about chasing him away.

Karen strolled in, mug in hand. She wore a crisp lavender blouse over a long gray skirt, and had coiled her thick auburn hair atop her head. "Ah, you're dressed. I was going to offer you the use of my tub." She occupied the master suite, which had a private bath.

"Thanks, but I woke early." Melissa had showered and thrown on jeans and a short-sleeved cotton sweater. "Figured I'd finish in the bathroom before Zora got up."

"These are my favorite." Karen transferred a muffin to her plate. "Listen, I know it'll be tricky once Rod moves in, sharing a bathroom and all. You can use mine whenever there's a crunch."

"Will do."

"He's coming over this morning." Karen's grin made her appear younger than her forty-two years. "We're switching Rod's stuff with Anya's as a welcome-home present for the honeymooners."

"You're putting her stuff in Jack's apartment while she's out of town?" Melissa wasn't sure she would appreciate someone else handling her property without permission. Still, it would save Anya and Jack the trouble.

"Anya's already packed the personal items," Karen pointed out. "And Rod gets lonely, rattling around in that apartment by himself."

"He's here for dinner nearly every night."

"You don't mind, do you?"

While Melissa wasn't crazy about adjusting to another man on the premises, she enjoyed Rod's sense of humor, and as Edmond had noted, having a physician down the hall might be valuable. "He's excellent company. Jack claims his uncle can't cook worth a darn, though. Are you sure the main attraction for him isn't the meals?"

Karen laughed. "Partly, no doubt. But he helps pay for the food and does the dishes without being nagged."

"What more could one ask for?"

"Precisely."

When her friend picked up the entertainment section, Melissa resumed reading the newspaper. A few pages later, a headline leaped out at her: "Driver to Be Sentenced in Street Fair Robbery." An unflattering photo showed Barbara Everhart, her hair pulled back and her expression grim.

Most of the details in the article were familiar, but Edmond hadn't mentioned that the setting had been a street fair or that there'd been three robbery victims, all vendors. Simon Greeley, the alleged robber, had traded gunfire with a police officer and suffered fatal wounds. No one else was hit, almost a miracle in such a crowded venue.

How did a sweet sixteen-year-old girl get mixed up with that awful man?

Of course, Barb wasn't sixteen anymore. The article listed her age as twenty-four; in the photo, she looked older. There was no mention of her daughter.

Melissa lowered the paper. How strange that Edmond, the last man on earth to become a father, had accepted guardianship of his niece. Was it mostly from a sense of duty, or had he truly bonded with the child?

Meeting Dawn again yesterday had reminded Melissa that, in her heart, she was still the little girl's aunt. Divorces might divide a couple, but they didn't necessarily sever emotional connections to other family members.

The doorbell rang. "That'll be Rod." Karen rose and cut through the den.

Melissa glanced at the muffin platter. Four remained.

She doubted they'd last long with Rod on the premises, not that she'd planned to save any.

From the front, she heard Rod's light tenor voice say, "Guess who I found casing the joint."

"Just remedying a mistake," came a deeper male response. "I forgot to send a wedding present, so I'm dropping this off."

Melissa's pulse sped up. She hadn't expected to run into Edmond again so soon. Swallowing, she chided herself for overreacting.

Yesterday, they'd sniped at each other. She regretted her testy remark about uncaring fathers, since her situation had nothing to do with Edmond. But his crack about not knowing herself had hit painfully close to home. Much as she treasured the triplets, she'd never expected to raise three babies by herself.

She realized now that what she'd longed for was a family with kids *and* a husband to love and care for. But she'd fallen for the wrong man, and then she'd chosen a path that led away from him. If only she'd known her own mind sooner...

Then what? *Sometimes you don't know your own mind now.* Or, as she'd concluded before, perhaps she simply couldn't have everything.

The quiet den filled with people as Lucky emerged from his lair. Amid the exchange of greetings, Melissa caught Edmond's gaze.

She managed a simple, "Hi."

With a nod, he set down a wrapped box bearing the logo of Kitchens, Cooks and Linens, the store where Anya had her bridal registry. "Those muffins smell fantastic. They remind me of Italy."

"Me, too," she said.

"I'm amazed you can smell anything after that whiff out front." Rod, wearing a deerstalker hat worthy of Sherlock Holmes, grimaced. "I may have to have my olfactory nerves removed."

"I've smelled worse," Lucky said.

"Really? Where?" Rod demanded.

"Accident scenes. I used to drive an ambulance."

Melissa didn't hear the rest of their conversation. She was too busy trying to remain relaxed as Edmond approached. "You could have mailed the gift," she observed.

The light reflected on his glasses, obscuring his eyes. "I had an ulterior motive," he said. "To apologize for being so rough on you yesterday."

"It's fine."

"You sure?"

"I pushed you," she conceded. *Now let's change the subject.* "It was good to see Dawn."

He shifted closer. "Being around you meant more to her than I expected."

"She means a lot to me, too," she replied honestly.

Rod brushed past them to snare a muffin. "Great! An energy boost."

Edmond took one, also. After the first taste, he released an appreciative sigh. "These are just like the muffins in Sorrento."

"Close." Melissa still believed her version lacked something—perhaps the taste of the local water.

"Sorrento. Is that in Mexico?" Impossible to tell if Rod was kidding. "So, Ed, you're helping us move the bride's stuff, right?"

"Uh…"

"Right this way."

As Rod shepherded Edmond to the stairs, Melissa released her grip on the newspaper and smoothed the crumpled page.

When Edmond tasted the muffins, he'd remembered one of their happiest times together, just as she had. *If only...*

If only they could travel and simply be a couple? But she couldn't lead that alternate life of her imaginings. Wisps of memory were no substitute for planning a future together.

And there was no way they could have a future.

It served him right to be drafted into hard labor, Edmond reflected as he backed down the stairs, supporting one end of Anya's desk. He'd had no business intruding on Melissa's Sunday.

Embarrassed at forgetting to bring a gift to the wedding, he truly had meant to drop it off and leave. But the scent and taste of those muffins had given him pause. Melissa's choice of recipe indicated that she, too, cherished the memory of their trip. That didn't necessarily imply she cherished *him, though*—the barrier between them loomed larger than ever, literally. So why couldn't he stay away?

After the divorce, Edmond had tried dating others. None of them had measured up, and this year he'd been absorbed in his family's troubles. Now he wondered if that was the only thing preventing him from finding a new relationship.

He and Lucky eased the desk down the front porch steps. The estuary smell didn't bother Edmond as much today. He supposed one could get used to it.

"Interesting how Rod left the heavy lifting to us,"

Lucky observed as they carted the desk toward a rental van in the gravel parking area.

"Is that typical of him?"

"I wouldn't exactly call him lazy." Lucky's amused tone indicated that he liked his new housemate. "But he does have a knack for arranging matters to suit his convenience."

"I'm surprised an anesthesiologist hasn't bought his own house by now." Edmond would love to do that, but he'd only recently paid off his educational loans.

"He spent all his money fighting for custody of his daughters, the two little flower girls at the wedding." Lucky led the way in maneuvering the desk up the ramp. "And lost to Portia and Vince Adams."

"As their father, Rod has rights." Edmond hefted his end of the desk.

"He found out six years ago during the divorce that Portia had cheated on him and the girls weren't genetically his, even though he'd raised them as his own." Lucky shook his head. "They aren't Vince's, either, but he's rich enough to afford the best representation, if you consider scummy bottom-feeders the best. Sorry, I don't mean to speak ill of lawyers. Well, maybe I do, but I'm sure you're an exception."

"I hope so." Edmond had heard his share of lawyer jokes, along the lines of *Why don't sharks bite attorneys? Professional courtesy.* He chose not to take the cracks personally.

As for Rod, under California law, he was the children's father regardless of genetics, since he'd been married to their mother when they were born. However, a guy as rich and reputedly unscrupulous as Vince could grind an opponent into the dust with one courtroom tactic after another.

"I try to avoid contentious cases," he said. "My preference is for both sides to reach a compromise."

"Are people really willing to do that where children and divorces are concerned?"

"Not always." Edmond understood Lucky's skepticism. "But if they can move past their initial insistence on winning, most prefer to do what's in the best interests of the child. They can also save themselves money and stress."

With the desk stowed, he brushed off his hands and descended the ramp. On the driveway, Lucky stretched. "Let's hope Melissa won't be requiring your services."

What a strange remark. "Which services?"

The other man laughed. "As an attorney."

"Why would she?"

"The embryos."

Usually, Edmond was quick to grasp people's meanings, but not in this case. "She said there's no father involved. Since I assume the sperm donor signed a release, I don't understand why she'd require legal counsel."

"You haven't heard the story?" Lifting a hand, Lucky shaded his eyes against the midday glare. "She didn't use a sperm donor."

Surely Melissa hadn't been rash enough to involve a man simply on the promise that he'd stay out of the picture. "Who's the father, then?"

"The father *and* the mother are clients who donated their unused embryos." Lucky glanced toward the house. "I'm sure they signed off on the whole thing, but people can be unpredictable."

"The babies aren't hers?" That was an inaccurate assessment, Edmond realized as soon as he said it. "Genetically, I mean."

"You got it."

She was carrying babies that weren't related to her. Edmond assumed she felt a strong attachment, yet many women served as surrogates and willingly relinquished the infants. Not that he expected Melissa to do any such thing.

The more he learned, the less he understood her. When he'd moved to Safe Harbor, he'd hoped he might finally grasp what had gone wrong between them and possibly how to fix it. Instead, the picture kept getting muddier.

Yet hadn't he cherished their differences during their marriage? She'd been his refuge when he felt overwhelmed, and he'd been her strength when her world had fallen apart after her parents' deaths.

When she'd brought up the idea of becoming parents, he wished now that he'd listened to her rather than reacting the way he had. But ultimately, they'd still have stood on opposite sides of a great divide.

The front door opened. Karen emerged, toting a couple of suitcases. Behind her, Rod hefted a box, grimacing as if about to collapse beneath its weight. Either it contained heavy books or he was milking the situation.

Preoccupied by what Lucky had revealed about the embryos, Edmond was in no mood to stick around for polite chitchat, with them *or* with Melissa. After a brief farewell, he went to his car.

As for the triplets, Melissa ought to be safe from a legal perspective. And surely she loved these children. Still, these babies were the blood kin of another couple, a mom and a dad. They'd presumably borne other children, so what *were* the implications for Melissa of raising triplets who had full siblings living nearby?

Embryo donation wasn't as regulated as adoption or surrogacy. In many respects, the legal status of embryos remained unsettled, but their transfer was governed by contract law as if they were property.

This discovery changed nothing between him and Melissa. So why did he feel sucker-punched?

Chapter 6

"You can't be serious!" On the examining table, Melissa tugged the ridiculously small hospital gown around her protruding abdomen. It still failed to close. "I thought I was doing well."

"You are." Dr. Zack Sargent appeared surprised by her outburst. "I didn't say you have to go on bed rest right now. But in a couple more weeks, we should consider it."

With an effort, Melissa curbed her irritation. Her obstetrician cared about her. Zack had worked her into his Monday schedule to give her an extra checkup due to the increased risks of her pregnancy.

"My only symptoms are dry skin and trouble getting comfortable in bed," she reminded him in a calmer tone. "You said I'm in great shape for eighteen weeks."

"That's true." Zack regarded his computer terminal.

An earnest man in his mid-thirties, he was the driving force behind the hospital's grant program for financially strapped clients. He was also married to Melissa's boss, Jan. "Blood pressure, weight gain, glucose levels, babies' heartbeats—everything's normal. Impressive, actually. But keeping you all healthy until delivery will be a balancing act."

"Surely lying around for months can cause problems, too." The prospect dismayed Melissa. She had too many responsibilities at work.

"Lack of activity can raise the risk of blood clots and decrease bone mass, which is why I don't recommend complete bed rest unless absolutely necessary," he said. "However, bed rest can mean simply staying home and doing less than usual. I'm also concerned about you operating a car as you get bigger."

"Karen offered to give me a ride to and from work whenever I'm ready to stop driving." Melissa was grateful for her generous friend. "And my housemates said they'd pick up groceries for me. I don't need them to do any of that yet, but I'll accept it as soon as I do."

"Good," Zack said. "Pay attention to what your body's telling you."

"It's telling me that staying home would drive me crazy." Aware of how much he cared about the fertility program, she noted, "And it's not as if Jan can throw a temp into my position."

From the doctor's expression, she saw that her point had registered. "Talk to her about working remotely," he advised. "There's no reason you can't keep up with your email and meet with clients from home."

"I can come into the office as long as I feel okay, though, right?" Melissa pressed. "I'll put my feet up.

And it should be easier for you to monitor me here at the hospital than at home."

Zack typed a note into the computer. "All true. But don't forget, there's a sixty percent chance that multiple babies will be born prematurely, plus your entire body is under stress. It's working hard even when you're resting."

Melissa closed her eyes, willing herself to relax. "I know that pregnancy is temporary and well worth the trouble. That doesn't make this easy."

"Of course not."

If she were married, things would be different, she reflected. Despite the assurances of her friends, the hospital's paid maternity leave and the staff day-care center, she experienced moments of panic about how she would cope with three babies.

If only Edmond... But that was ridiculous. He had problems of his own, and his attitude toward fatherhood hadn't changed. Also, his departure yesterday without saying goodbye puzzled her.

"Continue eating well and exercising mildly, as you've been doing," Zack concluded.

"I will." Melissa enjoyed the gentle stretching exercises she performed every morning.

"Any questions?"

She shook her head.

"I have one." He smiled. "Have you chosen their names?"

"People keep asking me that, but no." She wasn't ready. Besides, the only names in Melissa's mind today were Dawn and Barbara, whose sentencing was scheduled for this afternoon.

"Something wrong?" Zack asked.

"Nothing we haven't covered." It wasn't her place to discuss Edmond's family problems.

He assisted her off the table. "Let's schedule you for another appointment in a week. Sooner if you experience problems."

"You bet." Regretting her earlier sharpness with him, Melissa added, "I appreciate your working me in this way."

"Glad to do it."

As she dressed, she was glad she wouldn't have to face house confinement just yet, especially when she wanted to be there for her niece. Well, with luck she had a few weeks to spare. And perhaps the sentencing wouldn't be as bad as she feared.

Sitting in a row of tiered seats at the back of a room in Orange County Superior Court, Edmond was only peripherally aware of the people around him in the gallery. When he'd entered, he'd recognized witnesses from the trial and some news reporters. The only person who mattered right now, however, was the middle-aged man in a robe seated behind the bench.

By now, the judge would have reviewed the presentencing reports and statements. Surely they mentioned that Barbara had no prior criminal record. Yet although Edmond wasn't an expert on body language, to him the judge appeared stern.

After a few introductory remarks, His Honor addressed Barbara directly. "You have been convicted of participating in a robbery spree that endangered both the victims and other bystanders. It also resulted in your partner's death." Near Edmond, a woman nodded agreement. "Although your incarceration will deprive your daughter of her mother's care, it's only by luck that the shootout that killed Mr. Greeley didn't also deprive other children of their parents, or parents of their children."

Edmond's fists tightened. While he couldn't disagree with the judge, this boded ill for his sister.

Briefly, His Honor reviewed the counts on which she'd been convicted. Then he pronounced sentence: six years on each of the three counts of robbery, to be served concurrently.

Six years. While other members of the gallery murmured their approval, Edmond sat motionless, struggling to grasp the implications. Since the law required a felon to serve a minimum of eighty-five percent of the term, Barbara faced five years in prison even if she received a reduction for good behavior.

Edmond had understood there'd been a risk of a long sentence. Yet, emotionally, he'd hoped for a year followed by probation. His backup plan of moving in with Mort and Isabel simply wasn't feasible for longer than a year.

"Six years may seem like an eternity, especially to a woman your age," the judge continued. "However, this is not only a punishment. It's also a chance to learn from the bad choices that brought you to this point and separated you from your daughter. I hope you'll avail yourself of the educational opportunities in prison and determine to set a better example for your child in the future."

He asked the court clerk to notify the Department of Children and Family Services to check on the daughter's well-being. Edmond felt a wave of gratitude that he already had temporary guardianship and had also filled out the paperwork for permanent guardianship. While a social worker would still have to review Dawn's situation, there was no reason for her to be removed to a foster home.

Dawn. Oh, Lord, how would she take this news?

"You are remanded to the Orange County Jail for transfer to the state Department of Corrections." The judge's severe expression softened. "I wish you luck, Miss Everhart. You still have a chance to make something of your life."

He rose to leave the courtroom. At the defendant's table, Barbara stood along with her attorney. In her orange jumpsuit, she looked small and helpless. Her light brown hair, pulled back in a ponytail, was thin and lank and still held traces of purple dye, a relic of another lifetime.

As the bailiff approached, Barbara turned until her gaze met Edmond's. Tears ran down her cheeks. "Take care of Dawn," she mouthed, and then the bailiff led her away.

"You have to pity her," a woman nearby said to her companion.

"I pity her daughter, not her," the other woman responded. "One of those bullets nearly hit my son."

In the hall, Edmond caught up with the attorney. A man in his mid-forties, Joseph Noriega had a weary air. "I know it isn't what you hoped for, but it's fair," he told Edmond.

"What about an appeal?" Edmond asked. "She has sixty days to file, doesn't she?"

"I'll talk to her," Noriega said. "But I recommend against it."

"Why?" If his sister might have her conviction overturned or her sentence reduced, that was worth pursuing.

"The evidence against her was overwhelming,"

Noriega explained. "If the conviction is reversed, the district attorney will retry the case. He might aim for the jugular."

"Prosecute her for Simon's death?" To risk a murder conviction was inconceivable.

"That's right." The attorney shifted the position of his briefcase. "As for resentencing, the judge could set her terms to run consecutively instead of concurrently." That would mean eighteen years, also unthinkable.

Nevertheless, Edmond wasn't ready to give up their last glimmer of hope. "It's my sister's decision."

Noriega cleared his throat. "Yes, it is. She doesn't have to decide immediately, but I'll need time to prepare an appeal."

Edmond moved to the next subject on his mind. "Can I talk to her?"

"Not now. The courthouse isn't set up for visits."

"What about once she gets to jail?"

Noriega glanced at his watch. "I doubt you'll be able to see her tonight, but I'll try to arrange a phone call. She should be in state custody by tomorrow."

"Thanks." Edmond knew the man was doing his best. While Noriega might not be a high-flying celebrity defense attorney, he had a solid reputation.

Left alone in the wide corridor, Edmond gathered his thoughts. His father and stepmother would be anxiously waiting for news. Although Isabel had arranged for Dawn to spend the afternoon with friends, she'd be home in a few hours. A smart little girl, she must be aware of what was happening and worried about her mother.

The responsibility for her and for everything that lay ahead rested on Edmond's shoulders. Barbara's pleading expression in the courtroom remained seared into his heart. Because she was nine years younger, he'd always been protective of her and tried to compensate for their father's absences and their mother's withdrawal. So when Barbara cried, it had often been Edmond who went to soothe her. They'd become close, and even when his responsibilities chafed, he'd tried not to let her down.

She'd never been the eager student that he was. When she entered her teen years, she'd lagged academically just as Edmond became caught up in college and law school. Still, he'd commuted from home, and tried to supervise her homework.

In retrospect, he realized Barb's relationship with their parents had worsened after he moved out and married Melissa, even though their dad had changed jobs to be closer to his family. Naïve and strong-willed, Barbara had been easy prey when she met Simon at the fast-food restaurant where she'd worked after school. Four years older and an ex-con who'd served a term for assault, he'd manipulated Barb into moving in with him. Despite Edmond's protests, their dad had insisted he'd done all he could to rein her in and had refused to call the police. Their mom had pleaded with Edmond not to make waves, afraid Barbara would cut off contact entirely.

I shouldn't have listened. She was underage and he was an ex-con.

But Edmond hadn't fought his parents' decision. As a result, his sister was headed for a long stretch in state prison.

He hoped Noriega could arrange that call tonight. Contact would be difficult after she left the county jail.

Although he didn't often deal with criminal cases, he knew she'd be transferred to a prison reception center for an evaluation that could take weeks. Depending on such factors as the length of her sentence and how big a security risk she posed, she'd then be assigned to an appropriate facility. With luck, she'd serve her term at the women's prison in Fontana, about an hour's drive from Safe Harbor. Once she was transferred, he could arrange regular visits with Dawn.

In the interim, his sister faced a frightening adjustment away from her loved ones, in a strange and intimidating environment over which she had no control. She'd be locked up with gang members, drug users and other women far tougher than she was. Picturing how terrified she must be, Edmond went cold.

From another courtroom, a group of people emerged, possibly jurors being released for the day. He stepped to the side.

But when he took out his phone, he couldn't bring himself to press his parents' number. He needed to figure out how to explain the situation and provide a reassurance he was far from feeling.

If he could just bounce his concerns off someone, someone he trusted with his most sensitive emotions. And only one person fit that description.

Melissa nearly called Edmond several times that afternoon. But much as she was worried about Barbara and Dawn, Edmond had more important matters to deal with. She'd wait and try him later this evening.

Also, concerned about the issues her doctor had raised this morning, she kept an eye on her supervisor's office across the reception area. Jan had been with clients and staffers all afternoon.

Spotting her alone at last, Melissa went to confer

with her. Crossing the outer office, she paused when the receptionist asked, "Any word from Edmond about his sister?"

"How do you know about that?" Melissa hadn't discussed Barbara's situation with the young woman, who was noted—or notorious—for tapping into the office grapevine. At times, Melissa suspected Caroline *was* the office grapevine.

"Someone must have mentioned it." She ducked her head. "Honestly, I swore off gossip when the neighbors were jawing about my parents splitting up and I discovered how much it hurt. They're together again, by the way."

"I'm glad. And to answer your question, I haven't heard anything from Edmond today." Melissa edged toward her supervisor's office. "I have to talk to Jan before she takes off again."

"Okay." Caroline spread her hands. "If there's anything I can do, just say the word."

"Thanks." Hurrying away, Melissa tapped on the coordinator's open door, glanced inside for permission and entered.

It didn't take long to sketch the bed rest situation for Jan, which surely she'd expected. Small and intense, Jan Garcia Sargent moved from behind her desk to a chair beside Melissa's.

"I'm delighted that you plan to continue working and consulting as long as possible." After a busy day, Jan's normally smooth dark hair tumbled breezily over her suit collar. "You're an important member of this team. We'll work around your confinement, if I may use such an old-fashioned word. Multiple pregnancies aren't to be taken lightly."

"I wonder if I bit off more than I can chew." Melissa halted, embarrassed to have revealed that. "It's just that I'm a single mom. There's three of them and only one of me."

"I was a single mother, too, although not to triplets," Jan observed. "I only had Kimmie, but my life was a lot more messed up than yours when she was born. Not that yours is messed up."

"I understand." Melissa took no offense.

"This is a rough period, but it will pass." Jan's gaze strayed to a two-part frame on her desk. The faces of her nine-year-old daughter and ten-year-old stepdaughter, Berry, beamed out. "It's worth the sacrifices."

"Still, I feel like I pushed off down a ski slope without realizing how steep it is." *Enough about that.* Melissa shifted to less personal matters. "I'm glad you understand about my work situation."

"Karen and I can handle some of your duties," Jan assured her. "And thank heaven for teleconferencing."

"As long as clients don't mind me being as big as a whale," she said ruefully.

"That's what most of them are hoping will happen to them," Jan reminded her.

"I suppose so." As she took her leave, Melissa felt better. She doubted many bosses—especially those who didn't work in a fertility program—would be as supportive.

It was nearly five o'clock when she returned to her desk. Might as well close up for the day.

Her cell rang. Heart thumping, she glanced at the readout. *Edmond.*

"What happened?" she asked without preamble.

"Six years." His voice shook.

Six years? Barbara would be thirty when she was released. Melissa ached for her former sister-in-law and for Dawn. "Is she all right?"

"I imagine she's in shock," he said. "In retrospect, I should have been prepared for it, but this is hard for me to accept."

His honesty meant a lot. In the past, he'd had a tendency to put up a brave front, even when she'd suspected he felt otherwise. "How did your parents take it?"

"I haven't filled them in yet. I'm still at the courthouse."

He'd called her first? This news must have jolted him to the core. And he'd reached out to her, of all people.

"It will be easier if I break the news face to face," Edmond said. "We have a lot of decisions to make."

Underneath the statement, Melissa detected a plea for help. Nurturing her friends and especially Edmond had always satisfied a profound need in her, and she couldn't refuse him now.

"Do you want me to come with you?" Although her only contact with her in-laws since the divorce had been to exchange Christmas cards, she doubted they'd mind.

In spite of everything, she still felt a part of this family. They'd meant so much to her after she lost her own parents.

"Yes!" He sounded relieved. "I value your perspective and I think they would, too."

"Do they still live in the same place? I could meet you there."

"I'd rather we drove together so we can talk en route." He named a restaurant where she could safely leave her car near the courthouse in Santa Ana, which lay about a third of the distance between Safe Harbor and Norwalk.

"I'll get there as soon as I can."

"I'll be waiting."

What did it mean that he'd called her first? Melissa mused as she locked her desk. Nothing, she told herself. In a crisis, people pulled together and set their differences aside.

She hurried out to her car.

Chapter 7

Edmond's new car—new since the divorce, anyway—
was a black sedan that suited him, Melissa reflected as
she slid into the cushiony passenger seat. High-tech and
well engineered, it was sophisticated yet down-to-earth.

In the enclosed space, his light spicy aroma surrounded her. Inhaling it, she instinctively relaxed.

"Thanks for joining me." Edmond waited while she
adjusted the seat belt around herself before shifting into
Drive. "My mind keeps running in circles. I hate things
being so out of control."

"I understand." Melissa didn't mention the red rim
around his eyes. Had he been crying, or had he merely
worn his contact lenses earlier? He rarely wore them,
since they caused irritation.

Edmond eased the car up a ramp onto the freeway.
With the traffic lighter than usual for a weekday rush

hour, the navigation computer estimated their trip at twenty minutes.

"My parents fixed up a bedroom for Dawn," he began. "She and Barbara have been staying with them, so she's comfortable there."

"Is that where she lived while she was in school?" Being spared a change of schools would be a plus if her grandparents pressed to keep her with them.

"No, my sister and Simon had an apartment, or rather, several. They moved a lot, probably because they were behind on the rent." Then he added, "With Isabel and Mort, she has a real home, although it's relatively new to her. It may not be wise to uproot her."

"But you have guardianship," Melissa reminded him.

"I have emergency temporary guardianship, but the court could transfer that to her grandparents, if it's for the best." Edmond spoke as if examining the possibilities from all angles.

His attitude disappointed Melissa. She'd observed at the wedding how much Dawn trusted him. But then, he'd sacrificed their marriage rather than become a father.

Striving for a low-key approach, she said, "I'm sure her grandparents dote on her. Still, your dad was never the warm fuzzy type."

"Isabel makes up for that."

"In some respects." A kindly divorcée with no children, Isabel had been a nurse's aide who'd attended Edmond's mother as she lay dying of cancer. Six months later, when Mort Everhart married her, Melissa had been happy for them both.

"We have to act fast," Edmond continued, transitioning into the carpool lane. "I presume family services will be preparing a report and it's best if we can show a stable living environment."

"What kind of report will it be?" Melissa asked.

"A credit and criminal background check on all adults who'll be supervising her, for starters." In the open lane, he stepped harder on the gas. "The state has to ensure that prisoners' children are safe."

"Will there be a home visit?" In connection with her work, Melissa was familiar with procedures in adoption cases, where home studies were required.

"Probably, and they'll interview any adults involved in her care." Edmond grimaced. "When I laid out the procedures for clients, I never understood how intrusive it feels."

Melissa's thoughts turned to the little girl's emotional reaction to her mother's sentencing. "Did you and her therapist discuss how to explain about prison to Dawn?"

He slanted her a smile. "You ask the right questions. Yes, we did go over that. Also, the counselor, Franca Brightman, gave me a list of what children need when their parents are incarcerated."

"What's on the list?" Melissa had never before known a parent or child facing such a situation.

"What you'd expect, for the most part." A freeway sign indicated they were entering Los Angeles County. "To receive full information about what's happening and how it will affect them. To feel safe and be able to express their emotions openly. To understand that they can stay in touch with their parent."

"Is that possible? I mean, on a regular basis." There must be a way to visit Barb, although the impression Melissa had from TV shows involved clanging prison doors, body searches and Plexiglas barriers. How intimidating for a small child. *Or an adult.*

"Yes, we'll work it out once she's assigned to a specific facility," he said. "Right now, though, Barbara's in transition."

"Poor kid." Although Melissa knew her former sister-in-law was in her twenties, she still pictured Barbara as a teenager.

"Her poor daughter," Edmond said. "Sessions with a therapist, visits to Mom in prison, living with relatives. That's hardly a normal childhood."

"Children adjust." That's what Melissa had heard, anyway. "I'm grateful that my parents were wonderful. I had it easy."

"Did you?" He shot her a skeptical look. "They never recovered from your brother's drowning when he was a toddler. It felt to me like they tiptoed around you, and each other."

Melissa hadn't considered how much her childhood had been shaped by the tragedy that had occurred when she was five and Jamie only two. She'd taken her family's tensions for granted. "That's true, I suppose."

"But as you say, you adjusted."

Now that he brought it up, she could see the pattern she'd adopted. "I went to great lengths to avoid conflict, or any behavior that might upset my folks." They'd never talked about Jamie, and only years later had her mother shared how much she regretted letting grief and guilt dissuade her from having another baby.

"We both took on the role of good child," Edmond noted. "We tried to protect our own parents."

"That's true. We had a lot in common." Melissa sometimes forgot how similar they'd been in most respects.

Edmond concentrated on the road ahead as they exited the freeway. A wide boulevard led through the business district of Norwalk, a city of about a hundred thousand people. A few signal lights later, he followed a series of side streets lined with unpretentious homes until they reached the place Melissa remembered well, a one-story house with a small, patchy lawn.

As Edmond parked, she took in the fading paint and scrubby bushes. She didn't recall the place having such a tired appearance.

On the sidewalk, Melissa started to reach for his hand, then thought better of it. Much as she longed to help Edmond, she was only here as an observer.

For his sake, she hoped he and his parents could figure out what was best for Dawn.

When presenting options to clients for divorces, custody issues or other family matters, Edmond prepared thoroughly. As a result, he was accustomed to experiencing a sense of calm as he geared up for action.

Not today. Although his initial near-panic had abated, he had to focus on breathing regularly as he rang the doorbell. Reviewing the situation with Melissa had reinforced his conviction that Dawn belonged with his father and stepmother, yet an undercurrent of uneasiness remained.

Inside, the floor creaked and the door unlatched to reveal Isabel Everhart, her stocky figure still robust at age sixty-three and her brown hair only lightly touched with gray. Her gaze moved past Edmond to Melissa. "Well, this is a nice surprise."

"I'm glad to be here." Melissa reached to hug her former mother-in-law. "Edmond and I are coworkers at the hospital now—I'm sure he told you that."

"He didn't tell me about this." Ushering them inside, Isabel patted Melissa's bulge.

"Long story," she said apologetically.

"I wasn't asking." Isabel had always respected other people's privacy. It was one of the many qualities Edmond liked about her.

"I wouldn't blame you if you did," Melissa said. "But we have more important things to talk about today."

"Yes, we do."

In the living room, Edmond's father clicked off the TV and arose from the well-worn couch. In his late sixties, he had thinning white hair and weathered skin, the deep creases testifying to years of smoking. He'd quit during his first wife's final illness.

"About time you got here," he grumbled to Edmond. To Melissa, he said, "Dare I hope my son finally showed some smarts and won you back?"

"It's good to see you, too, Mort." She shared a light hug with the old man.

"You're together again?" He'd always had a soft spot for his daughter-in-law.

"We're friends, that's all." Edmond didn't want his ex-wife's presence to distract them. "Dad, Isabel…"

"If you didn't knock her up, who did?" Mort demanded.

"That's none of our business," Isabel spoke more forcefully than usual. "Edmond, the lawyer called and broke the news about the sentence."

Damn. He'd waited too long. "That should have come from me. I assumed this might be easier in person."

"None of this is easy," Mort growled.

"That's neither here nor there." Isabel continued briskly, "Mr. Noriega said he'll have Barbara call you in about a quarter of an hour, and Dawn should be home any minute. We'd better talk fast."

Edmond agreed. "Okay. About where Dawn's going to live…"

"I haven't had dessert," Mort growled. "Be in the kitchen." With that, he stomped off.

Although his dad had never been the sociable type, this was abrupt even for him. "He must be angry about the sentence. Or at Barbara," Edmond guessed.

"Both, I suppose, but that's not the whole story." His stepmother took a seat in a flowered armchair, leaving the couch to her guests. "I'll be frank with you."

"Please do." Now what? Edmond was grateful for Melissa sitting quietly beside him, hands folded in her lap.

"I know we discussed keeping Dawn here, but that's no longer possible," Isabel said.

Perhaps she didn't understand how much support Edmond planned to provide, both financially and in practical terms. "This is a longer sentence than we expected," he conceded. "However, I can arrange things…"

"Hear me out." Isabel didn't sound angry. In fact, he'd have pegged her emotion as sadness. "I have something to tell you."

"Is it Dad's cancer?" Edmond had believed that was no longer a threat.

"No." In the early-evening light through the window, his stepmother's square, plain face showed a sprinkling of age spots. "But Mort's oncologist observed some behaviors that concerned him and referred us to a specialist."

"Behaviors?" Edmond queried.

"Your father is showing signs of dementia."

In the shocked silence that followed, Edmond became aware of random noises—the hum of electricity, the rattle of a truck on a nearby street, a dog barking in a neighbor's yard. "I wish you'd said something to me earlier." He'd assumed they were keeping him in the loop.

"We just found out this morning," Isabel said.

"I'm so sorry." Melissa regarded her in dismay. "What a horrible thing. And the timing is terrible."

No wonder Mort had left the room before this discussion. "How severe is this? Is it Alzheimer's?" Edmond asked.

"Too soon to be sure." Isabel swallowed. "We're arranging for further testing."

"How's Dad taking it?"

"He rejects the whole idea." His stepmother shrugged. "Claims he's fine."

"That's natural," Melissa said. "It's a scary diagnosis."

"There's no actual diagnosis yet," Isabel corrected. "Just a suspicion."

"He has to face up to this." Edmond had heard that with dementia, early treatment could make a big difference.

"Face up to losing his grip on reality? His memories, his personality?" Isabel's voice broke.

"You're right." Until now, Edmond hadn't viewed this development from his parents' perspective. "It's devastating news."

"We're taking it one day at a time." His stepmother sighed. "Obviously, we can't raise a child under these circumstances. She'll have to live with you."

Dawn deserved a nurturing home with experienced

adults. She faced a difficult adjustment. What chance did she have with an uncle who'd failed miserably when he'd tried to be there for his sister?

Edmond had confidence in his ability to handle challenges at work and in court. But when it came to raising a child, he was lost. If he failed Dawn—if she grew up consumed by anger, or so desperate for masculine attention that she ran to a man like her father—it would be even worse than what had happened with Barbara. He'd have no one to share the guilt with. The entire responsibility would fall on him.

Around him, the silence lengthened, and he appreciated the women's willingness to let him struggle with his inner turmoil. Ultimately, what choice was there? Edmond had promised to supervise his niece's care if necessary. And necessary it seemed to be.

Outside, a car door slammed and a childish voice called her thanks to someone. "She's home," Isabel said, unnecessarily.

He'd run out of time.

"No!" More like a two-year-old than a seven-year-old, Dawn thrust out her lower lip, folded her arms and sat rigid on her chair. "I can't go live with Uncle Eddie."

Melissa noted the frustrated exchange of looks between Edmond and Isabel. They'd spent the past few minutes gently explaining about the sentence and assuring the little girl that she'd be safe and happy with her uncle.

"I'll rent a larger place where you can have your own bedroom." Edmond was hiding his doubts well, in Melissa's opinion. "You'll enjoy Safe Harbor. Remember how much fun you had at the wedding?"

"You can take your furniture with you," Isabel added. "And of course your books and toys."

"No." The little girl blinked back tears.

"Honey, Grandpa Mort has serious health problems." Isabel peered toward the kitchen, but there was no sign of the old man. "And your uncle loves you."

"A lot," Edmond added.

"I love you, too, but I can't live with you." Dawn hunkered down. Even her short brown hair seemed to bristle with defiance.

Melissa glanced worriedly at Edmond. She knew it had been hard enough for him to accept his role as surrogate parent without this rebelliousness.

However, only the tightness around his mouth revealed his impatience. "All these changes are a lot for you to accept, sweetheart. But I'm not such a bad guy, am I?"

"No." She sniffled.

"You can stay with Grandpa and me for a week or two, until your uncle's prepared a place for you," Isabel assured her. "That'll give you a chance to wrap your mind around this."

"I can't!" More quietly, Dawn said, "I'm going to prison with Mommy."

Her innocent loyalty brought Melissa near tears. What a brave little soul her niece was.

"Whatever gave you that idea?" Isabel shook her head in dismissal.

"They don't allow that," Edmond said edgily. "None of us is happy about this long sentence, Dawn, but we have to adapt."

"I *am* adapting!" she insisted. "I'll wear an orange jumpsuit like prisoners on TV."

"This isn't a game of dress-up. You can't play pretend prisoner." At Edmond's sharp tone, the little girl cringed.

Melissa had tried to stay out of the discussion. The problem was that, in their different ways, both Edmond and Isabel were so intent on persuading Dawn to accept the inevitable that neither questioned the cause of her stubbornness.

"Dawn, of course you're upset about your mommy." Melissa gazed into the little girl's misty eyes. "But why should you go to prison with her?"

"If I'm not there, who'll take care of her?" The question emerged breathlessly.

"What do you mean?" Edmond asked.

"She skips breakfast," Dawn said earnestly. "She forgets to put the laundry in the dryer."

"Believe me, in prison that won't be a problem," he muttered.

"You can't be sure of that!"

He frowned. "I'm a lawyer, honey. I'm aware of how prisons operate."

He was missing the emotional context, Melissa thought, and spoke again. "Dawn, do you believe it's your job to take care of your mom?"

"Somebody has to," she said. "I'll stay with her. I don't mind."

"Prisons aren't for children." Edmond spoke more gently.

"You could ask them," Dawn responded.

Melissa stroked the child's hair. "It's loving of you to try, but your mom's grown-up. She has to take care of herself now."

"And prisons are very well run. They have kitchens and laundry rooms and— Hold on." Edmond drew his vibrating phone from his pocket. "Yes, Mr. Noriega? Thank you! Of course I'll talk to her."

The attorney must be about to put Barbara on the line. Melissa hoped her sister-in-law wasn't in meltdown. That would only make things harder for Dawn.

Edmond carried the phone into the hall. As the little girl jumped up, Isabel touched her granddaughter's arm. "Give them a minute, sweetie."

Dawn plopped down again. Lips pressed together in a firm line, she sat shaking with tension.

Chapter 8

"In court, I could tell the audience was pleased about the sentence." On the phone, Barbara's words rang with pain. "It's awful how close those bullets came to hitting bystanders. I screwed up. I guess I deserve this. But I'm scared, Eddie."

"Has anyone hurt or threatened you?" he asked, careful to face away from the living room to prevent his voice from carrying.

"No, but in this place they're taking me to, I'm sure there'll be women who've done all sorts of things. I've seen prison movies."

He pictured his little sister's frightened green eyes, much like Dawn's. "Remember what I told you before. Be polite to everyone and don't make friends or enemies. Don't ask questions or accept favors." Behind bars, there were different rules of social behavior. "I'll arrange to visit as soon as possible."

She hurried on. "Don't bring Dawn till I'm assigned somewhere. At the reception center, I'm not allowed to touch anyone, and it would drive us both crazy. Mr. Noriega said I can't have phone calls while I'm there, either, just paper to write letters. Oh, I wish I could hug her!"

"She's worried about you." That was an understatement, he thought. "Seeing you might reassure her."

"Or terrify her. She has to get used to her new life. Please keep a close watch on her. Isabel means well, but…" The sentence trailed off.

"Isabel has her hands full with Dad." Edmond summarized their father's tentative diagnosis. "I'm sorry to drop this on you. I'm sure you wish you could be here for him."

"Isabel will cope fine," Barbara said. "You'll take care of Dawn as you promised, won't you?"

There was no room for hesitation. "Absolutely," he said. "As soon as I find a bigger apartment, she'll move in with me."

"You'll be a great dad."

His sister was overestimating his abilities. "I don't understand children," Edmond admitted. "Melissa's much better with her than I am."

"Melissa's there?"

"She came with me today," he confirmed.

"That's wonderful. I was hoping you'd reconnect." Barbara had been enthusiastic on Saturday morning when he'd mentioned having run into his ex-wife.

No sense emphasizing that he and Melissa were merely friends. He hadn't brought up the pregnancy, either, and wasn't about to now. "She's very fond of her niece."

A small figure darted into the hallway. "Can I talk to Mommy?" Dawn demanded.

"My baby!" Barbara cried in Edmond's ear.

"I'll put you on speaker." He tapped the phone. "Go ahead."

From the front room, Melissa ventured into view, arms folded over her middle. They shared an apprehensive look as Dawn blurted, "I want to go with you, Mommy. Where are you?"

"Honey, I miss you." Despite a catch in her voice, Barbara forged on. "Mommy did wrong. I broke the law and I can't be with you for a while. Uncle Eddie and Aunt Lissa are there. You behave."

Dawn broke into tears. "Mommy, you need me!"

Still holding out the phone, Edmond wrapped an arm around her. "It's okay, sweetheart. I'm here."

"Dawn, it's the grown-ups' job to take care of you." Barbara spoke with more maturity than he'd heard from her before.

"Who's going to cook for you?" the little girl persisted.

"They serve regular meals in prison. It's like having my own restaurant."

"What about your dirty clothes?" Dawn asked.

"Prisons have a laundry." Barbara assured her. "Honey, until we can visit again, I'll write you letters, real letters, not email. You can practice reading them."

As his sister struggled to put up a brave front for her daughter, Edmond's chest squeezed.

"I'll write you, too, Mommy," Dawn said. "Aunt Lissa, will you help me?"

"Of course," Melissa assured her. "We can send pictures, too."

"Mel? I'm glad you're there. Oh, damn, I have to

go." Barbara sniffled. "I love you all. Eddie, take care of my baby."

"I will." His breath came fast but he held his emotions in check. No sense in all of them breaking down.

After a round of farewells, the call ended. Edmond flashed on a memory of his sister at about Dawn's age. Sixteen and newly licensed, he'd picked her up one day after school.

Beaming, she'd bounced in her seat as he drove at a snail's pace, stopping at every yellow light and signaling for a quarter mile before each turn. "Go faster!" she'd cried.

"Drivers have to obey the speed limit," he'd said.

"Nobody's watching."

"That isn't the point. I might I hit someone." Even as a teenager, he'd had a strong awareness of consequences.

"You won't," she'd responded confidently.

"I won't because I'll be careful not to."

She'd laughed. "You should have more fun, Eddie."

They'd had contrasting personalities from the start. Sadly, she hadn't learned from his example or from her own experiences. Now she was paying a high price for her recklessness.

So was her daughter, Edmond reflected, holding Dawn close while sobs racked her little body. Prepared or not, he'd become her guardian in every sense.

He hadn't been able to save his sister. He hoped he'd do better for his niece.

Melissa had always been organized. On school nights, she'd laid out the next day's clothes over a chair and placed her books and homework in her backpack. She'd also maintained a wall calendar where she'd tracked upcoming tests and field trips. Friends had considered her weird, but her parents had approved.

Being on top of things had felt right. Sudden changes of plan, however, had distressed her unduly. Suffering stomach flu the morning of a math test, she'd hidden her symptoms from her mother and thrown up in the school hallway. Seeing her mother's worry when she'd arrived to take her home, Melissa had burst into tears.

It's okay to get sick, her mom had said. *Everybody does.*

Melissa hadn't shared the fear that gripped her because she hadn't clearly understood it herself. Losing control meant spinning loose without a mooring. Organization was her coping strategy, her security.

Once, just once, her mom had failed to watch two-year-old Jamie as closely as usual. At a neighbor's house during a party, he'd fallen into the swimming pool. He hadn't cried out or thrashed in the water, and no one had noticed. It had been Melissa, only a few years older, who'd spotted his little body at the bottom of the pool. The sight had been so surreal, she'd had to look twice before she started screaming.

Later, she'd tormented herself, wondering if he could have been saved had she reacted sooner. That fear had persisted for years, and she'd realized later that it had contributed to her sense that she'd be happiest without children. Only after a confidence from her mother, shortly before her parents' deaths, had Melissa released that nagging guilt and been able to acknowledge her deep desire to be a parent.

She understood Dawn's wish to accompany her mother behind bars. Some kids felt they were to blame for anything that went wrong around them. She figured it was even more true in a dysfunctional household, where the child might assume an adult role as a coping mechanism. In Edmond's home, with his father often away and his mother rather passive, he'd believed it was up to him to supervise his sister.

In the car, Melissa studied Edmond's profile as he navigated the freeway on-ramp.

"I admire you for taking in your niece," she said. "I know how hard it is for you."

He gripped the steering wheel. "Part of me is angry with Barbara, even though I feel rotten about what's happened."

Melissa watched him intently. "This situation isn't fair to you or to Dawn."

Seconds ticked by while he merged into traffic, which had thinned as rush hour passed and twilight descended. "I'll do everything I can, but is it really best for her to live with an uncle who has no idea how to be a dad?"

"I'm no expert on being a mom, either," she pointed out. "Especially to triplets. But my friends assure me you get on-the-job training. Plus, there's no single way to be a parent. Every person is different, although there are ground rules."

"Like feeding them and washing their clothes?" he asked dryly.

"And holding them when they cry," she said. "You've already mastered that part."

He shrugged. "I can do the obvious stuff, but I lack the right instincts."

She weighed her words, wary of pushing too hard. "There's a learning curve for everyone. But you *are* sensitive to your niece."

"Not as sensitive as you. Would you be willing…?"

He cleared his throat. "I hate to impose, but can you help while we settle in? I'm a bit overwhelmed by what lies ahead, and Dawn's attached to you."

Despite Dr. Sargent's cautions and her awareness that she'd soon have to limit her activities, Melissa's spirits rose at the request. Being able to nurture others had always been central to her happiness, and at this crisis point, both Edmond and Dawn clearly needed her.

"Of course." She shifted in her seat to ease the tugging of her abdominal muscles.

"It's only for a few days," Edmond went on. "I should draw up a parenting plan, the way I advise my clients to do in a custody situation."

"Smart idea." Being a family attorney had prepared him in a lot of ways, at least for the practical aspects of his new role.

Edmond shook his head. "On top of everything else, I'm worried about Dad."

"Dementia is terrifying." Melissa would prefer a physical disease, however deadly, to mental deterioration, but people didn't get the choice. "However, it will probably develop gradually, and Isabel's handling the doctor appointments. Let's stick to what has to be done right away."

"You always anchor me." Edmond slowed to let a truck shift into their lane.

"Glad to do it."

He flicked on the car lights in the growing darkness. "To begin with, I'll have to rent a bigger apartment with a bedroom for Dawn."

"What about a house?" Melissa recalled her receptionist mentioning a three-bedroom place for rent down the block from her family's home. "I heard of a vacancy a mile or so from the hospital."

"I'd like a house." The tension in Edmond's shoulders eased. "Compared to an apartment, a house has a greater sense of permanence, and a yard to play in."

Taking out her phone, Melissa opened the organizer. "I'll start a list."

He gave her a crooked grin. "You and your lists."

"You do the same thing!"

"We have that in common," he agreed. "Will you send it to me when we're done?"

"No, I was planning to keep it to myself and charge you for access," she teased.

His answering chuckle warmed her. "Okay, let's have at it. Put down renting a house. I should buy more household supplies, too. I'm always running out of detergent— I certainly don't want Dawn assuming she's responsible for *my* laundry now."

"Don't forget about day care." Melissa recalled a nurse discussing her child's activities. "The community college runs a summer sports camp for kids, with two-week sessions. At Dawn's age, that should be more interesting than parking her in the hospital's child center."

"I'm not sure she's the athletic type," Edmond said. "Barbara never talked about that."

"Sports camp offers gymnastics, swimming and other fun stuff geared to little kids," she said. "I can check it out online."

"I don't mean to lay too much on you," he cautioned. "Especially in your condition."

"Mostly I'll handle things from home." Melissa jotted another note. "You'll have to enroll her in school soon. It starts in August."

"I'll discuss that with Geoff Humphreys's wife. She teaches second grade." Keeping his gaze on the road, he said, "I'm glad you're tracking all this."

"Thumbs of steel," she kidded as she pressed the tiny buttons.

"Oh, and remind me to keep tabs on Barbara's status," he said. "We'll visit as soon as she's placed."

"Got it."

"I should stay in touch with her lawyer about an appeal, too," he went on. "He recommends against it. Still, she has sixty days to decide."

The list was lengthening, and Melissa hadn't finished. "I'll check with Isabel about Dawn's favorite foods."

"Ouch. Meal preparation is *not* my strong point." Beneath his glasses, Edmond rolled his eyes. "Please don't tell me to take a cooking class."

"Just hang out at my house," she assured him. "You'll learn by osmosis."

"Your roommates wouldn't mind?"

"They like Dawn. And you, too." Melissa suspected the group would enjoy teaching Edmond to fix meals for his niece. "It's fun when there are guests at meals."

"I'll chip in for the cost, of course."

"Definitely."

Ideas flowed between them. Maintain Dawn's schedule with her counselor. Contact child services and provide information for the social worker's report. Use Isabel's email address to provide daily updates to her and Dawn about their preparations so the little girl felt involved in the process.

At the same time, a cloud of "if-onlys" swarmed inside Melissa's head. If only Edmond hadn't refused to consider parenthood, they'd still be together. If only they'd had a baby, they could welcome Dawn into an established family. If only his heart had room enough for a houseful of babies.

What a ridiculous notion. She was projecting her longings onto a man who'd made his position crystal clear.

For the few weeks remaining before she had to restrict her activities, she'd do her best to serve as Dawn's aunt and Edmond's friend. She'd be a fool to fantasize about anything more.

She would never allow him, or her own vulnerability, to break her heart again. That didn't mean she had to abandon him or her niece.

She was stronger now than she'd been during their marriage, Melissa reflected. And surrounded by friends.

They were on a roll. Edmond's spirits, which had hit bottom after his sister's conviction, resurged. Not that he underestimated the difficulties ahead, but he'd regained a sense of order, thanks in large part to Melissa.

Stealing a glance at her, he admired the luxurious flow of her fair hair and the velvety texture of her skin illuminated by passing car lights. The adjectives he associated with her—*graceful* and *radiant*—were especially apt since her pregnancy.

Yet a question nagged at him, one that he should have asked years ago. Raising it now might roil the waters, but it lay between them, a thin, nearly invisible barrier that blocked any possibility of drawing closer.

"Mel," he said. "May I ask you something?"

She must have registered the difference in his tone, because she set her phone in her lap. "Shoot."

"I never understood why you changed your mind

about having children." He didn't wish to provoke an argument, but a sense of fairness propelled him to clarify, "You always seemed as happy as I was with our marriage."

"Lots of women change their position on motherhood when they get older." Despite the defensive words, she sounded more introspective than angry. "You've heard of the infamous biological clock. And because I work in the fertility field, I'm around babies and maternal hormones. They have a powerful effect."

That was the explanation she'd given previously. It hadn't satisfied him then and it didn't now. "There had to be more. You just sprang it on me."

She gave a startled jerk. "No, I didn't."

"It was as if you turned thirty and suddenly I hardly recognized you." He tried not to sound accusatory.

"I didn't spring it on you," she said. "We'd discussed having children."

"When?"

"After my parents died." That had been several years before they split up.

Vaguely, Edmond remembered her talking about the meaning of parenthood, but he'd associated that with the shock of losing her parents in a car accident while the couple was vacationing in Hawaii. "Maybe in the theoretical sense."

"It was more than that," Melissa insisted. "We talked about regrets, about not being able to go back and undo our choices." She had a much sharper memory of this conversation than he did, Edmond gathered.

"And that related to having children?" He'd failed to grasp the implication.

"I cited parenthood as an example of things we might regret."

"As I said, it was a theoretical discussion." Freeway lights banished the darkness as they neared the restaurant where Melissa had left her car. "Then you dropped it."

"Not exactly." She adjusted the seat belt, which kept slipping around her bulge. "I didn't want to hammer too hard because your mom was sick."

That failed to explain her abrupt insistence on having children. "If it mattered that much to you, you should have pursued it, not ambushed me with it."

"What difference would it have made?"

Acting evasive was out of character for her. "There's something you're not saying."

"Stop interrogating me. We aren't in court."

Edmond's marriage, his vision of the future and his happiness had crashed because of his wife's sudden demand. Granted, he'd contributed to the mess with his high-handed response, but the discovery that she was hiding her reasons, or a significant part of them, disturbed him.

"Tell me what you withheld," he said. "Please."

He'd gained enough perspective to understand that she instinctively avoided conflict. That hadn't usually been a problem between them, but in the grip of strong emotions, he must have spoken more forcefully than he intended.

This time, Edmond resolved to listen carefully. But he wouldn't let up until she told the whole truth.

Chapter 9

Distressed, Melissa shook her head. "I can't."

"Not acceptable." He'd read once that you had to clean out a wound before you had any chance at healing. That struck him as true for relationships, too. "Married couples aren't supposed to keep secrets."

"It wasn't my secret to keep."

What an odd statement. "Whose was it?"

"My mother's."

How could a secret of her mother's have destroyed their marriage? he wondered as he exited the freeway. "Melissa, she's not in a place where she needs you to protect her anymore."

She shivered as if her mother were watching from beyond the grave. "I promised never to betray her confidence."

"This is ridiculous." Hearing the dismissiveness in

his voice, Edmond amended, "I understand that you're upset. But I have a stake in this, too."

For a moment, the only noises were the rush of traffic and a siren wailing in the distance. Finally she spoke.

"Before they left for Hawaii, Mom apologized to me." She swallowed. "She knew how traumatic it had been for me, discovering my baby brother's body at the bottom of a pool."

He hadn't heard that part of the story. "I didn't realize you were the one who found him."

"I spotted him under the water. It was surreal, like a bad dream." Melissa took a couple of breaths before continuing. "I had nightmares."

"I can imagine. Did you get therapy?"

"No, and Dad was a psychologist. Isn't that ironic?" She shook her head. "For years, Mom refused to discuss anything about that day. She believed it was her fault because she didn't watch Jamie closely enough."

"Any parent would, I expect." Edmond had handled several divorces in which one partner blamed the other for the serious injury or death of a child. Sometimes they blamed themselves.

"It was more than that." She paused.

Aware of her emotional struggle, he quashed the urge to prod her for how her family's long-ago tragedy had affected her desire for parenthood. He *had* learned something in their three years apart.

"My mother explained that, at the pool party, the hosts were fixing margaritas. Mom rarely drank, but she didn't taste much alcohol in the margaritas, so she had several," Melissa said. "She wasn't sure how many. Three or four."

"That's why she wasn't watching Jamie closely," he guessed.

"Yes. The guilt haunted her." Tilting her head back, Melissa closed her eyes. Picturing her mother's face? Mary Fenton had been a classic beauty like her daughter, but she'd had deep-etched lines around her mouth and eyes. "Dad urged her to have another baby, but to her the risk was intolerable."

"You believe she was punishing herself?"

"Maybe, or terrified of screwing up again," Melissa replied. "After we were married and I made it clear we didn't plan on having kids, she feared her negative attitude had poisoned me against motherhood."

"Had it?" While she mulled his question, Edmond turned onto the street leading to the restaurant and swung into the parking lot. A scattering of cars bordered the coffee shop, with Melissa's white sedan sitting slightly apart. He pulled into an adjacent space and cut the engine.

"In retrospect, yes. After that conversation, I started to reevaluate my assumptions," Melissa said. "I talked about it to you a little, but then we got the news that they'd been killed. We were just recovering from that when your mom's cancer entered the terminal stage. There was a lot going on."

That might explain why he'd overlooked her subtle clues about motherhood. "I didn't notice a change in you, beyond what one might expect from losing loved ones."

"I wasn't entirely aware of it myself," Melissa conceded. "But I began to find kids fascinating. I realized that at some level, I had blamed myself, too, for not responding faster when I saw Jamie under the water. It was only a matter of seconds, but it felt like minutes. Somehow Mom's confession took that guilt away."

"So when you agreed with me that kids weren't necessary for a happy marriage," Edmond said slowly, "underneath that you were really afraid you couldn't protect them." He understood her fears, considering his regrets about not intervening with Barbara.

"I guess so, but I hated to cause problems in our marriage, particularly at such a difficult time for you. For a while I figured this desire for a baby would pass, so I tried not to dwell on it," Melissa admitted.

"What pushed you over the edge?" He assumed there'd been a trigger.

"One day at the lab where I worked, a woman who'd been on maternity leave brought in her baby." Melissa unsnapped her seat belt. "She offered to let me hold him. Feeling his little body in my arms, inhaling his baby scent, I just… I understood that having children was the reason I was put on this earth. That discovery must have been building inside me, but it hadn't hit me until then, and when it did, I had to share it with you right away. I suppose I should have eased into the conversation with more care."

A chill ran through Edmond. *That* conversation remained burned into his memory. "To me, your announcement came out of nowhere. It was as if you rejected everything we'd built together. As if you rejected *me*."

She stared at him, aghast. "I assumed it would bring us closer together."

"How could you imagine that?"

"I figured that once you got used to the idea, you'd be as excited about the new adventure as I was." She swallowed hard. "It meant so much to me, and then you went out and destroyed any possibility of compromise."

"Compromise?" Edmond didn't see how one could compromise on the subject. "You either have children or you don't."

"I believed you would discover that you'd grown, that you'd...matured since we first talked about kids."

Despite his resolve to listen patiently, he couldn't let the remark pass. "That's unfair. My decision not to have children *was* a mature one, based on my experience and my beliefs—beliefs we both held." His old anguish still burned. "When you changed your mind, you basically chose motherhood over me."

"When you had a vasectomy, you chose childlessness over *me*," she answered unhappily.

"That's not what I meant at all. I *was* choosing you, I was choosing the happy life that we shared.."

"To me, it seemed like I'd shared what mattered most to me, and you threw it in my face. How could I ever trust you again?" Melissa scooped her purse off the floor. "It's too late to undo any of this, even if we wanted to."

Edmond's chest hurt. More than that, his entire body hurt. Yet unfortunately, she was right. It was too late. "I hope we can still cooperate for Dawn's sake."

"Certainly." She opened her door. "We just have to keep our emotions out of it."

"And if you need anything during your pregnancy, don't hesitate to call me." Edmond knew she was facing serious challenges.

"Thanks." She stepped out into the night and walked to her car.

Sitting there and mentally replaying the conversation,

he wished he'd grasped her perspective at the time. He wouldn't have arbitrarily obtained a vasectomy—that had been arrogant. Still, it was doubtful their marriage could have survived. Edmond didn't want to be a father. He loved Dawn and he'd do his best as her guardian. But that didn't make him daddy material.

He waited while Melissa started her car and backed out. Then he followed the white sedan onto the freeway, watching over her until their paths diverged in Safe Harbor.

They might have no hope of reconciliation, but he still cared about her safety. He still cared about her.

Tuesday afternoon

Sender: Edmond Everhart
Subject: Our new home
Cc: Melissa Everhart

Dear Dawn and Isabel,
At lunch today, Aunt Lissa and I visited two houses for rent in Safe Harbor. One is a cottage near the beach, with a small yard and two bedrooms. The other has three bedrooms and a nicer yard and patio, but it's farther from the beach. I'm attaching pictures. Which looks better to you? I can't guarantee we'll get your pick, but I'll try.

Also, is it okay if I sign you up for sports camp during the day, while I'm working? You can play games and go swimming. Everyone says it's fun.
Love, Uncle Eddie

"I'd pick the house with more space," remarked legal secretary Lisa Rosen, removing a yogurt from the refrigerator in the law firm's lunchroom. Edmond had shared the pictures with the staff, who took a keen interest in his domestic situation.

"It's smart to include your niece in the process," added the fiftyish receptionist, Marie Belasco, who was replacing coffee supplies in the cabinet. "Fresh pot will be ready in a minute."

"I've had too much caffeine today anyway." Edmond had been running on full speed since early morning, returning phone calls and preparing pleadings for clients while starting on the list of things Dawn would need. He'd emailed Children and Family Services to ask the name of the social worker and checked out the sports camp website. Melissa had been a champ, setting up their lunchtime tour of rentals and accompanying him.

They were an effective team. He'd observed the overall condition of the houses, the square footage and the floor plans. She'd noticed the state of the kitchen appliances, the color schemes and the ages of the children playing in the neighborhood.

"The best houses go fast, so don't delay." Lisa, tanned and slim as befitted a sailing enthusiast, leaned against the counter while opening the carton. "Have you talked to Paula about registering Dawn for school yet? My son Fred was in Paula's class last year and she's fantastic."

"I plan to." Until recently, Edmond hadn't paid much attention to his coworkers' family situations. Now he could reel off the statistics: Lisa and her husband, both in their thirties, had a son and daughter ages eight and ten; Marie was divorced and an experienced foster mom whose adopted kids were in their teens. Geoff and Paula had two girls, ages eleven and fourteen.

His other perceptions were changing, too. How had

he managed to drive down Safe Harbor Boulevard for a year without noticing either Krazy Kids Pizza or the Bear and Doll Boutique? This morning, their signs had jumped out at him. He suspected he'd be visiting those places with Dawn in the near future.

Since he really had consumed too much coffee—half a dozen cups by late afternoon—Edmond excused himself, cut through the outer office and passed Marie's desk. No clients waited in the small reception area—a far cry from the large law office where he'd worked as an associate. A few more years there and he'd have been in line to make partner, but in that high-pressure environment, what had once been a major life goal had loomed like a prison sentence.

The term *prison sentence* hit Edmond painfully. Today was Tuesday, which meant Barbara should be en route to the reception center in central California. He had a vision of his sister huddled in her seat, shaken by every jolt of the bus carrying her farther and farther from home.

He hadn't realized that Geoff had stepped into the room until he heard the man's soft voice say, "I won't ask if the situation's getting to you, because you wouldn't be human if it weren't. But since you've been standing here staring at the blinds for several minutes, why don't you take the rest of the afternoon off?"

Embarrassed, Edmond tilted his head in acknowledgment. "I *was* thinking about my sister, but I assure you, I'm on top of things."

"I never doubted it." Geoff Humphreys gave him a genial smile. Although only forty, the guy projected a fatherly air. His receding hairline and tendency to wear wrinkled suits wouldn't have stood him in good stead in L.A., but he had a gift for putting clients at ease. *And me,* Edmond conceded. "You don't have to maintain a stoic front, Edmond. If I can help, just ask."

"I could use some advice from your wife," Edmond said. "I hear she's a great teacher, and my niece will be entering second grade."

"Paula loves animals and uses them in her lessons because kids really respond to them," Geoff said. "She's even converted me, and I'm allergic to cats and was never keen on dogs. But now we have a houseful of pooches."

"That's great." The stray dog hairs on the man's suit were part of his down-home charm.

"Pets are great for kids, too," his boss added. "Your niece like them?"

"It's hardly fair to bring a pet into a home that's empty all day." Diplomatically, Edmond added, "Unlike yours, I'm sure."

"Don't worry. I'm not offended," Geoff said. "Besides, the dogs keep each other company. That's the trick. Don't stop at one."

"I'll remember that." *And run in the opposite direction.*

Edmond's cell phone sounded. As he answered, he gave Geoff a farewell nod and headed for his office.

It was Mark Rayburn. "Got a minute?"

"Sure."

"I'm hoping you can bail us out of a jam." The administrator's pleasant manner didn't hide the determined undercurrent of his words. "We have a lecture series here at the hospital called the Medical Insight Series. On Friday, a speaker from D.C. was scheduled to discuss changes in health care laws."

"Excellent topic." Through the window, Edmond noted a few cars traversing the narrow parking lot. The office's location in a strip mall might be far from glamorous, but the busy convenience store and dentist's office brought in foot traffic.

"Unfortunately, he's had to cancel." Frustration underscored Mark's tone. "I wondered if you'd be willing to step in."

That was a tall order. "Wouldn't Tony be more knowledgeable about changes in health care laws?" That wasn't Edmond's field, nor did he have time to research it this week.

"I didn't mean you had to address the same subject," Mark assured him. "How about new directions in family law? There *are* new directions in family law, aren't there?"

"Collaborative law," Edmond confirmed. "It's an area I'm focusing on more and more."

"Yes, I recall discussing it with you," the administrator said. "That would be fine."

"This is called the *Medical* Insight Series, though, not the Legal Insight Series," Edmond noted wryly. "Won't that topic disappoint the audience?"

"Just weave in a few case histories that relate to surrogacy and such," Mark replied. "After all, Safe Harbor specializes in family medical issues."

Preparing a speech would add to a heavy week's schedule. Still, Edmond appreciated the honor, and Geoff would be pleased at the publicity. "Sure. I'll be happy to step in."

"Thanks. I'm glad we can count on you."

Within minutes after the call ended, Edmond had already thought of several examples to enliven the talk.

The prospect of headlining an event was invigorating, reminding him that he loved practicing law despite the pressure and the occasional frustration. Every day brought unique personalities and challenges that stimulated his mind and drew on his creativity. He enjoyed steering people through difficulties, analyzing their situations, mapping strategies and finding solutions.

Swiveling to his computer, Edmond opened a file and began jotting notes for his speech, energized for the first time in weeks.

Chapter 10

Tuesday afternoon

Sender: Isabel Everhart
Subject: From Dawn

Hi, Uncle Eddie and Aunt Lissa,
Please rent the house with three bedrooms. Then Mommy can stay with us if she comes to visit. [From Isabel: I told her this can't happen, but she insists on including it.]

Grandpa helped me find the sports camp website. It says I can pick my favorite sports from a list. That will be fun.
XXX (kisses)
Dawn (and Isabel)

"Ask her what she likes to eat," Karen prompted as Melissa drafted a response on her laptop.

She paused with her fingers above the keys. "You really don't mind if they join us for dinner once in a while?"

"Are you kidding?" Karen sat beside her at the breakfast table, which doubled as a community desk in the evenings. Tonight, they had the house to themselves. Rod and Zora had gone to Jack's apartment to put away Anya's things. Lucky was out eating pizza and playing video games with his buddies. "Growing up, I wished for a houseful of brothers and sisters, plus cousins and aunts and uncles at the holidays. Heck, I'd have been grateful for a father who joined us for meals."

Karen's mentally ill father had rarely ventured down from the second floor, she'd explained to Melissa when they'd first become friends. He'd died when Karen was nineteen, more than twenty years ago. Her mother, a nurse, had supported the family, working until her sixties, when Parkinson's disease forced her to quit. Divorced from an abusive husband, Karen had moved in with her mother until the elder woman's death the previous December.

"You're about to get your wish for more people. It's going to be a full house soon." Melissa adjusted her bulge beneath the lip of the table. "Even fuller than usual."

"We should throw a baby shower for all three of you mommies." Karen loved organizing social events.

"Let's wait till the dust settles, okay?" They'd barely finished cleaning up after the wedding. "Besides, I'm borrowing so much stuff from our coworkers, I'm not sure what I lack."

"We should start a list."

Melissa groaned. "Not another list."

"I'll do it." Her friend tapped on her tablet computer to wake it up. "It'll be fun to coordinate. Even if we don't have a shower, your friends will want to buy gifts for you, and I'll make sure we don't duplicate stuff that you and Zora could share."

"Such as what?" With triplets, Melissa figured she'd be using everything from a changing table to high chairs practically nonstop.

"How many baby bathtubs will you and Zora use?" Karen responded.

"None for me. Too much trouble. My babies will have to be content with sponge baths." That gave Melissa an idea, though. "I'll bet there are lists of suggested baby gifts posted online. You could start with one of those."

Her friend checked in her tablet. "Found one! Ooh, it's long, and thorough." Karen scanned it. "Let's add a fund to hire Nanny Nancy."

"Who's Nanny Nancy?"

"A newborn care specialist who works with multiples." Karen was jotting notes as fast as her fingers could fly. "Several staffers at the hospital have used her. Don't forget, between you and Zora, we'll have five babies in the house. Too bad there isn't a spare room for a nursery."

"We could kick Lucky out," Melissa teased. She didn't mention Rod.

"I wouldn't do that to him." Her friend grew serious. "Although he may have to move if he can't find a job locally with his new administrative degree."

"One problem at a time."

"I'll post the list on my blog as soon as it's ready." Karen usually blogged about the pluses and minuses of sharing a house, without revealing too many personal details. "Don't forget, Anya's due in September. That's only a little over a month away."

"I can't think past Sunday." As she'd explained to Karen, Edmond was planning to collect Dawn that day. It was fortunate the girl had chosen the three-bedroom, which had already been vacated by its previous tenants and was ready for occupancy. The beach cottage wouldn't have been available for two weeks. "Speaking of which, I'd better finish my email to Dawn." Melissa and Edmond had agreed that their niece should hear from both of them.

Melissa and Edmond had only been married a year when Dawn was born, and she'd been surprised by the rush of love she'd experienced when she first held her niece in her arms. She and Edmond hadn't been around Barbara much during her pregnancy, due to Simon's hostility, but they'd been invited to the hospital.

The infant had gazed inquisitively up at her aunt, her little mouth working and her hands waving. Helpless, sweet, filled with potential, but starting off in difficult circumstances—Melissa had instantly sensed that their lives would forever be entwined.

Whatever fears she'd harbored about having a child of her own didn't apply to her niece. Being an aunt was pure pleasure. Over the next few years, they'd spent as much time together as Melissa and Edmond could manage, dropping in when Simon wasn't around or running into each other at family gatherings. But after the divorce, Barbara had become hard to reach, and Melissa had reluctantly eased off her relationship with Dawn. It felt like fate that she and Dawn were once again connected.

"Don't forget to ask about her favorite meals," Karen prompted.

"Okay." On her laptop, Melissa typed, What are your favorite foods? Maybe Isabel can send the recipes.

"I'm not sure if I should say anything about Barbara," she told Karen. "It bothers me that Dawn is hoping her mom can visit, as if she were away at college."

"The truth will sink in gradually." Despite being childless, Karen had excellent intuition. "Focus on the things she can look forward to."

"Us reading together. Fortunately, I'm well stocked." During the past few months, Melissa had bought picture books for her triplets, including the favorites she and Dawn had once shared.

Remember *Goodnight Moon* and *The Runaway Bunny*? she wrote. I'll bet you can read those aloud to me now that you're entering second grade. And the triplets can listen, too. Scientists say babies can hear while they're inside their mothers. Karen set down her tablet. "How about some hot cider?"

"That would be great." Even in midsummer, an ocean breeze cooled the house, especially at night.

While her friend bustled around the kitchen, Melissa closed her eyes, hearing the distant murmur of the ocean and the call of night birds from the estuary, her mind wandering to the conversation she'd had with Edmond last night and the mixed emotions she'd experienced. Observing how much he cared about Dawn had reawakened her belief that Edmond had a deep capacity for fatherhood. Yet people could only be pushed so far outside their comfort zone, and Edmond was already way past his.

Karen returned with two aromatic cups of cider en-

hanced by cinnamon sticks. Melissa inhaled with pleasure. "That smells fabulous."

"Netflix just posted new episodes of one of our favorite series," her friend said. "You in the mood?"

"You bet." After double-checking that she'd copied
the email to Edmond, she hit Send.

Wednesday morning

Sender: Isabel Everhart
Subject: From Dawn

Hi, Uncle Eddie and Aunt Lissa,
My favorite food is peanut butter sandwiches with grape
jelly. I love Grandma Isabel's fried chicken with peanut
butter, too. It's supposed to be spicy but she takes the
hot stuff out. I like bacon, freezer waffles and shredded-
wheat cereal and orange juice. Artichokes are disgusting.

I'll read picture books to you and the babies. I'll sing to
them, too. My favorite song is "The Wheels on the Bus."

Can I play with my new friends Tifany [Isabel: unsure
of spelling] and Amber? They're nice.
Love,
Dawn (and Isabel)
Note from Isabel: As soon as I get a chance, I'll write
down the chicken recipe and send it to you.

Wednesday afternoon

Sender: Edmond Everhart
Subject: We got the house!
Cc: Melissa Everhart

Dear Dawn and Isabel,
I signed a lease today for our house. I'll move my furniture in on Saturday, and I'll pick you up on Sunday afternoon, if that's okay.

Aunt Lissa will help me figure out what groceries and other items to buy. Also, don't forget I'll be there tomorrow (Thursday) at 5:30 for our 6 o'clock appointment with Dr. Brightman.

I enrolled you in sports camp starting Monday morning. I'll talk to Tiffany and Amber's parents about a playdate.
Love,
Uncle Eddie

Arriving "home" from work, Edmond slid his car into a parking space between a station wagon with an Arizona license plate and a hybrid sedan from Utah. The Harbor Suites rented rooms and one-bedroom apartments—furnished or unfurnished—by the day or week. During his yearlong stay, he'd noticed that many occupants or their relatives appeared to be undergoing treatment at the hospital.

When Edmond had moved in, he'd planned to find a better place within a few weeks. However, the rent was reasonable, with Wifi included, and what more did a guy need than a bedroom, living room and kitchenette? After he sporadically checked rental listings the first month, inertia had set in.

Walking between one-story buildings to his unit, Edmond had to admit he wouldn't miss the courtyard's squatty palm trees and nondescript shrubbery. Nevertheless, the prospect of renting an entire house and supervising a child elevated his stress level.

What was the big deal? he wondered as he unlocked the door of his apartment. He hadn't been nearly this uneasy about transitioning from a big L.A. law firm to Geoff's small office.

Inside, he flicked on the lights. At five-thirty the summer sky was still bright, but the unit had a gloomy air. He set his container of take-out pasta in the kitchenette for later and wedged his briefcase against the small table.

Melissa had texted that she was leaving the hospital shortly and would be stopping by on her way home. They'd agreed to split the shopping duties. Despite his aversion to cooking, Edmond was more comfortable buying groceries than towels and other household items, perhaps because he'd had to learn his way around a supermarket by necessity.

He hadn't realized how much he'd valued having a teammate at home. During their marriage, he and Melissa had divided responsibilities smoothly, both pitching in, planning little surprises, always homing in on exactly what the other person would enjoy. What a relief it was, knowing he could count on her.

Edmond went into the bathroom to clean his glasses and brush his hair. He contemplated changing into a fresh shirt, but decided not to risk getting caught half-dressed.

Returning to the front, he took a hard look at the room. When they'd divided the furniture, his wife had taken a love seat rather than the full-size couch and a white wrought-iron ice cream set over the bland kitchen table. It wasn't until he arrayed everything around his new apartment in L.A. that Edmond had been struck by the coldness of his impersonal furniture.

He'd believed it didn't matter, since he spent such

long hours at work. The only thing he'd posted on the walls, there and here, was a photo montage from his and Melissa's trip to Italy. The happy memories the photos stirred outweighed the tinge of sadness he experienced about what he'd lost.

A tap at the entrance spurred Edmond into motion. When he opened the door, soft light haloed Melissa, highlighting the green and gold glints in her hazel eyes.

"Congratulations," she said.

"I'm sorry?" Standing close to her, he remembered that, in flat shoes, she only came up to his nose. In heels, she matched his five-feet-ten-inches.

"On the rental."

"Oh, right." He'd scored a victory in the housing market. "They received three applications. Luckily, your receptionist vouched for me with the landlord. Apparently her word carries weight."

"Caroline arranged for another renter a couple of years back, and that turned out well." Melissa stepped inside. "In fact, I was going to mention her. Harper Anthony, one of the nurses, has a daughter about a year older than Dawn and she's in sports camp, too. Harper's new husband Peter is the assistant director of the camp. Being a stepfather, he's sympathetic to kids in transition."

"I'll make a point of introducing myself. I presume the director will be there early." Sports camp opened its doors at 7 a.m. for the extended day program, which was convenient for working parents.

"Probably. Peter's very conscientious." Producing a pad and pen, Melissa prowled into the kitchen. "Shall we start in here?"

"Be my guest." Edmond opened one of the cabinets

to reveal its limited contents. "I already have peanut butter, soup and canned vegetables."

"You should buy more of all. Also fresh fruit and vegetables." While jotting notes, she poked through the other cabinets and the fridge. "Stock up on nonperishables such as instant mashed potatoes, pasta and tomato sauce, and frozen meals. You're low on eggs and milk, too."

Edmond had had no idea how much food he'd need to stock in the house for him and Dawn, since as a bachelor he often grabbed a bite on his way to work or ate something from the vending machines. "I appreciate this. Dawn's list wasn't exactly comprehensive." The prospect of planning meals for the whole week intimidated him.

And not just one week. Week after week. Month after month, unless Barbara successfully appealed. He ran his hand through his hair, scarcely caring that he was mussing it.

"Take Dawn shopping with you next week. I'm sure she'll have ideas." Melissa's sensible suggestion restored his equilibrium. "I read on the website that sports camp includes a segment on nutrition. Still, you should buy her favorites to start, including bacon."

Bacon was one of the foods that Edmond ate only at restaurants. "What's the best way to fix it?"

"You can fry it in a pan or bake it in the oven," she said. "The internet's full of directions for cooking practically anything."

Ah, yes. "I'm good at searching."

"And you're a quick study."

"About some things." Edmond had soaked up information in school and he enjoyed exploring the law as it evolved. Cooking was another matter. When he'd been newly single, he'd learned the hard way that mistakes in cooking resulted in a pan full of charred ingredients.

As they proceeded through the apartment, the length of Melissa's second list surprised him. He'd figured he'd have to buy more towels, but hadn't considered a range of other items, including extra blankets, more pots, pans, flatware and kitchen utensils, and a stool to help Dawn reach higher shelves.

"After you're in the house, I'm sure there'll be additional shopping," Melissa advised.

"For what?" Edmond asked.

"Curtains, for one thing. As I recall, the blinds in that house provide privacy but they aren't decorative."

"Where does one buy curtains?" That was alien territory.

"Kitchens, Cooks and Linens sells ready-mades," she advised. "And don't forget gardening equipment. I'll bet Dawn will enjoy planting flowers."

"There are flowers there already." He'd noted a lively array near the front steps.

"Not in the backyard," Melissa said. "Then there's the lawn."

"The lawn," Edmond repeated in dismay. He hadn't mowed a lawn since his teen years.

"You can hire a gardener," Melissa assured him with a hint of a smile.

"Oh, right." While he'd considered the cost of child care, he hadn't factored in yard care. "And a cleaning service, too. Any recommendations?"

"We clean our own house, so I'm not sure. Just ask at work. You'll be inundated with suggestions." She was grinning widely.

"What's so funny?"

"You're usually on top of every situation." She slipped her pad into a pocket. "It's refreshing to see you out of your element."

"Refreshing?" That wasn't the word Edmond would have chosen. "Awkward, maybe. Embarrassing."

"No, it's cute." She'd never called him *that* before. "Human."

"As opposed to my usual robotic self?" he asked.

"In a sense," she teased. "It's fun to watch the ice melt."

He traced her temple with his thumb. "Only with you." Her radiance drew him in, drew him close. He tilted his head, longing for her, but holding back.

And then, as if it were the most natural thing in the world, she looped her arms around his shoulders and their mouths met. Edmond pulled her against him, shifting slightly to accommodate her midsection, and got lost in the joy of holding and treasuring this incredibly lovely woman.

Chapter 11

Edmond's spicy scent replenished Melissa's soul, while her body responded with a glorious ripple of desire. This was what home felt like.

She rubbed her cheek over the end-of-day stubble on his face, hardly daring to ease back enough to meet his gaze. When she did, she nearly got lost in the passion blazing from his eyes.

Breathing hard, he rubbed his chest over hers, arousing delicious sensations in her ultrasensitive breasts. Eagerly, Melissa angled her hips against him, and relished his hard response. Heat flashed through her.

His mouth claimed hers again, and they shifted through the bedroom door. Such a tidy room, yet infused with his male essence. Melissa unbuttoned his shirt, a shade of light blue with a pin-stripe, just like the ones she used to pick out for him.

Edmond caught her wrists gently to stop her. "Could this hurt you?"

"My doctor said it was okay at this stage unless there's bleeding." She hadn't thought she'd need to pursue any further information.

"I'd hate to cause you problems." His hoarse voice vibrated through her.

"It won't." She refused to stop now. Her usually guarded self had transformed into a driving force, fueled by three years of longing. No matter what issues divided them, Edmond had always been the standard against which she measured all men.

He nibbled her earlobe. With a sigh of surrender, Melissa buried her nose in his neck.

His hands caressed her as he unzipped her dress, a rose-colored maternity outfit she'd worn today to please him. But she'd never imagined this would happen.

When his hands cupped her bare breasts, Melissa gasped. "That's unbelievably intense."

"Does it hurt?" He paused, his eyes large and dark now that he'd removed his glasses.

"No, no."

"You're incredibly voluptuous." His gaze trailed down her nude, enlarged body.

"Does that mean coarse?" She'd been uncertain how the changes in her body might appear to him.

Edmond's palm stroked her stomach. "Just the opposite. It's as if you're complete, the way you were meant to be."

That was the sexiest thing he could have said. Melissa reached for the buckle on his pants. "Take those clothes off, mister."

"Yes, ma'am." Edmond grinned.

When they were both splendidly naked, they went to the bed. He yanked down the comforter and lowered her to the sheets. "Side, back, front, or some of each?" he teased.

"All of the above."

His long, lean frame fitted against her, each brush of his skin over hers arousing a cascade of sparks. Because of her size, front-to-front didn't work, so they shifted into a position they'd never before tried, his larger frame spooning hers from behind. When he entered her, a wave of joy carried her above her own body. Edmond's moan indicated his disbelieving pleasure.

Slowly, carefully, he probed her until excitement overwhelmed them and they thrust, writhed and clung to each other. Melissa lost track of her separateness, entangled with him in spirit as well as flesh.

They lingered in a state of bliss. After it ebbed, she nestled into him, wishing she could stay there forever. But unless Edmond's heart had room for three babies, that was impossible.

Gradually, she grew aware that it was getting late and she was hungry. She scooted up, her hair tumbling around her shoulders. "I'd better go."

Sitting beside her, Edmond kissed her temple. "I've missed you."

"Me, too." She ran her palms over his chest.

"Losing you cut me off from so many things. Even aspects of myself." His voice grew hoarse. "Melissa, what we had should have been enough. Why'd you have to throw it away?"

Her happy mood evaporated. "I'm not the one who threw it away, Eddie."

He raised his hands in a stop gesture. "Let's not get

into that. I only meant—well, that our marriage was everything to me."

And to me...when we were younger. But she'd changed. Still, she'd have worked with him, delayed having children for a while and tried to find a way to satisfy both their needs, had he met her halfway. But much as she'd loved him, in the end, he hadn't been everything to her. "I wanted more," she said. "A family." A family that should have included him.

"I understand, or at least I'm trying to."

She moved to the side of the bed. "By the way, my housemates offered to help you move on Saturday. I can't do any lifting, but I'll bring the towels and stuff to your new place."

"Thank you," Edmond said. "For that, and for today."

Despite the pain he'd reawakened with his comment, Melissa didn't regret making love with him. Tonight had been an unexpected gift from life. Even though he couldn't make room in his heart for her babies, she doubted she'd ever find anyone who aroused her this way. With the babies due and her own activities soon to be limited, their moments together were precious.

When she stood up, Edmond hurried around to lend a hand. In the bathroom, Melissa washed up quickly. Returning to the living room, she paused in front of the photo collage.

Earlier, she'd been too busy to spare it more than a passing glance. Now, she took in the scenes with enhanced emotion: a picture of her looking radiant that Edmond had shot in Pompeii; a romantic image of them against the Bay of Naples, snapped by a tour guide; a photo of Edmond gazing in awe at a jewel-like stained-glass window in a church on the Amalfi coast. She'd never have believed on that trip that their marriage wouldn't last.

"Do you ever wish we could go back and stay in Italy?" Edmond murmured beside her.

Sometimes. But that was her alternate life, and she'd chosen this one. "Since it's impossible, why worry about it?"

"Because we still mean something to each other," Edmond said. "But you're right."

After a brief hug, Melissa went out to her car. A part of her yearned to remain in Edmond's bed, curled against him until the rivers all ran dry. But then, in Southern California, the rivers ran dry every summer.

As she angled into the driver's seat, flurries in her abdomen reflected the babies' activity. Her daughters. Ironically, if Edmond had agreed to have a child three years ago, these babies would have been implanted in someone else. Yet she was convinced they were meant to be hers.

At her first meeting with Nell and Vern Grant, Melissa had experienced a strong sense of recognition. Although the two were a few years older than her and Edmond, their coloring and builds were similar. Nell, a kindergarten teacher, was more emotional than her husband, with a bubbly sense of humor. Vern, an accountant, appeared earnest and almost humorless, yet his loving glances at his wife reflected his devotion to her.

She'd followed their journey through *in vitro* more keenly than with most clients, sharing their heartbreak when the first attempt failed. After they'd undergone the stressful process of egg harvesting a second time, she'd rejoiced when they produced six viable embryos. What a miracle it had been when the first three implanted. Nell's pregnancy had flourished until she suffered a dangerous rise in blood pressure several weeks before her due date.

Mercifully, the babies—all boys—had been delivered safely by Caesarian section. Melissa had joined the parents in their hospital room—at their request—posing for photos with a baby in her arms while Vern cradled his other two sons.

As she held the little boy, a blond infant who could have passed for her son, tears had run down Melissa's cheeks. Overwhelmed by the ache for a baby of her own, she'd replaced the boy in his bassinet, invented an excuse and hurried off.

Nell must have noticed her emotions. In a vulnerable moment during the year-long fertility process, Melissa had confided to Nell the facts of her divorce and that she was considering artificial insemination.

Six weeks after the birth, the couple had concluded they couldn't risk a second pregnancy and would donate the surviving embryos. When they offered them to Melissa, Nell explained she'd had recurring dreams of Melissa as their mother. But the Grants had insisted that she decide quickly so they could settle the matter. If she delayed, they'd have chosen another recipient.

Now, she stared into the dusk beyond the windshield, revisiting her turbulent emotions as she'd weighed the unexpected proposal. Although Melissa had identified with the Grants and their babies, she knew these children might have been better off with a married couple.

But the chance to realize her dreams, especially given her bond with the Grants, had overridden her doubts. Although there'd been no specific agreement that she allow regular visits after the babies' birth, Melissa liked the idea that the families could remain in touch.

Ironically, once the initial excitement over the implantation faded, the Grants had been too overwhelmed caring for their triplets to keep up contact. In an email, Nell had noted that one little boy had required surgery to fix a newly discovered heart defect. Although he was doing well, she had no energy to spare.

Melissa's hand rested on her abdomen. Her body still vibrated with Edmond's lovemaking, yet these little girls weren't simply someone else's embryos. They were her daughters.

Despite the joy they'd shared today, despite the fact that she longed to share her future with a husband as well as her babies, she'd made the right choice.

The counseling clinic occupied a small white building on a busy street in the city of Garden Grove, midway between Norwalk and Safe Harbor. Edmond had chosen Franca Brightman, Ph.D., based on a recommendation from Paula Humphreys.

He'd brought Dawn for weekly sessions after Simon's death and Barbara's arrest, fearing that the events would traumatize his niece. Edmond had learned during his family law career that counseling could be vital. He'd seen fiercely antagonistic divorces defused by a counselor's insights into the couple's underlying issues.

His sister had consented to Dawn undergoing therapy, although she hadn't been thrilled. Resisting the possibility that she, too, might benefit, she'd only attended once, early in the process. That had relieved her concerns, although she'd still refused Edmond's offer to fund counseling for her, as well.

Initially, he'd believed that the point of therapy was to "fix" the child. But Franca had explained that the goal was to allow Dawn to integrate her experiences and gain the emotional tools to cope in the future. Edmond had wondered how such a thing was possible with a child her age—she'd only been six at the start—who would have trouble articulating her feelings.

Allowed to observe her first play therapy session, he'd tried not to be impatient, although the pace had seemed slow. Franca—she encouraged them both to use her first name—had allowed Dawn to choose among an array of toys and art supplies.

When the little girl began drawing, he'd expected the therapist to steer her toward depicting scenes that would reveal her inner landscape. Instead, Franca had simply observed, with occasional comments such as, "You enjoy using bright colors," or, "The way you sniff the crayons shows me that you enjoy the smell."

She wasn't praising or directing the little girl; instead, she was making Dawn aware of her own reactions. After several sessions, he'd found that his niece *was* better able to process her emotions and to communicate them.

Tonight, once Dawn went into Franca's office, Edmond sat alone in the waiting room. He no longer observed the play sessions, after Franca explained that Dawn should be free to interact with her away from him. Also, despite an impulse to keep close tabs on his niece, he didn't wish to control her. Mutual respect was important in their relationship.

Would a father—a worthwhile father, not a jerk like Simon—be so quick to loosen the reins? Edmond did care about Dawn, very much. Beyond that, he had to trust the therapist's recommendations and hope his instincts weren't seriously out of balance.

After checking his email on his phone, he glanced at

the reading material arrayed on a low table in front of him. Choosing a parenting magazine, Edmond scanned an article about online safety, then flipped to a page about preparing for the start of school.

A photo of a woman with light hair, hazel eyes and a classic oval face reminded him of Melissa. Last night after she'd left, he'd slept still engulfed in emotions from their incredible lovemaking—regrets about their quarrel, a touch of anger that she'd pushed him away again. Confusion, too. Why couldn't he move past their relationship? Why was he still haunted by the sense that they belonged together?

After the divorce, he'd had one brief, unsatisfying relationship with a woman at his old law firm that had dissuaded Edmond from pursuing further affairs. He'd told himself he was waiting for the right woman. Making love to Melissa again had brought home the searing awareness that *she* was still the right woman. If only she'd waited before becoming pregnant, perhaps mothering Dawn would have satisfied her.

He didn't mean to resent those three little infants. And it was his own fault because he'd stupidly rushed to "solve" the situation.

The inner door opened. Dawn emerged, her little face more relaxed than when they'd arrived. "Franca wants you to go in."

He arose. "You're okay out here?"

"Yep. Don't forget to lock the door."

"Right." At the entrance, Edmond flipped the bolt, as he always did when leaving his niece alone in the waiting area.

As Dawn selected a picture book from the rack, he

went inside. "Hi," he said to the slim, red-haired woman as she rose to greet him.

"Big changes this week." Franca, who could almost have passed for a teenager with her heart-shaped face and sprinkling of freckles, shook his hand firmly. "How're you holding up?"

He'd emailed her about Barbara's sentence and Dawn's planned move. He'd also sent her information about the social worker along with permission to provide input for the woman's report.

"My head's spinning," Edmond said as they sat in adult-size chairs. Surrounded by mostly tiny furniture, he felt like Gulliver among the Lilliputians.

"Dawn talked a lot about her Aunt Lissa. I presume that's your ex-wife." Earlier, he'd described the circumstances of his divorce to Franca. "She's expecting triplets?"

"That's right." Edmond set aside his instinct to keep personal matters private. That was counterproductive with a therapist. "It's an embryo adoption."

"That's unusual." While her calm manner revealed only nonjudgmental attentiveness, Edmond sensed there was a point to this discussion.

"She works in a fertility program in Safe Harbor Medical Center, where I'm consulting." He sketched their interaction over the past week, including the preparations for Dawn's arrival, but omitted their intimacy. That really *was* nobody's business. "Being around Melissa seems to be beneficial for my niece, especially since I have virtually no experience with parenting."

He expected the therapist to agree. Instead, she replied carefully, "It's understandable that you'd rely on her, since you have a friendly relationship with your ex-wife, and Dawn has a bond with her." As usual, Franca summarized complex matters succinctly. "But what happens after the triplets are born? Melinda—sorry, Melissa—will be up to her ears in babies. No matter how attached she is to Dawn, they'll have first claim on her."

"Well, of course." Because of the speed of the week's events, Edmond hadn't thought that far ahead.

"That will be another loss for Dawn, and imagine how she'll feel," Franca said earnestly. "She'll be devastated if she's counting on her aunt and is set aside for the babies."

Much as he wanted to deny that that might happen, Edmond couldn't. This pregnancy had to be Melissa's top consideration. "What do you propose?"

Franca spread her hands. "I'm not suggesting you break off contact with your ex-wife, only that she remain on the sidelines. You have to be the constant in Dawn's life. So spend time alone with her. Find activities you enjoy doing together. Other people may come and go, but it's vital that she's assured she can count on you, always."

Always. He nearly blurted that Barbara was still Dawn's parent and that hopefully she'd be out of prison in five years or less. But by then, Dawn would be nearly a teenager. Furthermore, Barbara would be an ex-con with no job. How long would it take Barb to reestablish her life, and at what point should he hand over his niece? She might stay with him until she was grown. Dawn deserved to be his first priority.

"Well?" The therapist watched him closely.

"You're right," Edmond said. "I'm Dawn's anchor." With those words, he sealed his commitment. No more hedging; no more considering this a temporary situation.

"This transitional period will involve a lot of ups and downs," Franca went on. "During what's called the honeymoon phase, your niece may strive to please you, to conform to whatever you ask. Once she's more confident, she'll test you by flouting the rules. When that happens, it may seem as if you're taking two steps backward for every step forward, but that's natural. She has to figure out where the boundaries are in her new landscape."

"And my job is to steer a steady course," Edmond said.

"Yes. Fortunately, you're up to the task." Her freckles stretched as she smiled.

"As I've explained, my plans didn't include fatherhood." He'd been open on that score. "But I understand my responsibilities, and Dawn's needs. I won't let her down."

"You may be pleasantly surprised to discover that parenting your niece is more rewarding than you expect," Franca said.

"I hope so."

As he rose to shake her hand, Edmond tried not to show how rattled he was at the prospect of distancing himself from Melissa. For Dawn's sake and in some ways his own, he couldn't entirely keep them apart. For starters, he'd promised to bring his niece to her house for Sunday dinner. And then there was his longing for Melissa, which defied reason.

You can handle this. As Franca said, you're up to the task.

In the waiting room, the little girl's face brightened when she saw him. And reaching for her hand, Edmond decided that finding things to do, just the two of them, might not be difficult after all.

Chapter 12

Sitting at the small desk in her bedroom, Melissa listened to Edmond in dismay. He'd called to explain the counselor's recommendation that she put distance between herself and Dawn.

"I love her," she protested.

"This isn't the end of your relationship," he assured her, his voice slightly rough at this hour. It was only nine-thirty, but no doubt he'd had a long day. "However, in your condition, you can't guarantee you'll be there for her when she needs you."

While Melissa assumed he was quoting the counselor accurately, she couldn't shake the suspicion he was deliberately pushing her away. "Are you angry at me?"

"About what?"

"We…sort of snapped at each other the other night."

Surely he'd played their discussion through his mind as often as she'd played it through hers.

"No, I'm not angry," he said thoughtfully. "But, Melissa, even after all these years, we're both clearly still hurt and a little raw."

So he *was* pushing her away. "Are you going to change the plan to bring her over on Sunday night? I was just drafting an email to thank Isabel for sending the chicken recipe."

"No. She'll enjoy that, and so will I." His tone lightened. "And for what it's worth, Franca didn't say *I* had to avoid you."

If only he'd be clearer about what he meant! Melissa confined herself to a clipped response. "Well, I'll see you Friday, then."

"Friday?"

"At the hospital. I'm curious to hear your talk."

"Oh, yes. Great. Until then." On that note, the call ended.

Frustrating man! Irritably, she reread the draft email.

Thursday night

Sender: Melissa Everhart
Subject: Thanks for the recipe
Cc: Edmond Everhart
Hi, Isabel and Dawn,
Isabel, thanks for the chicken recipe. My friend Karen plans to fix it for us Sunday night. Dawn, I can't wait to have you over! It'll be fun having you live so close. I'm sure we'll get together often.
Love,
Aunt Lissa

She'd have to revise it to sound more impersonal. Melissa blinked away tears—maternal hormones kept her emotions close to the surface these days.

Inside her, the babies were squiggling. Her palm traced the shape of her abdomen, which seemed to expand almost hourly.

When her daughters emerged into the world, they'd have only their mother to depend on. She would have to be all things to them, an intimidating prospect. Adding to her concern was the uncertainty about when they would arrive and whether there'd be complications. She supposed the counselor had a point.

All the same, she'd never shut out her niece. Quite the opposite—she longed to share her family-to-be with Edmond and Dawn.

For now, she'd have to retreat, but it hurt, both for her niece's sake and for Edmond's. The man deserved a slap to bring him to his senses. At the ridiculous image of herself punching out her ex-husband, Melissa laughed.

Then she rewrote the email, and hit Send.

Friday morning

Sender: Isabel Everhart
Subject: From Dawn
Cc: Edmond Everhart

Hi, Aunt Lissa,
    Grandma Isabel's been helping me pack. I can't wait until Sunday!
    Here are my favorite names for my little sisters [note

from Isabel: that's how she refers to the triplets]. Bunny,
Bambi and Belinda.
Love,
Dawn

On Friday afternoon, Edmond was pleasantly surprised to find the hospital auditorium nearly full for his
talk. In view of the change of topic and speaker, he'd
half expected attendance to be low.

Waiting on the side of the stage with public relations
director Jennifer Serra Martin, he scanned the crowd.
Immediately, he pinpointed Melissa between Karen and
their supervisor, Jan Sargent. Meeting his gaze, his ex-
wife nodded encouragement.

Although she'd accepted Franca Brightman's advice,
he knew she was upset. He didn't like it, either. He and
Melissa had been soul mates from the day they met, and
it had torn him apart when they divorced.

Their lovemaking this week had shown how strong
the bond remained, but it was no longer just the two of
them. There was no question of bringing her three babies
into his household, even if he'd been willing to consider
it, because he couldn't risk letting his niece get lost in
the shuffle. Dawn urgently required stability, reassurance and his full attention.

And, despite his best intentions, he still felt a twist of
resentment about the pregnancy. If only she'd waited. If
only she'd loved him as much as he'd loved her.

Edmond surveyed the rest of the attendees, recogniz-
ing a number of people including Vince Adams, who
filled a center seat beside the administrator. Why was
the gruff billionaire attending his talk?

Perhaps Mark had suggested it to further involve

Vince with the hospital. The administration was hoping he'd give a major donation, as much as twenty million dollars, Tony had mentioned.

Adams, his wife and their daughters would be returning to their main residence in San Diego next month. They'd rented a beach cottage in Safe Harbor for the summer so the girls could be near their maternal grandmother, but school would be starting soon. And everyone in fund-raising knew that absence made the heart go wander.

"Let's get this show on the road," murmured Jennifer, a dark-haired woman with a throaty voice. Adjusting her note cards, she rose and approached the microphone. The audience chatter died.

"I'm Jennifer Martin, public relations director at Safe Harbor Medical Center. Welcome to our latest Medical Insight lecture." Her formality reminded Edmond that the talk was being recorded and would be available on the hospital's website.

What he said and how he said it would affect many people's opinions of him, now and in the near future. It might also change a few lives. He couldn't wait.

Melissa joined the round of applause as Edmond took the mike. In a blue shirt, dark brown jacket and tan slacks, he struck a balance between professionalism and Southern California informality.

Following a few introductory remarks, he launched into his topic. "When I worked for a large law firm in L.A., I witnessed the ugly side of divorces, custody battles and cases involving adoptions and surrogacy. As many of you may have observed, nice people can become monsters when they feel as if their family is threatened.

Sometimes the level of rage in those cases made me glad no one's invented a personal-size nuclear weapon."

A chuckle ran through the auditorium. Melissa's fists unclenched. She hadn't realized how tense she was on his behalf. During their marriage, she'd often experienced his emotions as if they were her own, a habit she'd picked up again, making it impossible to stop caring about him. If he didn't care about her, too, he shouldn't have moved to Safe Harbor. But then, he hadn't known about the triplets.

"Traditionally, for an attorney, handling divorces and custody cases means that your client either wins or loses. That's similar to criminal law, yet the overwhelming majority of our clients *aren't* criminals. I began to wonder why they, and we, acted as if they were."

The auditorium had fallen so quiet that a neighbor's sneeze startled Melissa. Everyone seemed mesmerized by Edmond's narrative.

"Over the past two decades, attorneys who share my aversion to these destructive processes have developed a field called collaborative law." He didn't bother to glance at the notes in his hand. Obviously, this was a subject he knew intimately.

"Collaborative law requires participants and attorneys to commit to the process of working together to seek reasonable solutions," he said. "We negotiate at group meetings, seeking to avoid going to court. The big savings in time and money appeal to many parties who initially resist the idea."

"What if all this collaboration stuff doesn't work?" The question, which Melissa considered rude since Edmond hadn't finished speaking, boomed from a man behind her. Swiveling, she recognized the speaker as Vince Adams, Tiffany and Amber's stepfather.

Privately, she doubted the billionaire would ever consider negotiating when his vast wealth allowed him to squash opponents through court battles, as he'd done with Rod Vintner over custody of the girls. She doubted that the youngsters' happiness had entered Vince's mind.

"Unfortunately, negotiations can fail, but we try to prevent that," Edmond responded. "Many collaborative law attorneys will not represent their clients should either side choose to litigate their dispute. The prospect of having to start over with new representation encourages clients to work harder for a solution. So does the awareness that they'll be running up a huge bill with no guarantee they'll get favorable results."

"Sounds good in theory, but it has to be damn hard in practice," Vince responded, as if this were a conversation between him and Edmond.

"It can be," Edmond agreed. "We have to educate clients that the desire to punish someone else is counterproductive. Breakthroughs occur when both parties are able to accord each other genuine respect."

He provided a few case histories of extended suits involving surrogacy and adoptions, with names and details changed to protect privacy, and compared these to cases where negotiations had brought about agreements.

"It's faster and more humane," he said. "And a lot easier on the attorney's nervous system."

Amid chuckles, Edmond opened the floor to further questions. Melissa admired how carefully he listened and how thoughtfully he responded. In several instances in which staffers appeared to be referring to a current situation, he offered to talk to them privately later.

The applause when he finished resounded in Melissa's ears. She swelled with pride.

In their own divorce, Edmond had behaved decently, dividing their assets down the line. Due to his higher income, he'd conceded to her attorney's demand for alimony, but that hadn't felt right to Melissa. While Edmond earned more, he'd also had law school debts and often sent money to his family. She'd inherited enough from her parents to pay off her student loans and tuck away a nest egg. So she'd declined the alimony, and had been rewarded by the gratitude in his eyes.

From an objective viewpoint, they'd behaved well. Internally, however, she'd been devastated. So, she was discovering, had he.

Why couldn't the man move past his rejection of fatherhood? He was doing so for his niece's sake. And while taking on three kids would be asking a lot, this man had far more internal resources than he realized.

The idiot needs to be part of a family. And so do I. But Melissa had no idea how to penetrate his bullheaded resistance. He'd have to discover the truth for himself. And that, she feared, might never happen.

Jennifer arose to thank the speaker and the audience. As the crowd dispersed, Edmond descended from the stage alongside the PR director. Melissa edged toward them to say a few words.

He was handing out business cards to a cluster of people, offering to meet with them during his office hours. Before she could move closer, Vince barreled into their midst, all but elbowing her and everyone else aside.

With Mark trailing apologies, everyone departed, including Melissa. Her congratulations could wait until tomorrow, and she didn't envy him having to talk to Vince.

* * *

Edmond's guard shot up as Vince approached, although he steeled himself to appear courteous. Fortunately, the interruptions during the talk hadn't thrown him off; lawyers had to be able to adjust their strategies quickly to challenges in a courtroom.

Furthermore, he had a favor to ask of Vince. Although to most men approving a children's playdate wouldn't qualify as a favor, he suspected that it might with Vince.

"I liked what you said about respect," Vince remarked in ringing tones as they shook hands. "Now if you can explain how to impress that on my wife, I'd be grateful."

What a personal thing to say, Edmond reflected, and how disrespectful of Portia Adams. "Is your wife here?"

"Oh, she's off with her mom and the kids, spending my money at the mall," the man responded. "I've had to commute from San Diego all summer because they miss Grandma. You see how I indulge her."

Edmond caught a meaningful glance from Mark. *Keep this guy happy* was the interpretation. "I'm sure she appreciates it."

"The hell she does." Vince didn't appear to care who overheard his remarks. Luckily the auditorium had emptied out. "You're probably aware, as the rest of the world is, that part of my interest in this hospital was to consult Dr. Rattigan about my infertility."

"How's it going?" Edmond didn't mean to pry, but Vince *had* raised the subject.

"The man's brilliant. The best in his field." At close range, Vince's breath carried a note of alcohol. While imbibing at lunch wasn't unusual, Edmond wondered if Vince was aware of how easily it had loosened his tongue. "He can't fix what's wrong with my sperm, but

I could father a child using their high-tech magic—if my wife weren't so uptight."

"Maybe things can be worked out." Edmond deliberately kept his response vague.

"With all I've done for her, my wife refuses to undergo *in vitro*," Vince groused. "Doesn't want to take the hormones or some such thing. *I'm* willing to do whatever's necessary—a procedure that involves sticking a needle into my balls—but she's too finicky to do her share."

Despite a wince at the man's crudeness, Edmond maintained a bland expression. "That's too bad."

Actually, he didn't blame Portia. From what he'd learned, egg retrieval for fertilization in the lab required lengthy and stressful preparations that had serious potential side effects. Portia must be in her early forties, which meant carrying a child would also involve extra risks.

"What about a surrogate?" the administrator asked. "Anything you need is available here."

"I don't want a stranger involved, especially when my wife's presumably still fertile," Vince growled. "Now I wish I'd never started this business, consulting a men's fertility specialist. The word's spread that I'm less than a man. You have no idea what it's like, having people look down on you for being unable to father a child."

"Nobody looks down on you," Mark said.

"Yeah? I can sense how the staff reacts when they think I don't notice." Vince appeared to be building up a head of steam. "It's time I took my toys and went home."

Alarm flashed across the administrator's face. Although Edmond hated to cater to this egotistical man just for the sake of a donation, there was a lot riding on the proposed expansion. Mark had explained that the hospital hoped to convert a nearby former dental building to provide not only labs and treatment facilities for the men's program but also office space for a wide range of doctors. It would mean some of them, including Jack, would no longer have to work odd hours in shared quarters. And Melissa's housemate Lucky might be able to use his newly minted administrative degree here at home.

"I do understand some of what you're experiencing, although it's my own doing." In the interest of male bonding, Edmond forced himself to overcome his repugnance at sharing personal details. "I got a vasectomy without considering all the consequences."

"Such as?"

Might as well tell the whole story. "My wife left me."

"Ever consider reversing it?" Vince asked, his interest piqued.

"Not really, although if I had it to do over…" Edmond couldn't finish the sentence, because he wasn't sure how it ended. Instead, he said, "In any event, I have other priorities at the moment. I have to take guardianship of my niece, the little girl who was with me at the wedding."

"How come?"

"Dawn's father is dead and her mom, my sister, is dealing with her own issues." That provided a chance to bring up Dawn's request. "By the way, your daughters were a hit with her. It would be great if they could play together before school starts."

"So that's who the girls were chattering about—Dawn, you say?"

"That's her."

Vince produced a card. "Here's my cell number. Sure, let's set it up."

Edmond reciprocated with his own card. "I'm in

learning mode when it comes to parenting. Any tips you can provide would be welcome." Not that he seriously expected Vince to have worthwhile insights, but even a stopped clock was right twice a day.

"Here's my advice. Don't let them get the bit between their teeth or they'll run you ragged," the man boomed.

"I'll remember that."

Vince beamed in satisfaction. "The hospital made a smart move when they hired you. You're my kind of guy."

Edmond couldn't honestly return the compliment. Instead, he ventured, "Don't give up on fatherhood yet. Your wife might change her mind."

"I suppose so. With Dr. Rattigan right here, this is too great an opportunity to pass up," Vince agreed.

"Maybe we can take the girls to the Bear and Doll Boutique in town," Edmond suggested. "I understand they offer children's craft classes." Geoff Humphreys had suggested the trip, since his mother owned the shop.

"I'll let you sort that out with my wife," Vince said.

On that note, they shook hands, and Vince departed with the administrator. Edmond debated stopping by Melissa's office, but it was after five o'clock and he had to finish preparing for tomorrow's move.

As he reached his car in the parking structure, his cell rang. It was Mark. "Thank you for bringing Vince down from the ledge," the administrator said. "You're a born diplomat."

"I was planning to ask him about the playdate anyway." Edmond didn't want to leave the impression that he enjoyed cozying up to donors.

"Well, he stopped talking about leaving for San Diego right away," the administrator told him. "Hopefully we're on track again, especially after I reminded him that the program and the building would bear his name."

"I'm glad I could help."

This had been a productive afternoon, Edmond reflected after the call ended. Scoring a success in his consulting job helped restore his sense of balance, which had been shaky since Monday's sentencing.

He'd been drawn to the law because of its logic, its order, its appeal to the rational. Edmond was most comfortable when employing his intellect, and most like a fish out of water when relying on his instincts.

That was Melissa's specialty. Facing the next few weeks without relying on her was a daunting prospect, especially since this weekend marked Edmond's transition into being Dawn's full-time guardian. Maybe he'd ask her for some last-minute tips....

Chapter 13

You're officially out of your mind. Ruefully, Melissa watched Edmond sleep in the morning light, his body sprawled across the bed, his tousled hair and bare torso tempting her to rouse him for another round of lovemaking. She should be more restrained, she supposed, but in view of her pregnancy and the fact that Dawn was moving in today, this might be their last such encounter.

Yesterday, while she'd folded the new linens and organized the kitchen, Lucky, Rod and Jack—back from his honeymoon and relieved to find Anya's belongings already in the apartment—had hauled Edmond's modest furnishings in his rented van to his new home.

She and Edmond had required only a glance or a few words to decide which item belonged in which room and how to orient the larger pieces of furniture. They shared an aesthetic about such matters.

After the others left, he'd invited Melissa to stay and share takeout. He'd seemed more open and vulnerable than usual, and it had occurred to her that he might be ready to begin a shift in his views about family. To be honest, she'd also craved this last chance to be close to him.

After dinner, they'd watched a documentary about the rapid expansion of Shanghai, one of the cities they'd visited during their marriage. Memories had surged of viewing the city's impressive museum, enjoying a river cruise at sunset and touring the waterfront Bund area with its colonial-era buildings. How carefree they'd been.

She had no excuses for sliding on his lap and enjoying his caresses save that she wanted to be that lighthearted just once more. With Edmond, she wasn't just a mother and a counselor, she was also a woman. And there was only one man who'd ever made her feel like one.

But she was putting her heart at risk, and for what? Dreams that refused to come true.

Beside Melissa, Edmond stretched and let out a groan. "I'm stiff as a—is there anything stiffer than a board?"

"An iron rod, although you already have one of those," she teased.

He laughed. "I'm afraid it may not live up to its reputation right now. Any chance of a massage?"

"I can try." Leveraging herself to sit on his back, Melissa kneaded the muscles along Edmond's spine and shoulders. Gradually, his knots dissolved beneath the pressure. He'd kept his body in excellent shape, she noted appreciatively, and his skin was smooth.

"You're next." Lazily, he helped her lie on her side. One leg resting lightly atop her thigh, he massaged her from behind, sending tingles of pleasure along her nerve endings. His hands hadn't lost their expertise in probing exactly the right points.

When he finished, they lay spooning, one of his palms cupping her abdomen. She scarcely noticed the ripple, but he gave a start. "What's that?"

Melissa sighed. "My girls are playing kickball."

"Does it hurt?"

"No. It tickles a little, though," she admitted.

His hand, which had jerked away, rested on her belly again, the heat soothing into her. "Can they feel it when I touch you?" he asked.

"I doubt it. But they can hear your voice."

"How about this?" Putting his mouth to her stomach, he blew on it, creating a raucous noise.

Chuckling as she pushed him away, Melissa retorted, "That tickles even more!"

"You said they were playing." His eyes widened in mock innocence.

Could he be changing, viewing these little ones as children instead of a burden? Melissa knew better than to push the issue, though.

"Just wait till they're crawling all over the carpet. Remember how destructive Dawn was when she was little?" What a cutie their niece had been, Melissa recalled. "They'll be grabbing things and climbing in our laps and sticking stuff in their mouths."

"Speaking of putting things in our mouths, how about a cheese Danish?" he asked. "On Sunday mornings, nutrition doesn't count."

"Yes, it does, but I'll make an exception."

They ate in the kitchen, reading the advance edition of

the newspaper they'd bought last night. It might not have the morning news, but all the inside sections were there.

Resting her feet on Edmond's thighs beneath the table, Melissa reflected that all Sundays should be so companionable and peaceful. Yet before too long, her daughters would be old enough to enjoy the comics with them.

With me, she corrected sadly, and barely restrained the urge to kick him.

Time to go. Although she'd have liked to greet Dawn here at her new home, Melissa didn't intend to press for that. Also, the pair would be joining her household for dinner tonight.

And maybe talking about the triplets had planted a seed in Edmond's fertile brain. At the image, she had to hide a smile.

She wasn't ready to give up on him. Even if that did make her the world's biggest numbskull.

"Are Tiffany and Amber here?" Dawn's wide-eyed gaze met Melissa's as she opened the door to welcome her niece and Edmond for dinner.

"I'm afraid nothing's been arranged yet." Heavens, the child had only moved into her new home today, and already she was eager for a playdate. "Your uncle's working on it."

"I sent their parents an email Friday night." Edmond, his brown hair still damp from the shower, ushered the little girl inside. He'd obviously cleaned up after the move.

Melissa transferred her attention to Dawn, who wore a crisp pink dress and a fresh ribbon in her bouncy brown curls. "My, you look pretty."

A pucker formed between Dawn's eyebrows as she peered into the living room. "Where did the chairs go?"

"We were only renting them for the wedding." Melissa closed the door behind her guests. "It's nice to have the couch in its proper place."

Dawn sighed. "I miss the flowers."

"So do I," Melissa agreed.

"Something smells wonderful." Edmond inhaled for emphasis. "Very spicy. Though I'd hoped Karen would wait to show me how to fix the chicken."

"She had to marinate it for a few hours," she explained.

"It has to marinate?" He ducked his head. "This is more complicated than I expected."

"It's worth it," Dawn told him.

"I'm sure it is." He gave her shoulder a pat. "Your uncle's a beginner chef. *Very* beginner."

"That's okay," his niece said earnestly. "We all have to start somewhere."

He gave a startled laugh, and Melissa grinned. "You're right, Dawn."

"She often is," he said, flexing his shoulders. He must be sore; Melissa's mind flashed to their erotic massage.

"I want to visit your room, Aunt Lissa." Dawn said.

Edmond's eyes narrowed, but since they hadn't broken the news to Dawn that her aunt was supposed to keep a distance, what reason could they give? "Sure."

"I'll try to learn something in the kitchen," Edmond said. "Dawn, don't stay up there too long. You're the expert on peanut-butter chicken and we may need your advice."

"I have to read Aunt Lissa the letter Mommy wrote."

From her small patent-leather purse, Dawn retrieved a wrinkled sheet of paper.

"You heard from Barbara?" This must have been a relief to Dawn. "How is she?"

"The letter arrived at my parents' house yesterday." Edmond explained. "She seems in upbeat spirits, considering." Or she'd tried to appear that way for her daughter's sake, Melissa gathered.

"Don't tell her what it says!" Taking her aunt's hand, Dawn tugged her toward the stairs. "I'll read it to the babies, too."

"I'm sure they'll like that." *And so will I.*

While Karen showed Edmond how to dredge the marinated chicken in flour and fry batches of it in oil, Lucky chopped vegetables from the garden. He had a large pile, including carrots, onions, zucchini, green beans, tomatoes, yellow squash and assorted greens.

"I'll stir-fry these with tofu, since I'm a vegetarian," the male nurse explained when Edmond asked what he was preparing.

"Zora fixed a salad earlier," Karen added, repositioning the clip that held her reddish-brown hair out of her face.

"Where's Rod?" Edmond missed the colorful anesthesiologist, who'd provided humorous commentary during yesterday's move, although he hadn't done much heavy lifting.

"He took Jack and Anya out for dinner," Lucky said. "There's just five of us tonight."

"Oh, is that all?" Edmond murmured.

Karen laughed. "The house feels empty without a crowd. I appreciate you and your niece joining us."

"I can't tell you how great this is for us." With Isabel's input, he'd planned a week's worth of meals. Preparing them still loomed as a major challenge.

While the chicken was frying, Karen carried dishes into the dining room to set the table. Edmond assisted Lucky at a second cutting board. "There sure is a lot of chopping involved, not that I'm complaining."

"That's the fun part about cooking vegetables." The man's knife flew, dicing a white globe that might be a turnip. "You can start with a basic sauce, such as sweet and sour, and throw in whatever's handy. If you have a couple of this and a few of that, it all goes into the dish."

Karen returned for silverware. "Did I hear you say earlier that you're arranging a get-together with the Adams girls?"

"Dawn asked to play with her friends again," Edmond confirmed. "I was planning on taking them to a workshop to learn how to sew doll clothes."

"Sounds fun," she said.

"To you maybe," Lucky muttered.

"How does this playdate thing work, anyway?" Edmond asked. "Do the parents stick around?"

"Depends on the activity, I presume," she said. "Since I don't have kids, my knowledge is theoretical."

Lucky handed Edmond several large tomatoes. "Don't chop these too small. Quarters will be fine."

"Start by inserting the point of the knife," Karen warned. "If you slice straight down and the knife isn't super-sharp, you might use too much pressure. Then, squish."

Edmond glanced at the red splotch blossoming on his apron. "Too late."

"You'll live," she assessed, and walked back into the dining room.

Following her directions, he did a neater job with the rest of the tomatoes. Then he started in on a carrot. *That* wouldn't squirt him.

"Rather than sewing classes, why not volunteer at the animal shelter?" Lucky said. "More fun for everyone, and you might do some good."

"I'll look into it." The prospect of cleaning cages didn't thrill Edmond. Still, he wasn't eager to spend an afternoon hunched over a table in a doll shop, either.

"Word of warning," Karen interjected as she reentered. "Rod volunteers at the shelter on Saturday afternoons. Running into him could be awkward."

"He should stay home that day." Lucky had no hesitation about ordering people around, Edmond mused.

"Surely it isn't that terrible if he runs into his daughters," he said.

"Vince has threatened to slap him with an injunction." Karen scowled. "I try not to hate that man, but it's hard."

"I have to admit, I'm torn, too." Lucky set his pot of vegetables on the stove. "An expansion of the men's fertility program could mean a lot to my career. And it'd be a good thing for our patients," he added. "But the guy's a creep."

"It's too bad." Rod obviously loved his daughters, regardless of not being related to them genetically. *Just as Melissa loves her babies.* Edmond had grown up hearing the philosophy that blood was thicker than water. Technically, that might be true, but now he was viewing relationships in a different light.

Dawn and Melissa appeared. "I'm hungry," the little girl announced. "Aren't you hungry, Aunt Lissa?"

"Pregnant women are always hungry," Melissa said.

"That's 'cause you're feeding the babies." Beaming, Dawn patted her aunt's belly.

"The chicken's done." With tongs, Karen transferred the pieces to a plate. "Would somebody please call Zora?"

"Zora!" Dawn yelled.

Everybody laughed. Edmond made a mental note that kids tended to take things literally. Or maybe his niece was joking. She had all sorts of hidden qualities, he was happily discovering.

Everyone dug into the meal with enthusiasm. Flavored with allspice and cayenne as well as buttermilk and peanut butter, the chicken proved delicious. The prep time had been rather long, in Melissa's view, but this was a special occasion.

Overexcited by the day's events, Dawn ate only a few mouthfuls before plying Zora with questions about her twins. In short order, the little girl learned that they were a girl and a boy, that Zora hadn't selected names yet and that the father was her ex-husband.

"You used to be married like Uncle Eddie and Aunt Lissa?" Dawn asked.

"Kind of." Zora shifted uncomfortably.

"Has *he* picked out names?" the little girl pressed.

"He doesn't know he's going to be a daddy," Zora said.

"Not all former spouses get along as well as Uncle Eddie and I do," Melissa advised.

"Also, your uncle's a decent chap who takes care of his family," Lucky put in. "Whereas Andrew…"

"Lay off him, would you?" In her prickly mood, Zora's short ginger hair gave her an electrified appearance.

"I should expect you'd be heaping insults on him, considering how he's treated you," Lucky said.

"That's my decision," Zora answered.

Melissa toyed with her fork, reluctant to interfere yet unhappy that the pair were sniping. For some reason, Lucky seemed to take Zora's situation personally, although neither of them showed any romantic inclination toward the other.

"As long as your attorney's here, why not ask him about notifying Andrew that you're pregnant?" Lucky persisted. "I'll bet the father has a legal right to be informed."

"Does he?" Zora addressed Edmond.

He finished a mouthful of Lucky's tofu dish. "When the baby's born, you'll be asked to identify the father for the birth records."

"But then Betsy will find out, and she'll tell him," Zora protested.

Dawn listened wide-eyed. "Who's Betsy?"

"Andrew's mother," Lucky said. "She's the nursing supervisor at the hospital. And if you ask me, a grandmother has a right to know, too."

Karen clinked her spoon against her plate. "Lucky, Zora's told you to stay out of it. Being her housemate doesn't give you big-brother privileges."

"Someone has to put her straight," Lucky grumped. "Otherwise she'll go right on making one bad choice after another."

"Like my mommy," Dawn said. "That's why she's in prison. She says so in her letter."

Zora, who'd opened her mouth to reply, turned her

attention to the little girl. "I'm sorry your mom's in trouble. But Lucky has no right to compare my situation to criminal activity."

"I didn't," he protested.

Karen slapped the table, rattling the dishes. "Enough!"

To distract her niece, Melissa said. "Dawn, you've hardly tasted your chicken."

The little girl heaved a melodramatic sigh. "Why do grown-ups always stop talking at the most interesting parts?"

Melissa wished she had an answer. No one else did, either, until Edmond spoke.

"As grown-ups, we should be mature enough to solve our problems without fighting." He traced a finger over his niece's temple, brushing away a curl that had drifted close to her mouth. "We should show children the right way to work out differences, which is to be kind and respectful."

"That's not how people act on TV," she protested. "They do mean things to each other."

"Which is an excellent argument for avoiding the boob tube," Lucky said.

Dawn giggled. "The boob tube! That's funny."

"TVs used to have an actual tube inside, called a cathode ray tube," Edmond informed his niece. "That might be where the term comes from."

"What's inside them now?" Dawn popped a forkful of salad in her mouth.

"Something called a liquid crystal display," Lucky said. "I won't go into the tedious details, mostly because I'd have to research them."

From there, the conversation veered to speculation

about the upcoming fall TV season. Her eyes glazing over, Dawn focused on her meal.

Melissa wasn't sure boring a child was the best way to avoid ticklish topics. For the moment, however, a whole tableful of adults had no better idea. How was Edmond going to manage parenting on his own?

The alarm woke Edmond an hour early Monday morning. He'd set it early so he had extra time to introduce Dawn to sports camp. Even though he'd signed her up online, he wasn't about to drop off a seven-year-old without a close look at the situation. Also, afterward he had to prepare for his office hours at the hospital, with several consultations scheduled as a result of Friday's talk.

Blinking his eyes open in the unfamiliar light of his new bedroom, he switched off the alarm and stretched. Ouch. His muscles ached in places he hadn't been aware of since he'd done construction in college.

Too bad Melissa wasn't here to massage him. And kiss him. And… But they'd both understood that couldn't continue. Still, this wasn't a bad way to start the week, swinging out of bed to the tantalizing scents of bacon frying and coffee brewing.

Wait a minute. Who was cooking breakfast?

The last trace of sleepiness vanished as Edmond leaped to his feet, pulled a bathrobe over his pajamas and raced down the hall.

Chapter 14

Dressed in jeans and a T-shirt, Dawn stood on a stool by the stove, flipping bacon over with a fork. The frying pan sizzled and spattered. Nearby, slices of bread had emerged nicely browned from the toaster, while a full pot of coffee hissed as the last few drops fell into it from the coffeemaker.

Edmond's urge to yell "Stop!" faded as he caught his niece's proud smile and heard her cheerful greeting. "Good morning, Uncle Eddie!"

"Good morning, cutie." He debated whether to order her away from the stove before she burned herself. However, he hated to spoil her happy mood. Also, since he had no experience in frying bacon, his fumbling might only emphasize that she'd been right to take charge. "Thank you for fixing breakfast."

"It was fun. You bought my favorite stuff." After

switching off the burner, she lifted slices of bacon and set them atop paper towels. "I love bacon!"

"Me, too." Still debating how to approach the topic of safety, Edmond took out plates and napkins, along with flatware.

"There's coffee." Dawn regarded him expectantly, waiting for a compliment.

"You're a talented little girl." He poured himself a cup. "You don't...do you drink this stuff?"

Her nose wrinkled. "Ugh."

Thank goodness. There was one bad habit he didn't have to break her of. After taking a sip, Edmond said, "This is great."

"Daddy showed me how to make it nice and strong." Dawn fetched a tub of margarine from the refrigerator along with a carton of juice.

After opening a jar of orange marmalade, Edmond sat at the table across from her. "Did you cook for your parents every morning?"

"Only when they were over hung," she said.

"Hungover?" The revelation chilled him. "Both your mommy and your daddy?"

Nodding, she spread marmalade on her toast. "This smells like oranges. I never had it before."

"I like it better than grape jelly."

She took a bite. "Me, too." .

Edmond ate in silence for a while, processing what he'd learned. He'd always assumed that his sister, for all her faults, took decent care of her daughter. Instead, he'd just learned that Barbara had drunk to excess and allowed her little girl to risk serious burns. Simon had actually instructed Dawn in brewing coffee so the child could cater to him, instead of being concerned about *her* well-being. And his sister had allowed that, too.

With a jolt, he reflected that if Barbara did appeal and gained release, he wasn't about to relinquish Dawn without making absolutely certain she'd have proper supervision. If his sister sought to reclaim her daughter, he'd be even tougher on her than child protective services would be.

To his niece, he said, "You're a wonderful little girl and I appreciate this breakfast."

Dawn's forehead creased with worry. Clearly she'd detected a "but" fast approaching.

"From now on, it's fine for you to get out cereal, bread, milk and juice, but please don't use the stove or the oven when I'm not around," he said. "If you want to set up the coffee, that's okay, but don't turn it on."

Her mouth trembled. "Why?"

Edmond hadn't meant to upset her. "You didn't do anything wrong. But even though you're a good cook, you might get burned, and it's my job to protect you." Another point occurred to him. "No using sharp knives unless I'm around, either."

"That's silly." Her mouth clamped shut, as if she were afraid to say more.

"You can still cook when I'm with you."

"What about when you're sleeping?" she demanded.

Clearly, his point hadn't sunk in. What did parents do in such a situation? Simply ordering her to obey might backfire.

In persuading a jury, he'd learned that people responded best when explanations made sense to them. "Here's the thing," Edmond told his niece. "Family services has to make sure I'm a fit guardian for you. If they find out I'm letting you do something they consider dangerous, I could get in trouble."

"Will they take me away?" Tears glimmered in her eyes.

"That's not likely," Edmond said. "But it's important that we follow the rules. You won't always know what those are, so if I correct you, please don't assume I'm angry."

"You're not mad at me?"

"Oh, honey, no."

When she scooted onto his lap, Edmond hugged the little girl, and discovered his eyes were wet.

In his ear, she murmured, "Can I still use the toaster?"

Edmond laughed. "You bet. Just keep a close eye on it. And thank you again for breakfast."

Maybe he wasn't so bad at this guardian thing after all.

The shouts of children and coaches rang through the community college gymnasium as Edmond walked in. Dawn, marching beside him with her backpack, grabbed his hand and hung on tight.

Around him milled parents with their kids, who ranged from preschoolers up through sixth graders. Edmond noted banners designating which age groups were to gather in what parts of the gym. College-age counselors in red T-shirts cheerfully directed kids, as well.

The website said the camp had been established both to keep kids active during the summer and to train college students who planned to work in physical education. Parents seemed willing to trust their kids to these youngsters and depart, but Edmond gazed around until he spotted a man of about thirty in a black T-shirt bearing the red-lettered words *Head Honcho.* Roughly Edmond's height, the man had the build of a wrestler. He must be Peter Gladstone, the director.

According to Melissa, Peter was a high school biology teacher during the school year. His wife, a nurse, had previously rented the house Edmond and Dawn now occupied. Safe Harbor was definitely a small town, he mused as they approached Peter.

"Mr. Gladstone? Edmond Everhart." He thrust out his hand, which Peter grasped firmly. "This is Dawn."

"Hello, young lady." Peter reached to shake her hand, too, but Dawn scurried behind Edmond. "This place can be scary, can't it? It's loud, too."

Her head bobbed.

He waved over a girl with a snub nose and honey-brown hair. "My stepdaughter will explain to Dawn how things work. Mia turned eight a few weeks ago, so she's in the next older group, but she's a sports camp veteran."

"Hi!" Mia gave Dawn a high-five. "My Mom told me about you. We used to live in your house. I have a black-and-white kitty named Po. Do you have any pets?"

"No."

"Come on, I'll show you where you're s'posed to be." Mia linked her arm through Dawn's. "I have two baby brothers. A surrogate mommy gave birth to them last month. Their names are Jacob and Jason."

"I'm going to have three baby sisters," Dawn said. "They don't have names yet."

Mia whisked Dawn away before Edmond could correct that the triplets weren't her sisters. Besides, he had a more pressing question, in view of the number of people milling around and the openness of the facility. "How do you maintain security?" he asked Peter.

"We check off each child's whereabouts repeatedly

throughout the day." Peter showed him the tablet computer where he kept track. "Visitors are strictly monitored." He indicated the badge Edmond had received when he signed in at the door. "You're welcome to stop by at any time. Things appear hectic right now, but it's quite different once the kids split into separate activities and the parents go home or to work."

Reassured, Edmond yielded when another parent broke in with a question. This seemed as safe a locale as any for his niece.

Preparing to leave, he spotted Dawn standing with Mia near the bleachers under a banner reading K-2. Kindergarten through second grade, Edmond translated mentally. Soon the jargon would become second nature, no doubt.

The two girls were talking animatedly. When Edmond waved, Dawn waved back almost perfunctorily.

Already she was making friends, Edmond thought as he wove his way through arriving parents and campers. Funny thing was, he had a twinge of disappointment at being so readily displaced.

Maybe that was how real parents felt, too.

Edmond arrived at the hospital half an hour early for his first appointment and decided to stop by Melissa's office. If she was busy, he could leave, but he found he wanted to tell her everything that had happened since she'd left the other day.

Edmond walked down the hallway to the fertility program offices. He'd expected to pop in to see Melissa unobserved, but he hadn't reckoned on the eagle eye of the receptionist.

"Hey there!" Caroline Carter swung around from a

file cabinet, setting a manila folder atop the open drawer. "How do you like the house?"

Since she'd recommended it and provided a referral to the landlord, she deserved more than a superficial answer. "Lovely. A bit cavernous until I buy more furniture, but it's nice not bumping into the walls every few steps."

"Is Dawn enjoying sports camp?" she asked. "I'll bet Mia showed her the ropes. She's a little sweetheart."

Did the woman track everything? Edmond didn't mind, considering how helpful she was.

"Dawn and Mia have become fast friends, and Peter Gladstone's a nice guy." Since Melissa had just appeared in the doorway of her office, Edmond addressed his summary to her, as well.

"That reminds me, the Gladstones write children's books about backyard biology," Caroline said. "I brought you one."

"That's very kind of you." Edmond was impressed by her generosity. "You didn't have to do that."

"I ordered a whole stack," Caroline said. "I'm proud to know the authors."

"Harper takes the photos and Peter writes the text," Melissa added.

"Where do they find the energy?" As Edmond recalled, the couple had one little girl, two babies and two jobs.

"I doubt they've done any writing since the twins were born." From a desk drawer, Caroline handed him a book with a stunning cover photo of a butterfly. "It explains how to identify insects in your yard. Mia added her photos and comments, too."

"That little girl's an author?" Leafing through it, Edmond was impressed with the quality of the pictures and the easy-to-read layout and text. "They've done an impressive job. Thank you, Caroline."

"Enjoy!"

"Many of those were shot in your yard," Melissa noted as he followed her into her office. "Dawn should love that."

"I love it, too." He looked forward to sharing the book with his niece.

"Things went well this morning?" Melissa closed the door behind them.

"Sports camp, yes. However, we did run into a rough patch earlier." He described the cooking incident and how he'd handled it.

"That was wise." As she sat in her chair, Melissa rubbed her belly. Forestalling his question, she explained, "Just some stretching pains in my abdomen. I have a doctor's appointment today. I'm hoping I won't have to limit my activities for another few weeks."

Concern jolted through him. How frustrating that, just when the risks from her pregnancy were increasing, his obligations to Dawn limited his ability to assist her. Now he might not even see her at work, and, to be honest, he'd come to rely on her as a friend and a sounding board. "Let me know what I can do."

"I will." She folded her hands on the desk. "Now, let's hear about sports camp. How's Dawn taking it?"

He sketched the experience, drawing a smile as he described the girls' busy chatter. "Mia seems very secure, considering the changes in her life."

"Yes, she does."

His thoughts turned to the twins. "Do the Gladstones leave their babies in the hospital child center while they work?" He presumed Melissa would do the same with her triplets.

"Harper's on leave," she said. "Twins are a challenge, even for an experienced mom, although not having to recover from a pregnancy makes things easier, I'm sure."

What about you? He wondered how she as a single mother could cope with so many babies alone.

Melissa always seemed organized and in control, the person that everyone else depended on. Only once during their marriage had she fallen apart, after her parents' deaths, crying in his arms and admitting she felt overwhelmed by the details of arranging funerals and settling their estates.

Edmond had been grateful for the chance to comfort her and take on some of her burdens. Then, just as she was recovering from her grief, his own mother had died, and Melissa had slipped into support mode.

He certainly didn't wish for her to fall apart again. But he hoped she'd lean on him if she needed to.

Her next question pulled him out of his musings. "How are you coping with fixing meals?"

"Tonight, we're eating with Dad and Isabel," he said. "I want her to stay in close touch with them. But tomorrow night, I'll be cooking—under Dawn's supervision."

She smiled. "That's funny."

Yes, it was. "The problem is what to do after dinner. How do I entertain her?"

"You can explore your yard with the book," she suggested.

"Terrific idea." That should occupy an hour or two. "And we can write about it to Barbara."

"Also a chance for Dawn to practice her writing skills."

"Right." So they'd come up with enough activities

to fill one evening. That only left 364 in the year. "Any suggestions for what we can do on Wednesday?"

"Edmond!" Melissa started to lean forward, then cried out.

For a shocked moment, he feared she was suffering premature labor and might lose the babies. The intensity of his dread surprised him. So did the fact that he pictured the triplets for the first time not as blurry squiggles but as small precious girls like Dawn. Well, that's what they would be, eventually.

"Don't panic," she said, smiling. "Just normal aches and pains again."

"What a relief."

"I was about to point out that you don't have to entertain children every minute," Melissa said. "Dawn's seven, not a toddler. Once you share the book with her, let her poke around the yard on her own."

"Unsupervised?"

"The yard is fenced," Melissa said. "If you prefer, you can sit on the patio or watch from the kitchen."

"I suppose she is old enough for that. Still, I'll keep a close eye on her until I know her better." After all, Edmond had never anticipated Dawn would cook breakfast on her own. Who could guess what else she might do? "Now I have clients to meet and I'm sure you do, too."

"Pardon me if I don't stand up."

Rising, he came around the desk for a quick kiss. "I'll let you know if there's any news about my father's condition."

"Please do. I've been reluctant to trouble Isabel."

As soon as he left, he thought of a dozen other things to mention, the kind of small matters that married couples discussed over breakfast or supper. Would the two of them ever be like that again?

Edmond set the thought aside. Obviously, events had made that impossible.

Melissa could have sworn she had read fear on her ex-husband's face in response to her cramp. Had that been purely for her safety, or for the babies, too?

Being around Dawn was changing him or, she believed, bringing out a capacity for fatherhood he'd long suppressed. Edmond cared deeply about his sister, but taking on responsibility for her too young and then running head-on into her teen rebellion had apparently convinced him that parenting brought only disappointment and stress.

Damn his stubbornness! If only he wasn't too stubborn to see what was so obvious to her. Maybe then they could all be a family....

Voices in the outer office reminded Melissa that she had clients arriving, and her daydreams were getting her nowhere. Opening the notes in her computer, she prepared to guide another couple on their journey to parenthood.

Chapter 15

"What kind of butterfly is that?" Peering into the bushes in the early-evening twilight, Dawn squinted through the camera. It had been her idea to take pictures for her letter to her mother.

Edmond searched fruitlessly for a matching shot in the book. "The plain white kind," he improvised. "Or else it's a moth."

"Uncle Eddie!" she protested as she pressed the button. "Try harder."

With a sigh, he flipped further into the book. They'd had fun cooking dinner. Dawn had showed him how to stir the pasta and how long to heat the sauce in the microwave. He'd demonstrated tossing the salad, and although some had landed on the floor, he'd been rewarded when she discovered that, to her surprise, she liked salad—with a generous dose of ranch dressing.

Afterward, Edmond had been intrigued by the first half hour of insect-watching, mostly because of Dawn's excitement. After a long day at the office, however, his energy was lagging.

"We might have to wait till tomorrow to find out what it is," he said. "We can ask Peter at sports camp."

"You promised we'd write Mommy tonight!"

Although Barbara wouldn't care whether they identified the butterfly, it mattered to Dawn, so he tried again. Peering at the book in the fading light, Edmond spotted a prospect. "Here! It's a Cabbage White butterfly."

Dawn studied the page. "It's pretty."

"Yes, but it's a pest," Edmond noted, reading the text. "The larvae—the baby caterpillars—eat vegetables."

"So do we," his niece retorted. "Does that make us pests?"

He laughed. "You have an unusual view of the world." Still, it was getting late. "Now that we've identified it, let's go write the letter."

"Okay." Dawn might be stubborn, but she complied readily when he proposed something she'd enjoy.

Inside, they downloaded the picture to Edmond's laptop, where he opened a blank document. The completed letter would be printed out and sent by regular mail.

He wished phone calls were allowed, but Barbara was still awaiting assignment to a specific prison. Much as he wanted assurance of how she was doing, he was grateful she'd requested no visits until she was settled. The long drive would be grueling, especially while he and Dawn were establishing a routine.

He helped his niece insert the photo into the document and let her write about their insect hunt, taking over only when she became frustrated by her mistakes.

Also, he told his sister that their father had set up an appointment with a specialist.

During dinner with his parents last night, only Dawn's chatter about sports camp had prevented an awkward silence. Mort had been withdrawn and ill-tempered, while Isabel had been unusually low-spirited. Edmond omitted that from the letter, though.

After they proofread, printed and signed it, Dawn kept flexing her fingers. "Is there something else you'd like to write?" Edmond asked as he folded the paper into an envelope.

"I wish I could write to Daddy." She shot him an apprehensive glance.

Edmond weighed how to respond. Much as he'd despised Simon, the man had been Dawn's father. Recalling that Dr. Brightman had urged him to validate whatever emotions she experienced, he said, "You must miss him."

"Yes." Sitting at the kitchen table where they'd been working, she stared down at her hands. "Is it wrong to love somebody who did bad things?"

"Feelings aren't right or wrong. They're natural, and they're okay." Therapy had taught him that. "You told me once that you were mad at your daddy. You aren't still angry?"

"I got mad when he was mean, but he could be nice, too." Tears trembled on her eyelashes as she gazed up at her uncle.

That raised a topic that worried Edmond, even though Dr. Brightman had detected no indications of abuse. "Did he ever hit you, or touch you in a way that was uncomfortable?"

She blinked, frowning. "He just yelled when I got in the way."

"Anything else?" He waited, in case she had more to say.

Out the rear window, he had a view of the darkening rear yard, with only a few lights from neighboring houses peeping through the bushes. What a peaceful place, the opposite of the apartment complex where he'd once visited Dawn and his sister. Graffiti had festooned the walls, angry voices had echoed, and a couple of slouching teenagers in gang-style clothing had lounged out front, watching Edmond as if weighing whether he posed a threat. Or perhaps whether they wanted to threaten him.

"Daddy took me to meet Santa Claus at the mall." Dawn's little chest heaved. "He said he always wished his daddy had done that for him."

Even that crook Simon had once been a vulnerable child, Edmond reflected. "If you want, I'll take you to the mall next Christmas."

She nodded. "I'd like that."

Abruptly, Edmond recalled a holiday when he'd escorted Barbara to the North Pole display at the mall while their mother was buying Christmas presents. Although his sister had been older than Dawn was now, her face had shone the same way, full of innocence and trust. *If she went so wrong despite my best efforts to guide her, how can I be sure Dawn's life won't get messed up, too?*

He'd put that question to Franca a few weeks ago, hoping for a definitive answer. The counselor's response had been that each person reacts differently to adolescence. Even the most ideal parents have no guarantee of how a child will develop.

Edmond closed his laptop. If only he could wrap Dawn in a cocoon and keep her safe until she was grown.

"Can Aunt Lissa come over?" she asked out of the blue. "I want to see how the babies are growing."

He searched for an excuse. "Honey, she shouldn't do any extra driving while she's pregnant."

"Then let's go over there."

He was tired of beating around the bush. And hadn't he resolved to be honest with her? "Remember at breakfast yesterday, when we talked about rules?" he said.

Dawn pressed her lips together. "Mmm-hmm."

"This isn't exactly a rule," Edmond admitted. "But Dr. Brightman believes it's important for you and me to spend time alone together, without anyone else. You've lost your dad and have to live apart from your mom. I'm the person who'll always be here for you."

"But can't I still see my aunt?" she asked earnestly.

"Yes, occasionally. But Dr. Brightman's afraid you'll be hurt when Aunt Lissa gets busy with the triplets."

"I can help," Dawn assured him. "In our old apartment, I used to babysit for the lady next door."

"You did?" Surely neither the mother nor Barbara had been negligent enough to leave this child alone with an infant. "By yourself?"

"I mean, while Mrs. Lawrence was napping," Dawn clarified. "She showed me how to change Ginny's diaper and feed her a bottle, too."

"Ah." He supposed that was all right, as long as the mother had been on the premises. "Mrs. Lawrence must have been fond of you."

"When she was pregnant, I rubbed her feet," Dawn continued proudly. "Can I do that for Aunt Lissa?"

"Let's not give Family Services the idea we're treating you as a servant." And now for a distraction. "How about some popcorn?"

"Sure."

Among Melissa's purchases had been an air popper and a jar of popping corn. "Let's fix a bowlful and eat it while we play with your jigsaw puzzle." A gift from her grandparents last night, it featured a colorful image of fish swimming through a coral reef. The printing inside the lid contained facts about tropical fish and coral.

Dawn scrunched her face. "Our hands will be greasy with butter. We'll mess up the puzzle."

"Good point. Let's work on it for a while and then break for popcorn."

"Okay."

They set it up on the coffee table, where they could leave the puzzle in place until it was finished. Edmond showed his niece the trick of finding the edge pieces first, and she concentrated intently.

Nearly an hour later, when they paused for a snack, Edmond realized he was enjoying himself. But eventually Dawn would feel secure enough to challenge him, and he still had no idea how to respond.

Despite her curiosity about how Edmond and Dawn were faring on their second night alone, Melissa resisted the urge to call on Wednesday. If only she could magically peek in to make sure everything was going well.

She understood it was important for Edmond to relate to his niece without her running interference. But didn't she belong anywhere in the equation? Maybe he couldn't love the triplets but...but, then again, why couldn't he?

She supposed she ought to be reasonable. But she'd spent a lifetime being reasonable. It was wearing thin.

Melissa had just slipped into her nightgown when her phone sounded. His name on the readout gave her a buzz, just as it had when they were first dating.

Sitting at her desk chair, she asked, "How'd it go?"

"It's ridiculous to be pleased about such a small thing, but I was able to let her play in the yard while I fixed dinner." Amusement infused Edmond's voice. "I only checked on her every five minutes."

"Lucky you didn't burn the food."

"It's hard to burn beef stew," he said.

"No, it isn't." She'd done that once, shocked to discover that despite the liquid, the ingredients stuck to the bottom of the pot. "Dare I ask if you made it from scratch?"

"Yes," Edmond replied cheerily. "I believe that was the name on the label."

"What else did you do?" Every detail fascinated her.

"We made progress on the puzzle," he recounted. "Then we knocked off to read aloud."

"Something educational?"

"The newspaper," he replied.

"Seriously?" That might be rather deep for a seven-year-old. "Which section?"

Edmond cleared his throat. "The comics." The *Orange County Register* ran two pages of them daily, in color.

"Of course."

"I never figured fatherhood could be this fun," he said. "But Dr. Brightman cautioned that there'd be a honeymoon period, and I guess this is it. What if we clash in the long run?"

"You and she have a lot in common," Melissa ventured.

"Aside from our relatives, name three things."

"You're both smart." That was easy. "You have strong personalities."

"And?"

"And you both have the good taste to like me."

He chuckled. "Very much. Oops. She just got up to use the bathroom. If she suspects you're on the phone, she'll insist on talking to you, and then she'll never get to sleep."

Reluctantly, she acquiesced. "Sleep well."

"You, too." He clicked off.

From the next room, Melissa heard Karen and Rod laughing together. They weren't lovers yet, as far as she knew, but they grew closer almost daily.

How lovely to be at that stage of a relationship, when the future spread before you filled with possibilities. Those possibilities were still there for her and Edmond, if he would quit being so hardheaded.

But they were making progress. She hoped so, anyway. Or else she was setting herself up for another crushing disappointment.

During Edmond's scheduled hospital hours on Thursday afternoon, Melissa was tempted to venture up to the fifth floor and poke her nose into his office, but her increasing size made every excursion a major effort. Stretching, she rubbed her sore abdomen.

At twenty weeks she was only halfway through a fullterm pregnancy, yet she was already as large as many women at forty weeks. She'd be glad when she finally held these babies in her arms.

A tap drew her attention to Caroline's anxious face at the door. "Were you expecting Mr. Grant?"

Melissa hadn't been in touch with her daughters' genetic parents for weeks. "No. Is Nell here, too?"

"Just him," Caroline said. "And he seems agitated."

"About what?"

Rolling her eyes to signal that she didn't dare say more, the receptionist stepped aside. The man who stalked past her gave the impression he'd have thrust the other woman out of his path had she not moved.

Melissa avoided reacting to his body language. "Vern. Welcome!"

He glared at Caroline. "Privacy, please."

The young woman's gaze met Melissa's, silently asking permission. Receiving a nod, she scooted out and closed the door.

"What's up?" Although his attitude alarmed her, Melissa kept her tone pleasant.

"We want our babies back."

"What?"

Vern scowled. "You took advantage of us."

Dread squeezed her throat at the accusation. This had to be a misunderstanding. Or a bad dream. "Why would you say that?"

"My wife's in tears every night." He paced across the office, his light brown hair disheveled—a contrast to his usually trim appearance.

"What's wrong?" Melissa noted dark circles under the man's eyes. Caring for seven-month-old triplets must be stressful, yet sleep deprivation alone couldn't account for his barging in and throwing around wild claims.

"What's wrong?" he repeated mockingly. "You took our girls, that's what's wrong."

"I took your girls?" She felt foolish, echoing his words, but the charge blindsided her.

"You caught us in a weak moment." He planted himself in front of her with his hands in fists. "You were desperate for babies and you manipulated us into giving you ours."

His unfairness was so shocking that she hardly knew where to start. "I was far from desperate. As far as I'm aware, I could have conceived on my own."

He leaped to another point of attack. "You saw how cute our babies were, and you wanted our embryos for yourself."

"Vern, please sit down." Arguing was fruitless. They needed to get to the root of this situation. "Where's Nell? She should be part of this discussion."

"There's nothing to discuss," he snarled, still on his feet. "When our daughters are born, you're handing them over to us."

Aghast, Melissa gripped the edge of the desk. "These are my daughters now. You signed a contract."

"Under duress."

She blinked in astonishment. "What duress?"

Vern resumed pacing. "What you did was wrong. You played us."

As much as Melissa tried to remain objective, she couldn't. "The embryo transfer was your suggestion, yours and Nell's, not mine."

"That isn't true." A muscle bulged in his jaw. "My wife and I would never have agreed to give away our daughters if we'd been thinking straight. You were supposed to be there for us, not for your own gain."

Did he speak even a grain of truth? Melissa tried to recall what they'd said at the time, but her brain refused to cooperate. One matter stood out, however. "You and

Nell insisted I decide immediately or you threatened to choose someone else."

He ignored the remark. "I could go to the administrator and have you fired for unethical conduct, but I'll give you a chance to fix this. You have until tomorrow to tear up that contract and agree to our terms." With that, he pivoted and stomped out.

Melissa could hardly breathe. Of all the possible problems that might arise, it had never occurred to her that the Grants would try to claim her daughters and threaten her career.

Overwhelmed, she burst into tears.

"It's not as unusual as you might imagine," Edmond told the clients seated across from him. "About a quarter of surrogates are friends or relatives."

Bev and Mick Landry, the couple he'd met a few weeks earlier while they were conferring with Melissa, had scheduled the meeting to ask about Bev's younger sister serving as their surrogate.

"I'd feel more comfortable sharing the pregnancy with my sister than with a stranger," Bev said.

"Let's review the issues." Edmond brought up the question of whether Bev's sister would use her own eggs and whether her insurance would pay part of the medical expenses. They'd also have to resolve in advance how they'd respond if anything went wrong with the baby, whether the brother-in-law fully agreed to the surrogacy, and what they'd tell the child about her "aunt."

"This sure is complicated," Mick grumbled.

"Of course it's complicated," his wife said. "Most people would think we're weird for even considering it."

"There's a surrogate mother in the Bible, so it's not that weird," her husband retorted.

"On the other hand, I don't recall anybody suing anybody in the Bible, which is why I advise covering all the bases," Edmond answered calmly. "It would be wise to draw up a contract, including what expenses you'll pay and whether your sister-in-law will have visitation rights. Both sides should bring their own lawyer, and your brother-in-law should sign the surrogacy agreement also."

Bev toyed with her purse strap. "Could we hire you as our attorney?"

"Certainly, but in my private practice. I'm only a consultant at the hospital." Quickly Edmond added, "Or I'd be happy to suggest other family law firms in the area." While part of his motive in affiliating with the hospital had been to expand his business, it was important that clients chose the representation that suited them best.

When the couple departed, it was almost five o'clock. He wouldn't mind picking up Dawn earlier than scheduled, especially since this was their evening to visit the therapist, but first he checked his email. There was welcome news: Portia Adams had agreed to his suggestion of a playdate for the girls.

"Saturday morning at the Oahu Lane Shelter is fine," she'd written. "However, a certain person volunteers there in the afternoon and we do not want to run into him."

That would be Rod, Edmond reflected. He typed a quick response, promising to set up the volunteer stint at a time when they wouldn't run into "a certain person."

He pressed Send and had begun collecting his belongings when his phone rang   Melissa.

Smiling, he answered, "Hi."

"Can you come down?" A sob shook her voice. "Something awful has happened."

"I'm on my way." Barely pausing to click off the phone, he sprinted for the stairs.

Chapter 16

The urgency in Melissa's words flooded Edmond with fear. He had to force himself to slow for a gurney in the corridor, barely avoided skidding down the last flight of stairs, and raced through the empty reception area where Caroline usually sat.

His heart was still pounding when he entered Melissa's office. It was a relief to find her sitting upright rather than lying down, screaming in pain, as he'd feared. "Are you okay?"

"I didn't mean to scare you." Sniffing, she wiped her eyes on a tissue. Her skin was unusually pale, he noted. "Thanks for coming. Do you need to pick up Dawn?"

"Not yet." Keeping track of his niece's schedule was becoming instinctive. "What happened?"

Her voice breaking, she described a threatening visit

from Vern Grant. The man was completely out of line, in Edmond's opinion.

"I don't think they can force me to do anything but I'm not sure," she concluded.

"Legally, you're the mother." Edmond had researched the subject after learning the facts of Melissa's pregnancy. "Embryos are considered property, and the Grants transferred ownership to you. They can't simply change their minds, walk in here and demand the babies."

"Vern just did." She hurried on. "Whatever the law says, he contends I took advantage of him and Nell when they were vulnerable. Given my position of trust here at the hospital, I'm terrified he might have a case."

"Didn't you say the embryo transfer was their idea?" It infuriated Edmond that the man had hurled such accusations and upset Melissa in her condition. Or any condition.

"Yes, but..." She released a ragged breath. "Even if they can't win in court, they could wreck my reputation. I hope Mark would stand by me, but he has to answer to a corporation based on the other side of the country. And if this damages the hospital's reputation, I'd feel awful."

Now that he'd learned she was in no immediate danger, Edmond's wrath focused on the person who'd put her in this position. "What he's saying could be considered slander."

"So I should spend years and all my money suing him?" Melissa asked. "Even if I won, between the internet and the press, it'd still ruin my career."

His outrage refused to yield. "One might make a case that they manipulated *you* into serving as their surrogate, without your consent."

"I don't believe they planned this," she said unhappily. "But there's no time for tempers to cool. They're insisting that I agree to their terms by tomorrow."

"What terms?" Edmond countered.

"Tear up the contract and give them my babies." The devastation on her face cut him to the core.

"What about your terms?" he responded. "Even if you went along, which you won't, are they proposing to pay for your lost work and suffering? Surrogates are paid between twenty and forty thousand dollars, plus expenses."

He paused, aware that he was letting his emotions control him. Melissa had a right to his best advice and clearest thinking.

"I hadn't considered that." She folded her arms as if holding in her emotions. "I want to fight, only I keep seeing their side of this, too. They must miss their little girls, now that their little boys are getting bigger."

Edmond ached to defend her with all his expertise, but this wasn't his decision. Also, he still believed in collaborative rather than adversarial family law, even with people who ticked him off.

Reaching across the desk, he stroked her hands. "As soon as fire stops shooting out of my ears, I'll call the Grants and suggest we meet. I'll explain that I'm attending as your friend, but that they're welcome to bring an attorney if they'd like."

"My schedule's packed tomorrow," Melissa said worriedly. "But if necessary, I'll rearrange it."

"This weekend should be soon enough. As you said, everyone's tempers need to cool." He'd find a sitter for his niece. That raised another point. "We should avoid mentioning this to Dawn. This is a touchy subject."

"Especially while it's unresolved." Tears flowed down

her cheeks again. "It feels like a judgment. I've wondered if I'm capable of caring for three babies."

"If you weren't frightened about raising triplets by yourself, you wouldn't be human," Edmond assured her. "But you aren't by yourself anymore. I'll support whatever you choose."

Melissa's mouth quirked with a hint of a smile. "I appreciate that."

A few minutes later, possessed of the Grants' phone number and with Melissa in slightly better spirits, Edmond headed for his office. As he climbed the stairs to burn off nervous energy, he recalled his impulsive statement that he'd support whatever she chose. Melissa must be wondering what he meant by that, and in truth, so was he.

He'd begun to imagine a future in which he and Dawn frequently visited Melissa and her babies. He'd pictured the triplets becoming toddlers, old enough to read stories to and play games with.

But that didn't mean he could be their father. Despite his progress with Dawn, Edmond wasn't convinced he could succeed with even one child. But it was unthinkable for Melissa to be forced to give up the daughters she loved.

At his office, he decided he'd calmed enough to place the call. Besides, the Grants had set tomorrow as a deadline, which meant he'd better contact them before then.

Holding himself steady, Edmond dialed their number.

That night, Melissa barely touched her dinner. Luckily, Jack and Anya had joined the group and the conversation flowed merrily around her. The newlyweds laughed a lot and occasionally finished each other's sentences as they recounted their adventures snorkeling and swimming on Catalina Island.

Only a little over a month from her due date, Anya also reported on the flood of gifts from her large family for baby Rachel Lenore. "There's more clothing than she can possibly wear," she told Zora and Melissa. "I'll share them with you guys, although you'll probably be inundated, as well."

"I'll organize a shower in September." Karen slanted a concerned glance at Melissa. She'd been the only one at the table who'd noticed her friend's withdrawal that evening.

"What a great idea." Anya bubbled over with ideas. Even Zora, whose pregnancy weighed more and more on her mind as well as on her body, brightened at the prospect of games, refreshments and a party at the house.

Melissa held it together until the newlyweds, Lucky and Zora went out to a movie. Then she collapsed on the couch in the den, ready to explode into a thousand pieces.

Karen joined her. "You're upset. I presume this has to do with Vern Grant's visit this afternoon."

Melissa stretched along the couch to elevate her feet. "Caroline told you?"

"She was worried." Sheepishly, her friend admitted, "And I heard raised voices. Not the words, but the general tone." While the walls between offices were thick enough for privacy, they weren't soundproof.

"Caroline means well, but please don't repeat any of this to her." It would be awful if her plight became gossip.

"Of course not." Glancing toward the kitchen, where Rod's dishwashing activities had grown suspiciously quiet, Karen called, "House rules forbid repeating anything you overhear, Rod."

His inquisitive face poked through the doorway. "Since you bring it up, I might as well join you." Removing his apron, he added, "I'm done in the kitchen."

Melissa wasn't thrilled about sharing confidences with a third party. However, since Rod had been deprived of his daughters, he might have insight into her situation.

She repeated Vern's claims and Edmond's comments. "Edmond emailed to say they've agreed to meet us tomorrow night at their house. They didn't say if they're bringing a lawyer."

"On a Friday evening?" Rod quirked an eyebrow. "It'd be a wonder if they found one of those bottom feeders to work such odd hours."

"Rod!" Karen narrowed her eyes at him.

"I didn't mean Edmond," he amended.

"Besides, the Grants don't have a lot of money." *Which might give them an additional motive to sue me,* Melissa reflected unhappily.

"I'll watch Dawn," Karen offered.

"Thanks. I'll let Edmond know." She sorted through her turbulent thoughts. "I keep wondering… *Did* I do something wrong? It's true that they suggested the embryo transfer, but I could have refused."

"As I recall, they pressured you," Karen said loyally.

"All the same, I was in a position of trust." Inside Melissa, flutterings indicated the girls were playing again. She hugged herself, hoping the little ones sensed the strength of her love.

"The embryo transfer happened after their sons were born, right?" Rod didn't wait for confirmation. "Seems to me you'd fulfilled your responsibilities as a counselor."

"Except that the embryos were at Safe Harbor, which means the Grants were still our clients." Her chest felt heavy. "If I'd been more objective, maybe I'd have stepped aside."

"But they'd already ruled out bearing the children themselves, hadn't they?" Karen probed.

"That's true."

"Had they chosen to donate to anyone else, they'd have never dared make a claim like this," Karen said.

Melissa wished the matter were that simple. "Maybe not, but I put myself in this situation by acting on impulse."

"These people changed their minds, pure and simple," Rod chimed in. "If you ask me, they're taking advantage of *your* vulnerability. They assume they can manipulate you into giving them what they couldn't afford and weren't willing to risk themselves."

His dismissive tone, Melissa suspected, sprang from resentment at his ex-wife's betrayal and the loss of Tiffany and Amber. He'd only reconnected with them this year after Tiffany ran away from San Diego to see him and her grandmother, who lived in Safe Harbor. Since the grandmother had a fondness for her former son-in-law, she occasionally arranged for Rod to join her and the girls, without the parents' knowledge, although Portia must suspect.

She *had* persuaded her husband that there was no harm in allowing Tiffany and Amber to be flower girls at Jack's wedding, since he'd been close when they were little. But in Melissa's opinion, Portia and Vince simply liked to act important at social events, especially those involving the hospital staff.

What if her own daughters grew up amid court battles and conflicting claims? The legal fight had drained Rod's savings. If Melissa lost hers, how would she raise three children?

"Surely the Grants will come around." Karen's guarded optimism contrasted with Rod's skepticism.

Melissa shivered. "I'm dreading tomorrow night."

"You'll do fine," Karen said. "Edmond will be with you."

"Yes." That was the one positive note in this experience.

Rod's phone beeped with a text. "It's Tiff," he reported. "The girls are spending the night at their Grandma Helen's house and the coast is clear."

"Helen invited us over for game night," Karen explained. "I hate sneaking around to see the girls, but the Adamses leave us no choice."

"I don't hate sneaking around," Rod responded cheerfully. "I enjoy it."

"Because you're thumbing your nose at Vince," Karen said wryly.

"You bet."

To Melissa, Karen asked, "Are you okay alone? I don't have to go."

"I'm fine." To forestall further offers, she said, "Go! I insist."

The house fell quiet after they departed. Gazing through the glass doors into the summer night, Melissa had a startling idea.

Fate had presented her with a strange opportunity, if she chose to view it that way. Saying yes to the Grants might not only save her career, it might also clear a path for her and Edmond to be a couple again. To be a family with Dawn.

A wave of despair washed over her. *I can't give them up. They're my daughters.*

Melissa had always been sensible, and tonight the arguments lined up like bowling pins. But her heart ordered her to throw the ball and smash them to bits.

To hell with being sensible.

Thrilled to see her aunt on Friday even though she'd been warned that Melissa and Edmond had to leave after dinner, Dawn bounced in her chair through the meal at Karen's house.

"What do the triplets look like?" she asked eagerly.

"They're about six inches long," her aunt said. "And— Oh, you mean what *will* they look like when they're older?"

"Yes!"

If this was a touchy subject for her, Melissa hid it well, Edmond reflected. "They'll probably be blonde, but they aren't identical. That means they were born from separate eggs, so they'll be as different as any three sisters. One might have darker hair, for instance."

"I'll bet they'll be cute," Dawn said.

"No cuter than you."

The little girl beamed.

Edmond saw no harm in bringing his niece to visit her aunt after keeping them apart all week. Dawn was doing well in her new home, as Dr. Brightman had agreed at Thursday's consultation.

"We aren't out of the woods yet," she'd told Edmond. "But you're handling this very well." Strangely, the praise mattered more to him than the fact that his law practice was growing and that he'd received compliments from both Geoff and Tony this week.

Tonight, however, Edmond was entering alien territory. If only he had some idea what to expect at the meeting with the Grants. On the phone, Vern had been calmer than Melissa described him, but there was little chance he'd changed his mind. He might even have hired an attack-dog attorney to lie in wait for them.

Should that happen, Edmond would have to work at controlling his temper. The saying went, "An attorney who represents himself has a fool for a client." But he was only participating as Melissa's friend. If this matter did end up in court, he'd hire someone who didn't have a personal stake in the outcome.

After dinner, Edmond reminded Dawn that he and Aunt Lissa had adult business to take care of.

"Karen borrowed some games from Tiffany and Amber," she said. "We'll have fun."

"I'm sure you will." He hugged her.

"Thanks for babysitting," Melissa told her friends. "I owe you."

"No, you don't," Karen answered. "We'll enjoy this."

Assisting Melissa along the driveway to his car, Edmond noticed how much larger she'd become—again. "Are you sure you're well enough for this?"

Melissa adjusted a clip in her hair. "Yes. I'm still able to work, remember? Although I'll start riding with Karen on Monday."

"I approve." He'd have offered to drive her himself, but he had to take Dawn to sports camp. And starting in a few weeks, to school.

In the car, Edmond navigated across town toward

the address Vern Grant had provided. "I wish you'd reconsider about formulating a strategy," he said. Melissa had declined his earlier suggestion to discuss tactics.

"I'd rather just listen to them." In the fading light—the days seemed shorter already, although July had barely yielded to August—her gaze sought his for understanding.

"You're more comfortable relying on intuition," Edmond summarized. "It's still best to have an opening gambit, a fallback position and a bottom line."

"How do you strategize options about losing the children you love?" She rested her forehead against the passenger window. "The opening gambit, the fallback position and the bottom line are all the same. My answer is no."

"We used to discuss best and worst case scenarios in difficult situations, remember?" *Until the divorce, anyway.* "That helped prepare us."

"Sure, like when we heard my parents were in an accident in Hawaii," Melissa said bleakly. "Best case scenario was that they'd recover. But we got our worst case." Her mother had died a few hours after arriving at the hospital, while her father had passed the next morning.

"But it gave us a chance to research how to handle funeral arrangements while we were still in a hopeful mood," he pointed out.

She sighed. "This isn't making me feel any better, Eddie."

"I guess not." Weaving through the Friday evening traffic on Safe Harbor Boulevard, he searched for a way to lighten her mood. "If something goes wrong, it doesn't have to be the end of your dream of becoming a mother."

"Doesn't it?" she asked tearfully. "If I lost my little girls, I'm not sure I could go through another pregnancy."

That heartbroken expression on her face tore at Edmond. These children meant the world to her. She was their mother. But he was not their father, and he reminded himself that the best way to help Melissa and the triplets was to remain impartial, even if he wanted to defend them to the ends of the earth.

He halted the car in front of a one-story bungalow with shutters and a wide porch. Such a pretty place. But they were facing a scene that might not be pretty at all.

Determined, he got out and circled to help Melissa.

Chapter 17

Vern didn't immediately launch into an attack as he admitted them, but his taut body language told Melissa he hadn't lost his determination. Holding on to Edmond's arm, she gazed around their small living room, which she'd never visited before.

Playpens, stuffed animals, a changing station and a bounce chair obscured whatever the décor had been pre-parenthood, while the scents of baby powder and laundry soap lingered in the air. Nell sat on the carpet watching a blond baby creep toward a glittery ball.

The new mom rose, revealing a tall, slightly pudgy figure, and removed a towel from her shoulder. "The other two went to sleep, but Tommy's our explorer." Nell brushed back short hair a shade lighter than Melissa's. She'd cut her once-flowing locks during her pregnancy.

"They never all sleep at once," Vern said. "It must violate their union rules."

Edmond gave a polite chuckle. Melissa wasn't sure how to respond. In the past, she'd joked and chatted with the Grants like a close friend. Now, she hesitated about what to say. Who could tell what remark might set off a tirade of accusations?

"May I sit down?" she asked.

"Of course." Nell hurried to remove a baby blanket from the couch. "My gosh, you're huge. How far along are you? I've forgotten."

"Almost five months." Melissa lowered herself to the seat. "I have to stop driving soon. You remember that stage."

"I'd put it out of my mind." Nell glanced uncertainly at Edmond. "You're her ex-husband?"

"I'm here as a friend." He stood with hands clasped in front of him. But behind those glasses, his brain was measuring and assessing. While Melissa appreciated his analytical powers, she'd much rather be assured that he was fiercely in her court, committed to her and to the babies. "Is anyone else joining us?" An attorney, he meant.

"It's just us," Nell said.

"We can speak for ourselves," her husband added with a touch of belligerence.

On the floor, Tommy scooted for the ball. It rolled a few inches off, arousing a dismayed grunt from the child. Another scoot, and the ball rolled again. The baby's complaint rose to a wail.

Vern scooped him up. "Can't have him waking the others," he said. Nell stretched her shoulders and neck.

Melissa decided to raise the painful subject that had

brought them here. "I was surprised to hear from Vern yesterday," she ventured.

"I didn't know he intended to drop in on you," Nell said.

Melissa doubted Vern had acted without some encouragement from his wife. "He indicated you've been upset."

"That's right." Vern adjusted the baby on his shoulder. "She misses her little girls."

Edmond's eyes narrowed. He was probably wondering how the woman could miss what she'd never had. But before this pregnancy, Melissa had missed having a child, so she understood.

Don't be too understanding. You're not here as their advocate.

"It's been hard caring for triplets, I won't pretend otherwise." Nell perched on the arm of the couch. "But that doesn't mean I've forgotten my other babies."

These are no longer your babies, she thought, struggling against a flare of temper, but Nell's attention was fixed on Melissa's belly. "How are the girls doing?"

"Fine."

"Can I feel them?"

Edmond took a step forward as if to block any such attempt. Much as Melissa appreciated his protectiveness, she doubted it could do any harm. "Go ahead."

Easing down beside her, Nell laid her palm on Melissa's bulge. After waiting a minute, the other woman appeared disappointed. "Nothing going on right now, huh?"

"Sorry, they're not being very active at the moment."

Nell removed her hand. "They'll soon be active all the time. I want to be part of this."

"Excuse me?" Melissa asked.

Nell took a deep breath. "Giving away our daughters—I wasn't thinking clearly. And to a single mom! The girls deserve a father."

"I raised that point myself." Melissa couldn't believe the woman was revisiting the issue now. "You said it didn't matter."

Nell cleared her throat. "You should have counseled us to keep our options open, that we might change our minds."

Melissa strained to hold in her frustration. "I did."

Vern glared. "Like hell!"

Edmond raised a cautionary hand. "Let's keep this civil, shall we?"

The two men faced each other as if they were a pair of, well, male animals. Edmond had never been hotheaded, however, and luckily Tommy's fussing distracted Vern.

"I reviewed my notes today," Melissa said, glad she'd kept careful records. "I advised you repeatedly that frozen embryos can remain viable for years. However, you informed me if I didn't take them during my next cycle, you'd find another recipient."

"It hurt to picture them cold and alone," Nell admitted, then put in, "I might have been suffering from postpartum blues, which you should have understood."

"I asked you about signs of depression. You denied experiencing any. All the same, I urged you to consult a counselor before deciding what to do with the embryos."

"I don't remember any of that," Vern said.

"Neither do I." Nell lifted her chin. "Those are our daughters you're carrying, our genetic children. From now on, Vern or I will attend all your doctor's appointments and ensure you're eating the right diet. When the girls are born, we're taking them home. Otherwise we'll go to the hospital administrator and have you fired."

Intrude into her medical exams? Run her life and commandeer her children? Fury powered Melissa to her feet.

"What do you think I am, your slave?" she demanded. "Was this your scheme, to trick me into serving as your unpaid surrogate?"

She could see Edmond staring at her in surprise. And with a hint of admiration, too.

Nell's eyes widened in shock. "How can you accuse us of tricking you?"

"I never considered embryo adoption until you brought it up," Melissa retorted. "Then you pressured me to implant the embryos immediately."

"It was still your decision," Nell protested.

"You urged me to hold your little boys, when you should have realized that would remind me of how much I wanted a baby." Melissa had no idea where these words sprang from, but they kept flowing. "You told me you'd dreamed that I was meant to be the mother of these babies." She was so angry, her hands shook.

Edmond hurried to her side. "Your blood pressure might rise—"

"You bet it's rising!" Melissa roared. "These people are treating me like a brood mare and trying to steal my babies!"

Nell and Vern were speechless. Tommy had stopped squirming in his daddy's arms to gape at her.

"Let's table this discussion until we've all calmed down." Gently, Edmond drew her toward the door. "Mr. and Mrs. Grant, I'll call you tomorrow."

They nodded without a word.

Outside, the evening air cooled Melissa's skin. As they walked to the car, every twinge from her stretched abdomen reminded her of what she was enduring and risking for the sake of her daughters. How dare the Grants presume to attend her doctor visits and supervise her diet!

"I've never seen you like this," Edmond said as he held the car door for her.

"Neither have I." Once he was behind the wheel, she added, "I was fighting for my children."

He gave her a wry smile. "I'm impressed."

"Did I make things worse?" She recalled the outrage on the Grants' faces when she'd accused them of manipulation.

"Doubtful," Edmond said. "You stuck to the point and didn't throw in random accusations."

"The way Vern did in my office?" As they drove to her house, she reflected how sad it was that the Grants' contentions had destroyed her old sense of comfort around them. "What happens next?"

"Let's see how they react when I call," Edmond said. "Maybe they'll change their minds after hearing your side of the story."

Melissa shuddered. "They'll probably hire a lawyer, and the next thing we hear he'll be in Mark Rayburn's office demanding my dismissal." Much as she hated dwelling on the negative, she had to prepare for that possibility.

"In my opinion, that would be a serious miscalculation on their part." He kept his attention on the spottily illuminated road. "They'd have more leverage by merely threatening to hire an attorney. Once they do, the hospital will be reluctant to admit any wrongdoing."

"Oh, that makes me a whole lot happier," she muttered.

"Sorry." With the car halted at a red light, Edmond turned his gaze on her. "Honey, the law's on your side. You're the girls' mother. I haven't reviewed the contract you and the Grants signed, but I'm assuming Tony drew it up, and he's damn smart."

She waited, hoping for more—a declaration that they'd get through this together, that he'd begun to feel something for the babies. *Tell me you've started to care about them.*

When he didn't, Melissa asked, "What if the law isn't enough? The Grants might not be able to take the babies, but they can ruin my career."

Edmond shrugged. "Worst case scenario, you might have to decide whether you'd rather lose the career you've worked for so hard, or relinquish the babies."

How could he placidly propose the devastation of her dreams? "I guess I should have expected that from you," Melissa snapped.

"I beg your pardon?" His mouth tightened.

"I must have been out of my mind, to imagine you and I could ever truly be close again." Anguish combined with her fury at the Grants, and she unleashed it all on this man for whom she'd risked her heart. "You still resent my request that we consider having children."

"Okay, I resented it," Edmond replied. "That doesn't mean I'm trying to punish you. One of us has to view things logically."

"That's right, I'm completely irrational." If he'd deliberately set out to infuriate her, he couldn't have done a better job. "The worst part is that you're lying to yourself. Anyone watching you with Dawn can tell you were meant to be a father."

"Now I'm the one who's irrational?" he asked grimly. "Despite everything I've experienced in my life, everything I've learned about myself, I'm clueless. Only you can show me the truth."

"That's about the size of it." Melissa clamped down on her impulse to shoot more barbs at him. Until tonight, she'd never imagined that she could speak to Edmond, or anyone, this way.

Now she'd destroyed whatever might have existed between them. But hadn't it only been a mirage, anyway?

Edmond remained silent, too, until they reached her driveway. "I'll call the Grants tomorrow."

"Thank you." She made her way into the house, declining his offer of help.

That night, after Edmond read a story to Dawn and tucked her into bed, Melissa's tirade still twisted and burned inside him. She was more than a lover and more than a friend, she was the only person he'd ever truly opened up to and depended on. Now she'd rejected the person he knew himself to be.

He didn't deserve the anger she'd hurled at him, but he supposed she'd been holding some of that inside since he first informed her about the vasectomy. Had she lashed out then, would it have made any difference?

Instead, she'd sat frozen in shock. He'd probed for a reaction and tried to reassure her that he loved her. When she didn't respond, he'd hoped his words would gradually sink in.

The next day, he'd arrived home from work to find

that she'd moved out. From then on, she'd coolly handled the details of their divorce, avoiding any discussion of what had set it off. After a few attempts to persuade her into counseling, he'd accepted that their differences were irreconcilable.

In all honesty, even if she'd roared at him, Edmond doubted he'd have reversed the vasectomy. Despite his willingness to serve as Dawn's guardian and his desire to help Melissa through her pregnancy, he wasn't cut out for fatherhood. In bed, he tossed and turned until he finally fell into a troubled sleep.

On Saturday morning, Dawn grew overexcited with eagerness to join her new friends, asking every five minutes if they could leave yet. At nine o'clock, when they arrived at the Oahu Lane Shelter in a light industrial complex near the freeway, Edmond had to catch her arm to prevent her from dashing across the parking lot.

"Always look both ways," he warned. "Drivers can't see you."

"There they are!" Waving, she tugged against his grasp. "Tiffany! Amber!"

Beaming, the red-haired girls waved back. Their mother, a slender woman with auburn hair, nodded a greeting to Edmond, who had been introduced to her at the wedding. In her late thirties, Portia Adams wore a hot-pink designer jogging suit. Faded jeans might be more appropriate for today's outing, but Vince Adams's wife could afford to discard an expensive outfit if it got stained.

When they reached the rambling one-story building, a young woman in a blue blazer checked their names off a list. "Ilsa will be right with you," she said.

"Ilsa?" Portia asked.

"That's the shelter's director, Ilsa Ivy." Edmond had noticed the name on the website.

"She provides the orientation for new volunteers," the blazer-clad woman said. "How many shifts a week do you plan to sign up for?"

It hadn't occurred to Edmond that they'd be expected to volunteer on a regular basis. "We're exploring our options."

"Can we come every Saturday, please, please?" Dawn peered into the hallway as if expecting little animals to trot into view. Judging by the chorus of yips and meows from within, there were quite a few on hand.

"I'll consider it," he told her. A regular volunteer shift might bring them closer, and the cause was worthwhile. However, once Barbara received her prison assignment, they'd have to take some Saturdays to visit her.

"I wish *we* could. But with school starting, we have to go back to San Diego." Amber made a face.

"We'll visit our grandma, though." Tiffany took Dawn's hand. "Like we did last night."

Portia gritted her teeth just as the shelter's director, a tall woman with thick gray hair, arrived to escort them and a handful of fellow newcomers through the building. She pointed out recent improvements.

"We now perform spay and neuter operations here on the premises, instead of transporting the animals to another location," she announced. "We're very grateful to have received a large donation."

Beside Edmond, Portia murmured, "I suppose we'll have to contribute something to keep the girls happy."

Politely, he said, "That's generous of you."

For the girls' sake and because she and her husband were important to Safe Harbor Medical, Edmond wished he could like this woman. That hope faded as the morning passed, however. She wrinkled her nose at the odors from the cages, although Edmond considered the shelter well maintained, and yawned openly while Ilsa explained the need for volunteers to foster animals.

"I wish we could adopt a kitten," Amber said wistfully as they viewed a newly rescued litter. "We have room, Mommy."

"Please don't mention that idea to your father," Portia warned, nostrils flaring. "He hates cats."

"I heard you have a new house," Tiffany commented to Edmond. "You could get a pet."

"We're renting so we'd need the landlord's approval." He glanced at Dawn. Eventually, adopting an animal might be feasible, but not yet.

To his relief, she shook her head firmly. "We can't. I'll be too busy helping my aunt with the babies."

"You will?" Tiffany exchanged a look with her sister. Now, what was that about?

Ilsa paused at the end of the corridor. "We don't normally put volunteers to work without training, but we just received a large load of newspapers that have to be folded to fit inside cages."

Portia's expression grew pinched. "Does she seriously expect us to sit around folding newspapers all morning?"

"I'll talk to her." Portia's attitude irked him, but he *had* been the one to suggest they meet here.

As their group dispersed, Edmond took the director aside to apologize for bringing a guest who didn't understand what they'd be asked to do. When he mentioned that his companion was Mrs. Vince Adams, Ilsa gave a start of recognition.

"Actually, we could use her advice," she said, "We're

planning a charity ball next Christmas and I'm sure she'd have great ideas."

Edmond thanked her. "I'm happy to fold newspapers."

"We'd appreciate it." The older woman smiled in approval. "As for the girls, they can play with some kittens who're ready for adoption."

Portia showed a spark of interest at Ilsa's request, especially when she learned that social leaders from Irvine and Newport Beach were expected to attend. By the time a teenage volunteer returned the girls an hour later with cat fur on their clothes, Portia had provided contact information and permission to use her and Vince's names as supporters of the shelter.

"Naturally, we'll send a donation," she informed Ilsa.

"That would be most appreciated."

As for Edmond, he didn't mind a few paper cuts and ink-smudged hands. After washing up, he shepherded the group out.

The girls hugged each other goodbye in the parking lot. Tiff and Amber were kind little souls, very different from their parents. Edmond credited their grandmother and Rod's influence during their early years.

Not being related genetically to his daughters obviously didn't matter to Rod. And the way Melissa had fought for her children last night showed as tight a bond as any mother had with an infant. He realized now that implying she might give them up had been ill advised, but he'd been thinking in terms of best and worst case scenarios.

Meeting the Grants—despite the unpleasant circumstances—along with their little boy had provided Edmond with a sharper picture of the tiny girls within Melissa. A scene flashed into his mind: his house filled with playpens and toys and three adorable girls rolling and crawling and clamoring for attention. How exhausting. But strangely appealing, too.

He gave a start. Had Melissa sensed that would be his reaction even before he did? Edmond respected her intuition in most instances. But then his mind conjured another image, of his sister, alone and scared in a prison cell. And his idle fantasy about babies fell apart in the face of his complete lack of understanding of where he'd gone wrong with Barbara.

He and Dawn were almost home before he noticed how quiet she'd grown. "Did you have fun with your friends? It's obvious they care about you."

Staring out the window, Dawn shrugged.

Something had upset her, and he had no idea what. Grasping for straws, he asked, "Are you worried about the kittens finding homes? This is a no-kill shelter. They'll all be placed eventually."

Another shrug.

At their driveway, Edmond pressed the garage opener. "Honey, I can't read your mind. Can you say what's wrong?"

"Nothing." Her tearful tone belied the response.

"Obviously, something is." In his pocket, his phone sounded. What rotten timing! He couldn't ignore it, though, in case it was the Grants. Glancing at the readout once they were inside the garage, he saw his stepmother's name and grew concerned. Normally she only emailed about routine matters. "Isabel? What's up?"

Dawn opened the passenger door. Holding the phone, Edmond exited, too.

"Your father met with the specialist yesterday," Isabel said.

Damn! Events had pushed Mort's appointment from his mind. "What did you find out?" he asked as he let his niece into the house.

"There's good news, mostly."

"What do you mean, mostly?"

"Mort doesn't have dementia," Isabel said evenly.

"That's fantastic." A weight lifted from Edmond. Despite his preoccupation with more immediate issues, the prospect of his father's long-term decline had troubled him deeply. "Dad's okay, then?"

"Medically speaking, yes."

"What do you mean?" Peripherally, Edmond noticed Dawn disappearing toward her bedroom, head down. Well, one crisis at a time.

There was a noise on the other hand, and his father's gruff voice spoke into his ear. "I'd better explain this myself, son."

Chapter 18

Perplexed, Edmond paced through the front room. "What's this about, Dad?"

"Something I should have admitted years ago." His father sucked in a raspy breath. "I've let you carry too much of my burden."

Was he feeling guilty because he'd been away so much driving a truck? "You had to earn a living." Edmond pictured Mort's strong face with the etched lines of a smoker.

"I don't mean that," his father growled. "My diagnosis isn't dementia, it's something called pseudodementia. That means I act like I'm nuts, but I'm not."

"You don't act nuts." Realizing he should simply listen, Edmond said, "Go on."

"The specialist they sent me to was a shrink." His father pronounced the last word with disdain. Although he'd accepted Dawn's therapy, it wasn't the sort of thing Mort would have undergone himself. *Until now.* "He says I'm suffering from depression."

That was understandable. "It's been a rough year."

"Not the normal down-in-the-dumps kind," Mort said bitterly. "The kind that's been eating at me for years. The kind I deserve."

"You need to get something off your chest?"

"That's right. This was hard enough for me to tell the shrink and I'm only saying it to you once. So listen hard."

"I'm listening." Edmond wandered into the kitchen.

Gruffly, Mort described his sense of losing control with Barbara, then sixteen, after Edmond married and moved out. Although he'd switched jobs to be closer to home, Barb had acted like a stranger, plus he'd been dealing with his wife's cancer.

"Made me damn furious when your sister ran around, drinking and cutting school," he said. "I figured she was old enough to be a decent human being while her mother was sick." Their arguments had escalated, with commands and reproaches on Mort's side and defiance on Barbara's.

One afternoon after taking his wife to chemotherapy, Mort had driven home to pick up a book she'd forgotten and interrupted Barbara nearly naked on the front couch with her new boyfriend. The sight of Simon—covered with tattoos and obviously much older than her—had been the last straw.

Furious, he'd sent Simon away with threats to call the police. Then Mort had forbidden Barbara to see him again and grounded her for a month. She'd responded with a rude gesture and told him with a four-letter-word what he could do to himself.

"I lost it." Mort's voice tightened. "Took off my belt and lit into her."

"You didn't." Horrified, Edmond had an image of his outraged, hulking father beating his half-dressed sister.

"I stopped when I realized I'd raised welts on her back," his father said shakily. "She grabbed her clothes and ran to her room." Mort was breathing hard now. "I had to return to your mom at the infusion center. By the time we got home, Barbara had packed a suitcase and gone."

"That's why she left." Edmond had believed he was to blame for being selfishly wrapped up in his happy marriage. But why hadn't his sister confided in him? He'd tried to call her after she left, only to receive the cold-shoulder treatment.

"Simon took pictures of her welts and she threatened to report me to the police if I interfered again," Mort said angrily.

"No wonder you refused to act against Simon." On further reflection, Edmond supposed Barbara might have feared that if he learned the truth, he would report both Mort *and* Simon's misdeeds to the police. *Well, I might have. And if I had, maybe she wouldn't be in prison now.*

"She never felt she could return home, no matter how bad things got," Mort said unhappily. "Rotten as Simon was, I don't believe he ever beat her."

Edmond recalled Dawn saying her father had yelled at them, but nothing more. "I don't think so, either."

"That's the whole ugly story," Mort finished. "I've been holding it inside, and this past year, when everything blew up, it was driving me crazy. I couldn't focus on anything except how I drove your sister to this."

Dismayed as he was, Edmond couldn't let his father take all the blame. "Dad, Barbara's twenty-four years old and a mother. She should have had better sense than to take part in a robbery."

"I owe her a big apology," Mort said. "But there's no undoing the damage."

"An apology would be a start." Aware of how difficult this conversation had been, Edmond said, "Thanks for telling me."

"Better late than never."

His emotions in turmoil, Edmond said goodbye. His heart went out to Barbara at sixteen, betrayed by their father. And, to some extent, to Mort, who'd been eaten by guilt and just as hurt.

Edmond sat staring at the phone, mulling the implications for himself. He'd been certain after what happened with Barbara that he lacked the instincts for fatherhood. Would he have changed his mind if he'd known the real reason for his sister dropping out of school and moving in with Simon?

Melissa had accused him of deceiving himself about his aptitude as a parent. It hadn't been a deliberate deception, but he might have been blinded by events beyond his control. And with her intuition, she'd understood him at a deeper level.

A noise from the hallway drew his attention.

Dawn stood holding a suitcase, an edge of cloth peeping out where she'd packed in haste. Confused, he said, "Are you planning to spend the night with your friends?"

"No." Only then did he notice her red-rimmed eyes.

"I heard you say grandpa isn't sick anymore. Take me back."

Edmond sure hadn't seen this coming. *So much for my fatherly instincts.* "Yes, Grandpa's better, but I'm still your guardian. You're staying with me."

"No." She blinked, her little chest heaving. "I want to go home."

Barely a week ago, he'd have been relieved. Now, giving her up was inconceivable. "I know I'm not the best uncle in the world, but you're my little girl, Dawn."

"Take me home!" she repeated in a fiercer tone. "I don't want to stay here."

Why was she mad at him? "Have I done something wrong?"

"I hate you!" Bursting into tears, the little girl dragged the suitcase back to her room and slammed the door.

Edmond couldn't imagine what had provoked her. Although news of Mort's good health might have prompted the idea of returning to her grandparents, Dawn's reaction seemed excessive. Also, her mood had been subdued ever since they left the animal shelter.

There was a lot at stake, maybe his entire relationship with his niece. He had to keep trying.

Edmond walked down the hall and tapped on her door. "Can I talk to you?"

"Stay out!" she cried. "You're not my father! You don't even like children. You'll be glad when I'm gone."

Every word stung with old truths that no longer held. In the space of a few days with Dawn, Edmond's perception of the world had changed. Sharing breakfast, watching her skip into sports camp each morning to join her new buddies, picking her up and learning about her day—he loved those things. How had he let her down?

He couldn't—wouldn't—return to being the uncle who dropped in once a week to take her to therapy. As Melissa had fought for her babies, he was going to fight for Dawn.

"I'd be miserable if you left," Edmond said through the closed door. "Please let me in."

"You and Aunt Lissa don't need anybody else," came the ragged answer. "Now you can be happy."

What on earth was she talking about? He tried the knob, and found the door locked.

He supposed a stern, old-fashioned father would force the issue. But Dr. Brightman had said defiant behavior was natural, and Dawn's actions weren't placing her in danger. Edmond chose to let it ride and change tactics. "What should I fix for lunch?"

"I'm not hungry."

"Are you kidding? Your stomach's growling so loud, I thought it was thunder."

For a moment, it seemed Dawn might not answer. Then she said, "Peanut butter."

"With jelly or marmalade?"

"I don't care."

"Okay. I'll call you when it's ready." Grateful that she'd spoken to him, Edmond went to fix lunch.

He'd have to play this by ear. Edmond hoped he'd developed some essential paternal sensitivity, even if it hadn't come naturally.

"It's almost like cheating." Reaching the bottom of the steps, Melissa set the lock on the chair lift and eased out of the seat.

"Cheating?" Karen planted hands on hips. "With you and Zora both pregnant, I'm glad I didn't remove this after Mom died." She'd installed the device while caring for her mother, who'd battled Parkinson's disease.

She had to admit, having an easy way to go up and down—including a remote that allowed her to summon the seat should Zora leave it on the other floor—would be invaluable.

"You're wonderful," she told her friend. "I'd be lost without you."

"What am I, chopped liver?" Rod demanded, descending from above, where he'd posted himself to keep an eye on Melissa's maiden journey.

"Thank you, too." She gave him a weary smile.

Following last night's altercation with the Grants and her blowup at Edmond, Melissa hadn't slept well. A short while ago, when Edmond had called, she'd assumed for a moment he might be willing to discuss their quarrel. Instead, he'd had more pressing issues on his plate.

He'd filled her in about Mort's depression and the reason for it. Although she was glad the older man wasn't suffering from dementia, the revelation about his brutality to Barbara turned Melissa's stomach—and Edmond's, too, she gathered. He'd also mentioned Dawn's rebellion but assured her he would figure out the cause on his own. With no further comments, he'd ended the call.

She missed being on his team. On Dawn's team, too. But it seemed her outburst last night had permanently closed that door.

"Something wrong?" Karen asked.

Melissa had no intention of mentioning either her quarrel with Edmond or his father's revelation. Since her friend already knew about her other problem, she focused on that. "I'm worried about what to do if the Grants get me fired."

"I'll organize a protest." Karen accompanied her to the kitchen to start lunch. "I remember when they proposed giving you the embryos, how uncertain you were and how much they pressured you."

Nevertheless, Melissa doubted that would save her job. "I suppose I could find a laboratory position like I used to have. But I'd hate to give up working with our clients and my friends on the staff."

"Screw that," Rod said.

Karen glared at him. "Language!"

"Sorry." Rod didn't appear regretful, though. "Being around my daughters last night reminded me how important it is to fight for what you love, even if you lose. They know how much I love them because they understand how far I was willing to go."

"I *do* intend to fight," Melissa responded heatedly. "I'm talking about accepting the loss of my job, not giving up my daughters."

Karen raised her hands. "I'm declaring a moratorium on arguments, spats, quarrels…"

"We weren't quarreling," Rod said.

"Much," Melissa qualified.

"And sharp tones of voice," Karen finished. "Okay, what kind of sandwiches does everyone want?"

"Depends on what's available." From the fridge, Rod extracted bread, cold cuts and condiments.

Melissa pitched in. Yet the moment she let her thoughts wander, they fixed on another kitchen a few miles away. What were Edmond and Dawn discussing over lunch? Had he uncovered the source of her rebellion?

For three years, Melissa had believed that her ex-husband had been wrong for her and that her closeness to him had vanished forever. Then, these past weeks, experiencing his tenderness, his devotion to his niece and his concern for his sister and parents, she'd let down her guard. No, she'd gone far beyond that. She'd fallen in love with him again.

But however she might feel about him, her loyalty to her daughters came first.

Edmond had hoped Dawn would emerge from her room for lunch in better spirits. Instead, the little girl stared down at her plate throughout the meal, although she did consume most of her sandwich and several cream-cheese-filled celery sticks, She responded to his questions in monosyllables.

As soon as she was done, Dawn grabbed her camera and scraped open the rear sliding door, avoiding Edmond's gaze as she darted out. While she hadn't repeated her insistence on leaving, neither had she unpacked her suitcase, he noted when he peered into her room.

Edmond considered placing an emergency call to Dr. Brightman. However, he wasn't ready to admit failure.

After cleaning up the lunch dishes, he glanced out the window. Dawn's small figure prowled through the bushes at the rear of the lot, halting as she spotted something. He adjusted his glasses and then he saw it, too, a flash of emerald hovering in front of an orange trumpet-shaped flower. A hummingbird.

How magical, and how endearing he found his niece's fierce concentration as she took aim. Lowering the camera, she continued to watch the tiny bird.

I can't give her up. Especially after what he'd learned about his father. Not that his dad was likely to hit her, but Edmond could never entrust Dawn to them. She was his child now.

Still, he had no clue why she was pushing him away. Since he was batting zero on that, he decided to seize this chance, with Dawn out of earshot, to call the Grants. Stiffening his composure, he pressed their number.

Nell answered. After greeting him, she said, "Vern's not home."

"Can we just talk?" Through the window, he watched Dawn. She'd moved on to investigate a neglected flowerbed where a few scraggly marigolds lingered. "This needn't be formal."

"I suppose it's all right. Hold on." In the background, a baby was crying. A minute later, the wailing stopped, and then Nell spoke again. "Okay, I'm settled."

"How did you feel about last night's discussion?" Edmond said.

Nell sighed. "I was picturing her the way she used to be, smooth and in charge. So it came as a shock to witness a different side of her."

Unsure of her mood, he framed his response with care. "She caught me off guard, too."

"I understand how uncomfortable and scary it is to carry triplets," Nell said. "I can't blame her for being upset."

"She'd do anything for those kids," Edmond said. "And I'd do anything to help her." He hadn't registered until he spoke how strongly he meant that.

"How do *you* feel about babies?" she asked.

"Me?" Tricky subject. "I don't have much experience."

"Ever hold one?"

"My niece." Edmond responded, instantly hit by a sweet memory of her baby scent and wide-eyed gaze.

"How did you react?" Nell probed.

"I was afraid I'd drop her." Edmond chuckled. "She's seven years old now, and I haven't dropped her yet." Firmly, he steered back on course. "About the triplets..."

"I guess it was unrealistic to hope she'd accept our terms." Nell's frankness made him want to stand up and cheer. But they hadn't won yet.

"I'd hate for Melissa to land in trouble at work," Edmond said. "But she's the mother of those triplets, and she'd put her life on the line for them, let alone her job."

"How about you?"

The woman had a talent for throwing curve balls. "Excuse me?"

"How do you feel about these babies, specifically?"

He might as well be frank. "I'm still growing into the reality of being a father, but it's astonishing. Transformative. Utterly unique..." The words choked off as he recalled Dawn's anger. What if he *couldn't* figure out what was wrong with her?

"I understand," Nell said. "Vern and I will talk this over and call you again."

"Thanks." Edmond waited in case she had more to say, but she clicked off.

Only then did it occur to him that she'd misinterpreted his comments about fatherhood. He'd been referring to Dawn, not the triplets. Hadn't he?

The screen door slid open. "Who was that?" Dawn asked. "Why were you talking about the babies?"

Damn. He'd forgotten to keep an eye on her and protect her from this conversation. Too late, and if he lied, she'd sense it. Moreover, he'd be setting a bad precedent. "It was the donor mommy of Aunt Lissa's babies. We were just discussing—"

Her face crumpled. "Don't give away my sisters!"

"What on earth?" Surely she hadn't drawn that conclusion from anything he'd said. "Where'd you get that idea, Dawn?"

She scuffed her shoe against the floor. "If I tell you, will you promise I can still play with them?"

"Amber and Tiffany?"

A short nod confirmed his guess.

"Of course you can play with your friends, whenever they're available." Edmond reached for his niece and, hesitantly, she scooted closer. "What did they say?"

"They heard Karen and Rod talking at their grandma's house." The story spilled out—the Adams girls had believed the babies might be given away to save Melissa's job. Tears rolled down her cheeks.

Distressed, Edmond lifted Dawn onto his lap. "That's the problem with gossip. It doesn't give you the whole story. Aunt Lissa and I hate this idea. It didn't come from us and we're fighting it."

"You used to not want children." She must have heard that from Barbara. Or maybe she was remembering something he'd said during the divorce, he thought remorsefully.

"That was a long time ago. People change," Edmond said. "I have, a lot. I'd never been a father before. You're teaching me all sorts of important things."

His niece sniffled. "You wouldn't be happier if it was just you and Aunt Lissa?"

"I'd be terribly sad without my little Dawn," he assured her gruffly. "Nobody's giving anybody away. Not you, and not the triplets."

Her cheek rested against his shoulder. "You promise?"

"I'm not letting anyone take you. We're a family." His

chest hurt from the swell of emotions. "As for the babies, they're family, too. And so is your aunt."

Could he honestly claim to be Melissa's family, especially after their argument? But he was. He'd never stopped loving her, no matter how hard he'd tried over the years. He couldn't bear to lose her again, or Dawn, or those three little girls who had become real to him before he knew it.

How ironic that, for so long, he'd carried the guilt of failing his sister. Although he still didn't fully understand why Barbara hadn't confided in him, he no longer believed that her actions were his fault.

And he no longer believed he was hopeless as a father. Today, he'd been sensitive enough to elicit the cause of Dawn's unhappiness.

No wonder Melissa had been frustrated at his refusal to acknowledge his fatherly instincts. He had plenty of them. That left the hard part: what was he going to do about it, and about their disagreement?

What's your best and worst case scenario? No, scratch that. What's your goal?

Suddenly, his path became obvious. "I have an idea," Edmond said. "But I need your help."

"Okay, Daddy." Snuggling against him, Dawn didn't seem to notice the endearment she'd used.

Although Edmond suspected he might not hear that term often, it marked an important step. That was how love grew, he was discovering. Sometimes gradually, in fits and starts, and sometimes in a big leap.

He was ready for a leap. "Let's get started."

Chapter 19

"I should have remembered not to play Scrabble with you." Zora studied the board with disgust. "You always win."

"I had lucky draws." Collecting the tiles for storage, Melissa smiled at the picture they made, sitting at the table barely able to reach the board due to their swollen bellies. "We may not be able to play again for a while. My arms won't stretch that far."

Draped over an armchair in the den, Lucky glanced up from his computer tablet. "We ought to measure you guys to see who's bigger."

"Who cares?" Zora shot back.

"It would be in the interest of science," Lucky continued. "Twins due in three months versus triplets due in four."

"Our doctors already have that information." Melissa had no desire to turn their pregnancies into a contest.

"Also, Melissa's two inches taller than Zora," Karen observed from the couch. "That might affect the results."

"It's an interesting idea, though," Rod murmured from beside her as he lowered his medical journal. "Considering that we're all sitting around like dullards on a Saturday afternoon."

"Exactly." Lucky ran a hand over his short dark hair. "My old roommates would have placed bets."

"Your old roommates were slobs," Zora said.

"But never boring."

A phone rang. Everyone reached for pocket or purse before pausing in recognition of the ring tone. It was Melissa's.

Her heart skipped at the name on the readout. "Edmond," she answered. "What's up?"

"Any chance your friends could babysit Dawn for a while?" He spoke with a cheerful lilt. "I'll bribe them by bringing dinner."

"If you're bringing dinner, why do you need them to babysit?" Melissa asked.

"You and I are going out," he said.

"Is that how you ask for a date these days?" she teased, grateful for his willingness to reach out to her.

"We have a few things to discuss," Edmond responded lightly. "Okay?"

"Sure." Never mind that those things might be uncomfortable, as long as they were friends again. "How's Dawn?"

"Much better. I ferreted out what upset her." He explained about Rod and Karen's indiscreet remarks and

Dawn's conclusion that children—both her and the babies—were expendable.

"That's horrible." Around the room, everyone was trying to appear busy, all the while listening so hard their ears must hurt. "I'd be happy to join you for dinner."

"Give me an hour, okay?" he said. "Oh, and is it okay if Dawn shoots pictures in your yard? The Gladstones' book inspired her."

"You bet. We have plenty of bugs, birds and so on. See you in an hour." Ending the call, she took a deep breath, ignoring the curious looks from her friends.

Edmond was ready to talk. A twinge of fear warned that he might be planning to withdraw further, yet if so, why the upbeat tone? Belatedly, she recalled that he hadn't mentioned the Grants. Had he phoned them yet?

Their unreasonable demands had wrecked her night's sleep and the fallout had hurt Dawn, too. Much as she'd rather skip chastising Rod and Karen, their gossiping had added to the problem.

In the past, Melissa would have avoided the confrontation, but now she'd learned it was better to address the issue. Firmly, she faced the couple on the couch. "Remember the rule about not discussing any of our personal business around others?" she began.

Parking his sedan in the driveway, Edmond recalled his first visit to the blue-trimmed white house. Had the wedding been only a month ago? Since then, his entire life had changed.

And he intended to change it much more. "Well, kid?" he asked Dawn.

She clutched her camera. "Ready for action, Uncle Eddie."

"This is a fantastic place to take photos."

"I can't wait to show them to Mia." School started on Monday and, although her friend was a year older, Paula Humphreys had assured Edmond the girls could sit together at lunch. She'd also arranged, at his request, for Dawn to be in her class.

He retrieved two of the three large sacks he'd bought at Papa Giovanni's. The aromas of tomato sauce, oregano, garlic and other spices covered the familiar scent of the estuary.

In the driveway, Dawn placed her hand into the crook of his arm. "We're a team, aren't we, Uncle Eddie?"

"Now and forever," he said.

Since Melissa's childhood, the glory of the sun setting over the ocean had delighted her. Tonight, as golden and scarlet streaks transformed the western sky above Safe Harbor into a painter's palette, her spirits soared.

She and Edmond were alone in a small grassy park that divided the harbor from a beach, currently empty of sunbathers thanks to the nippy evening breeze. With the waves unusually calm, surfers were taking the evening off, as well. Only a few joggers and dog-walkers passed by.

While Edmond spread a cloth over the picnic table, Melissa glanced toward the harbor, where sailboats skimmed toward their moorings. At this hour, the swimwear and surfboard shops along the quay had closed, although the Sea Star Café was serving food outdoors beneath warming lamps, an ironic touch considering that it was August. Melissa welcomed the cool breeze.

"Comfortable?" Edmond removed containers of food from a large sack. "Sorry about the hard bench."

"No worries. That smells divine," she said. "This is a treat."

"For me, too." On paper plates, he served a pesto dish along with salad and bread, and sparkling grape juice in plastic glasses.

He'd been gracious earlier with her housemates, Melissa reflected. Karen and Rod had apologized for their negligence. They'd believed themselves out of the girls' earshot. But they shouldn't have run that risk, they'd admitted.

All's well that ends well, Edmond had said.

Thank you, Karen had responded. *I've learned my lesson.*

Me, too. Rod's face had gone red with embarrassment. For once, he didn't attempt to joke about the situation.

I forgive you, too, Dawn had added. *Just don't do it again.* She'd been in a buoyant mood after the frank discussion with her uncle.

"I'm impressed by how well you and Dawn talk," Melissa told Edmond as they ate.

Fork in hand, he paused to gaze at her, his contact lenses emphasizing the rich brown of his eyes. "It's astonishing what a difference it makes when people actually listen."

"You've always been an excellent listener." That quality had impressed her from the start.

"I'm a better one now." He cleared his throat. "Which brings me to something I wanted to discuss."

Her phone trilled. Melissa checked the readout. "It's Nell Grant." Anxiety pumped up her heart rate.

Although reluctant to risk spoiling their evening if this were bad news, Melissa couldn't bear to delay. "I'm sorry but I have to take it." Receiving his understanding nod, she answered. "Hi, Nell."

"Hi." The woman hesitated. "I hope I'm not interrupting your dinner, but I promised Edmond this afternoon that I'd call."

"You did?" She was surprised he hadn't mentioned that conversation.

"Vern and I have been reconsidering our position," Nell continued, barely audible above the intermittent rumble of waves. "There's a part of me that will always wish we could have raised our little girls."

Melissa gripped the phone so hard it dug into her hand.

"But your condition reminded me what my pregnancy was like and the reasons I can't go through it again," Nell said. "You're right. You didn't agree to serve as our surrogate. You undertook this pregnancy out of love, and you're their mother now."

Melissa released a long breath. "You won't seek custody?"

"No, and I'm sorry we upset you," Nell said. "It was a knee-jerk reaction, pure emotion and no common sense. Honestly, we're in no position to raise three more infants."

Melissa had to be sure this drama was truly over. "You won't file a complaint with the hospital?"

"You did nothing wrong," Nell conceded. "If you'd refused, we'd have given the embryos to someone else, and there wasn't anyone I trusted more than I trusted you. My dream confirmed what I already knew, that these babies were meant to be yours."

Over the sea, the moon rose above the last wisps of sunset, and it struck Melissa as the most exquisite sight in the universe. *We're safe.* "I'm a little intimidated about what lies ahead, but we'll be fine."

"I'm sure you will, especially now that you've reconnected with your husband," Nell said. "He'll make a terrific father."

Melissa wasn't sure how the woman had drawn that conclusion, but what mattered was that she no longer faced an agonizing battle. "I'm thrilled. Thank you for calling."

"Can we keep the kids in touch, as we planned?" Nell asked. "We could hold a once-a-year reunion between Thanksgiving and Christmas. Our own way of giving thanks."

Melissa doubted she'd ever be completely comfortable with the Grants again, but the children deserved to know their siblings. "We'll figure something out."

"I'll send you an email to confirm what I've said," Nell went on. "You don't have to worry that we'll change our minds."

"I appreciate that." The extra reassurance reminded Melissa of how much she'd always liked the Grants. "Have a great evening."

"You, too."

After clicking off, she recounted the conversation to Edmond as relief seeped through her entire body.

"Congratulations." Tenderness lit his gaze. "You're incredibly beautiful when you're happy. I'd love for you to be happy all the time."

"Me, too." Part of her conversation with the other woman still puzzled her, though. "Whatever you said to Nell earlier had quite an impact."

"What in particular?"

"She has the impression we've reconciled and that

you're ready to be a father." Melissa raised her hands, palms outward. "I don't mean to criticize."

"It's all right." Edmond leaned forward. "The more perspective I gain on the past, the more I want to kick myself."

"That sounds painful."

"Not as painful as the last three years have been," he said. "Do you remember when I proposed to you?"

"Yes, of course." They'd been walking hand-in-hand on the Santa Monica pier at sunset.

"I promised to love and cherish you forever," Edmond mused. "It seemed easy, since we were on the same wavelength in almost every way. That was part of the problem."

"What do you mean?" Melissa had considered harmony to be among their greatest strengths.

"Since we were always in sync, we never learned to handle serious conflict," he explained. "When I got the vasectomy, I assumed that you'd understand what it signified to me."

She'd taken his action as a dictate: my way or the highway. "What exactly did it signify?"

"That what we shared was too precious to risk." Edmond spoke with grave intensity. "When you left, I believed you didn't love me as much as I loved you."

"But I did!"

"I understand that now." From the table, he picked up a manila envelope she hadn't noticed and removed a sheet of paper.

Even at a glance, it didn't resemble a legal document. "What's that?"

It turned out to be a computer-printed picture of them with two-year-old Dawn in front of a Christmas tree. In black ink, someone had drawn three babies, angled as if held in their arms. Each infant had a bow in her hair.

Underneath, Edmond had written in his bold hand: "Marry me again—for keeps. Let's be a family."

Tears sprang to Melissa's eyes. Could he have changed that much? "You're willing to accept my daughters?"

"Our daughters." He moved close, and his arms encircled her. "I don't just accept them—I love them. I'm not sure how it happened, but while I was becoming Dawn's father, I became theirs, too. Raising four children won't be easy, but I'm looking forward to it."

Much as she longed to shout her agreement, it was hard to accept what she'd longed for but never believed could happen. Melissa had to be careful, for all their sakes. "Do you have any idea what lies ahead? The sleepless nights, chaotic schedules, financial sacrifices."

"Sleepless nights? I'm an old pro," Edmond joked, then grew serious. "I'm not sure anyone can be one hundred percent prepared for this kind of situation, but I want to spend my life with you and Dawn and the triplets. There's nothing more important than that." His embrace tightened. "You're the other half of my soul, Melissa. Please marry me."

She leaned against him, her last doubts vanishing. He was the only man she'd ever loved or ever could love, and by some miracle, he loved her, too. "We can skip the fancy ceremony. We had that already and, besides, I can't picture myself waddling down the aisle like a boat in full sail."

Edmond peered down, his eyes narrowing in mock sternness. "No fair, dodging the best part. Let me hear a loud 'Yes, Edmond, I'd love to be your wife!'"

As the sun glimmered below the horizon, it seemed

to Melissa that the waves receded and the world grew still. Her voice rang out as clear as a clarion call. "Yes!"

"Yes what?" he prompted.

"Yes, I love you and I'll marry you, and you better not change your mind because I'll never let you go again!"

"Perfect," he said. "That goes double for me."

When he kissed her, his warmth dispelled the chilly air and filled the empty spaces in Melissa's heart forever.

Forever. That was her favorite word.

Chapter 20

Edmond and Melissa remarried the first week of September at the historic Old Orange County Courthouse, with Dawn as flower girl, Geoff Humphreys as best man and Karen as maid of honor. A handful of friends, along with Isabel and Mort, joined the festivities.

To Edmond, the intimate ceremony was as special as their elaborate wedding eight years earlier, although he knew Melissa missed her parents. And they both missed Barbara, who'd been maid of honor at their first wedding.

A week later, after submitting paperwork and obtaining approval from the state department of corrections, he took Dawn to the women's prison where her mother had been assigned. Although he wished Melissa could accompany them, the trip would have been too strenuous.

During the hour-long drive, Dawn peppered him with

questions. She considered it funny that they weren't allowed to wear blue jeans because that was what prisoners wore, or forest-green pants with tan tops, which would resemble prison guards' outfits.

But at the sprawling facility, she scarcely spoke during the screening process. And when she first spotted her mother in a large room echoing with the conversations of other prisoners and their families, she clung to Edmond.

His sister appeared healthier than she had in court, he was pleased to note. Her brown hair, free of purple streaks, was neatly brushed and her hollow cheeks had filled out.

"It's me. Mommy," Barbara assured her daughter. "Give me a hug, Dawnie."

The girl ventured out for a quick embrace, then darted back to Edmond. They took seats across a table from Barbara.

"Do you have pictures of the wedding?" she asked.

"Of course." He'd been allowed to bring them, subject to review by the guards.

As Barbara flipped through the half dozen shots, Dawn went to peer over her shoulder. Soon she was chattering away about her new dress and her bouquet.

"You look beautiful," Barbara said. "And Melissa's *very* pregnant."

"I'm going to have three sisters," Dawn crowed, although that was hardly news. They'd written to her mother at length about the triplets and the wedding.

"Sisters?" Barbara frowned. "They're your cousins."

"No! They're my little sisters," her daughter declared.

At the rise in her voice, a guard glanced over. The woman didn't move in their direction, though.

Edmond understood Barbara's instinct to hold on to

Dawn as tightly as possible. However, he was glad when she said to him, "They *are* her sisters, aren't they? You and Melissa have to serve as Dawn's parents now. I'll always be her mom, too, but I blew it."

"If I'd had any idea why you left home…" He let the sentence trail off, cautious about discussing the painful topic in front of Dawn. Although Mort had written a letter of apology, Edmond doubted his sister's emotional wounds had healed.

"I should have told you about my fight with Dad, Eddie," his sister said. "I was too embarrassed and too stupid to get the help I needed. Well, I'm getting it now—the hard way."

"What kind of help?" Dawn frowned. "Like Dr. Brightman?"

"Yes, I do receive counseling," her mother said. "Also, while I'm in prison, I can earn a high school equivalency diploma. Maybe an A.A. degree, too. That's the same as two years of college."

"Terrific. That should help you get a job after you're released."

"I'm not sure if anyone will hire a convicted felon, but I'll worry about that later." Barbara cleared her throat. "I guess Mr. Noriega told you I decided against appealing the conviction. My sentence was fair, and I'm not willing to risk a longer term."

"Yes, he did." Edmond hurried on to share news of his own. "The court has approved my permanent guardianship. We passed the family services review with flying colors." The social worker had interviewed him, Melissa and Dawn, as well as conducted a home visit.

He waited uncertainly for Barb's reaction, unsure of how she'd feel about the word *permanent*.

"That means until she's eighteen, doesn't it?" his sister said slowly. "But I can ask to get custody when I'm released."

"Yes, if you have a job and a stable living situation." Despite an effort to sound neutral, Edmond couldn't avoid the edge to his voice. "Once she's twelve, she'll have the right to choose, though."

Dawn stared at them both, lips pressed tightly. Although he'd explained this to her earlier, it was bound to be a sensitive topic.

"You want to keep her, don't you?" Barbara asked.

"Of course."

Sadness shadowing her face, she gazed at her daughter. "I'd rather have her with me, but she needs stability. Dawn, you can stay with Uncle Eddie and Aunt Lissa till you're grown-up if you want to."

"Can I still see you?" Dawn touched her mother's arm.

"Absolutely!"

"I'll bring her once a month while you're here," Edmond promised. That seemed often enough to maintain the relationship while allowing Dawn to adjust to her new home and school.

"Thank you." Barbara sighed. "This is for the best. I'm the one who let her down."

Much as Edmond yearned to disagree, he couldn't.

Barbara steered the subject to their preparations for the babies. The third bedroom, which they'd designated as the nursery, was filling with toys and baby equipment donated or loaned by friends, Edmond said. The Grants had given them many items that their boys had outgrown.

"Will you send pictures when the triplets are born?" Barbara asked wistfully.

"Yes, Mommy," Dawn said. "I'll take them myself."

"You're a natural photographer." A few minutes later, as Barbara hugged them farewell, her eyes glittered with unshed tears. She faced a hard road ahead, Edmond reflected, but she wouldn't walk it alone.

He told her that, quietly, before he left, and his sister smiled.

"Can't I choose one, please?" Dawn wheedled, sitting between Melissa and Edmond on the patio lounger. It was a late afternoon toward the end of September. "Not Bambi or Bunny, I promise!"

"Not Belinda either," Melissa replied gently, with what struck Edmond as admirable patience. She must be very uncomfortable these days, with the triplets growing rapidly. After a few weeks of riding to work with Karen, even that had become a strain, and she'd begun telecommuting on a reduced schedule.

The little girl released a melodramatic sigh. "Okay. But we've been through *all* the books. We have to call them something!"

In Edmond's lap, the international-themed book fell open to a page filled with O's—Omorose, Ophelia, Orma. Moments before, they'd been staring at F's—Fayola, Fritzie and Fulvia. Gently rocking the lounger with one leg, he stifled a yawn. It was the third such volume they'd flipped through this afternoon.

"We could draw names from a hat," he joked.

"No, Uncle Eddie!" Dawn scolded.

"I was kidding."

"Let's rest for a minute and enjoy the sunshine," Melissa said. "Maybe the names will sort themselves out in our brains."

Dawn bounced in her seat. "Flowers!"

"They are beautiful." Melissa beamed at Edmond as she regarded the planter overflowing with petunias. "I'm glad you had them planted."

"So am I." He'd hired a gardener as well as a cleaning service.

Dawn waved her hands impatiently. "I mean how about flower names, like Daisy?"

"Maybe not that particular one, but it's a good idea," Melissa responded.

They ran through floral names, including some that Edmond found on his phone. Most he considered too old-fashioned. Blossom. Chrysanthemum. Poppy. "Alyssa is nice."

"My favorite is Lily," Dawn announced.

"That's pretty," Edmond mused. "It reminds me of Tiger Lily in *Peter Pan.*"

"Lily of the valley was my mother's favorite scent." Melissa clapped her hands. "We've picked a name!"

"Lily," Dawn said happily. Edmond was glad she'd been able to propose one of the names.

"One down, two to go," he said. "How about other names starting with L?"

"I'd rather not." Melissa half closed her eyes as he continued rocking the lounger. "The girls will have a hard enough time establishing unique identities without that."

On the lawn, a bird alighted and began pecking industriously. "How about bird names?" Dawn asked. "Like Robin or Jay."

"Pelican?" Edmond joked.

"Flamingo," said Melissa.

"You guys, cut it out." The little girl folded her arms.

Melissa took a deep breath. "Now that I think about it, a name caught my attention in one of the books, but I'm not sure it's right. It isn't a bird name, either."

"Out with it," Edmond commanded.

"Simone," she said.

His jaw tightened. Did she really want to call a baby after Dawn's dad? "Why Simone?"

"I had a high school friend named Simone, an exchange student from France," Melissa explained. "Unfortunately, we lost touch over the years."

"Sih-mone," Dawn pronounced. "It sounds sophisticated." That was one of her favorite new words from a story she'd read.

"It's a variation on Simon…" Edmond pointed out.

Melissa stretched her neck. "That's why I was reluctant."

Dawn drooped. "Never mind."

Her disappointment touched him. Of course she had positive feelings about her dad, too. "It's okay that you loved Simon. He loved you, too."

"I don't want Simone to grow up to be a robber," the little girl said.

Melissa stroked her niece's hair. "She doesn't have to be like him in the bad ways."

"Just the good ones." Dawn studied them hopefully. "Okay?"

Melissa quirked an eyebrow at Edmond. "Do we all agree on Simone?"

He did, actually. "Let's go for it. Naming kids after family is a wonderful tradition."

"Excellent idea," Melissa said. "But we tried that, remember?"

None of their female relatives' names had quite hit the mark. Then Edmond came up with one they hadn't considered. "What about your brother?"

"Jamie." Melissa spoke the name gingerly.

"The little boy who died?" Dawn had heard the story. "It can be a girl's name, too, can't it?"

"You bet." Melissa ran a finger across Edmond's cheek. "It's a wonderful suggestion."

"We each picked a name," their niece observed.

"So we did. Lily, Simone and Jamie," Melissa said "They're lovely."

The lowering sun and his rumbling stomach reminded Edmond that the dinner hour was approaching. "Who's hungry?"

"Me!" said Dawn.

"Me, too," Melissa chimed in.

"It's lucky I know how to cook." He'd learned a lot these past few months, he reflected as he assisted his wife to her feet. Now he had a heart full of love, a house about to be full of babies, and a box full of recipes.

Hard to say which was more important. Grinning to himself, he slid open the patio door and ushered his family inside.

* * * * *

Melissa Senate has written many novels for Harlequin and other publishers, including her debut, *See Jane Date*, which was made into a TV movie. She also wrote seven books for Harlequin's Special Edition line under the pen name Meg Maxwell. Her novels have been published in over twenty-five countries. Melissa lives on the coast of Maine with her teenage son; their rescue shepherd mix, Flash; and a lap cat named Cleo. For more information, please visit her website, melissasenate.com.

Books by Melissa Senate

Harlequin Special Edition

The Wyoming Multiples

The Baby Switch!
Detective Barelli's Legendary Triplets
Wyoming Christmas Surprise
To Keep Her Baby
A Promise for the Twins

Furever Yours

A New Leash on Love

Hurley's Homestyle Kitchen (as Meg Maxwell)

A Cowboy in the Kitchen
The Detective's 8 lb, 10 oz Surprise
The Cowboy's Big Family Tree
The Cook's Secret Ingredient
Charm School for Cowboys
Santa's Seven-Day Baby Tutorial

Visit the Author Profile page at Harlequin.com for more titles.

The Baby Switch!

MELISSA SENATE

Dedicated to the one, the only Gail Chasan,
editor extraordinaire.

I can't thank you enough for everything.

Chapter 1

Liam Mercer's agenda for Friday, April 14:
*Negotiate 2.4 million-dollar acquisition of Kenyon Corp.
*Take six-month-old son for first haircut at Kidz Kutz, where apparently there was a baby seat in the shape of a choo-choo train, and a puppet show video to distract criers.
*Preside over four meetings, sign countless documents, approve hiring of VP in New Business Development, prepare quarterly report for board of directors.
*Repair lifetime rift between his father, the imperious Harrington Mercer, and his I'll-do-what-I-want-it's-my-life younger brother over the weekly family dinner tonight at the Mercer ranch.

Just another Friday. Well, except for the haircut. That was new. Liam loved firsts when it came to Alexander and noted them all in the leather-bound baby book his cousin Clara had given him, along with a seven-foot-tall stuffed giraffe, the day after Alexander was born. The first notation of the first first: at barely a half hour old, Alexander West Mercer wrapped his tiny fist around Liam's pinky. Every worry and fear that a single, twenty-eight-year-old corporate president who'd had no idea he was even going to be a father could actually raise a helpless living creature on his own, fell away. Of course, every one of those worries returned two seconds later, but his heart had been swiped by the little guy. A love he'd never felt before had come bursting out of Liam's chest. And that was that.

He shifted Alexander in his arm, nudged the heavy baby bag higher up on his other shoulder and pulled open the door to Mercer Industries. Despite the fleece jacket with its bear-ears hood covering his son's dark hair, the silky wisps were getting so unruly they were peeking out. The plan was to knock off the acquisition, deal with two of the meetings, then slip away at lunchtime to Kidz Kutz and be ready with his camera.

"There's Wyoming's luckiest baby!"

Liam turned around in the reception area. Clara, his favorite cousin and right-hand woman, VP of Mercer Industries, bent forward to coo at Alexander. As it was just before nine o'clock, employees began streaming through the doors, smiling at Alexander as they passed through to the elevator bank.

Clara gave the baby a little tap on the nose. "Yup, luckiest. Millionaire at birth, gorgeous gray-blue eyes and the Mercer dimple and a doting extended family, including myself. Oh, and let's not forget a daddy who refuses to hire a nanny and instead keeps him close by at the cushy company day care and visits twice a day."

"Three times, actually," Liam said. He couldn't spend enough time with his son.

And at least it was Friday. Even though Liam always had work crowding his weekend, he was looking forward to his plans to take Alexander on a hike up Wedlock Creek Mountain to see the huge Cottonwoods. Alexander would watch the scenery from his perch in the backpack carrier, one of the zillion baby gifts he'd received from family and friends and coworkers in total shock that Liam Mercer, who wasn't exactly a playboy but lived for work, had become a father.

After the hike it would be library time, where he'd sack out on the huge bean bags dotting the children's room and read Alexander's favorite book three times, the one with the talking pear named Joe. On Sunday they'd head to his family's ranch, a huge spread with a small petting zoo that his father had created just for Alexander. He was a good eight months away from feeding a goat pellets from his hand, but his dad wanted the zoo in place "because clearly Alexander is advanced." His father was way over-the-top when it came to Alexander, but Liam had to admit the grandfatherly pride was touching. Especially from Harrington Mercer.

Liam's phone buzzed in his pocket, as it had been doing for the past half hour, par for the course for the president of Mercer Industries. But he couldn't reach his phone with Alexander in one arm and his baby bag in the other. "Hold him for a sec, will you, Clara?"

She wrinkled her nose. "And risk baby spit-up on my

dress for the big meeting with Kenyon Corp? No way."
She did a few rounds of peekaboo, covering her face
and opening her hands to reveal a big smile to a rapt Alexander. "Peekaboo, I see you! And I swear I love you
even if I won't risk what happened last month at your
grandmother's birthday dinner. Oh, yeah. I know you
remember, drool-boy." She blew a kiss at Alexander,
then headed through the frosted-glass double doors on
her very high heels.

Liam rolled his eyes with a smile. Six months and a
day ago, he'd been the same way. He'd no sooner go near
a sticky baby than pet an animal who'd get white hairs on
his Hugo Boss suit. But six months and a day ago, Liam
hadn't even known he was about to become a father.

Life could change just like that. And had.

And now Liam knew how wrong he and Clara were
about their expensive clothes and perfect hair. Spit-up
didn't bother him at all. Changing diapers—no problem. Alexander's new favorite solid food—Toasty Os
cereal—thrown at his hair with a giggle? Good arm, kid.
It was amazing how Liam had changed in six months
because of one tiny baby. His baby.

And Clara was wrong about something else. Alexander wasn't the luckiest baby in Wyoming. He didn't
have everything.

He didn't have a mother.

After the shock had worn off, when Liam had stepped
into his new role as someone's father, when he'd sit with
Alexander in the middle of the night in the rocking chair
in the nursery, feeding him a bottle, holding him, rocking him, breathing in the baby-shampoo scent of him,
staring at every beautiful bit of him, all Liam could really focus on was the fact that his baby's mother had

died during childbirth, that this innocent child in his arms was motherless.

Liam was doing okay as a father, maybe even better than okay. It had been some learning curve. He'd forced himself to take two weeks off from the office, hired a baby nurse to teach him the ropes, which had involved waking up every few hours, warming baby bottles, changing diapers, acquainting himself with ointments and lotions and baby bathtubs, and figuring out which cry meant hungry or diaper rash or gas or *pick me up*. Now, six months later, he basically knew what he was doing. But no matter that Liam was there, really there, he was no substitute for a mother.

The problem with finding a mother for his son was that Liam wasn't looking for a *wife*.

"There's our little heir," came the voice of Harrington Mercer. The fifty-eight-year-old CEO took Alexander and held him high in the air, his own expensive suit be damned. "Good, Alexander, you're all ready for a day of soaking up the corporate culture. You'll intern here through college, then get your MBA, and you'll be in line to take over Mercer Industries, just like your father and your grandfather did from great-granddad Wilton Mercer."

Liam mentally shook his head. "Dad, he's six months old. Let's get him sleeping through the night before he starts as a junior analyst at MI."

His father waved his hand in the air. "Never too soon to immerse the heir in the learning process. Anyone knows that, it's you, Liam. Heck, you grew up in this building." His dad smiled and kissed Alexander on the cheek. "Oh, I have a little present for you, Alexander." He set his briefcase on the reception desk and opened it, and pulled out a tiny brown Stetson. "There. We may be businessmen, but we're Wyoming men and cowboys at heart."

Harrington Mercer took off Alexander's hood and settled the little hat, lined with fleece, on his head, nodded approvingly, then handed him back to Liam and headed through the double doors.

"One minute I don't understand your grandfather at all," he whispered to Alexander. "And the next, I want to hug him. People are complicated. Life lesson one thousand five."

Alexander smiled and reached out to squeeze Liam's chin.

"You know what's not complicated?" Liam whispered as he shifted his son to push open the door. "How much I love you."

Liam took the elevator to the fourth floor, which held the company's health club, cafeteria and the day care, using his key card to open the door to the day care center. The main room, separated from the door with a white picket fence-gate decorated with grass and trees and flowers, was for the toddlers and preschool-age kids. Liam waved at one of the teachers, then headed into the nursery for babies under fourteen months. The room, with its pale blue walls bordered with smiling cartoon animals, was cozy with its decor and baby gear, the play mats and bouncers and bassinets with little spinning mobiles playing lullabies. Two babies were already there, having tummy time on the thickly padded mats. There were seven babies currently, ranging in age from three to twelve months.

"Morning, Liam," the nursery director said with a smile. "And good morning, Alexander. I like your hat."

Liam signed in his son and handed him over, always feeling like he was handing over a piece of his heart. Another employee came in with her four-month-old and stood for a while by the window, nuzzling her little daughter's cheek before finally giving her to the director with a wistful smile.

I know how you feel, he thought, staring at his baby son. *It's so hard to say goodbye, even for a few hours.*

The day care center had been started almost sixty years ago by his grandmother, Alexandra Mercer, for whom Alexander was named. Back then, when the brilliant businesswoman, then president of Mercer Industries, became a mother, she'd insisted that her husband, Wilton, the CEO, agree to open a day care center on site for all employees. She'd hired the best nannies in Wedlock Creek to staff the new corporate day care and told off anyone who dared say that she should be at home, raising her child herself. Back then, not many employees partook in the service offered. But now, with women comprising over half the employees at MI, the day care center was almost always filled to capacity. Knowing their babies and toddlers and preschoolers were well taken care of just an elevator ride away made for happier, more productive employees. Liam could attest to that firsthand.

He kneeled down on Alexander's play mat and pulled out his phone to take a photo of Alexander in his cowboy hat, noticing an unfamiliar number on the screen. The same number had called three times in the past half hour. As he snapped the photo of Alexander, the phone buzzed again.

"Can I throw this thing out the window?" Liam asked the director.

She laughed. "You go ahead—answer it, I mean. We'll take good care of Alexander."

Liam smiled and nodded. "See you in a few hours for lunch and a haircut, cowboy," he said to Alexander, then finally answered the call on his way out the door.

"Liam Mercer," he said.

"Oh, thank goodness we finally reached you," a female voice said. "Mr. Mercer, my name is Anne Parcells. I'm the administrator of the Wedlock Creek Clinic. We need you to come to the clinic right away and to bring the minor child, Alexander West Mercer, and your attorney."

He froze. The minor child? His attorney? What the hell was this?

Liam frowned. "What's this about?"

"We'll discuss everything at the meeting," Parcells said. "If you can get here by 9:15, that would be appreciated. The others will be here by then, as well."

"The others?"

She didn't respond to that. "Can we expect you by 9:15, Mr. Mercer? Please come to my office, two doors from the main entrance."

Liam glanced at his watch. It was 8:55. "I'll be there."

There for what, though? Alexander was born in the Wedlock Creek Clinic. If the administrator was referring to his son as "the minor child" and talking attorneys, there was probably some kind of liability issue regarding the night he was born. A class action lawsuit, maybe. Liam closed his eyes for a second as memories of the snowstorm came back, memories he'd tried to block. Alexander's mother phoning him, a desperation in Liza Harwood's voice he'd never heard before, not that he'd known her very long.

Liam, there's no time for explanations. I'm nine months pregnant with your baby and in labor. I should have told you before but I'm telling you now. I'm on my way to the clinic. The snowstorm is so bad. If anything happens to me, I left you a letter...

Nine months pregnant with his baby. And something had happened to Liza.

Most of Wedlock Creek had lost power that night, and the clinic's backup generator had blinked out twice. There had been so many accidents in town—from tree limbs falling on houses to car wrecks and pickups in ditches. Liza had made it to the clinic in one piece but had not survived childbirth. A tragedy that had had nothing to do with the storm or the clinic.

Liam closed his eyes again, then shook his head to clear it. He had to call his lawyer, reorganize his morning and get to the clinic.

He headed back inside the nursery for Alexander. At least he'd have some unexpected extra time with his son this morning, after all.

Shelby Ingalls sat in an uncomfortable folding chair in the Wedlock Creek Clinic's administrator's office, holding her baby son against her chest in the sling he was fast asleep in. She glanced at the doorway, hoping the woman would come back and get this meeting—whatever it was about—underway. Opening time at Treasures, her secondhand shop, was ten o'clock, and Shelby wanted to display the gorgeous antique frames she'd found at an estate sale the other day and the cute new mugs with napping beagles on them. She knew several of her regular customers would love those.

She'd been about to head down to the shop when

Anne Parcells had called, asking Shelby to come in and "bring the minor child" and her attorney. The phrasing and the word *attorney* had freaked her out, but the administrator had refused to say anything else. Shelby had been so panicked that it had something to do with Shane's blood test, that he was terribly ill after all. A week ago she'd brought him into the clinic for a stomach virus and had been waiting for the results, which she'd been sure would reveal nothing since the virus had cleared up and Shane was back to his regular happy little self. But despite the director assuring her that Shane was perfectly healthy, Anne Parcells again requested that she come immediately to the clinic—and to bring an attorney.

First of all, Shelby didn't have an attorney, and despite the size of her extended family, there wasn't a lawyer in the bunch. Nor did she want this weird request from the director to become family fodder until she herself knew what it was all about. Her sister, her mother, her aunt Cheyenne and a bunch of cousins would be crowded in the back of this room if she'd let anyone know. So she'd called her sister, Norah, who despite being a chatterbox who knew everyone and all the town gossip, could keep a secret like no one else. Turned out, Norah was newly dating a lawyer, an ambulance-chasing type, and so much of a shark that she was thinking of breaking up with him because of it. A few minutes later Norah had called back and assured Shelby that David Dirk, attorney at law, would meet Shelby at the clinic by 9:10—and that the meeting was probably about some lawsuit from the night Shane was born because of the storm and the generator failing twice. In any case, Norah had promised to keep mum about the meeting and texted:

I get to know what it's about, though, right? Call me the minute you're out of there!

Shane stirred against her chest, and she glanced down at her dear little son, caressing his fine brown wisps. A moment later, an attractive guy in his early thirties appeared in the doorway. He had a baby face and tousled hair, but he wore a sharp suit and had intelligent eyes behind black-framed glasses. Not Norah's typical brawny rancher type.

"David Dirk," he said, extending a hand and sitting down beside her. "When the administrator arrives and says her spiel, don't comment, don't agree to anything, don't answer anything with yes or no. In fact, let me speak for you."

"I always speak for myself," Shelby said. "But I'll listen to your advice and we'll go from there."

Before he could respond, two other men appeared in the doorway, and at the sight of the one holding a baby wearing a brown cowboy hat, Shelby almost gasped.

She knew him. Well, she'd seen him before. And she'd never forget his face. Not just because he was incredibly good-looking—six feet one or two and leanly muscular with thick, dark hair and gorgeous blue eyes, a dimple curving into the left side of his mouth. It was that she'd never forget the combination of fear and worry that had been etched into his features, in those eyes. The night she'd given birth, he'd been sitting in the crowded waiting room of this clinic, his head in hands, when the ambulance EMTs had rushed her inside on a gurney. He'd looked up and they'd locked eyes, and despite the fact that she was already in labor and breathing and moaning like a madwoman, the complex combination of emotions on the man's face had so arrested her that for one single moment, she'd been aware of nothing else but him. Given the pain she was in, the contractions coming just a minute and a half apart, that was saying something. A second later she'd let out a wail that had even her covering her ears, and the EMT had hurried into a delivery room.

She'd wondered about the man in the waiting room ever since, if whomever he'd been waiting on had been okay. There had been one hell of a storm that night, so much blinding snow that a ten-minute ride to the clinic from her apartment above her shop had taken almost an hour.

Because she was now staring at the man with the baby cowboy, he glanced at her, and she could see he was trying to place her.

"Good morning," a woman said, her voice serious as she appeared behind the two men in the doorway. "I'm Anne Parcells, administrator of the Wedlock Creek Clinic. All parties are here so let's begin. Please," she said, gesturing for the men to enter and to sit in the two chairs positioned to the left of her desk. Shelby and her attorney were seated to the right. "Thank you for coming, Ms. Ingalls and Mr. Mercer." Introductions were made between attorneys and parties, the door was closed and everyone was now seated.

Please get to the lawsuit or whatever this is about so that I can get back to the store, Shelby thought. Three of her favorite regular customers, the elderly Minnow sisters, came in every Friday morning at the shop's opening time of ten o'clock to see what she might have added to the shop for the weekend rush. She hated to keep them and any new customers waiting. Wedlock Creek was a small town, but had its own rodeo on the outskirts and a bustling downtown because of it, so folks came from all over the county to enjoy a bit of the Wild West, then walk the mile-long Main Street with its shops and restaurants and movie theater with the reclining seats. Business was semi-booming.

The administrator cleared her throat, her expression almost grim. Shelby felt for the woman. The Wedlock Creek Clinic, a nonprofit that included an urgent care center, was a godsend for so many in the county, since the county hospital was forty-five minutes away. A lawsuit had the potential to close the clinic.

"I'm going to just say this outright," Anne said, looking up from some paperwork. "A week ago, Ms. Ingalls—" she gestured to Shelby "—brought her six-month-old son, Shane, to the clinic with a stomach virus. A standard blood test was run. This morning our lab returned the results, noting a discrepancy with Ms. Ingalls's blood type and Shane Ingalls's blood type."

A discrepancy? Huh? Shelby leaned forward a bit, staring at the woman, who glanced at her for a moment, the expression in her eyes so compassionate that the hairs rose on the back of Shelby's neck.

Anne Parcells looked down at the papers in her hands, then back up. "Based on the results, it would be impossible for Ms. Ingalls to be Shane's biological mother."

What the ever-loving hell? Shelby bolted up, her arms around Shane in the sling. "That's impossible! Of course he's my son! I gave birth to him!"

The administrator's expression turned grim again. "The test was run three times. I'm afraid that Shane Ingalls cannot be your biological son, Ms. Ingalls."

Shelby's legs shook and she dropped down on her

chair, her head spinning. She tried to make sense of the words. *Not your son. Discrepancy. Impossible.*

This had to be a mistake—that was the only explanation. Of course Shane was her son!

Dimly, she could hear her sister-appointed lawyer requesting to see the paperwork, the ruffling of sheaves of paper as Anne handed over the stack and David Dirk studied them, flipping through the various documents.

"Jesus," David mutter-whispered.

Shelby closed her eyes, trying to keep hold of herself despite the feeling coming over her that shΔe was going to black out. She felt herself wobble a bit and grabbed David's chair to steady herself.

He put a bracing arm around her. "We'll have your and Shane's blood drawn again and retested in a different lab," he said.

She sucked in a breath and nodded. Yes. Redone. A different lab. It was a mistake. Just a mistake. The results would prove she was Shane's mother. She was!

"Excuse me," Liam Mercer's lawyer said, darting a compassionate glance at Shelby. "But what does this have to do with my client?"

The administrator took a deep breath. "Based on the results and a discussion with a night-shift nurse who retired three months ago, we believe your babies—Shane Ingalls and Alexander Mercer—born within minutes of each other in the early-morning hours of November 5, were accidentally switched at birth."

Chapter 2

Shelby gasped.

"That's impossible," Liam Mercer said, his gaze narrowed on the administrator, then on Shelby. "Come on."

The woman glanced from Shelby to Liam, then said, "In the chaos of the storm, the nurse didn't follow procedure to secure an identifying bracelet around the male babies until the generator kicked back in. She was positive she'd put Ms. Ingalls's baby in the left bassinet and Ms. Harwood's in the right. But because we now know that Shane Ingalls can't be the child Shelby gave birth to, she thinks she must have made a mistake."

Liam stood up, tightening his hold on the baby in his arms. "That's ridiculous. Like Mr. Dirk said, the blood test results are a mistake. A mislabeled vial, and voilà, mother and baby are suddenly not related. There was no switching of babies."

"Mr. Mercer," Anne Parcells said. "I wish that were the case. However, given that the generator failed at precisely the time when both babies were taken, within minutes of each other, to the pediatric clinic to be weighed and measured and cleaned up, it's entirely possible that the nurse accidentally switched the babies. I also wish that the blood type issue could be a mistake, but Ms. Ingalls's blood was drawn twice on prior visits to the clinic during prenatal care—and documented, of course. Her blood type is not compatible with Shane's."

Oh, God. There went her last hope.

"*Entirely possible* isn't good enough," Liam said, his voice ice-cold. "Either the nurse did switch the babies or she didn't. If you don't know for sure, then…" He shook his head, then stared at Anne Parcells. "Wait a minute. Alexander was born here, so you must have his blood type on record and his mother's. Are they compatible? I'm sure they are."

The administrator nodded. "Alexander's blood type, one of the most common, is a match for Liza Harwood's. However, it's also a match for Ms. Ingalls. Which leads to next steps. DNA tests must be conducted."

"There," Liam said, "Alexander's blood type is compatible with his mother's. And mine, I'm sure. He's my son."

"You visited the urgent care center twice in the past five years, Mr. Mercer. Your blood type is on record. Your blood type is compatible with Alexander's, as well."

The relief that crossed Liam's face almost had Shelby happy for him. But she was barely hanging on.

"This is all some mix-up with Ms. Ingalls and her son's blood type but it has nothing to do with me." He looked over at Shelby then, his expression a mix of confusion and worry. Just like the night she'd first seen him. "I don't mean to sound cavalier at your expense, Ms. Ingalls, but this is a mistake," he said to her. "It has to be."

"He's right!" Shelby shouted, panic and bile rising. "It's *all* a mistake. It has to be a mistake!"

"There were four babies born the night of November 5," the director said. "Two boys and two girls. If there was a switch, it was between Shane Ingalls and Alexander Mercer."

The lawyers began talking, but Shelby's ears felt like they were stuffed with cotton. As Liam began pacing, she glanced at the baby in his arms—and gasped.

"What?" Liam asked, freezing, his gaze narrowed on her again.

"The little birthmark on his ear," she whispered, standing up. "I have it, too. So does my grandmother." Norah didn't have it. Her mother didn't have it. But Shelby *did*.

Everyone peered at the tiny reddish-brown spot on the baby's earlobe. Then at Shelby's ear.

"Oh, for God's sake. It's nothing," Liam said, shifting Alexander in his arms so that he was out of view. "It's a mark that will fade away."

Shelby's legs shook to the point that she dropped back down in her chair. She stared at Shane's dark hair, so unlike her own, which was blond. But Shane's father, a bronc rider she'd foolishly married after a whirlwind courtship and who'd left town with another woman the moment Shelby told him she was pregnant, had Shane's same dark hair. He had blue eyes, too, just like Shane.

But the baby in Liam Mercer's arms was also darkhaired. Also blue-eyed.

In fact, the babies looked a lot alike, except for the shapes of their faces, and Shane's features were a little sharper than Alexander's. Did Shane look like Liam Mercer? Okay, yes. But he also looked a little like Shelby. Even if no one ever commented on that. *He must look like his daddy,* she'd heard someone say a time or two as they'd peered in Shane's stroller, then at her.

She suddenly felt dizzy and put her hand on her lawyer's chair to brace herself again. Oh, God. Oh, God. Oh, God. This could not be happening.

It was a mistake. Shane was her son.

Liam's lawyer also flipped through the paperwork, then looked up. "As there's no reason to believe that Alexander West Mercer is not my client's biological child, based on blood type, we'll await DNA results before any further discussion."

Shelby's lawyer nodded. "We'll have Shelby's and Shane's blood tested for type at a separate facility. Until those results come in, we also will proceed with the understanding that Shane Ingalls is Shelby Ingalls's biological child.

Thank God Norah was dating a lawyer. Shelby's mind was in such a state that she'd never have thought of that.

"If that is agreeable to both parties," the administrator said. "Of course I'll need you both to sign some documents."

Shelby stared down at Shane, the voices retreating as everything inside her went numb. She held him as close as she could without squeezing him. He was her son.

"I saw you," Liam said, a reluctant awareness edging his deep voice.

Shelby looked up. Liam was standing in front of her and staring at her.

"The night Alexander was born," he said. "I was in the waiting room and you were suddenly wheeled in, but another gurney was blocking the doorway. I was afraid you'd deliver right there in front of me."

"I remember," she said. *The sight of you, the way our eyes met, gave me something concrete to focus on.*

"I'd like to confer with my client," Liam's attorney said.

"As would I," Shelby's lawyer said.

Liam and his lawyer stepped to the back of the room. Shelby and hers stayed at the front.

"Until we have your blood tested again, Shane is your son same as he was a half hour ago," David said. "Even if the results indicate that you and Shane can't be biologically related, operate under the assumption that he is your child under the law until the DNA tests are in."

He is. He is my son! But she heard herself ask the impossible. "What if he isn't?" she said, her voice strangled on a sob. "What if he's not my son?"

"Then the four of us will meet again, Shelby. But until we know for sure, don't agree to anything Mercer or his attorney asks of you and for God's sake, don't sign anything. Do you hear me?"

She nodded. "I hear you."

The administrator took Shelby and Liam and their attorneys into a room, explained in detail how the DNA test worked, then had a technician swab the inside of their mouths and draw blood for good measure, vials labeled with their names. In addition to their attorneys, two techs served as witnesses and the entire process was videotaped to assure all was handled correctly. Shelby and Liam both watched, eagle-eyed, as the swabs and vials were sealed into separate bags.

"I'll also have my and Shane's blood drawn at Cottonwood County Hospital today," Shelby said. "I'll ask for the results to be forwarded to all parties."

Finally, after another clipped speech about how sorry the administrator was and that she'd call the moment the DNA test results reached her desk, the attorneys left, and Shelby and Liam Mercer were alone.

Liam had the same expression on his face that Shelby had to have on hers. Shock. Confusion. And fear. He was looking down but not at his son or at the floor.

"I'm hanging on to useless hope," she said. "If Shane isn't my biological son, if the babies were switched, then the baby in your arms is my child?" She shook her head. "This is crazy."

"Alexander is my son," Liam practically growled, his expression so fierce she took a step back. "Sorry," he said. "I know you're going through the same thing I am. I don't mean to take this out on you, of all people."

She bit her lip and let out a breath. Was the baby in Liam's arms her son? Had she walked out of this clinic six months ago with someone else's child? And left her own behind? Tears pricked her eyes.

"May I see him?" Shelby asked, blinking back hard on the tears. "Up close?"

Liam hesitated, then stepped toward her. Shelby tried to stifle the gasp. Alexander Mercer did look an awful lot like her. Down to the shape of the eyes, his face, something in his expression and the little Ingalls birthmark. But he had a dimple—like Liam. None of the Ingallses had a dimple.

But Shane's father did.

Still, hair and eye color and a birthmark and a dimple didn't mean Shane wasn't her son.

Even if the baby in her arms looked a lot like Liam Mercer.

Shelby shook her head, suddenly unable to speak. She sucked in a breath. "I love Shane with all my heart. I'm his only parent. I'm his mother. He's my son."

"I feel the same way about Alexander," Liam said. "His mother died in childbirth."

Oh, no. That was why he looked the way he had that night. "I'm so sorry." She let out a breath. "And I'm scared. Really, really scared."

"I don't say this often, Ms. Ingalls. But so am I."

That made her feel better. Especially because he was a Mercer. And the Mercer name in Wedlock Creek meant two things. Power and money. Shelby barely broke even every month. And her lawyer was on loan.

"Liam," she said. "My son looks a lot like you. And your son looks a lot like me."

He turned away, then stared down at the baby in his arms. Then at her. Then back to his son. "Yeah. I know. And I'm worried as hell. That the babies actually could have been switched. I mean, I saw you here, in this clinic, in labor, at the same time Alexander's mother was in labor. I saw you with my own eyes. You gave birth to a baby boy. That's not in dispute. If Shane isn't yours, then…" He shook his head, then stared at the ground.

She expelled a breath. "So now what?"

Alexander gurgled and cooed, "Du, wa," his gaze on Shane. The two babies eyed each other, smiles forming. Alexander reached out to touch Shane's arm and Shane smiled, reaching to touch the brim of the little Stetson.

"They like each other," Liam said softly, his voice hollow. "Look, let's go to the hospital and get your and Shane's blood drawn for typing. For all we know, the clinic here has been making mistakes for years. Let's find out for sure that you and Shane *can't* be related."

Should she go anywhere with Liam Mercer? Maybe she should run it by her lawyer. But then again, there was only one person on earth who knew what this insanity felt like: Liam. She wanted to hear what he had to say. She needed to be around him right now.

She let out a breath and nodded. "I'm in no position to drive. My hands will shake on the wheel."

"I'll drive. I'll install Shane's seat in the back of my SUV."

Which meant he was calm. Outwardly, anyway. Because he knew that no matter what, he wouldn't lose anything? That was very likely how things were for Mercers. Money and power talked.

"I want to make something clear, Mr. Mercer. I know the Mercer name. You and your family are wealthy and powerful and own half the commercial real estate and the rodeo. I'm a single mother without much to my name but a secondhand shop. Regardless, if you push me, if you try anything underhanded, I'll fight you with everything I have."

"Whoa," he said, his blue eyes steady on her. "We're going through the same thing, Ms. Ingalls. We're in the same position. Money and power are meaningless here. If Alexander isn't my biological son, all the money in Wyoming won't make it any less true."

She stared at him. He was right—to a point. Money and power *could* take Shane away from her. He could end up with *both* boys.

"I might be rich, Ms. Ingalls. But I'm not underhanded. I'm a single parent, just like you are. And I'll swear on anything you want. I'll never do anything to hurt you or these babies."

The sincerity on his face made her feel better. And truth be told, she needed to believe him or she'd spontaneously combust. "Call me Shelby."

He nodded. "And call me Liam."

He gestured for her to walk ahead out the door. "Let's get the hell out of this clinic."

As she watched Liam zip up his son's fleece bunting, the tenderness on the man's face almost stole her breath.

He loves that baby. Like I love Shane.

Dear God, this was a mess.

You're my son, no matter what, she whispered silently to Shane.

As they left the office, each holding a baby, Shelby was barely hanging on. If the DNA tests proved the impossible, that they'd each taken home a baby who wasn't theirs, *would* Liam try to seek custody of both babies and win because of his power and money and influence? Right now it was easy for him to say he'd never do anything to hurt her. His back wasn't up against a wall— yet, anyway. Not like hers was.

Stop getting ahead of yourself, Shelby. He might be a Mercer, but she had a loud, bossy, big family in Wedlock Creek. They'd have her back. Her sister had managed to supply her with a lawyer in less than five minutes, after all. *One step at a time, one piece of information at a time.*

Feeling a little stronger, she watched as Liam headed across the parking lot to his car, a sleek, black SUV, settled Alexander in his car seat, then drove it over to where she stood next to her twelve-year-old Ford.

She could not, would not, lose Shane. But the little boy in that black car was very likely her baby, too.

Oh, God. Suddenly she wanted to tear Alexander from his car seat, take him in her arms and explain it had been a mistake, she hadn't known, she was so sorry she let someone else take him home and raise him these past six months.

As tears slipped down her cheeks, she felt a hand on her shoulder.

She hadn't even realized Liam had gotten out of his car and had come over to her. "We'll figure this out together," he said.

At the word *together*, she calmed down again and looked up into Liam Mercer's eyes. She saw sincerity there. But the last time Shelby had trusted a man she'd ended up pregnant and alone.

Careful, she told herself. Proceed with utmost caution. *Agree to nothing. Sign nothing. You're a smart woman. Keep your head.*

She was glad when Liam let go of her shoulder and opened her car door to get Shane's car seat, busy with installing it in his SUV. They were not united. They were not anything. His use of the word *together* would likely only serve him. She didn't know this man at all.

She was on her own here and had to remember that. Or she'd lose everything.

Liam's hands had been steady on the wheel during the drive to the hospital, but inside he was a mess. Every time his mind latched on something that would make Alexander his biological son, three more *yeah, but what about xyz, yeah, but remember when the administrator said* socked him upside the head. Shelby had been silent for the almost hour drive, and he was glad. He didn't want to talk about any of it. He could barely handle thinking about it.

Alexander wasn't his son? He damned well was, no matter what a piece of paper said. That was the one thing that kept reverberating in his head. He was sure it was the same for Shelby, which made him want to be around her and never see her again at the same time.

Was the baby in the back seat, the one without the cowboy hat, his biological child?

Maybe. Probably? No. Yes. He went round and round as Shelby and Shane were ushered into the lab room to get their blood drawn. As he sat in the waiting room, Alexander playing his favorite game of squeeze Daddy's chin, women around him commenting on Alexander's cuteness and big cheeks, he could hear Shane crying behind the closed door. Which made him hyperaware of the timing; his tiny vein had just been pricked, a vial filling with his blood. Which would prove, once and for all, if the clinic hadn't made a mistake with the typing. From prior visits, at that.

Hell, it was unlikely, but he was hanging on to hope. If Shelby *could* be Shane's biological mother, then they could all just walk away, go back to their lives and live happily-ever-after. Liam would have one heck of a story for tonight's dinner at the Mercer ranch.

Shelby finally came out of the lab room, holding Shane, who had a little round Mickey Mouse Band-Aid in the crook of his right arm. Liam stared at his little tear-stained face, seeing not only his own expression in Shane's, but Liza's, also.

He almost fell out of his chair.

"Are you all right, Liam?" Shelby asked, rushing over.

He slowly shook his head. He was not all right.

Calm down and go back to hanging on to hope. Wait for the blood results. If they still say Shelby isn't Shane's mother, then you'll wait for the DNA tests. You're Alexander's father. You are.

As they left the hospital, Shelby told him that the lab had promised to expedite the results, based on a call from the clinic requesting it. She would know by three o'clock today.

"I want to stay with you and Shane until we know," he said. "I need you in my sight."

"Because you're afraid I'll run away with your heir?" she snapped. "If Shane is your son, then Alexander is *my* son," she reminded him, her green eyes flashing.

He stared at her. "You really don't trust me, do you?"

"I don't know you," she pointed out. "And I don't trust easily. Add in who you are…"

"I told you, Shelby, I—"

"Won't do anything to hurt me or Shane. I know. I've tucked that away to remind you of it when you really have to face the truth of what's happened."

He shook his head. "Let me change how I put it, then. I want you and Shane in my sight because I'm going out of my mind. I don't want to be alone, but I don't want to tell anyone about this yet. That leaves you. To be with someone who gets it without my having to say a word."

Her expression softened. "I know exactly what you mean." She glanced at her watch. "Oh, God, I really need to head over to my shop and put a sign on the door that we're closed for the day. The Minnow sisters are probably worried about me, and I had an appointment scheduled for ten-thirty to look through a bag of stuff."

"Minnow sisters? Bag of stuff?"

"For Treasures, my shop. The Minnows are three elderly sisters who stop by every Friday at ten to see what I've added for the weekend shoppers."

He nodded. "The secondhand store. Next to the bakery, right? My cousin Clara loves that place. I once complimented a painting of a weathered red barn in her hallway and she said she got it from Treasures. I stopped by one day to check it out but left when I realized it was a secondhand store."

She raised an eyebrow. "Why doesn't that surprise me? Honestly, you never know what you'll find at Treasures."

Like dust? Falling apart old junk even its owner didn't want? The painting had to be an exception. "Well, why don't we head over there? We can talk there or not talk there and just keep each other occupied until the call comes from the hospital lab. I could use a few cups of coffee. At some point later I'll drive you back to the clinic to pick up your car."

Forty-five minutes later Liam pulled into a spot in front of Treasures. As they got out of the car, Shelby taking out Shane, and Liam taking out Alexander, he saw Shelby craning her neck to look down Main Street.

"I can just make out the Minnow sisters heading into the library," she said. "They're easy to spot since they always walk three across the sidewalk. They must have waited all this time for me and gave up."

As she opened the door with an ornate gold key, he realized he actually had been in the shop once before with Clara. His cousin had insisted on dragging him along to find a present for her mother, who despite being Liam's dear aunt, was the biggest snob alive. Liam hadn't thought his aunt would want anything from a secondhand shop, but the next time he'd seen her, she'd been wearing the brooch that Clara had insisted she'd love. *It's antique, it's history, it has a story*, Clara had insisted. *Who knows where the brooch has been, what love story it was part of. It's so romantic!*

It's so...*used*, was what Liam had thought. He appreciated the shiny and new. But hey, if it worked for his cousin and aunt, all the better for Shelby, now that he actually knew the shop's owner.

"I'll keep the shade drawn on the door and the *closed* sign hanging," she said as they stepped inside. "I hate to disappoint my customers or keep new ones away, but I can't open the store. Not in my frame of mind."

"I know what you mean," he said, scooting Alexander a bit higher in his arms. The baby snuggled against his leather jacket. "I had a day full of meetings, including a very important one. I canceled everything and delegated what I could." His cousin had been incredulous when he let her know he was counting on her to seal the deal on the Kenyon Corp acquisition, that he had full faith in her. Incredulous that he was skipping the meeting and that he believed in her so much; that part of their relationship had never really been tested before.

"What the hell could be so important that you'd miss the negotiation?" Clara had asked when he'd called her after dropping off Shelby and Shane at the hospital entrance. He'd let Shelby know he'd park and meet her after alerting his office he'd be out for the day.

"I can't talk about it right now, Clara. Just knock them dead."

"Oh, I will. Hope everything's okay."

"Talk to you in a few hours," he'd said and ended the call, which he knew would worry her, but his very focused cousin would set her mind to the negotiating and nothing else and she'd do great. She'd burn up his phone later and ring his doorbell until he answered later, though. Of that he had no doubt. To both tell him about the meeting and to hear what had kept him from it. But he had no idea when he'd be ready to talk about what was going on. *If* he'd talk about it.

He turned his attention to the stuffed shop, every table, every bit of space, taken up by things, from lamps to flower pots and vases to cases of jewelry to paintings and knickknacks of every kind imaginable. There was a bookcase of old, leather-bound classics and an entire table full of various teapots with little cups and saucers.

He glanced up at the wall near the shop's entrance. "Look, Alexander, it's a cuckoo clock. The little bird is about to come out because it's almost the half hour." He walked a bit closer and as the clock chimed that it was 1:30 p.m., a gold bird with a red beak popped out.

Alexander giggled and pointed.

"Cuckoo," Liam said. "Cuckoo!" Yup, this whole thing was *cuckoo*, all right.

Alexander giggled, and Liam smiled, snuggling his little boy close.

She smiled. "Fatherhood agrees with you."

He looked at Alexander, the little boy he loved more than anything on earth. "Alexander changed my life. For the good."

"Must have been hard, though, going from Wedlock Creek's most prized eligible bachelor to the father of an infant. On your own."

"It was. I guess I was too shocked to pay attention to how hard it was and just went day by day. But every night, when I'd be up with Alexander at two and four a.m., the house dead quiet except for his tiny burp after having his bottle, I was just overtaken by devotion. By a sense of responsibility to this little life I helped create."

She bit her lip and looked at him, then set Shane down in a bouncy seat behind the counter and handed him a teething ring in the shape of a rabbit. "With this...new information, I hate to put him down, for him to be out of arm's reach for even a moment, but honestly, he's getting big. He's eighteen pounds now."

Liam smiled. "So's Alexander." He glanced at Shane, watching the little stuffed animals twirl around on the mobile attached to the bouncer. "This is some mess, huh? Everything we thought we know about our lives is suddenly turned upside down."

She was staring at Shane, and he could see tears glistening in her eyes. He wanted to hold her, to tell her they'd get through this, somehow, that they'd get through it together. But what comfort would that be? They were practically strangers.

The light shining through the windows caught on her blond hair and the side of her delicate face, and she looked so alone and lost that he reached out and took her hand and gave it a gentle squeeze. *I'm not the enemy,* the squeeze was supposed to say. *But yeah, this sucks.*

She looked up at him, surprise crossing her pretty face, and she squeezed back.

"I have another bouncer if you want a breather yourself," she said.

"Sure."

She disappeared into a back room and returned with a yellow bouncer with a stars and moon mobile. Alexander pointed at it.

"You like it?" Liam asked the baby. "Let's get you settled in it next to your buddy, Shane."

He put Alexander in the bouncer, buckling the little harness, and turned the reclining seat so that the boys could see each other. He stood and came back around the counter when Shelby's phone rang.

She glanced at the cuckoo clock. "It's only one forty-five. Could that be the hospital lab?" Her phone rang again, but she seemed frozen in place. On the third ring she grabbed it from her tote bag. "Shelby Ingalls speaking."

"It's them," she mouthed to him, the phone against her ear. He watched her listen, her eyes full of hope. *Tell me what I want to hear*, those eyes beseeched. But then the light went out of the green depths, and she clearly couldn't contain the sob that rose from inside her.

She croaked out a "Thank you for calling," then put the phone down on a table next to a teapot, her eyes welling, anguish dropping her to her knees on the circular rug.

"Oh, no," he said, closing his eyes for a moment. Oh, no. No.

She burst into tears. "It's official. Shane is not my son."

Chapter 3

Liam rushed over and knelt down beside her. He put his arm around her. "I'm so sorry, Shelby."

"It has to be true, then," she said. "The hospital switched the babies. How else could this have happened?"

Intellectually, he was beginning to believe it. In his heart, though, Alexander West Mercer was his son. Plain and simple.

Except it was no longer so plain or simple.

"The baby right there," she said, staring at Alexander in his bouncy seat, smiling up at the colorful mobile dangling above. "He's my son? That's what the DNA tests will reveal. I took home the wrong baby. How could I not know my own child? How?"

He felt his cells, his blood, the air in the lungs, come

to a dead stop. *My son. My son. My son.* He wanted her to stop saying those words. Alexander was *his* son.

But he was going to have to accept the truth. Two baby boys had been born early in the morning of November 5. One couldn't be Shelby's child. Which meant the other was.

"They do look alike," he said. "And given the chaos in those moments after they were born, you probably barely got to hold him, let alone study his face in the dark."

She bit her lip, squeezing her eyes shut.

"We both took home the wrong baby," he added, his gaze on Shane in his own bouncy seat, biting the little teething ring. When he looked at Shane Ingalls, he saw a beautiful baby boy, someone else's beautiful baby boy. He felt no connection. What did that mean?

"I want to talk to the nurse who switched them," Liam said. "I need to hear what happened. Of course I know she can't be certain, that it's only what makes sense, given the blood type issue and the delay in putting identification bracelets on the babies, but I need to hear her tell me herself."

Shelby wiped under her eyes and tilted her head. "*Can* we talk to her?"

"We can do whatever the hell we want. She's no longer employed by the clinic. The director said she retired three months ago."

Shelby nodded. "I'd like to hear it from her about what happened, too."

"I'll call Anne Parcells and ask for the contact information. She may be cagey about it. Anne has to be worried about a lawsuit. The nurse, as well."

"*Are* you thinking about a lawsuit?" she asked.

"Well, first we need back the DNA tests that conclusively prove we took home the wrong babies. But if the nurse made an honest mistake in the chaos of a blizzard that knocked out power…"

Shelby nodded. "An honest mistake is an honest mistake even if it's turned our lives around. And who knows what this will mean for Shane and Alexander."

"Meaning?"

She shrugged. "Well, what's going to happen now? What's going to happen when the DNA test says I have your son and you have mine?"

He sucked in a breath.

"I want to hold Alexander but I'm afraid to," she said, wrapping her arms around herself as if protectively.

He stiffened, everything inside him going numb. "I know. Because if you hold him, knowing what you know, you're afraid you won't be able to hand him back over. It's why I haven't asked to hold Shane." He'd have to face the truth, then, that Shane was his, that he'd left him behind, and he wasn't sure he could handle that.

She stared at Alexander, who was smiling at the mobile and then looking at his little buddy, biting on his teething toy. "He has my eyes and the Ingalls straight and pointy nose. We all have that nose."

"It's a good one," he said. Liam's nose was more Roman. And Liza's had been long.

"My head is going to explode," she said. "I can't think. I can barely stand up anymore."

"I know. Same here."

"I think I need to just go upstairs to my apartment, with Shane, and just let this all sink in."

He nodded. "I think that's a good idea. I could use some time alone to try to process this, too." He headed over to where Alexander sat in the bouncer.

"Liam, I'm very close to my family, particularly my sister. I don't think I can keep this from them until the DNA tests are in. Especially because I have no doubt anymore that the babies were switched. And to be honest, I don't want to keep it from them. I need their support."

He nodded again, letting his head drop back a little. "I can understand that. I'm not all that close to my parents or my brother, but I wish I were. I'm close to my cousin Clara, the one who likes your shop."

An idea started forming and he dismissed it. Then came back to it. It involved inviting Shelby to the family dinner tonight. Shelby and Shane. He could drop the bombshell and they'd all have a chance to meet the Ingallses. It would be a way to get the conversation over with.

"Maybe getting our families' takes on the situation is a good idea," he said. "The Mercers get together every Friday night for dinner, a tradition going back generations. Why don't you join us? You and Shane. We can tell them together."

"I thought you said your weren't close with your family. Weekly family dinners—on a weekend night, no less. That sounds close."

"I think we all keep doing it because we want something to change but it never does, and the weekly dinners make us feel like we're doing something to change it. But the evening always ends in arguments or stony silences, mostly because my brother won't go into the family business, which is nothing new. He's a cowboy on a cattle ranch."

"Well, he'll sure be glad to see me and Shane, then," she said. "Talk about taking the focus off him."

Liam laughed, and for a moment he was surprised he had any laughter in him. "I think he'll be thrilled. He may actually hug me."

"How do you think your parents will take the news?" she asked.

"Like we did. Who the hell can process this?"

She smiled, lighting up her pretty face. "Right?"

He smiled back. Then felt it fade. "But no matter what, Shelby, *we* decide what will happen. You and me. No matter how forceful or strong our families come on about this. I decide nothing without you, and you decide nothing without me. Deal?"

She stared at him hard for a moment. "Deal."

He picked up Alexander from the bouncer seat, darting a glance at Shane. At the baby he had to accept was his flesh and blood. But it didn't feel real or even possible. His head and heart were not computing, as was often the case.

"Pick you up at six-thirty?" he asked. "Cocktails at six forty-five, dinner at seven."

"I'd prefer to meet you there," she said. "I think. Yes, I'll meet you."

He nodded. "I'll drive you over to the clinic so you can get your car," he said, hoisting up Alexander and heading toward the door.

He felt numb as she scooped up Shane and followed him. They were both quiet on the ride to the clinic. He watched her open up the back door of her car and buckle in Shane. As she went around to the driver's side, she held up a hand as if saying goodbye. For now, anyway.

He held up a hand too, then started his car. Part of him was relieved to be on his own with his son, his beloved Alexander. *We're safe*, he thought the moment he pulled out of the lot.

But left behind, again, was his biological child.

Someone was ringing both doorbells—to the shop and the upstairs apartment—like a lunatic, pressing it so many times and holding it that Shelby's poor cat, Luna, darted under her favorite velvet chair.

"I'm coming, I'm coming," she called, turning around on the back stairs. She'd been on the way up to her apartment, Shane in one arm and her overstuffed tote in the other. Liam had just left five minutes ago. Could he be back? She hurried down the stairs and peered through the filmy curtain at the window.

Twenty-six-year-old Norah Ingalls, in her uniform of black pants, a white T-shirt and yellow apron with Pie Diner in sparkly blue letters across, looked frantic, her strawberry-blond hair pulled back in a messy ponytail. Shelby let her in.

"You haven't returned my texts!" Norah said, hands on hips. "Or my calls. The shop is closed at three in the afternoon. Four people at the diner mentioned it's been closed *all day*. What the hell, Shelby? What is going on? David wouldn't tell me a thing. Which freaked me out even more."

Shelby closed the door behind her sister. "Let's go upstairs. I need to be home for this, to actually say the words to another person for the first time."

Norah's hazel eyes widened. "Jesus, you're scaring me, Shel."

"It's a doozy," Shelby said, leading the way up the stairs to the apartment.

The moment Shelby unlocked the door at the top of

the stairs she felt better. Home. She'd lived here for the past five years, ever since she'd opened Treasures with a little help from an unexpected small inheritance the Ingalls sisters received from their late grandmother. The apartment was like the store—old but with some beautiful architectural details, arched doorways and big windows that let in great light. She'd decorated the place with finds from estate sales, where she bought most of her goods for the shop. Whenever she was up here she felt at peace. And she needed that feeling to tell her sister what was going on.

"Let me put Shane down for his nap and I'll be right back, Norah."

The hands were back on Norah's hips. "I can't take another second, Shelby Rae Ingalls. Tell me now!"

"Two seconds, I promise. Shane is zonked. He'll go right out."

She slipped into the nursery, painted soothing shades of pale yellow and blue, cradling Shane against her before putting him in the crib. He let out a cry, then a sigh, his blue eyes drooping. He fussed for a few moments, but Shelby sang his favorite song, about the itsy bitsy spider, and his eyes drooped even more.

She watched him for a moment, closing her own eyes, bracing herself against the truth and for having to actually talk about what had happened today. Norah would be the first person she'd tell.

She closed the nursery door and headed back into the living room, where Norah was holding two bottles of whiskey that a handyman had given Shelby a couple weeks ago for taking so long to fix the washing machine.

"I'm gonna need this, right?" Norah asked. "Both bottles, from the expression on your face."

"Yes," Shelby said, and this time her sister's eyes went even wider. She attempted something of a smile, took the whiskey bottles back into the kitchen and poured two glasses of white wine instead. Norah followed her in, standing in the doorway. "Okay. Here goes," she said, handing her sister a glass.

Norah gulped half the glass of wine. "I'm ready. Whatever it is, whatever you need, I'm here for you."

Tears streamed down Shelby's face. She stood there in her kitchen and bawled.

Norah burst into tears, too. "Oh, God. Oh, God. You're sick."

Shelby froze. She wasn't sick. No one was dying. *Get ahold of yourself, Shelby.* Perspective. With that, she launched into the whole story, starting with the meeting at the clinic, explaining about having her blood retested at the hospital and ending with being invited to Liam Mercer's family ranch for dinner tonight.

Norah's open mouth and chin kept dropping lower. She stared at Shelby with *what the?* shock on her face, then raced over and enveloped Shelby in a long hug, both of them sobbing. Her sister wiped under her eyes and gave Shelby's hand a squeeze before dropping down on a chair at the round table in front of the window. "I seriously think my legs are going to give out. I just can't believe this." She opened her mouth as if to ask a question, then clamped it shut. Then again. Then again. "It's not sinking in, Shelby."

Shelby sat down across from Norah. "I know. I don't even think I've processed it. It's just buzzing around at the forefront of my mind like a bee that won't go away."

"What's Liam Mercer like? I've seen him around. He's hard to miss."

Shelby took a sip of wine. "I know. Gorgeous. Amazing body. And surprisingly nice."

A strawberry-blond eyebrow shot up. "Really? He didn't threaten you?"

"About taking Shane? No. I don't think it's sunk in for him at all that Shane is his child. Or he's not ready to believe it. I think he'll need the results of the DNA test for that. His blood type is compatible with Alexander's, as is the baby's mother's. As is mine. So I guess he's still holding out hope that his life can go back to exactly what it was seven hours ago."

Norah shook her head. "If he does threaten you, we'll sic David on him."

Shelby reached across the table and squeezed her sister's hand, glad she'd rung the bell like a lunatic, after all. "It's good to be dating a lawyer. I'll tell everyone else tomorrow morning. I need to just lie down and breathe before getting ready for dinner at the Mercers'."

"God, have you seen that place?" Norah asked. "I didn't know ranches could have mansions on them."

She thought back to what Liam had said, that all the money and power in Wyoming couldn't make the truth any less true.

She wasn't sure if that helped or not.

As Liam watched his brother hoist Alexander high in the air in the family room, as close to baby talk with an "up you go!" as Drake Mercer got, he found himself studying Drake's face and hair and the dimple that deepened when he laughed every time Alexander giggled. Liam had been studying his family since he'd arrived ten minutes ago for the weekly Mercer family dinner. Last Friday night his mother had remarked over the Italian wedding soup course how Alexander was looking more and more like his handsome grandfather every day, especially around the eyes and "something in the expression." He wondered now if coloring was enough to make people see similarities where otherwise there was none—when people knew they were related.

He'd always figured Alexander must look more like Liza's side of the family, though he'd never really seen Liza in Alexander's face. And since Liza had been raised by a few different foster families, she'd never known her family.

"I knew you were going to be a rancher like me," Drake said, tapping the tiny Stetson Harrington Mercer had bought for Alexander.

"A *weekend* cowboy, like me," Harrington corrected. "That's how it's done. You devote your weekdays to the family business and the weekends to appreciating the land. Every Mercer has done it that way for generations."

"A real cowboy, weekend or otherwise, walks his own way, blazes his own path," Drake said, hoisting up Alexander again and earning a giggle.

"A real man puts family first, Drake," Harrington said, his tone its usual imperious don't-bother-arguing.

Drake didn't bother. He'd long stopped. He'd say his piece to a point, but he knew he was talking to a brick wall.

Liam admired his brother. He'd been blazing that own path since he was knee-high, doing things his way, taking the punishment and lecture rather than follow rules that didn't make sense to him or came from someone else's rigid vision for how he should act and think. Now, at twenty-seven, Drake was the foreman's right-hand man on a very prosperous cattle ranch and would likely take over the retiring-age man's job in the next year or two.

Liam had never thought he and his brother looked that much alike, but as he studied Drake, he could see how similar their features were. They had their mom's blue eyes and thick, dark hair, though Drake wore his a bit longer and messier than Liam did. Liam had his mother's strong, straight nose, while Drake more resembled Harrington Mercer.

How could someone who looks so much like me be so different from me in every way? their father would mutter at many a family dinner.

He glanced at his son, whom Uncle Drake was now setting down in the giant playpen by the sliding glass doors to the deck. Now that he knew that Alexander was very likely Shelby's son, he saw Shelby in his sweet little face.

"Must we have the same conversation every Friday?" Larissa Mercer asked, dusting her hands on her apron as she emerged from the kitchen, the smell of something delicious wafting out. His mother loved to cook and was working her way through one of the Barefoot Contessa's Italian cookbooks. "We're here together. That's what matters. Let's just enjoy ourselves."

Harrington Mercer gave Drake a half frown and poured himself a drink. Before he could respond, the doorbell rang.

Shelby. And Shane.

"I should have mentioned this earlier—I invited a friend to dinner," Liam announced. "She also has a six-month-old." He'd had a few hours to let his mother know. He also could have mentioned it when he'd arrived. But he'd found himself unable to get the words out.

Plus, he'd be hit with a barrage of questions about who Shelby was to him—with the assumption that they were a couple. Liam hadn't brought a woman to a family dinner in a couple of years, since he'd gotten his heart stomped on as a love-struck twenty-three-year-old bursting with a marriage proposal. Then two years ago he'd finally gotten serious again with another woman, a VP at Mercer Industries whom he'd discovered had been more interested in him as a stepping stone and left MI high and dry in the middle of a merger when she'd gotten a better offer from a rival company. Then a year ago there was Liza, whom he might have fallen for if he hadn't been so guarded against betrayal. But Liza had always said she had no interest in meeting his snooty, highfalutin family, which had made him laugh. All she'd wanted from Liam was his time and attention, and he hadn't even been willing to give that. She'd been right to dump him when he told her he wasn't interested in marriage or children—probably ever.

His mother's eyes lit up. "Ah, a new love interest!" She turned toward the family room, where her husband and younger son were ignoring each other in opposite corners. "Ooh, Harrington, did you hear? Liam's bringing home a girlfriend to meet us!" She turned back to Liam. "I had a feeling you'd fall for a single mother of a baby. Gives you quite a bit in common from the start."

Liam headed toward the door. "Actually, Shelby is just a friend."

His mother smiled slyly. "Sure she is. You've never invited a *friend* to Friday dinner before."

Liam pulled open the door, and the sight of Shelby stopped him cold. It wasn't just that she was beautiful; she was. But she suddenly seemed so…necessary, as if he couldn't get through the day without being with her and had just realized it when he saw her face.

That was nuts.

They were in the middle of one hell of a thing. That was it. She was like a lifeline. She was the other half in this. Not his other half, of course, but the other half in this insanity. It made sense that he needed her to feel some sense of grounding.

"It's good to see you," he said very honestly. "Hey there, Shane. You look very handsome in your lasso-print onesie." Sometimes he still couldn't get over that the word *onesie* was a big part of his vocabulary.

She laughed, setting him more at ease, and he was struck by her green eyes. He saw so much in those eyes. Worry. Confusion. Anxiety. But if he wasn't mistaken, she was also glad to see him.

She peered behind him, and he turned to find his entire family standing in front in the arched doorway to the family room, clearly eager to get a glimpse of the woman who'd gotten herself invited to the Mercer family dinner.

"Everyone, meet Shelby Ingalls and her son, Shane. Shelby, this is my mother, my father and my brother, Drake."

Everyone smiled and started talking about how cute Shane was. Everyone except Liam's father. In fact, Harrington Mercer was glaring at Shane. Really. His dad was glaring at a baby. What the hell was his problem?

"A word, Liam," his dad said, his tone cold, his expression…angry.

He glanced at Shelby standing next to his mother, oblivious to anything but Shane, whom she'd asked to hold. "Just going to talk to my dad for a second. Be right back."

Shelby nodded, and he followed his father to the library.

Harrington Mercer closed the door, then pointed his finger at Liam's chest. "Now you listen to me, Liam. I overlooked one illegitimate kid because of the circumstances and you're raising him. But if you think this other one is going to have the same privileges as Alexander, you're wrong."

Liam stared at his father, no idea what the hell he was going on about. *"What?"*

"Clearly, Shelby's child is yours. He looks exactly like you. And considering the babies are the same age, I'll say it now, Liam—use condoms for God's sake."

Liam might have laughed at how ludicrous this conversation was, but nothing about it was funny. "I have an announcement to make, Dad. I want to say it once and to everyone. So let's head back."

Harrington frowned. "Trust me, you don't have to announce anything. It's obvious just from looking at the baby." His father shook his head but followed Liam.

He stood beside Shelby, so close he could smell her shampoo. "Ready?" he whispered to her.

"Not really," she said. "But I'll never be."

"I have an announcement," he called out, and his brother glanced at him, then lifted his dark eyebrows at the seriousness of Liam's expression.

"What is it, dear?" his mother asked, coming closer and wrapping her arm around her husband's.

He cleared his throat, took one last look at Shelby, then said, "This morning, the Wedlock Creek Clinic called and asked me to bring in Alexander—and my attorney. Shelby got the same call." He looked at Shelby, so beautiful in her blue dress, her blond hair loose around her shoulders. He told them everything, from what the director had said to the DNA testing to Shelby getting the call to confirm that she couldn't be her baby's mother.

"We should get the DNA results in about a week," Shelby said, her voice a bit tight and strange-sounding.

"So now I have two nephews," Drake said. "That's kind of awesome."

Liam smiled at his brother. His younger sibling had a way of always defusing a situation.

"This is very sudden," Harrington said, frowning. "Of course, until the DNA results are in, there's no reason to assume that the babies were switched. Alexander is our grandchild, same as always, and Shelby's child is hers."

"But Shelby's child *can't* be hers biologically, Dad," Liam said. "Which means the two male babies born the night of November 5 were switched."

Harrington lifted his chin. "If that is truly the case, I'll call my own lawyer about getting the lawsuit going. That inept clinic needs to be shut down."

"No," Shelby said. "The clinic serves the entire county. It takes the poorest residents who don't have insurance. What happened was an honest mistake during the blizzard back in November when the power went out and the clinic's generators failed twice."

Harrington stared at her. "Well, the generators shouldn't have failed. The backup is supposed to *back up*."

"First of all, Dad, I don't have conclusive proof that Alexander isn't my biological son. I won't know for certain until the DNA tests."

"Proof that he isn't?" Harrington snapped. "You sound like you believe this nonsense."

Ha. A minute ago his father was *sure* Shane was Liam's child. "I'm facing facts."

His father stared at Alexander in his playpen, still wearing his little brown cowboy hat, then slid a glance at Shane in Shelby's arms. "So this," he said, pointing at Shane, "is my true grandchild?"

What the hell, Liam thought. *True* grandchild? "Alexander is your true grandchild, regardless, Dad," Liam and his brother said at practically the same time.

"This is quite a mess." Larissa Mercer patted at her ash-blond hair. "I say we sit down to dinner and talk about something more pleasant. As your father said, until the DNA results come in, there's no need to discuss it."

"We should prepare for the truth to come," Shelby said softly.

Liam glanced at her and had the urge to hold her hand, in solidarity, in needing her strength, in offering her his. "I agree."

"Do you like salmon, Shelby?" Larissa asked. "I've made a heavenly balsamic-glazed grilled salmon with new potatoes."

Liam looked at Shelby, his expression hopefully telling her that his mother just couldn't handle this right now. They would talk salmon instead.

"I love salmon," Shelby said with a gentle smile. She looked around the room. "I love your house, Mrs. Mercer."

Relief crossed Larissa Mercer's face, and she linked arms with Shelby. "Come, dear, you can test-taste a potato and tell me if it's ready."

As the women left the room, Liam watched his father walk across the floor and pretend great interest in rearranging the glasses on the bar.

"You okay?" Drake asked, taking Alexander from the playpen and holding him.

Liam stared at his son. His son. "Not really."

"This may get seriously complicated," Drake said. "You know that."

Liam frowned. "Shelby's a good person. I have no doubt of that and I barely know her."

"I'm not referring to Shelby," Drake said, his gaze moving to Harrington Mercer.

Liam felt a quick, hot poke at his gut. "Well, we'll find out what a real cowboy truly is, then, won't we?" he said.

Not even sure himself what he meant.

Chapter 4

Dinner had been an awkward nightmare. Shelby had never been so happy to leave anywhere in her entire life. Of course, she didn't know Liam Mercer very well, but even a total stranger could see the man was tense.

"Oh, Shelby, wait!" Larissa Mercer said as they stood in the doorway, about to make their escape. "I have something for your shop."

Shelby turned around and smiled, surprised. That was unexpected. Larissa opened the foyer closet and amid some coats and rain boots, Shelby could see a large plastic container marked *Donate*. She pulled out a medium-size plain brown bag with little handles and handed it to Shelby. "Here you go. Someone left it on the porch a few weeks ago and I've been meaning to bring it over to Treasures. It's one of those musical jewelry boxes. It works, too—plays one of my favorite Mozart piano sonatas."

Shelby glanced in the bag, but the box was wrapped in newspaper. "That's very kind of you to donate it to Treasures. I wonder why someone left it on your porch."

Larissa shrugged. "Harrington's name is on the bag," she said, pointing to the black script across the front. "Your father shrugged when I asked him about it. I guess someone left it as a thank-you for something or other. But there's not a drop of space for another thing in this house, so you take it, Shelby. It's lovely and someone will indeed 'treasure' it."

Liam reached over and hugged his mother, his shoulders relaxing. "Thanks for dinner, Mom."

"Ahlabawa," Alexander cooed, looking at his grandfather with his big blue eyes.

"Bye now," Harrington Mercer said, nodding at all of them and then turning away.

Larissa sighed and leaned forward. "It's a lot to take in. Let him digest it."

"It *is* a lot to take in," Shelby agreed. "Thanks again for the donation."

The moment the Mercers' stately red door closed behind Larissa, Shelby breathed a sigh of relief. Everyone—except for Drake—had eaten in record time and then made excuses for having to disappear. Dinner had taken all of fifteen minutes.

Liam half smiled in the illumination of the porch light. "Yeah, I know," he said in response to absolutely nothing. No words were needed.

She smiled. "Every Friday, huh? You're made of strong stuff."

They headed to their cars, Liam with a baby carrier in each hand, Shelby holding the bag Larissa had given her. Liam shrugged. "I don't know why I expect my father to be different, but I always do. I always wish he'll say: 'Whatever you need, Liam. I'm here for you.' My mom tries, but she's an ignorer, a rug sweeper-under." He shook his head. "I guess they have a right to their own take on things."

Shelby touched his arm, her heart going out to him. "Well, it had to be a shock for them. They're Alexander's grandparents. Their lives are turned upside down, too."

He frowned. "Pretending the situation doesn't exist and talking about gardening and the new gift shop on Main Street isn't going to make the situation any less crazy."

Truth be told, Shelby had appreciated the small talk about spring bulbs and how the gift shop sold a simply delightful rose-scented hand cream in the loveliest packaging. For the half hour she'd spent in the Mercer mansion, she'd almost forgotten the events of the day. Almost. Being forced to talk about something else, to think about something else, had been a good thing. "Your mom is right, though. Your dad just needs time to digest. To let it sink in."

He nodded and glanced down at Alexander in his baby carrier. "He's out cold."

"So's Shane," she said, reaching to caress a strand of silky brown hair in the breeze. "Liam, what are we supposed to do for a week until the results come in? Until we know for sure. How are we supposed to get through this? What are we supposed to *do*? I can't think straight."

"Me either. I could use a strong cup of coffee right now. That's all I know."

"I have a new bag of Sumatra beans," she said. "And really good chocolate cookies."

He smiled. "Your place, it is. I'll follow you."

Within a half hour they were on their second mugs of coffee and another cookie each in the eat-in kitchen in Shelby's apartment, both babies stirring in their carriers on the side table across from them. Shane began fussing, which made Alexander scowl and pipe up.

Shelby got up and was about to pick up Shane when she stopped and turned around.

"Liam?" She bit her lip, then rushed to get her thought out before she clamped down on it. "Maybe you should soothe Shane. And I'll pick up Alexander."

He put down his mug and stared at the boys in their carriers. Finally, he nodded and stood up, and she was suddenly so aware of his height and the breadth of him. Earlier he'd seemed like an adversary but now he felt more like an anchor somehow.

"You first," he said. "If that's okay."

She walked over to the table and kept her eyes on Alexander, trying not to let her gaze keep drifting to the little birthmark on his ear. Or how like her eyes his were.

"He can get a little fussy with newcomers," he said. "He likes his grandfather and uncle and two particular teachers at the day care. He's warming up to my cousin Clara and seems to save his spit-up for her."

He was being kind, she realized. Trying to let her know that if he squirmed and fussed in the arms of the woman who'd given birth to him, to not take it personally. She turned to him and smiled and he smiled back.

She undid the harness and scooped up the baby, cradling him against her. He slipped into her embrace as though he'd always known her, one little hand grabbing at her shirt, the other wrapping around a strand of her wavy blond hair. He looked up at her with those enormous blue eyes.

As tears pricked her own eyes, she turned away a bit, needing some privacy from Liam.

He seemed to get that. "I'll go pick up Shane now, if that's all right."

She whirled around, suddenly nervous despite this being her idea. "Okay."

She watched him walk over to the table and undo Shane's harness, then carefully pick him up and cuddle him against his chest.

"He feels like Alexander—like a six-month-old baby boy. But he's not Alexander."

"No," Shelby said. "He's not."

But as she looked down at the boy in her arms, the boy she knew was hers, too, all she could think was: *you're my flesh and blood. You're a part of me, a piece of me. But you're not mine.*

The tears threatened to spill over, and she blinked them back hard.

"He's been here in Wedlock Creek all these months and I had no idea," Liam said, his gaze on Shane, nestled in his arms. Shelby could see anger etched into his features, his jawline hard. "I've been denied my child and you've been denied yours."

And they both loved the babies they'd raised for the past six months, the babies they'd believed were their children. The babies who were their children. Shane was her son. Nothing, not a blood type, not DNA, not a court order, would change that.

"I see what you mean about not being able to give him back," Liam said. "I've missed out on six months."

"I know," she said, nuzzling her cheek against Alexander's head. "So what the hell do we do? What do we *do*?"

She couldn't leave Alexander, this precious bundle she held, this baby she'd brought into the world. She couldn't walk away, go home, open the shop, wait an endless week. She couldn't. She needed, wanted, to be around Alexander with the same fierce drive she needed to be around Shane.

"I don't want to put him down," Liam said, kissing Shane's head. "I don't want to give him back."

The tears did spill then. "I know. Me either. I don't want to leave him behind again."

"Exactly," Liam said, his gaze soft on Shane.

She felt Liam staring at her. When she looked up at him, she could see he was deciding something.

"Shelby, I have a proposition for you."

She tilted her head. "What kind of proposition?"

"Until the DNA tests come in," he said, "maybe we should think about the four of us being under one roof. Together."

"What? You're suggesting we live together? We don't even know each other!"

"Except you've been raising my son for the past six months and I've been raising yours. I want to know him, Shelby. I'm sure you want to know Alexander."

"Of course I do."

"I don't know how else to go about this. We've lost out on enough time."

"And if the results come back and the boys weren't switched?" she asked. "If the blood typing results were a mistake—even three times?"

"Then we can go back to our lives."

She stared at him. "And if the results come back and we know for sure the babies were switched at birth?"

"We'll cross that bridge if we get there, Shelby."

Live with Liam Mercer?

Live with Shane and Alexander. That was all she needed to know. "The kitchen floor slants a bit. And Drunk Pete likes to howl at the moon when he leaves the bar down the street every night. But the guest room bed is incredibly comfortable."

He raised an eyebrow. "I was thinking you'd move in with me. I live on a ranch on the outskirts of town. Well, it's not a working ranch, but I do have two horses. There's a lot of room and everything a six-month-old baby could want."

His turf? No way. She bit her lip. "I have everything a six-month-old baby *needs*. And three bedrooms. We can bunk the boys in Shane's nursery. I'd prefer to be here, Liam, for many reasons. Including the fact that people often stop by to see if I want to purchase their unwanted treasures for the store. They know to ring my apartment bell during off hours."

"You sure do make yourself available to look through someone's old stuff."

"You know the old saying. One's man's junk... But it's more than that, Liam. Sometimes people need to get rid of things to finally let go, to say goodbye to parts of their past. I get that."

"There are parts of my past I wish I could let go of that easily." He glanced around the apartment, his gaze stopping on the beads dangling down from a doorway. "Then I'll be back with my bags in a couple hours."

The day had begun with learning she wasn't Shane's mother.

It was ending with Shane's father moving into her home.

She didn't even want to fathom what tomorrow might have in store for her.

Nine p.m. was closing time at her family's Pie Diner, which meant Shelby would find her sister, her mom and her aunt Cheyenne in the main part of the diner or the kitchen, cleaning up and taking pies for tomorrow morning from the oven and leaving them to cool. She hadn't had much of an appetite at dinner, but she would never turn down a slice of pie, particularly chocolate cream, and on Fridays there was always chocolate cream. The Pie Diner was truly just that: pies, scrumptious, homemade and sliced generously. Every day there were various quiches, pot pies, and six kinds of dessert pies, and very few leftovers.

She entered the diner just as Norah was turning over the open sign.

Norah rushed over for a hug, and Shelby was so done from the day she practically went limp in her sister's arms. Norah took Shane's carrier and set it down on the counter. "One slice of chocolate cream pie and a lemon seltzer coming up. You okay?"

She waited until the fortifying pie was in front of her before answering. "Liam is moving in. With Alexander. Neither of us can bear to be away from Shane and Alexander, so it just makes sense to be together."

Norah's mouth dropped open. "Moving in? Shelby, are you sure?"

"I just know that I held Alexander tonight for the first

time and I couldn't give him back. I didn't want to give him back. And it was the same when Liam held Shane."

"Oh, Shelby. I can totally understand that."

She forked a piece of pie, her appetite for her favorite dessert barely there. "I can't think straight. I can't see straight. Up is down, right is left. I need him and Alexander around me. Liam's going through the same thing I am. I can be a mess without having to say a word. He instantly knows how I feel. It's a comfort."

Norah nodded. "Well, if he so much as talks about trying to gain custody of Shane, you call David, you hear?"

"No one is talking about custody—at least until the DNA test results come in. And then, who knows? I have no idea what's going to happen, Norah."

"What's this about custody?" Shelby's mother asked, coming through the swinging door of the kitchen, her blond hair in a short ponytail. "Ooh, there's my precious grandbaby," she said, beelining for Shane in his carrier on the counter. She smothered her grandson with kisses, then noticed Shelby's expression. "Hey, what's wrong?"

"I've got news, Mom. Can you grab Aunt Cheyenne?"

"Everything okay, Shel?" Arlena Ingalls asked, her hazel-green eyes worried.

She shook her head. "No."

"Oh, God." Her mother's eyes filled with tears.

"I'm not sick," Shelby assured her. "It's nothing like that. But something crazy has happened."

Her mother bit her lip and hurried into the kitchen, then came out with Aunt Cheyenne. The Ingalls women were strong stock and Shelby knew she could count on them—for support, for advice.

Norah squeezed Shelby's hand in commiseration, and as her mother and sister stood behind the counter, staring at Shelby, she launched into the whole story. Starting with the call from the Wedlock Creek Clinic's administrator and ending with Liam packing his bags to move in with Alexander.

And then after a barrage of questions she couldn't really answer, they hugged her one by one and sent her home with a quiche Lorraine, a chicken pot pie, and three kinds of dessert pie, her favorite chocolate cream, a cherry and Arlena Ingalls's famed Comfort Custard Pie.

"It's gonna be okay," her sister said at the door. "It will."

"Just be careful, Shel," her aunt Cheyenne said, tossing her long auburn braid off her shoulder. "You say this Liam Mercer seems kind and reasonable, but the DNA test results aren't in yet. When those results say that Shane is his biological son, all hell is gonna break loose."

"That'll make Alexander Mercer my biological son," she reminded them. "We're both in the same boat in very choppy, uncertain waters."

"I'm just saying, Shelby—he's a Mercer. His family is philanthropic and all that but they're also ruthless when it comes to business."

Shelby's stomach twisted. "Babies are hardly business."

"To Mercers?" her mother said. "Maybe they are."

Shelby frowned and was afraid she was going to burst into tears so she gripped the door handle.

"Honey, I'm not trying to scare you. I'm just trying to tell you to keep your guard up. Okay?"

Shelby hugged her mother, the tears pricking, anyway. "Oh, trust me. My guard couldn't be up higher."

Suddenly, three Ingallses were hugging her and then

Shelby picked up Shane's carrier and left, her heart so heavy she had to stop three times to catch her breath on the ten-minute walk to her apartment.

Chapter 5

As Liam pulled up into a spot in front of Treasures, he glanced up at the two-story brick building, lights glowing from behind curtains in the apartment windows above the shop. He had no idea how he was going to live in this tiny apartment with a woman who stole the air around him because she was so vital to him and with two babies who each made his heart stop for very different reasons.

He'd make it work. To have Alexander and Shane both living with him, anything would be worth it.

He made five trips from the car to the side doorway that led directly up to the apartment, then rang the bell.

When Shelby opened the door, he was again struck by how moved he was. Not just because she was so pretty, her face scrubbed clean, her blond hair pulled back into a ponytail, jeans and a yellow hoodie on her tall, lean form. When he looked at Shelby Ingalls, even when he just thought about her, he felt rooted in the world, which was nuts. He'd just met the woman.

But their lives, the most important thing in their worlds, were now so entwined that he wanted to be connected to Shelby at all times. Must be why he was okay with moving into this little, strange place above a dusty shop full of old things. He could have insisted on them all moving to his ranch house, which had even too much room for four people, especially when two of them were itty-bitty. But this was Shelby's domain and he wanted to be in it.

She was Shane's mother. The mother of his biological son. And she was the biological mother of Alexander. His life.

"I'm not sure my apartment is big enough for all that," Shelby said with a smile as she looked down.

"Well, I had to take Alexander's rocking bassinet—he sleeps it in like a champ. And his favorite bouncer seat. And his tummy time mat. And the lullaby player. A few packs of diapers, wipes, his clothes, pj's, favorite blankets, stuffed animals and chew toys, and I'm a walking baby store."

Shelby laughed. "I'll help lug it. First, let me take this little guy up." She smiled at Alexander. "You're going to like the apartment," she whispered to the sleeping baby as she took his carrier. "Your buddy is up there and you're going to share his nursery. I painted the stars on the ceiling myself."

Liam loved how sweet she was to Alexander, how she talked to him, the catch in her voice. He wanted to take the carrier out of her hands and just hold her for a few minutes right here in the illumination of the overhead light, tell her this new beginning was going to work out fine. But instead, he grabbed the bulky exersaucer and followed her through a side door that led directly up a flight of stairs to the second floor and bypassed the need to go through the shop. *Focus on why you're here—the babies*, he told himself. *And stop focusing on Shelby herself.* "I told him all about the nursery on the way over."

She glanced behind her, that smile lighting up the dimly lit stairwell. "Did he say anything back?"

"He said he can't wait to be Shane's roomie."

Shelby laughed and went into the nursery, where she left Alexander in his carrier for the meantime, and Liam put the exersaucer in the living room. They raced back downstairs. She grabbed the two garment bags, which held his suits for work, and Liam took the bassinet and two duffels. Three trips later, everything was inside.

"Well, Alexander is fast asleep in his bassinet," Liam said as they stood in the nursery.

"Shane, too," she said, reaching into his crib to caress his little head.

They backed out of the room, leaving the door just slightly ajar. He followed Shelby into the living room and sat beside her on the big overstuffed red couch. He liked the apartment more than he'd expected. It was both soothing and colorful, cozy and practical, particularly with a baby living here—correction, two babies—and just plain inviting. He was used to his ranch with its brown leather couches and more stark furnishings, but he liked it here.

"I told my family what's going on," she said when she came from the kitchen with a tray holding two mugs of coffee.

Liam added cream and sugar and took a sip of the needed hot brew. "Did they react like mine?"

She smiled. "Not quite, but they did warn me to be careful."

"Careful?"

"The Mercer name carries a lot of weight, Liam. You know that."

He put down his mug and took both her hands in his. "I'm going to say this again, Shelby. As many times as I need to. I will not do anything to hurt you. I will not attempt to take Shane away from you. I can't say it any more black-and-white than that. And I hope you won't attempt to take Alexander from me."

The relief that came over her must have been very strong because she flung her arms around him, and he held her tightly, resting his cheek against the top of her head. "We're in this together, Shelby."

She nodded, then pulled away. "I feel better." She tucked her legs underneath her and picked up her mug of coffee. "You weren't married to Alexander's mother?"

Liza's face floated into his mind and he tried to push it out. He couldn't think about Liza without feeling a hard punch of guilt.

He shook his head. "We only dated for a few weeks. My cousin Clara wanted to adopt a dog, so we went to the animal shelter to check them out. Liza worked there. That's how we met."

She smiled. "Did your cousin adopt a dog?"

"Sure did. She went in wanting a dog that didn't shed, bark and was completely trained in every regard. She left with a German shepherd mutt she fell in love with at first sight. He sheds, barks and is only a quarter trained. Meaning he'll do anything you say for a rawhide bone.

His name is Bixby and now she has about a hundred lint rollers."

"I've always wanted a dog, but I inherited Luna from my grandmother five years ago and I don't think she'd appreciate a dog in the place."

"Ah, so that's what that black-and-white fuzzy thing I almost tripped over was—your cat."

Anything to delay talking about Liza. And how he'd let her down.

She smiled. "So you met Liza at the shelter…" Shelby prompted.

So much for changing the subject. "We were as different as night and day, but I liked her a lot. She was a real free spirit, into hiking and nature. She couldn't believe she fell for a corporate stooge."

Shelby smiled. "I totally get it."

"Well, somehow, we connected. We spent a lot of time together. She liked being out at my ranch, despite the lack of animals. Just to breathe in all that country Wyoming air. But then honesty came between us."

"Honesty?" she asked, wrapping her hands around her mug.

"We were talking about what we wanted from life, and I told her I had no intention of ever getting married or having children. That I was a lone wolf."

He paused, that hot poke of guilt stabbing at his gut.

He felt Shelby staring at him but didn't want to give her time or room to ask questions, so he rushed on. "I mean, I liked Liza. A lot. But I also liked things as they were. No commitment. Just two people enjoying each other's company. No rules, no musts. Because she was a free spirit, I thought she'd understand."

"But she didn't?"

He frowned, remembering the look on Liza's face. Disappointment. Hurt. "She told me that just because she was a free spirit didn't mean she didn't believe in love or forever, that in fact, love was everything to her. She said she wanted five kids. She asked me again if I was absolutely sure, if I could say with conviction that I never wanted to get married or have children. I said yes. I was sure. So she ended things."

He put his mug down and turned away a bit, resting his elbows on his knees, his head bowed. He hated this part of the story.

"The night she gave birth was the first time I'd heard from her in about seven, eight months. She called me on her way to the clinic and told me she was nine months pregnant with my baby, in labor, and she was sorry she hadn't told me. She said if anything happened to her, she left me a letter."

He stood up and walked to the windows, staring through the filmy embroidered curtains at Main Street in the dark, the familiar landmarks somehow comforting. There was the general store with its weather vane and silver cowboy hat atop it. The small library his mother had funded. He could just make out the Pie Diner at the tail end of the street, Pie Diner flanked by two painted wood pies, a cowboy lassoing one. He closed his eyes and kept hearing Liza's voice.

I'm nine months pregnant with your child.
And the words in her letter.

I'd never want my child to have a father who's not interested in him or her, a father who doesn't want the responsibility. That's why I didn't tell you. If anything happens to me, Liam, you'll be the baby's

*only parent, his or her only family. I have no one
else, as you know. We only knew each other a few
weeks, but I know you're a good person and caring and will step up if need be. Since need be is all
I'll have, I'll take it. This is your child. That's all
you need to know to love him. But I guess you'll
have to find that out for yourself.*

"If I'd known she was pregnant, I would have been
there for her, making sure she had what she needed. Instead, she went through her pregnancy alone and she
had no family. She was all alone, Shelby."

There it was. People let each other down. People could
not be trusted, period. Even if you thought you meant
well, you ended up breaking someone's heart, ruining a
year or two of their life, scarring them. He'd been hurt.
He'd done the hurting. It never ended. He'd vowed not
to hurt Shelby because he wasn't romantically involved
with her, never would be, despite how badly he wanted
to kiss her, and could keep a solid emotional distance.
As long as he kept her at arm's length, everything would
be fine. So he would.

She got up and walked over to him, touching the back
of his shoulder. "She wasn't alone, Liam. Not really. She
had her baby. When I was pregnant and here by myself,
I'd just touch my belly and I'd feel better. I'll bet Liza
felt that way, too."

He appreciated that. He relaxed a bit, the knots in his
shoulders—particularly the spot where she'd touched
him—loosening. He let his mind wander to how Shelby
would feel in his arms. He wanted her in his arms.

Arm's length, he reminded himself. That meant no
touching her. No holding her.

"You planned to *never* marry or have kids?" she asked, heading back to the couch.

He turned around and sat down next to her, picking up his mug of coffee, and took a sip, wrapping his hands around the warmth of the cup. "I used to feel differently, years ago when I was young and naive. But no—I'm done with the idea of love and marriage. The kid situation took care of itself."

"So you adapted to parenthood, Liam. Maybe you could adapt to marriage. How could you be so sure you couldn't?"

"Because love doesn't last."

"My parents were married for twenty-two years until my father died. They were deeply in love until my father's last breath."

He glanced at her. "I'm sorry about your father."

"Love does last," she said. "It *does*. Or it can. Even if it hasn't for me."

"Or for me, Shelby. Twice I got my heart handed back to me in shards. I learned to not get emotionally invested. It's better that way." *And given the way I ended up failing Liza when she needed me?* Yes, he was done.

Shelby tilted her head at him, those green eyes regarding him. "I've never seen anyone more emotionally invested in another person than you with Alexander."

"He's my son. Not my girlfriend. And I don't have girlfriends anymore. Just dates here and there, three-week-long relationships where everything is clear and ends with no one disillusioned."

She picked up a cookie from the plate on the coffee table and took a bite. "You're a hard one. Are your parents happily married?"

He shrugged. "Honestly, it's hard to tell. Their marriage was all but arranged by my late grandmother, Alexandra. Alexander was named for her. She was something else. A brilliant businesswoman. My grandfather was smart and made her president of the company when the company started failing under his watch. She turned it around. She ran Mercer Industries and the family. My father really respected her. So when she pushed him to marry my mother, he complied. I guess they're happy enough. But their marriage certainly didn't make me think love is real or lasting or a reason to marry."

"A reason to marry?" Shelby repeated. "Love is the only reason!"

"There's also practicality."

"Well, I'm all for being practical and smart about how I live my life, but love and emotion can't be bulletpointed in a memo about how to live."

He laughed. "Sure it can. I make bullet-pointed to-do lists every day. Today's got blown to bits, of course."

"See? Life works that way."

"Don't I know it, Shelby."

She glanced at him, then sipped her coffee, her gaze landing on the brown bag his mother had given her at dinner. She jumped up and brought it back to the sofa. "It was nice of your mom to give it to me for Treasures."

"It was thoughtful. Larrisa Mercer can be very kind and loving. She can also be very, very practical."

Shelby reached in and lifted out a medium-size something wrapped in newspaper. She unwrapped it, stuffing the paper back in the bag on the floor. She gasped as she examined it. "Wow, it's absolutely beautiful! I can't believe your mother didn't want this." She turned it around in her hands, the ornately jeweled tin box sparkling when it caught the light from the floor lamp. She reached underneath and twisted the metal prong, Mozart playing softly. "Lovely. Honestly, I want it for myself."

He smiled. "Keep it, then."

"I love mysteries, don't you? Don't you wonder who dropped it off on your parents' porch and why?" She leaned down and scooped up the bag, looking at his father's name scrawled across it, then put it back down. "As your mother said, maybe your father once did the person a favor and this is a thanks."

"My father doesn't do favors unless there's one coming back."

She frowned at him and opened the lid. The box was about six by eight and lined in an unexpected pink velvet. Shelby smiled. "This is definitely not for sale. I'm going to keep it as a memento of the first time I met your family. The day I met you."

"It's been one hell of a Friday."

She laughed. "Sure has."

"Let's add Saturday to the mix, too, then," he said. "Let's go talk to the nurse who switched our babies."

Shelby turned to him, putting the jewelry box back in the bag. "Should we wait until we have the DNA results?"

"I feel like I'll go out of my mind if I don't have information, something, to help explain where we are now. Shane can't be your biological child. Something has to account for that. And it has to be the nurse."

Shelby nodded slowly, her expression so pained that he regretted his words, that Shane couldn't be her child. He was.

He reached for her hand. "I'm sorry this happened, Shelby."

"Me, too. Except—and this is going to sound crazy—

if it hadn't happened I wouldn't have Shane. I wouldn't have loved this little boy for the past six months. Granted, I wouldn't have known otherwise. But how can I regret having loved Shane all this time?"

He wanted to pull her to him and tell her he knew exactly what she meant. But he held back.

"Let's go talk to the nurse in the morning," she said. "I want to hear what happened but I'm scared, too. That she'll take any last, lingering bit of hope away. That somehow, this is all a mistake and Shane is mine and Alexander is yours."

"I know," he said. "I know."

In the middle of the night, Shelby woke up to the sound of a baby crying, and the different strain to the cries made her rush into the nursery. But it wasn't Shane crying. It was Alexander. And Liam was already there, soothing him on the rocker.

Half-naked.

Shelby was suddenly aware that she was wearing a tank top and yoga pants and showing more than she'd planned to her new housemate. *Note to self: from now on, grab bathrobe.*

"He's settling down," Liam said. "Maybe cutting his first tooth. I think I saw a little white nub on his gum."

"Shane cut his first just last week," she said, coming over and caressing Alexander's silky brown hair. His mouth quirked and his one hand shot up in a fist, then he scrunched his mouth around until he finally settled down, fast asleep. She smiled.

"Sorry we woke you," he said.

She was staring at his chest, she realized. His very muscular chest, dark hair whirling in the center. He wore sweats and was barefoot and he was so damned sexy that she had to look away.

"I'm used to it," she whispered, barely able to find her voice.

What she wasn't used to was a man in her apartment, taking care of business, taking care of a child. In the hours between her discovering she was pregnant and telling Shane's father the news, she'd had all these wonderful fantasies—fantasies that she thought would become reality. A scenario like this one, for example. Waking up to her baby's cries and rushing into the nursery only to find his father there first, holding their child, soothing him, rocking him back to sleep. And then the two grown-ups going back to their own room and making love, falling asleep spooned together, his arms around her. Shelby protected and safe in his love. She'd had those fantasies for just four hours before they were blown to bits.

Liam stood, and Shelby shook those thoughts away. She watched as he put Alexander in his crib and pressed a finger to his lips and then his son's cheek. "Sweet dreams," he whispered, and then they both quietly exited the room.

He stared at her for a good long moment, and she wondered what he was thinking.

God, I want to kiss him. That was her sudden thought. Was he thinking the same about her?

Adrenaline and panic were at play, that was all. She had to keep her lips and hands to herself. This situation was hard enough without falling for a man who wasn't interested in marriage or family life, despite being a great dad.

"Well, good night," she said. "Next cry is mine."

He smiled and headed back to his room and the moment he disappeared from her sight she missed him.

Chapter 6

In the morning Liam sat on the bed in the guest room at Shelby's, distracted by the sounds of two babies gurgling and Shelby's melodic voice asking who wanted apricot baby food and who wanted peaches. Then he heard her saying they could both have a handful of their favorite cereal, Toasty Os. He heard Alexander babbling happily and Shelby moving about the kitchen, the cabinet doors closing, a chair scooting in.

He liked the gentle noise. He was used to living alone—well, with a baby, who said a couple of words that sounded like da and ba but otherwise babbled or cried or let out various levels of shrieks, happy or otherwise. Now, someone else—a woman—was taking care of Alexander this morning. It felt funny. And nice.

He'd gotten up the moment he heard a baby stir and

fuss—turned out to be Shane, and Shelby had beaten him into the nursery.

"I've got this," she'd said, a baby in each arm. "Relax, take a shower, have some coffee."

Relax? He couldn't even imagine. Not for a long time. He'd thanked her, taken his coffee to his bedroom and had gotten busy on the telephone. He'd started with Anne Parcells.

The Wedlock Creek Clinic's administrator hadn't been comfortable giving out the nurse's contact information, citing a pending internal investigation, so Liam did some investigating of his own and easily found her name and then her address. Kate Atwood on Cumberland Road.

Liam had then called Mrs. Atwood, explained who he was and why he wanted to talk to her, and she was reluctant and nervous. He'd explained that both he and Shelby felt a bit lost and thought hearing what happened, what may have happened, from the night nurse who'd been there would be a comfort or provide a sense of grounding. She'd finally agreed to have them over this morning at nine o'clock.

Liam headed back into the kitchen. Shelby was scooping scrambled eggs onto plates just as toast popped up in the red toaster on the counter. "I was just about to call you for breakfast. I have no idea how you like your eggs. If you like eggs."

"I love scrambled eggs. And toast. And thank you," he said.

"Bwa!" Shane babbled. Alexander eyed him and said, "Tawaba!"

Liam smiled. "From lonely onlys to brothers."

Shelby's entire face lit up. "I hadn't really thought of

that. But you're right." Her gaze on the boys was so tender, so reverent, so…happy that he almost slid an arm around her and held her close so they could both just stare at these magnificent tiny creatures they'd created. Everything Shelby was going through, he was going through. He'd never experienced anything like it before. Liam wasn't entirely sure, but he thought what was going on was called *intimacy*. Real, true intimacy. They understood each other on a level that was surprisingly comforting—and made him uneasy.

Which was why he changed the subject. He explained about the calls and their appointment with Kate Atwood. The beautiful moment they'd shared—gone. And he instantly felt less tense.

"I think we should go without the boys, though," Shelby said as she put a few more Toasty Os cereal on each baby's high chair. "I think that might be too much for the woman."

Liam topped off his coffee, which had to be his tenth in the past twenty-four hours. "You're right. She may feel more comfortable talking to us if we're not holding the babies she switched."

"I'm sure my mom and aunt would love to watch both boys," she said. "They'll be at the diner but can take turns keeping an eye."

"People eat pie for breakfast?" he asked. "I never thought of that."

"No one needs a reason or a time to eat pie. Our fruit pies are popular for breakfast, but my aunt Cheyenne makes five kinds of quiches for the breakfast crowd. Egg pie—with the most heavenly additions you can imagine. For dinner there are chicken pot pies, meat pies. Pie isn't just apple pie."

"I'll never think of pie the same way again."

She smiled. "They'll make you take a few boxes for the road. It's just how they are."

"Good. I don't turn down pie."

He could talk about pie for hours. Anything but switched babies and retired nurses and clinic blackouts.

"I'll call my mom," she said, reaching for her phone.

While she was on the phone, Liam entertained the babies with a little peekaboo. Shane didn't like when his face was hidden. But he got a big smile when he opened his hands from in front of his face and exclaimed, "Peekaboo! I see you!"

Shelby put her phone back on the counter. "We're all set. My mom said she can't wait to meet Alexander. Cheyenne and Norah, too."

"Why do I doubt that your mom will react like my father? I don't even know your mother but if she's anything like you, I can't imagine her referring to Alexander as her *real* grandson."

"Shane will always be her grandson. Alexander will feel like a bonus for a bit and then within a couple of weeks she'll forget that she didn't know he existed for the first six months of his life. Maybe that's how it'll be for your dad."

"We'll see. But I won't hold my breath."

They packed up the babies and drove over to the Pie Diner, just a quarter mile down Main Street and well situated next door to the library. The diner had been in business since Liam was a little kid, and his grandmother used to take him there all the time. Alexandra Mercer was no baker, but she loved pie. He'd never paid much attention to the menu and always ordered his favorite: Key Lime.

"I love how the place has changed over the decades but still has the same feel it always had," he said as they pulled into the gravel parking lot. He'd always liked the painted cowboy on a horse lassoing five painted wood 3D pies on the other side of the sign.

They barely got out of the car with the babies in their carriers when the door burst open and three women emerged, all various shades of blond with Pie Diner aprons on.

"I just saw you last night but I can't get enough of you," said the one Liam assumed was Shelby's mother. She was tall and slender like Shelby with chin-length blond hair and Shelby's green eyes. She took the carrier from Shelby and kissed Shane on his forehead. "Don't tell your mom but I'm gonna give you a little taste of apple filling this morning. Just wait till you get a real tooth and get through my amazing pie crust."

Liam smiled and extended his hand. "Liam Mercer. And this little guy is Alexander."

"Arlena Ingalls," she said, shaking his hand. "I'd pull you into a hug but we're both short a hand." She turned to Alexander in Liam's arms. "Hello, Alexander. You are absolutely adorable."

Shelby smiled. "And this is my aunt Cheyenne and my sister, Norah."

"Nice to meet you all," Liam said.

Cheyenne's long, curly hair blew forward in the breeze but she didn't brush it back from her face. She was staring from Shane to Liam, from Liam to Shane. "My God, Shane is the spitting image of you," she said to Liam, her hand covering her mouth.

"He is," Shelby's mother said with a nod.

Norah was looking from Alexander to Shane, then

to Liam and Shelby. "And Alexander looks a lot like Shelby if you can ignore all that blond hair she has. It's in the eyes and the expression. And—he has the little Ingalls birthmark. Shelby has it. And so did our father."

Shelby nodded. "It all adds up to the babies being switched. That's why we have no doubt what the DNA tests will reveal. It may seem early to go talk to the nurse, but we just want to, need to."

"I can understand that," Norah said. "Was she nervous about the idea of meeting with you?"

Liam nodded. "I assured her we just need to talk to her off the record, nothing official, that this isn't about pointing fingers or looking to blame. It's just to understand, feel more connected to what happened."

"Well, you two take all the time you need," Shelby's mom said. "We're thrilled to watch both babies."

"Appreciate it," Liam said.

A few minutes later they were in Liam's SUV—alone. He looked in the back seat, sure he'd find Alexander and Shane back there, as usual, rear-facing in their seats. But just the bases were there. It was a funny feeling.

"Do you feel like we're missing something?" he asked.

She nodded. "I'm so used to having Shane with me at the shop that anytime he's not with me I feel like I lost something."

"You have a nice family. They seem like a very loving bunch."

She smiled. "They're in the pie business. It's a happy, loving thing."

"Happier and more loving than mergers and acquisitions and management, that's for sure."

"But you love your work?" she asked.

"I like it. I wouldn't say I love it. But I do love the family history, the tradition, to working on something started by my great-grandfather. I'm glad it's Saturday, though, so I don't have to have Mercer Industries on my mind. I put in a few hours on the weekends, but I try very hard to devote off time to Alexander."

She smiled. "You're a great dad."

He felt her compliment inside him. "Means a lot coming from a great mom."

That beautiful smile lit up the car again, and when a swath of her blond hair fell forward he was tempted to tuck it back away from her pretty face. He'd been so aware of her last night in the room right next door. He'd been tempted to get out of bed and pretend he heard Alexander fussing just so he could see her again, look at her, be with her. He wasn't sure how he'd feel about living in a small apartment above a shop, but the moment he'd arrived last night with his bags and Alexander's things, he'd felt at home because Shelby and Shane were there.

But he still didn't feel a connection to Shane yet. Maybe he'd need the DNA test results to make it feel real and then his heart would catch up with his head. Or maybe it would just take time. Just because Alexander wasn't his biologically didn't mean the baby was any less Liam's son. Liam had a feeling the space he was putting—emotionally—between himself and Shane was because of Shelby. At this point he wouldn't want her throwing herself into the role of Alexander's mother, just as he was sure she wouldn't want him to suddenly become Shane's father. They both had to move slowly—and were.

After fifteen minutes down a rural service road, Liam

turned onto Berrymill Road and slowed down as he approached the yellow Cape Kate had told him to look out for. "Looks like we're here."

A woman stepped onto the porch. She was petite and looked haggard and tired, as though she hadn't slept in days. Or since yesterday.

"Ready?" Liam asked Shelby.

She nodded and they both got out of the car. Liam held up a hand to the woman, and they headed up the porch steps. Up close, Kate Atwood definitely showed even more signs of not sleeping. There were dark circles under her eyes, and she looked as if she might break down in tears at any minute. Liam's research had revealed she was sixty-six years old and she looked quite a bit older. She was petite and thin with short, light brown hair shot through with gray, and brown eyes behind glasses.

"Come on in," she said. "I've made iced tea and have homemade oatmeal cookies, if you like."

Shelby offered a gentle smile. "I never pass up a cookie. I come from a long line of bakers. Pie bakers, but I do love cookies."

Shelby's warmth clearly set the woman at ease. Liam watched Kate's shoulders relax and her entire countenance changed. She still looked like she might cry, but the fear that had been in her expression, as though they might turn their anger on her, lightened up some.

They followed her into a cozy living room. Liam and Shelby sat on the love seat across from the recliner that Kate took. She gestured at the cookies, the pitcher of iced tea and glasses. "Please help yourself."

They did, more to ease in to what was to come than thirst or hunger.

Shelby took a sip of tea, then put her glass down and clasped her hands. "Mrs. Atwood, we understand that you were the nurse on duty in the maternity area of the clinic the night our babies were born. As you know, the clinic administrator has informed me that my son Shane can't be the baby I gave birth to. We're awaiting DNA testing but all signs do point to the two male babies being accidentally switched. Can you tell us what happened? What you remember?"

Kate looked at each of them and took a deep breath. "First, I am so sorry." Tears glistened in her eyes. "When Anne called me and had me come in to discuss that night, I had no inkling that I might have switched two babies. But when she said that one baby couldn't be the biological child of one of the mothers, I immediately knew that I must have switched the two male newborns."

"Can you tell us what was happening at that time?" Liam asked.

Kate folded and unfolded her hands in her lap. "It was terrible. The wind was howling so badly and we were all so afraid the power could go out and it did. The generator came on but then it failed, too. I'd just brought the Ingalls baby to the nursery to weigh and measure him and the lights came back on so I put him in the bassinet and ran to Ms. Harwood's labor and delivery room for her infant to bring him to the nursery. The lights went out again just as I approached. All of a sudden, a tree fell on the east wing and people were screaming in fear. I put the Harwood baby down in a bassinet for safety and wheeled both over away from the windows. I was sure the Ingalls baby was on the left and the Harwood baby was on my right. But in the chaos, I must have mixed them up. I must have put the bracelets on the wrong babies."

"You said you had no inkling you might have switched the babies," Liam said gently. "As you were braceleting them, you didn't think for a second that you could have switched them?"

She shook her head. "I was so sure. Ingalls left, Harwood right. And I remembered thinking, the Harwood baby had that tiny birthmark on his right ear."

"Like this," Shelby said numbly, pointing at her own ear.

"If only the lights hadn't gone out the moment Shane was born," Liam said. "Shelby would have noticed the birthmark—and noticed that it was gone when she next held her baby. Because she was holding the wrong infant."

"I'd mixed them up in my mind even before I put on their bracelets," Kate said. "How could I have done such a thing? I'd been a nurse for over thirty years. I am so, so sorry for what I did. I take full responsibility."

Liam looked at Shelby. He watched her get up and go sit down next to the retired nurse and put her arms around her. The woman looked so surprised that she burst into tears and held tightly on to Shelby.

"It was an honest mistake in the chaos of a terrible snowstorm," Liam said. "It happened and that's that. Nothing's going to undo it so we just all have to accept it and move on."

Kate wiped under her eyes with a tissue. "You sure are being kind about this. My daughter said we should expect to be sued."

"No one is suing anyone, Kate," Liam said. "I want you to put that worry out of your head."

The woman burst into tears again, covering her face with her hands.

"Kate?" someone called from upstairs. "Is it time for my soup? Where is my soup?"

Kate took a breath. "That's my mother. She's elderly and not very well."

"We won't take any more of your time," Liam said. "Thanks for meeting with us."

"Yes, thank you," Shelby said. "It was helpful to hear what happened. How it happened."

Kate walked them to the door, her mother calling about her soup again. "Are you going to switch the babies back?"

Shelby froze.

Liam felt momentarily sick.

It was the first time anyone had actually asked that question.

"No, ma'am," Liam said. "I have a better idea."

Shelby glanced at him, questions in her eyes.

"Where is my soup!" Kate's mother called again.

"You go ahead, Kate," Shelby said, stepping out onto the porch. "Thanks for talking to us."

Kate nodded and shut the door behind them.

Liam leaned his head back and he headed down the porch steps. "I need about ten cups of coffee or a bottle of scotch."

"I thought I might fall over when she asked about switching the babies back," Shelby said, her face pale, her green eyes troubled. She stared at him. "You said you had a better idea. What is it? I sure need to hear it. Because switching the babies is not an option. Right?"

"Damned straight it's not. Never will be. Shane is your son. Alexander is my son. No matter what. Alexander will also become your son and Shane will also become my son as the days pass and all this sinks in."

"I think so, too," she said. "Right now it's like we can't even process that babies we didn't know until Friday are ours biologically. But as we begin to accept it, I'll start to feel a connection to Alexander. Same with you and Shane."

He nodded. "Exactly. Which is why on the way here, I started thinking about a way to ease us into that, to give us both what we need and want."

She tilted her head, waiting.

He thought he had the perfect solution. The only solution.

"I called the lab running the DNA tests and threw a bucket of money at them to expedite the results. On Monday," he continued, "we will officially know for absolute certain that our babies were switched. Of course we're not going to switch them back. I'd sooner cut off my arm."

"Me, too," Shelby said, staring at him. "So what's your plan?"

"The plan is for us to get married."

Shelby's mouth dropped open. "What? We've been living together for a day. Now we're getting married. Legally wed? Till death do us part?"

Liam opened Shelby's car door, and she got in, her entire body feeling like rubber. He shut the door and came round and got in. "Let's get out of here and talk. We'll go to my ranch. Then we'll pick up the boys."

She nodded, all she could manage. Married? What?

"On Monday we'll know with certainty, Shelby. You have my child and I have yours. You've been raising my son and I've been raising yours. You love Shane and I love Alexander. If we marry, if we join together as a family unit, we each have the boys we've been raising and the baby we didn't know was ours."

"Join together as a family unit," she repeated. "So… we're getting married to become a family. For the boys' sake and ours."

"Yes. Precisely."

Her baby's father floated into her mind. *One day we'll get married and it'll be us against the world. We'll have a big old house in the country, a chicken coop, maybe even horses. We'll watch reality TV and go to the rodeo and die old, fat and happy.*

They'd gotten married at the famed Wedlock Creek Chapel. Legend said that those who married at the chapel would have multiples in some way, shape or form: twins, triplets, quadruplets, even quintuplets, whether through nature, science, marriage, or adoption. The town and county was full of big families with identical twins and fraternal triplets. Morgan Crawford had said he'd hoped they'd have quintuplets. Except by the time she did discover she was pregnant, Morgan had two other girlfriends. One of whom was the supposed real love of his life. When Shelby, who had no clue her new husband was cheating on her, told him she was pregnant, he said he was sorry but he was filing for divorce and that, "I'm sorry, Shel, but happiness has to come first."

She was around six months along when she'd heard he'd died in a car wreck. Shelby had been very sad about the whole sorry story for so long that her sister had moved in with her for two weeks and made her scrambled eggs and toast every morning and minded the shop, letting her just lie on her sofa, her hands on her growing belly, unsure what anything meant anymore. If you couldn't trust the word of the man you loved, the man you thought loved you, the man you'd *married*, what could you believe in?

Heck, she couldn't even believe in the legend of the Wedlock Creek Chapel. She was pregnant with *one* baby, which was more than fine with her. But maybe true love and legends only came true for others.

You believe in this, Norah had said, taking Shelby's hands and putting them on her stomach, where she'd felt a good, hard kick. That kick had made her burst into a smile, her first in weeks, and from that moment on, she'd been fine. She had her baby-to-be. She had her family. She had Treasures. Her trust had been breached, but who said she had to let another man into her life? She certainly didn't plan to. Not for a long while, anyway.

Now here was Liam Mercer proposing they marry for the most practical of reasons. Maybe she shouldn't pooh-pooh it, no matter how much she believed that love, deep, abiding, lasting love, was real and waiting for her. Right now her heart was guarded with barbed wire.

But marry a man without love as the main reason? Come on.

"Think about it," he said. "I think it's a good solution. The only solution, really."

"But what about the future? What about love, Liam?"

He snorted. "Love? That's for fairy-tale endings. No—I take it back. I do love Alexander. And I'm going to love Shane the moment I let myself go and trust me, I've been fighting it."

She felt herself go limp. "I know. Me, too."

"Monday, the results will say that Shane is my flesh

and blood. And the floodgates are going to open, Shelby.
I think the same will happen to you."

"I know it will."

He pulled over and put the SUV in Park and turned to
face her, reaching for her hand. "So, let's have our children. Both children. Together. A family unit."

She noticed he kept saying a family unit instead of a
family. Because family implied something else, whereas
a family unit sounded more like a business term. Because this would be a businesslike marriage. A merger,
a spousal acquisition for the benefit of both parties. And
both minor parties.

"I will think about it, Liam. But I won't give you an
answer until I see the DNA results."

"Understood."

He put the car in Drive and continued on, signaling
for the service road that would lead back into town.

Marriage. To Liam Mercer.

Chapter 7

Shelby had needed a break from their conversation, so instead of going back to Liam's ranch to talk, they picked up the babies and each went their separate ways with the plan to meet up for dinner at home—home being Shelby's apartment. When Liam had dropped her and Shane off, he hadn't mentioned the proposal, and she'd gotten out of the car so fast it was a wonder she hadn't dropped Shane on his head. Maybe getting married was a ridiculous idea. But it seemed the only good one. The only solution to one hell of a situation.

"How about we go see the goats at Grandma and Grandpa's?" Liam said to Alexander as they pulled onto Main Street.

Of course from his rearview mirror he only had a view of the back of the baby's rear-facing car seat, but he still imagined Alexander smiling and clapping his hands about going to see the goats. As for Liam, he needed the open air and the hundreds of acres of wild Wyoming land. His own property had almost a hundred acres but was closer to town and more developed than his parents' place twenty miles out. Besides, he needed a sense of familiarity, of grounding about who he was.

He also wanted his father to show him that Harrington Mercer was back to being the loving, doting grandfather he'd always been. He didn't like being on the outs with his dad; they'd always gotten along, and Liam had always prided himself on understanding his father when his brother wouldn't even try. He'd stuck up for Harrington Mercer in arguments with Drake so many times over the years. But the way his father had thrown around words like *real grandson* had sent shock waves through his gut. He didn't like it and he needed that nonsense over and done with. He was sure his father would be back to his old self today now that he'd had some time.

As he pulled up in the circular drive, Harrington Mercer was just coming back from the stable, his usually perfectly coiffed salt-and-pepper thick hair a bit mussed, which meant he'd been out riding.

"Thought I'd show your grandson the goats," Liam said as he got out of the car and took out Alexander. He turned toward the penned pasture where around ten goats of all colors were grazing.

"Sure," Harrington said, his voice strained. Liam noticed he didn't reach for Alexander. Or say one word to him, as a matter of fact. "Your mother and I have a fund-raising dinner, so just see yourself out when you're done here."

Alexander reached out his hands for his grandfather, whom he adored. "Ga," he said, one of his only words.

Harrington glanced at the baby. "I'd better hit the showers." With that he turned and walked away.

"Stop right now," Liam said, his voice so cold it surprised even him. "Your grandson is reaching for you."

"I just told you—"

"I know what you said, Dad. I want to hear what you're *not* saying."

"I'm preparing myself, okay?" Harrington said, a mix of anguish and resolve in his eyes. "You're expecting the DNA tests soon. They're going to say that Alexander isn't a Mercer. That he's not my grandson. I need to prepare for that, Liam. I need to take a step back."

Liam's legs actually buckled. He expelled a breath and tried to collect himself, to get over the sharp left hook his brain just took. "Not a Mercer? Not your grandson? Dad, he was your grandson two days ago. He's your grandson now. He'll be your grandson Monday, no matter what the hell the DNA tests say."

"The DNA results will say he's that Ingalls woman's child. He's her baby. He's her father's grandson."

Liam sucked in a breath. "And *that Ingalls woman's* child—Shane? On Monday is he suddenly going to become your grandson?"

"I suppose he is. I'll have to work that out in my own time, get to know him."

"Dad, Alexander is your grandson and will always be. Just as he'll always be my son."

"That's not how life works, Liam."

"It damn well is." He looked at Alexander for a long moment, then turned and walked away.

Red-hot anger was working its way up every nerve

in Liam's body. He stomped back to his SUV, put Alexander back inside as gently as he could given his mood and peeled out of there. Ten minutes ago he'd needed this land, the place he'd grown up, to soothe him, to ground him. Now he never wanted to step foot here again.

Shelby wrapped the adorable elephant salt-and-pepper shakers in pink tissue paper, put them in a Treasures bag and handed it over to her smiling customer. The woman had actually left five minutes earlier with a pricey tea set that Shelby had found at an estate sale a few weeks ago, but she'd returned, unable to stop thinking about the shakers. Her customers often did that. And that was how the heart worked. You might pass something up, but if you couldn't stop thinking about it, especially a minute after leaving, you had to come back and make it your own.

This afternoon had been good for business. Her sister, Norah, had filled in for her this morning while she and Liam had been out to see Kate Atwood. Shelby usually told Norah everything, but she found herself holding back the bit about the marriage proposal. Shelby could barely wrap her mind around it.

And she was grateful that the shop had been busy all day. Between answering questions about the origin of pieces—she usually had no idea—and whether lightbulbs came with the lamps—no—and if she'd go down ten dollars on the price—usually, since she expected to be asked—she'd barely had time to think about Liam's proposal. Marriage.

Her gaze landed on the brown paper bag that Liam's mother had given her last night; she'd brought it down to examine it further during slow times, and there was finally a lull. She glanced at Shane, napping in his bouncer seat behind the gated register area, then excitedly reached in the bag and pulled out the wrapped box, quickly taking off the newspaper.

The music box was so beautiful. And so old. Shelby guessed it was at least a hundred years old and had been passed down from generation to generation. She ran her hand on the pretty pink velvet lining, worn with use, and she imagined what had been in this box over the decades—brooches and earrings and pearl necklaces, beloved treasures. As her fingertip brushed the far edge of the lining, she realized there was something underneath. She tugged at the side and it released easily. The lining had a smooth edge that would easily tuck back under.

Under the lining was a folded-up piece of paper!

A secret note? A love letter? Should she read it or tuck it back and leave the writer the privacy he or she had expected by hiding it under the lining?

But the music box had ended up in her possession. So maybe it was okay to read it. Just the first line or two, and if it belonged to someone she knew she'd stop reading immediately and return it.

The bell jangled, and Shelby looked up. Liam. Looking absolutely awful. Well, looking absolutely gorgeous but angry. He was pacing, Alexander in his baby carrier, fast asleep.

Secret note, you will have to wait until later. She tucked it back under the lining and put the music box back in the bag and stowed it under her desk, lest anyone think the box was for sale.

"You okay?" she asked. He clearly wasn't.

Steam was practically coming out of his ears. "My

father doesn't think of Alexander as his grandson anymore. He's not a Mercer anymore, apparently. He's an Ingalls."

Shelby froze, the idea of that innocent baby being rejected by his grandfather too much to take in. "What?"

As three women came in to browse, Shelby smiled tightly at them, then took Liam's hand and pulled him closer to the wall. "Not his grandson? What?"

She watched his face as he told her what happened at his parents' house. So many emotions flashed—fury, hurt, bewilderment.

"No one turns their back on my son. Especially not my father," he growled under his breath.

"Alexander is your son, no matter what," she said. "And as you told your father, he always will be, also no matter what. What you feel for him is in here—" she added, touching her heart. "That won't change because of DNA."

"Well, apparently my father is heartless. That's the only excuse I can think of."

Except from what Liam had told her of his father, Harrington Mercer wasn't heartless. Why would he shun the baby he loved so much? It made no sense.

She reached for Liam's hand. "I'm so sorry. He must be going through some major adjustment issues over this. I'm sure he'll come around."

"Adjustment issues? He doesn't get the right. The situation is what it damned well is," he added on a harsh whisper. "Accept it and carry on. That's the only way to go."

"Maybe you're a lot stronger than he is, Liam. Maybe he just needs time."

"I don't care what he needs," he snapped. He stopped, leaned his head back and let out a breath, then looked at her. "Sorry. I don't mean to take this out on you. I need to go upstairs, put Alexander down for his nap and take a hot shower. I could use some time to myself so it's good that you need to work. See you at closing."

She nodded and gave him something of a commiserating smile and her heart went out to him as he trudged past her, hurt and anger so evident in his eyes.

Dammit.

An hour and forty minutes until closing. For a moment Shelby considered turning the open sign to closed and locking up for the day. Time alone or not, Liam needed her. But the Minnow sisters walked in just then.

"Missed you yesterday," Callie said, her emerald silky scarf lovely against her hazel eyes.

"We waited a half hour, but you never opened," Bea added. "We were so worried. I hope you're okay."

She smiled at the three kind elderly sisters. "I'm fine. I just had something unexpected to attend to and it went on a bit longer than I thought it would. Sorry about that. But come on in and look around. I did put some new things out. June," she said to the only redhead among the blonde sisters, "I found a wonderful framed old map of Wyoming from the turn of the last century. I know you love old maps."

The women excitedly began looking at the merchandise, June beelining for the art wall.

For the next fifteen minutes, she vaguely listened as the sisters talked about the history of Wedlock Creek, one eye on the cuckoo clock and the other at the door, which kept opening as post-rodeo Saturday shoppers came in.

In the next hour alone, Shelby made over four hundred dollars. Not bad at all. But nothing was worth thinking of Liam upstairs alone, stewing, hurt, angry. Finally, six o'clock chimed, and Shelby flipped the sign, grabbed Shane's carrier and headed upstairs. It wasn't until she'd unlocked the apartment door that she realized she'd left the music box downstairs behind the counter. Drat. She'd come back for it later. Now all she wanted was to talk to Liam.

She didn't hear a sound when she entered the apartment. She headed into the nursery and saw Alexander sleeping in his bassinet. She lowered Shane into his crib and kissed his forehead, then began tiptoeing out, her ears straining for any sign of Liam. The apartment was dead quiet.

It was only when she was about to walk through the nursery doorway when she spotted him, again deliciously half-naked in a pair of navy sweats on the glider chair in the corner, a book about a talking pear open on his lap. He was asleep, the dim lighting casting shadows on his handsome face.

She fought the urge to curl up on his lap and listen to his heartbeat, which was what she wanted to do. Their children were in this room. Liam was in this room.

Her heart was in this room.

She was falling in love with him.

The truth hit her upside the head to the point that she had to put her hand on the doorknob to steady her legs. *Yes, I'm falling in love with you*, she said to his beautiful, sleeping form. *You're caring and kind and a great dad and you've shown me so much consideration and tenderness. And God, look at you*, she thought, her gaze going from all that silky, thick, dark hair to his long eye-

lashes resting at the tops of his cheeks, the chiseled jawline with just a hint of five o'clock shadow, the strong
neck and broad shoulders and that chest, muscular and
practically hairless, the waistband of his sweats covering long legs. Even his bare feet were sexy.

She was going to marry this man? This man who
didn't believe in love and had proposed a marriage for
circumstances' sake? Try as she might not to consider his
proposal, she'd thought about it constantly. It did seem
like the only solution. They would be a family unit. No
one would lose anything. The babies would have their
parent and their biological parent, and Liam and Shelby
would have their sanity.

But would she really? Or would she go absolutely
bonkers? She was already feeling too much for Liam
Mercer. What if she fell whole hog in love with him
and he made it even more crystal clear that this wasn't
a romantic union, that love had nothing to do with it?

This isn't about your love life, dope, she reminded
herself. *It's about keeping Shane and raising Alexander. It's about the babies. It's about keeping your heart
intact.*

Yes, she would remember that. The whole point of
marrying Liam Mercer was so that she would have both
babies and not have her heart shredded. If she kept that
vital point at the forefront, she would remember that
that was where her heart had to lie—with the boys. Not
the man.

*I will marry you, Liam Mercer. If I got through that
meeting on Friday morning with the Wedlock Creek
Clinic administrator, I can get through anything.*

She'd let him know on Monday—when the results
came in.

* * *

Liam woke up just about every hour on the hour Sunday night, the anticipation of tomorrow too much for his brain to handle. He already knew, intellectually, that Alexander wasn't his biological son and that the DNA test would reveal that Shane was. But he still couldn't wrap his mind around it, believe it on a gut level.

He cursed and threw the blanket off and got out of bed, trying to be as quiet as possible. He needed a shot of whiskey. Something to turn his brain off and get him back to sleep.

The kitchen light was on, and he slowly approached, not sure if Shelby would want company at 3:12 in the morning. For a moment he stood in the doorway and just watched her, sitting at the round table by the window, her hands wrapped around a blue cup, steam still emanating. She wasn't facing him, but he could see the tightness in her face, her jawline.

"You, too, huh?" he whispered.

She turned and nodded and then burst into tears.

"Shelby," he said, rushing over to her. He leaned down and put his arms around her, and she shot up and wrapped her arms around him, sobbing full force. "I know," he soothed. "I know exactly how you feel." He tightened his hold on her and let her cry, resting his head on top of hers. Her hair was silky and smelled like coconuts.

Talk about getting his mind off tomorrow. Who needed whiskey when there was beautiful, sweet Shelby smelling like the beach?

"It's going to be okay," he whispered. "We're going to make it okay. You and me. We're going to be a family, Shelby."

He felt her nodding her head against his chest, her sobs subsiding, her breathing ragged. She sucked in a breath and just stayed in his arms. He reached a hand to her hair and stroked the silky blond mass, then lifted her face to his.

"Everything is going to be okay," he repeated.

She looked up at him, and he could see she was trying to believe it, to make herself believe it. "Sometimes I'll believe anything you say, Liam."

"Now's the time. Because we're going to make it okay. We just have to remember that everything we do is to keep our children. To have the children we were denied. If we remember why we're here, why we're doing this, we'll keep what's important at the forefront."

"I want Shane and I want Alexander."

"I want Alexander and I want Shane," he said. "Getting married makes that happen. And it'll make it a lot easier if we need to formally adopt the babies we've been raising for six months and the ones we haven't been."

She nodded and wiped under her eyes, and he pulled her close again. This time she just held on tightly, not saying anything.

The urge to kiss her was so overpowering that Liam loosened his hold on her. He wanted her so bad, to let his hands fall from around her shoulders down her back to her waist and up to her breasts.

Did he not just tell Shelby they had to focus on what was important: the children? Letting himself feel more for Shelby, giving in to his attraction for her, would make for a hot night, but would end up ruining everything down the line. Romance died. Love faded. People moved on. He and Shelby couldn't take the risk of a failed romance getting in the way of their family.

He pulled back and dropped his hold on her.

"Everything is going to be okay," she repeated, a wobbly smile on her face.

Now suddenly he wasn't so sure himself.

Chapter 8

Monday was a rainy, chilly mess. Good, Liam thought, glancing out the window of the Wedlock Creek Clinic. The perfect kind of day for absolute proof that you walked out the clinic with someone else's baby. That someone else walked out with your baby.

He glanced at Shelby sitting next to him. She sat ramrod straight, staring ahead, the strain on her face unbearable to him. He reached a hand down to squeeze hers, and she glanced at him for a moment and squeezed back, then let go.

The moment of truth had arrived.

The administrator handed each of the attorneys, sitting on either side of them, a copy of the test results. She cleared her throat and from the way she closed and opened her eyes very quickly, he knew without a doubt what the results said.

"Ms. Ingalls, you are not the biological mother of Shane Ingalls," Anne Parcells said. "You are the biological mother of Alexander Mercer. Mr. Mercer, you are not the biological father of Alexander Mercer. You are the biological father of Shane Ingalls. Based on the findings and discussions with the nurse on duty the night of November 5, it is our understanding that the babies were, indeed, accidentally switched."

This time, Shelby gripped his hand and held on.

"I meant what I said," he whispered. "It's going to be okay. We have a plan. Let's both remember that and we'll get through this meeting."

She bit her lip and nodded, her hold tightening on his hand. He couldn't even say this was the worst moment, finding out with absolute certainty that Alexander was not his child. No, that honor went to the first meeting, in this office, when a part of his brain was trying to understand what the administrator was saying—that the two male babies born the night of November 5 had been switched. He'd never forget it, the way everything in him had seized up. There had been times in his life when the world, including his own personal one, didn't make sense. But nothing would ever come close to how he'd felt when Anne Parcells had implied the babies had been switched.

Liam's attorney whispered in his ear about whether or not he'd changed his mind about the lawsuit. He had not. Shelby's attorney, whom Liam had learned on the way over was actually her sister's new boyfriend, also whispered something in Shelby's ear. He watched her shake her head.

Liam stood. "I speak for both myself and Shelby Ingalls. There will be no lawsuit. There be no litigation of any kind against this clinic, which serves a vital purpose to our county, or against the nurse, Kate Atwood. A mistake was made during a raging snowstorm. It wasn't about negligence. It was about act-of-God chaos."

"I appreciate that, Mr. Mercer," Anne Parcells said, relief visible on her face.

"I suppose you two have some things to work out between you, then," David Dirk said, glancing from Shelby to Liam.

"Actually, we have worked things out privately," Shelby said.

Did that mean she would accept his marriage proposal? Liam sure hoped so.

"Very good," Dirk said. "Shelby, please know if you need my services, just call. I'm here for you."

Shelby nodded. "I appreciate that, David."

With that, he left. Liam's attorney clapped him on the back, tapped Alexander on the nose and left, too.

Liam and Shelby stood, said goodbye to the administrator and headed out, and it wasn't until his face met the air that he realized he'd been holding his breath. Shelby stood beside him, her blond hair whipping behind her in the breeze, her expression fierce and sad and resigned.

He put his arm around her. "My son, your son, our sons. Doesn't matter which one we're talking about."

He saw her eyes glisten before she nodded. "My son, your son, our sons."

He pressed a kiss to Alexander's forehead and held him close. Shelby was doing the same to Shane.

"I accept your proposal, Liam. The family unit marriage. I accept."

"Good," he said. "Good."

"I suppose we'll go to the town hall and have the mayor marry us? She can probably do it this week."

"Town hall or whatever you want. Shelby. If you want a church wedding or the Wedlock Creek Chapel or the backyard at your mom's or if you want to clear an aisle in Treasures, I'll marry you wherever and whenever will make you happy."

She stilled and stared at him. "Happy? That's not really part of this."

"This might not be the traditional kind of marriage, Shelby, but it's legal and binding and we're going to be saying vows. I want you to have the wedding you want. Not what feels appropriate for the situation—who even knows what kind of wedding that would be."

She tilted her head. Not the beautiful Wedlock Creek Chapel, that was for sure. Been there, done that. "A town hall wedding. But I'll think on it. And thank you. Once again, there you go showing me a very thoughtful, kind side of yourself."

"I know this isn't easy, Shelby. I know this can't be what you dreamed of when you dreamed about your wedding day. But let's make it as special as it deserves to be. We're each getting a new son, six months after the fact, who happens to be our flesh and blood. That damned well deserves a parade."

She hugged him with her free arm, and he was glad he made her feel better.

"What kind of wedding do *you* want?" she asked.

"As long as I'm marrying you, I don't much care otherwise."

She bit her lip and turned away. "Well, I'm going to see my family, to let them know the results. They're waiting on pins and needles."

She hurried away and he wanted her to come back. Her and Shane. "I'll see you at home in about an hour, okay? We'll plan it all out."

He nodded and he watched her as she settled Shane in her little silver car, then got in and drove off, taking two big pieces of himself with her.

"Wait," Norah said, forkful of Shelby's mocha chip pie in midair. "He said 'As long as I'm marrying you, I don't much care otherwise'?"

Shelby sat in the cushioned booth of her family's Pie Diner, Norah next to her, her mother and aunt Cheyenne across. The café was pretty busy but the moment the three women heard the words *I'm getting married* come out of Shelby's mouth, they rushed around to fill orders and coffee cups and slap down checks, then slid in, her sister stealing bites of her pie.

"But that sounds like he has feelings for you," Erin Ingalls said. "Are you sure he doesn't?"

"Very sure. He meant it as in, you're Alexander's biological mother and Shane's mother in all ways that matter. He didn't mean in the romantic sense. For a man who doesn't believe in love, I'm the only logical woman to marry based on the circumstances."

"Men who don't believe in love wouldn't marry at all," Aunt Cheyenne put in on a whisper, pointing to the two huge gossips who slid into the booth behind Shelby's.

"Well, the marriage won't be about love," Shelby reminded them. "Except the love of two six-month-old babies. We're joining as a family for our sakes and theirs."

"Don't tell me he's jetting you off to Vegas for a quick ceremony," Shelby's mom said. "This may be a marriage of circumstance but if my girl is getting married, I don't want to miss it."

Shelby smiled but it took some doing. "The whole thing is just so… I don't even know the right word. It's not a sham marriage. It's not a real marriage. It's just the only thing we can do. I don't know that a big celebration is in order."

"Well, it's certainly not temporary, either," Norah said. "Church wedding? Wedlock Creek Chapel? Reception in the backyard?"

Shelby did love her mother's backyard with its woods and trees and the pretty white lights hung across the deck railing. But a church wedding and a reception at home? No. That was just going too far. She thought again about the gorgeous Wedlock Creek Chapel where she'd married Morgan after their whirlwind courtship. She'd dreamed of marrying there and that dream had been spit on.

Huh. Maybe she could take back the dream. Get married at the chapel again. It wasn't as if she and Liam would be having sex, so the old legend about newlyweds being blessed with multiples wouldn't even have a chance to come true.

Her mind made up, Shelby finally dug into her pie. Mocha whip-chip pie—delicious. "I think the Wedlock Creek Chapel, and afterward we can take the boys to the park."

"I'm so glad you didn't choose the town hall," her mother said. "I know the marriage is just about paperwork and legalities. But it's still a ceremony. And there's no more beautiful place to marry than the chapel."

Shelby nodded. "Agreed. The marriage is definitely only about the legality. And then we'll start the paperwork to each adopt our biological baby. Liam is looking into whether we need to legally adopt the boys we took home, too."

Aunt Cheyenne shook her head. "What a thing." She rested her hand on Shelby's. "It may not be a love marriage, but Liam Mercer sounds like a good man, and you'll both have both boys."

Shelby nodded. "That's what's important. Not my love life. And we're both entering this marriage knowing what's what. So it's not like anyone can get hurt."

She caught her mother, aunt and sister glance at one another. Who was she kidding? Someone was going to get hurt and that someone was Shelby. Because she was falling in love with her fiancé. Getting married, living together as husband and wife, watching him be a father to their children, would only make her love him more.

You just have to put up a wall between you two, she told herself, sipping her coffee. But how?

"So, how's this going to work exactly?" Norah asked. She leaned forward and whispered, "I mean, once you're married, will you…?"

Shelby tilted her head. "What?" Three pairs of Ingalls green eyes stared at her with various glints of curiosity, amusement and wonder.

Ah.

They were talking about sex. About the bedroom.

"We haven't exactly talked about any of that stuff," Shelby said. "Guess we'd better."

"You two should square away on everything before the wedding," her mother said, getting up as a man could be heard muttering that the waitresses were sitting down on the job. "*Everything*. Make a list."

"What should be on it?" Shelby asked. "Besides the bedroom question."

"Well, that's number one," Norah said, sliding out of the booth and holding up a "gimme a minute" finger at a customer. "The rest you two need to come up with together."

As her family hugged her and got back to work, Shelby tried to think of what else they should get clear on, but everything was jumbled around in her head.

All she could really think about was that she was going to marry Liam Mercer. The handsome, kind man she'd been unable to stop thinking about last night as she lay in bed, her cat snuggled in a ball beside her. She knew what he slept in, just a pair of low-slung sweats, and it had been difficult to get his incredible body off her mind. And then she'd gotten out of bed to have some herbal tea and he'd come into the kitchen and she'd lost it.

She'd sobbed in his arms and he'd held her so close, making her believe what he was saying, that everything really would be okay. When they'd finally left the kitchen and gone back to their rooms, she'd wanted to slip inside his room with him, curl up beside him in bed, just to have his strong arms around her. But there would be no curling and cuddling in this union. Her dear cat would have to continue in that role.

A romance-free marriage, given the circumstances, was entirely appropriate. It was the way to go.

After what had happened with Shane's father, the way he'd become Dr. Jekyll and Mr. Hyde, Shelby hadn't been planning on falling for anyone for a good long time. Her plan had been to be a good mother, build her business and spend time with her family—people she knew she could trust no matter what.

Now here she was, about to marry a man she barely knew but had to trust and—God help her—did.

She just couldn't afford to love him. As if putting the brakes on love was possible. It might be for Liam Mercer, who seemed to have amazing powers of self-control. But a little part of her held out hope that even he wouldn't be able to stop love at full speed if what was blossoming between them grew into more.

Unless she was mistaking his kindness and concern for something else. She'd mistaken her ex's lying personality for sincerity. So maybe Shelby had better take a big step backward and focus on the family. The family *unit*, she amended.

Feeling stronger, more grounded and comfortable with moving forward, she took another bite of pie.

When Liam arrived back at Shelby's apartment from the Chinese restaurant with their take-out order, he froze and panicked with an *Oh, my God, I forgot Alexander at China Taste!* Then he remembered he wasn't on his own anymore; he lived with someone, someone who was watching Alexander while he picked up dinner.

Someone he was going to marry.

The whole thing had been his idea but he still couldn't quite get used to it. He'd been solely responsible for his son and now Shelby would be equally responsible. As would he for Shane. That was the one absolute they'd discussed so far in terms of how their marriage would work. Shelby had brought up the idea of setting parameters when she'd come up from Treasures an hour ago, and since they both needed to think about what their must-haves and deal-breakers were, they'd agreed that Liam would go pick up dinner and they'd work it all out over lo mein and fried dumplings and General Tso's chicken.

As he set the bag on the big coffee table, Shelby hopped up and headed to the kitchen, and he could barely take his eyes off her. She'd changed into faded jeans that hugged her curves and long legs and wore a V-neck dark blue ruffly shirt that made her eyes even more emerald-like. She returned with a tray of plates, silverware, glasses and a pitcher of iced tea. Both babies were fast asleep in the nursery, so the timing was good for chowing down and having a very serious, important discussion.

They dug in before getting to the nitty gritty of the impending conversation. Liam tried to cut a dumpling in half and it went flying across the coffee table, immediately inspected by her cat, Luna, who'd finally warmed up to Liam. Luna wrinkled her nose at the dumpling and walked away.

They shared a good laugh over that, the tension abating somewhat.

"Ooh, vegetable fried rice—my favorite," she said, heaping some on her plate.

"Mine, too."

"Well, ordering Chinese as a married couple will be a snap," she said. "Except there may be arguments over leftovers."

"I'd always leave you the last dumpling," he said.

She tilted her head and looked at him. "You would, wouldn't you?"

He nodded. "I told you I'd never do anything to hurt you. That includes matters of the stomach."

She laughed. "Good to know." She ate a few more

forkfuls. "So I guess we'd better start figuring out what we both expect from this marriage-to-be."

"Well, we have our first thing, that we are both equally responsible for both babies. That Shane is no more yours than mine. That Alexander is no more mine than yours. They are *our* children."

"Right. That's number one. It may take a little time, though, and we both need to be okay with it. I already love Alexander and I've known him for a weekend. I've loved Shane for his entire six months on earth and of course our bond is very strong. Both of us just need to catch up."

Liam nodded and twirled a forkful of lo mein. "Exactly. And we will."

"Number two," Shelby began, pushing around her fried rice as though stalling for time. "The marriage is legal, yes, but we'll have separate bedrooms."

The emphasis on the word *separate* told him she was talking about sex—the lack of, actually.

"Separate bedrooms, like now," he agreed. But the thought had been put in his head, about sharing a bedroom and lying next to soft, sweet, smart Shelby. She was so lovely, so sexy, without a shred of makeup and in jeans. He could so easily imagine lifting that ruffly shirt off her, seeing what was underneath. A lace bra. Underwear sexy just by virtue of it being on her luscious body.

His mind was going places it had no business wandering. Especially because he'd just agreed that their marriage would be platonic—which he'd always known would be the case. Separate bedrooms. No sex. No making out.

"Separate bedrooms," he agreed.

"Good," she said, forking a dumpling and dipping it in soy sauce.

"Right, good."

Good for the marriage, bad for him on a personal level because the control and restraint he'd have to put forth would zap all his energy.

Get back to the marriage—the reason for the marriage, he told himself. *Forget sex. You'll have to, anyway.*

"I have a condition, as well," he said, "One that goes in tandem with number one. Neither of us can make a decision about either baby without the other's agreement. I'm used to being the boss, so this won't be easy for me, but I know I don't want you to make decisions without my approval so I won't make any without yours."

"Agreed. I trust that we both have the babies' best interests at heart. After all, that's why we're getting married in the first place. So they both have the two of us. So we have the two of them."

Liam nodded. "So far, we make a great team. We see eye to eye."

"I know," she said. "It does make things easier."

They saw eye to eye because they were just plain compatible. They had the same values. They found the same things funny. And sad. They cared about the same things: two six-month-old boys. And those boys were the most important things in the world to both of them.

The marriage would work out fine. He was sure of it. If he could keep his attraction to Shelby at bay, the marriage would be a real success. There would be no hurt glances, no disappointments, no arguments over perceived romantic slights.

But keeping his emotional distance from her would

be easier on his own turf. Here, everything *was* Shelby. It was all Shelby, all the time. At his ranch, there would be so much more space for the two of them. The four of them. It would be a hell of a lot easier to keep an emotional distance if he had a physical one.

And he'd need that, too. She was too close here, all the time.

He glanced around at her crowded apartment, then back at Shelby. "Is it important to you that we live here? I mean, it's cozy and I like being here, Shelby, but it's pretty small. I'd prefer we move out to my ranch. We can keep the boys together in the nursery, and you'll have a big bedroom. Plus, there's a family room and a lot of space for two boys to grow up."

"I'll make you a deal. We live here until they start walking. Then we'll move to the ranch since they'll need the space. But right now I need to be on my turf. Is that selfish? I know you probably feel the same way."

"I can understand, Shelby. You feel safe here. And your livelihood is downstairs. You're connected to your life here. We'll stay until they start walking."

He'd just deal with it. Power through. Try not to accidentally brush up against her in the small kitchen. Not imagine her naked in the shower in the one tiny bathroom.

Her smile lit up her entire face. But then it faded. "I've thought about the ceremony and all that. I decided on the Wedlock Creek Chapel, but maybe we should just go to the town hall and have Mayor Franklin marry us. After, we could throw a dinner party—at your ranch since this place couldn't hold one side of our families let alone both. Though my family will probably want to hold a part at the Pie Diner."

"Town hall? You sure that's what you want? Money is no object, Shelby. If you want a big wedding, I'm happy to give you the shindig of your dreams."

She put her fork down. "My dreams? Liam, the wedding of my dreams doesn't involve marrying a man I don't love. A man who doesn't love me. All the Mercer money can't change that."

"Understood," he said. "I just want this to be as... I don't even know. I'm asking a lot of you, Shelby. To—as you said, marry a man you don't love. I guess I just want to make it as easy as possible, to give you everything you want. Does that make sense?"

She smiled again. "Yes. And I appreciate it. But I come from a family of bakers, Liam, and we've known since birth that icing can't make a lopsided cake less lopsided."

"Well, then, let me tell you this. As your husband in this venture, Shelby, I'll always respect you in every way. You can count on me. Just know that. Maybe not in all the ways you used to think about. But you can count on me."

"It might take me a while to believe that, really believe it. So don't take it personally if I don't seem to trust you right away. Given my past..." Her cheeks pinkened and she pushed more rice around on her plate.

"Shane's father hurt you pretty bad," he said gently, hating the idea of anyone hurting Shelby.

"Oh, just the usual case of saying one thing and then doing the complete opposite. He said all the right things, all the right romantic things, and I fell big-time. We got married after a whirlwind relationship. But just when I discovered I was pregnant, I found out he had two girlfriends. I confronted him and he said he was young and a free spirit and 'wasn't that why I fell for him?' Uh, no. He filed for divorce and left town with the one girl-friend he said he was his true love. When I was around six months along, I heard he died in a car accident."

"Sorry," he said. "It couldn't have been an easy time to be pregnant and treated that way."

"I never felt so alone. Or scared. I just kept thinking, what about the baby? He won't have a father? It wasn't supposed to be like this."

"Life can be like that, huh?"

She gave him something of a smile. "Don't we know it."

He reached for her hand and held it for a second. "I'll never betray you, Shelby. I can promise you that."

"Well, this isn't a love marriage, so betrayal really isn't an issue."

"There are lots of ways to betray someone."

She looked at him, her expression serious. "Yeah. You're right."

"But it's true that we're not in this for love or romance. This is about both of us having our children, becoming a family. It's about family."

She nodded.

He could keep telling himself this wasn't about romance all he wanted. But he couldn't take his eyes off Shelby. Couldn't stop picturing her naked. Couldn't stop imagining his hands gliding up her shirt, exploring every inch of her skin.

He wanted her, but he'd control himself, of course; control was Liam Mercer's middle name.

He took a sip of his beer. "Tomorrow, let's apply for our marriage license and find out what we need to do there, then we can start the ball rolling on formally adopting the boys. I'm not even sure if we each need to adopt the babies we took home. We'll need to get all our questions answered."

"This could have gone so differently if we were different people. Or if one of us or even both of us were married or involved with significant others. I think I should be grateful to have this opportunity to have both boys."

"That's how I look at it." He was grateful. And marrying to make it all happen wasn't taking anything away from him since he hadn't planned on marrying anyone. Loving anyone.

"After everything you went through with Shane's father, you still believe in love and happily-ever-after?" he asked.

"That's moot now," she said.

He wondered if she didn't answer because she did still believe in love or because she didn't. But she was right. The topic was moot. They'd marry to have their family unit.

This was a business partnership, really, with family as the business and the partnership. He was good at business. He'd be good at this marriage.

"So we each know what to expect, what this marriage will involve, and we'll be off to a great start," he said.

"My sister, Norah, texted me earlier. If we choose to get married at the Wedlock Creek Chapel, Annie and Abe Potterowski, the caretakers and officiants, can marry us on Wednesday at noon. There are no waiting periods or blood tests required in Wyoming."

"I hate the words *blood test*," Liam said.

She smiled. "Me, too. I hate it more than any words in the English language." She bit her lip. "You know what

I also hate? The idea of marrying at the town hall. I love the Wedlock Creek Chapel, and since our marriage is going to be legal and binding, then we might as well have the ceremony in a beautiful, old chapel where I once—"

"Once what?" he asked.

She shook her head. "Doesn't matter. I'm set on the chapel."

He nodded. "Wednesday at noon, it is. Will you have your family there? I'm not sure about inviting my parents. My father and I are still on the outs. But I can't imagine getting married without my brother being there, no matter what kind of marriage it is."

"Let's have our families. Maybe it'll help your dad to understand why we're doing it, why it's so important."

"I don't even want to look at him," Liam said, turning away. He'd suddenly lost his appetite for the extra serving of General Tso's chicken he'd put on his plate. "I'm not going to think about him. I'm not going to let him get to me again. He can feel how he wants. I'm my own man."

"You are. But he's your father and that word is powerful, as you know. He'll come to see why he's on the wrong side of this, Liam. But you may have to be patient with him."

"He doesn't deserve my patience. He deserves a kick. He deserves to never see me or Alexander—or Shane—again."

"Well, that'll hurt him, yes. But it'll hurt Alexander and Shane, too. And you."

"Can we change the subject?" he asked, handing her a fortune cookie.

"We can change the subject," she said, taking the cookie from the wrapper and snapping it in half. "My fortune says, learn by going where you have to go." She raised an eyebrow. "Uh, what?"

"I guess that's what you're doing. What we're both doing. We have to get married. We'll learn en route."

"Yes, but learn what?"

"How to make it work?" he suggested. "How to live with each other? How to be parents to children we've just met?"

"I'm putting this fortune in my wallet. I like it."

He smiled and cracked open his fortune cookie, pulling out the small slip of white paper. "Mine says, the best year-round temperature is a warm heart and a cool head. I've got the cool head, I think. Except when it comes to my father. Warm heart for my children. So I'm good, right?"

"I think it means to be passionate but practical. I like that one, too."

"Passionate and practical cancel each other out, though. Like our marriage. It's practical. It can't be passionate. Can you imagine what might happen if we let attraction into the picture?" He shook his head. "Whoa, boy."

"What would happen?" she asked, leaning forward.

"The minute you let romance in, there's a heart waiting to be broken. We can't risk that in our situation, Shelby. So no matter how much I may want to make love to you, I'll never so much as kiss you on the lips."

"You want to rip my clothes off?"

"You're a beautiful woman, Shelby. I'm just saying that I'm going to keep a certain distance. This marriage is to let us both have both babies. That's it."

"Right," she said. "The family unit."

He nodded. "You know, before I found out about Al-

exander and Shane, I was thinking about how much I
wanted Alexander to have a mother. And how I was
going to make that happen given that I didn't want to
marry. At least that worked out."

She stared at him for a moment, then nodded slowly
as if she was working out something in her mind. Surely
she felt the same way after what she'd been through, no
matter that she still believed in love. She wouldn't have
to worry about heartache or loss and her baby—her babies—would have a father. A loving father who'd do
anything for them and her.

How he was going to keep his mind off Shelby as a
woman was going to take some doing, though.

Shelby turned over in bed and started at her alarm
clock. 1:37 a.m. She'd been tossing and turning all night
again, bits and pieces of Liam's words echoing in her
head. *Want to make love to you… Going to keep my distance… For the sake of our children…*

On Wednesday she'd be marrying him. For good reason. So she had to put everything else out of her mind.
Her plans, her former hopes, her future dreams. She
should be grateful that Liam Mercer was a single, gorgeous, sexy, very kind and loving father. He could have
been a total troll. So many could-have-beens would have
derailed any hope of her having Shane and Alexander
in her future. Now she wouldn't have any worries about
that. *Thank your lucky stars*, she told herself, throwing
off the blanket. She'd make herself a cup of herbal tea,
the chamomile that always soothed her back to sleep,
and wake up refreshed and ready to become Mrs. Mercer tomorrow.

She left her room, the apartment quiet. Liam's door

was ajar, and for a half second she was tempted to poke her head in and watch him sleep. Maybe he'd be half-naked again. Instead, she headed to the kitchen and rummaged in the cupboard for the tea and sugar, then filled up the kettle and sat down at the kitchen table. Her gaze landed on the brown paper bag containing the music box—the other day she'd put the bag on top of the refrigerator and promptly forgot about it. No wonder, given everything going on in her life.

The secret note! She popped up and retrieved the bag and set it on the table, eager to see if anything was written on the folded-up piece of paper hidden under the lining. She might not be having a hot and passionate romance herself, but perhaps the secret note-writer had and penned a love letter he or she had never intended to send.

Careful to get to the boiling kettle before it could let out its whistle and wake up the whole apartment, Shelby poured her tea and waited for it to steep, then took out the music box.

Once again, she edged back the pink velvet lining and pulled out the folded piece of paper—plain white unlined stationery, a bit yellowed with age. It was a letter, written in neat black script. Her gaze went to the bottom of the page. It was signed *Mama*. It was to: *My dear son.*

And dated fifty-eight years ago.

Wow. Over half a century old. Given its age and that there were no names, Shelby felt justified in reading it.

My dear child,
You'll be coming into the world any day now. I know I won't be able to care for you properly—I can barely feed myself, let alone make sure a new-born has what he needs, especially for the upcom-

*ing winter. A drafty, depressing apartment above
a bar is no place to raise a child. But that's all I
can afford and I just don't see any way out.*

*Mrs. Mercer says you'll want for nothing and
that you'll be so loved that you'll never know you
weren't her own flesh and blood. When she said
that, I admit I broke down and cried. But I know
what she meant. She'll love you just as I would.
And she can give you what you need, what you deserve, whereas you'd have a hardscrabble life with
me. You'd be called a bastard your whole life. I
want more for you, my precious baby. So you'll go
with Mrs. Mercer the moment you're born. You'll
be her child. But know that I did love you just as
much and always will, forever.*

Mama

Shelby stood up slowly, her legs shaky, and paced
the kitchen. What the hell? The letter was dated fifty-
eight years ago. Which meant the baby in question was
Liam's father?

She glanced at the name on the brown paper bag.
Harrington Mercer.

Someone had left the bag containing the music box
on Harrington Mercer's porch. Someone who knew the
letter was hidden under the lining and wanted him to
know the truth? Who? It would have been easy to miss
the hidden letter entirely. The Mercers had given away
the box without even knowing the letter was there—that
Shelby was sure of.

Perhaps the person who left it figured Larissa Mercer
would open the package out of curiosity, open the music
box, see the uneven lining and edge it back to find out

what was underneath. But that was a risk. After all, Larissa Mercer hadn't even gotten that far.

But Larissa had opened the package and unwrapped it. She'd even twisted the music prong to see if it worked because she'd mentioned it played one of her favorite sonatas. Perhaps whoever left it on the Mercer doorstep knew Larissa would at least open it? Maybe it was one of those *Well I'm going to do my part by putting the box where it needs to be and if the person meant to find the letter does, great. If not, at least I tried.*

Maybe the person who left the box was the mother herself? Or a friend or relative of the mother?

Shelby read the letter again. What was the mother's connection to Mrs. Mercer? How had they even met, given the difference in their "stations," especially almost sixty years ago? And *was* "Mrs. Mercer" Liam's grandmother—Alexandra, whom Alexander was named for? Or a different Mrs. Mercer?

Question after question flew at Shelby.

The biggest one at the moment was whether or not she should wake up Liam to show him the letter. Surely it could wait until morning, not that she'd manage to get a wink of sleep now.

But considering that Liam was suddenly standing in the kitchen doorway, in those sexy sweats and a University of Wyoming Cowboys T-shirt, it looked like it was going to be now.

Chapter 9

Liam had heard Shelby get out of bed because he'd been tossing and turning all night and his ears were trained on the nursery. But instead of hearing any middle-of-the-night cries from the babies, he'd heard Shelby get up and head to the kitchen. He'd thought about giving her privacy with her thoughts; he was sure it was the wedding—the entire idea of getting married—that kept her awake, but if he could ease her mind, he'd try.

"Couldn't sleep again?" he asked, coming in the kitchen and taking a mug from the cupboard. "Is there enough water in the kettle for another cup?"

She nodded. "I've been tossing and turning for so long I figured I might need a few cups to help me back to sleep."

He added a tea bag to the mug and poured the still-steaming water on it, then sat down next to Shelby. She held a letter, the old jewelry box his mother had given her beside her.

"Found something in the box?" he asked, adding cream to the tea.

"I did, Liam. A letter hidden away under the lining right in the main compartment."

"Hidden away? A secret letter?"

She nodded. "It's almost sixty years old."

"What does it say?"

She took a deep breath. "Liam, I think you'd better read it. There's a reason this music box was left on your parents' porch. Someone wanted your father to find the letter. Or at least have the music box where the letter was hidden."

"Huh? What does the letter have to do with my father?"

"I think it's *to* him," she said, handing it over.

Liam frowned and took the letter. It was signed Mama. Well, his mother didn't refer to herself that way, so he doubted this was from his mother. Or to his father.

My dear son, he read, saddened by the first paragraph, by a mother-to-be wanting the best for her child and having to give him up.

At the second paragraph, at the line *Mrs. Mercer says you'll want for nothing and that you'll be so loved that you'll never know you weren't her own flesh and blood*, Liam shot up out of the chair. He quickly read the rest, then his gaze focused on the date. The year his father was born.

"My father was adopted by Alexandra Mercer?" he said, voicing his thoughts aloud. "He never told me. He never let on that he was adopted."

"Maybe he doesn't know," Shelby said gently.

He stared at her. "Jesus. Maybe he doesn't." His gaze fell on the music box. "This was in there?"

"Tucked under this lining," she said, pointing at the pink velvet and showing how it edged away from the corners and could be inched over.

"So the box was his birth mother's? And she left it on my parents' porch? On the chance my rich, snobby parents might want some old music box and find a hidden letter? That hardly sounds plausible."

Shelby sipped her tea. "I know. I've been running through possible scenarios and nothing quite makes sense. I have the feeling someone who'd been close to the birth mother put the box on your parents' porch. A relative or friend. Someone who knew the secret and thought, well, let me finally deliver this letter that never got sent and if Harrington Mercer finds it, great, and if not, I tried."

Liam sat back down. "Why not just knock on the door and hand him the letter and explain everything?"

"Good question. I really don't know. Maybe whoever left the box made a promise never to reveal the secret?"

"God Almighty. Well, what the hell am I supposed to do with this information? Show him the letter? He obviously doesn't know he was adopted. And I told you how he reacted to the DNA results. DNA means a little too much to my father. It would kill him to find out he wasn't—in his own words—a *real* Mercer."

"Maybe we could investigate a bit. Try to find out the backstory and history. There must be a connection between your grandmother and the birth mother. Clearly, they crossed paths and a baby was passed between them. I could do a little surreptitious questioning of some of my elderly customers who've lived their entire lives in Wedlock Creek."

Liam nodded, his head about to explode. "Go ahead. I've had about enough of family mysteries for one weekend."

"Seriously," she said, covering his hand, and he was glad she was here.

"Do you have a family album? If Alexandra Mercer was pregnant in the months before your father was born, maybe this isn't about her and your father at all."

"That's true," he said. "I was getting ahead of myself for no reason. This probably has nothing to do with my grandmother and father at all."

Wasn't that what he said about Alexander being switched at birth with Shane?

Early Tuesday morning, Shelby watched downtown Wedlock Creek disappear as Liam drove them out to the ranch lands just fifteen miles out of town. Liam wanted to check out his family photo albums that he had at his house before heading to the office for the day. His plan was to take both babies to the Mercer Industries day care, unless Shelby wanted to stick with business as usual and take Shane to work with her at Treasures. Or both babies. But Shelby had been excited for Shane to spend the day with Alexander at the day care where they'd be doted on, and besides, it would free her up to dig into the family mystery behind the letter she'd found in the music box.

They drove down a long gravel drive that managed to reflect the Wyoming wilderness and be perfectly manicured in a rustic way. A half mile up was an open wrought-iron gate with a metal sign: The Double M.

"Double M for the two Mercers?" she asked.

He smiled. "I guess now I'll have to change the name to the Triple M." He glanced at her, eyebrow risen. "Quadruple M since you'll be a Mercer, too."

She stared at the sign at they passed it. She didn't feel like a Mercer, but then again, she wasn't one yet.

"Might be easier to stick with the Double M for old times' sake. Or just The Mercer Ranch."

"Probably," he said, pulling up in front of a beautiful white farmhouse with shiny black shutters and a barn-red door. There were acres of land as far as the eye could see and pastures and hedges but no cattle or horses. As Liam had said, this wasn't a working ranch.

"It's so beautiful out here," she said, getting out of the car and heading to the back seat to take out Shane.

Liam did the same with Alexander. "I've missed it, even though I've only been gone a couple of days. I sit out on the porch and just watch the land, the trees rustle in the breeze, and I can often figure out a problem."

Maybe she'd been hasty in insisting they live in her apartment—even until the babies turned into toddlers. Maybe they could both use all this fresh air and open space to think, to have room to breathe.

"Come on in," he said, taking Shane's carrier and easily handling both. He set Alexander's down and unlocked the door, then picked him back up and they headed in.

Shelby gasped. This was not what she was expecting at all. The entry led into a huge open space with floor-to-ceiling windows on the back wall. Exquisite rugs and leather couches made a living room around a massive stone fireplace, and across the room was a play area for a baby with floor mats and a walker and bouncer seat and everything a baby could want, just like Liam had said.

Huh. Shane sure would like that play area. And Shelby could imagine waking up here every morning, having this view with her morning coffee. Her mind would be clear until it focused on how her life had changed so dramatically so quickly. And then while she'd have a minor panic attack, she'd have the view and the natural beauty of this ranch to calm her down.

"I love it," she said. "Your home is beautiful."

"Wait till you see the room that would be yours," he said. "My cousin Clara decorated a guest room for me since the rest of the place is so masculine. I'll bet you'll like it."

She had no doubt she would. He carried the boys up the grand staircase to the second floor. He pointed out his room and a bit farther down the hall he opened a door. "This is the nursery."

She walked in and for the second time in five minutes, she gasped. "My God. This is a prince's nursery."

"Guilty," he said. "A little too much disposable income and loving the heck out of Alexander, and I ended up with this."

The crib was gold and she wouldn't be surprised if it was made out of twenty-four-karat gold. A mural of Winnie the Pooh with one of Shelby's favorite wise quotes from the sweet little bear was on one wall. A giant stuffed giraffe was in one corner, and one wall was lined with low, built-in bookcases full of board books and children's classics. A glider chair was by a window along with every type of baby paraphernalia imaginable. All the fanciest, the most expensive brands. The room was as grand a nursery as she'd ever seen.

"The nursery at your place is just as nice," he said. "It has everything they need—you were right about that. Fancy doesn't make the room better."

Tears poked at her eyes. "You know what I'm thinking about? The letter. How the birth mother wrote that she wanted more for her unborn baby than she knew she could provide."

He touched her shoulder. "Shelby, you're hardly destitute. I like your place just fine."

"I appreciate that. But even I wouldn't pass up the chance to live here. Alexander and Shane can be real Wyoming cowboys on this ranch."

"If you're sure," he said. "Why don't we move both of you in after the wedding?"

She nodded. "And either I'll take the boys with me to Treasures for the day or you'll take them to the day care. Maybe we'll split the week."

"Sounds good." He looked at her and reached for her hand. "We will make this work. I promise."

She nodded, needing to change the subject. She didn't want to talk about them, about their businessy marriage. "So where do you keep the family albums?"

"In the family room," he said. He picked up both carriers, and they went back downstairs. Liam set the babies in the gated play area, carefully babyproofed, she noted, and headed over to the wall of bookcases. He took out two leather albums and sat down on the brown leather sofa.

She sat beside him, eager to see a photograph of Alexandra Mercer—and if she'd been pregnant in the nine months before Harrington Mercer was born. "I hope there are pictures of her at the right time."

"There's an entire album devoted to her, my grandfather, Wilton, and my dad as a baby. I haven't looked in these albums in ages, but I'll bet there are lots of photos of her when she was expecting."

Except there weren't. Not one.

There were several photos of a nursery in various stages of development, so clearly Wilton and Alexandra had been expecting a baby. But as Liam flipped the pages of the album, there were no photos of her in the family way. One photo was dated January, nine months before his father was born. Alexandra Mercer was slim, her tummy washboard flat in a 1950s-style tucked-in sweater. The next photo was dated October, with Alexandra and Wilton holding infant Harrington. There were countless photos of Harrington as a newborn.

"Look!" Shelby said. "There's a photo of your grandparents leaving the hospital with your dad. Cottonwood County."

"So did she give birth there—or did the birth mother? And my grandparents brought my dad home."

The rest of the albums gave nothing away. They were all of Harrington Mercer growing up.

"Maybe there's another album of the nine months before your dad was born?" Shelby asked.

"Maybe. I only have these two. I'm sure my parents will have all the albums. They're not much into nostalgia but I'm sure they kept old photos."

"And you're all right with me doing a little careful poking into the memories of my elderly customers? The Minnow sisters were very involved in the town when they were younger and they've been in Wedlock Creek all their lives. Maybe they'll remember when your grandmother was pregnant. Or not pregnant."

"As long as you ask in a roundabout way. If my father was adopted and doesn't know, which I imagine he doesn't, I certainly don't want him and his story becoming gossip."

"I'll be careful, I promise. I trust the Minnow sisters."

He nodded. "Well, I'll show you around the rest of the house and property and then we'll both go to work. Like it's just a normal day." He laughed and shook his head. "As if there's anything normal about finding out on Friday that your baby was switched at birth, and then getting married on Wednesday to the mother of the baby he was switched with. And we can't leave out finding a secret half-century-old note about my father."

"It does feel good to go about our lives as normally as possible," she said. "Being at Treasures always makes me feel connected to myself. And I've been very at odds and ends this entire weekend."

He reached for her hand again. "I know. But hopefully once we're married and we're settled in here as a family, that'll become the new normal."

She smiled at his optimism. For someone who didn't believe in love or happy-ever-after, he sure was open to possibility. That was good.

But she couldn't imagine anything about any of this feeling remotely normal. Ever.

Shelby closed Treasures early for the day and met her sister, mother and Aunt Cheyenne at Finders Keepers, the one shop in Wedlock Creek that sold dresses.

"Um, Shelby, you can't get married in a denim jumper," Norah said, sliding dresses on the rack and shaking her head. "Oh, a turtleneck dress with long sleeves that goes to the ankles. Very bridal."

"I'm not really going for bridal," Shelby reminded her family.

"Sweetheart," her mother said, "you may not be going for bridal, but you are getting married. For real. Legally wed and all that." She paused in front of a pale pink dress. "How about something like this? It's pretty but not formal."

Shelby stared at the dress, which she did like. Very much, actually. It was silky and floaty. "I think I should wear something a little less pretty. More functional."

"Like this," Aunt Cheyenne said, handing Shelby a pale yellow sundress, simple and cotton with eyelet around the hem.

"That screams barbecue at the Mercer mansion. I'm thinking more…workish."

"This?" Norah asked, wrinkling her nose at how clearly plain and dull she found it.

Shelby smiled at the off-white, sleeveless shift dress. "Perfect."

Her relatives looked incredibly disappointed by the lack of adornment.

"At least wear amazing shoes," Norah said. "You'll have the photos forever."

"I have a pair of slingbacks that'll work," Shelby said. "Well, we're done."

"I hope you'll consider wearing Grandma's earrings," her mother said. "I wore them for my wedding and they brought me luck for over two decades."

Shelby could use some luck. "I'd love to. Thanks, Mom."

But the mention of her own grandmother reminded her of Liam's. Just what went on fifty-eight years ago between Alexandra Mercer and the woman who wrote the letter to Harrington? Who was the woman? How did they meet? And what happened to her? Shelby had so many questions and not a single answer.

"I'm closing the Pie Diner for a private party tomorrow from twelve-thirty to one-thirty."

"Oh?" Shelby asked. "What's the occasion?"

Her mother shook her head. "My daughter's getting married."

Shelby smiled. "Ah. That'll be nice, Mom."

"I'll leave it to you to invite the Mercers," her mom said. "We can meet and get to know one another at the party."

Shelby nodded. A casual wedding reception might be just the thing to bring Liam and his dad back together. She knew his father's attitude about Alexander had caused a rift between the men that both might be too stubborn to try to fix.

She thought about the letter, about the fact that Harrington Mercer was likely adopted and might not know it. Would finding out destroy him? If he couldn't handle his own grandson not being a "real Mercer," how could he ever accept not being one himself?

She was about to remind herself that this wasn't her business and should butt out and let Liam handle it. But she was marrying into this family. And Alexander and Shane were forever tied to the Mercers. So it was her business.

And wasn't she about to be a Mercer herself?

Chapter 10

On Wednesday morning, Liam set a jar of Alexander's favorite baby food, sweet potatoes, on the tray of his high chair, and a jar of Shane's favorite, apricots, on his, and did double duty, a spoonful to Alexander and a spoonful to Shane.

"Guess what, guys?" he said as both boys slurped around the spoons. "I'm marrying your mother today. We'll put you in your best sleeper outfits."

Shane stared at him with his big blue eyes. As Liam fed the baby another spoonful of apricots, he reached over and caressed Shane's cheek. The little guy wrapped his little hand around Liam's pointer finger.

"Bwabawa!" Shane gurgled, a big smile on his adorable face.

And just like that, something shifted inside Liam, a door opened a crack and love beams filtered through.

You're my son, Liam said silently to Shane, his heart about to burst. *We have a lot of lost time to make up for, don't we?*

At least I can feel it for babies, he thought, even if his heart was closed to romance. At least he wasn't a total goner.

"I'm your daddy," he whispered to Shane. "And I'm your daddy," he whispered to Alexander, spooning apricots into his open mouth.

"Bahababa!" Alexander babbled, picking up his toy key set and banging on the high chair.

His phone buzzed with a text. His cousin Clara.

We'll see you at the chapel at noon and then at the Pie Diner immediately following.

Did *we'll* include his father? Liam had called his parents yesterday to tell them about the wedding, and his mother had been surprised but happy and agreed it was a good solution. He'd heard his father grumbling about a prenup and Liam had sighed and told his mother the wedding plans and said a hasty goodbye.

He had no idea if his father would show up.

At least he knew the bride would be there. Last night Shelby had been quiet and had spent most of the night in her bedroom. Twice he'd knocked to see if she was okay and twice she said she was fine, just mentally preparing for a major event in her life.

He knew the impending marriage was keeping her up at night. Joining together as husband and wife solely to keep the family together. They'd make it work because they had to.

"I guess it's okay for you to see the bride before the

ceremony in our case," Shelby said, coming into the kitchen. "Anyway, I'll be getting dressed at my mom's house and so I'll meet you over there. You'll bring the boys or should I take one with me?"

"I'll bring them both."

He watched her take a deep breath. "Well, I'll see you at noon, then."

"Shelby," he said as she was about to leave the kitchen.

She turned around.

"Everything's going to be okay. I know I keep saying that. But it really will be okay. Better than okay. It'll be great. We'll make sure of it."

She managed something of a smile. "I'm holding you to that."

He wouldn't let her down. He might not be able to give her everything she wanted, but he'd give her a solid family.

"Bababa," Alexander said, slapping his tray.

"Bababa," Shane repeated happily.

Shelby smiled. "They're holding you to it, too."

He thought of the gold bands in his pocket. A symbol of strength and forever and infinity, of their vows to stand by each other. Yesterday he'd called Shelby's sister, Norah, for Shelby's ring size and he'd picked up two matching rings he thought Shelby would like.

Making good on the promise was everything to him. He wanted nothing more than for Alexander and Shane to have their mother and father, for him and Shelby to have both their babies. This way, everyone was happy.

Except *happy* wasn't how he'd describe the look on Shelby's face as she left.

His cell rang, and he was glad to avoid thinking too much about it.

His brother, Drake. "Sweating bullets?" he asked.

"Not in the slightest," Liam said. "Cool, calm and collected."

"Cut me a break, Liam. You're getting married. It's a big deal."

Liam put down the spoon and jar of apricots. "Shelby and I are getting married so that we can both keep our babies and have the ones we were denied. It's a partnership based on a fundamental need. Like most mergers."

Drake laughed. "You're more like Dad than you realize, big brother."

Liam frowned. "What is *that* supposed to mean?"

"It means that sometimes you need someone to kick you upside the head."

"About?" he asked. Drake, who had a steady stream of "women in his life," was hardly someone he'd take advice from on the subject of marriage. "I know what I'm doing, Drake."

"I'm just saying you might be in for a rude awakening."

"Again—about what?"

"About what marriage is really going to be like," Drake said. "It's not a business partnership. Shelby is a person. Shane is a mini person. You can't crunch them like numbers and make everything add up. Or not."

"And what makes you an expert on marriage?" Liam asked.

"I'm not. But I know you. You don't look at Shelby the way you look at acquisition reports."

"Acquisition reports aren't a beautiful woman."

"Exactly."

"Can I go now? I'm halfway through feeding my sons."

He froze, staring in wonder at Shane. At Alexander. His sons. Plural.

There was dead silence on the phone. "Jesus, Liam. You just said *sons*. You went from having one son to two in less than a week."

"I know. I think it was the first time I said that, actually. Sons. I have two sons now. And that's why I'm marrying Shelby. And it's going to be the best-run partnership I've ever formed."

"Well, I'd never miss your wedding. I'll see you at the chapel at noon."

Unsettled, Liam hit End Call and tried to focus on the happy babies in their high chairs. Liam offered Alexander a Toasty O but he flung it at his cheek. Shane threw his toy keys across the room.

Now *this*, he was familiar with. This, he knew how to handle.

How he actually felt about Shelby or getting married—really, deep down? That was something he didn't want to think too deeply about.

The Wedlock Creek Chapel was a beautiful white clapboard building that looked a bit like a wedding cake. Built in 1895, the Victorian chapel had scallops on the tiers and a bell at the top that almost looked like a heart. Shelby had been surprised that when she'd gone inside, her heart hadn't dropped; she hadn't been thinking about her first wedding in the chapel at all. Her mind was on Liam and Shane and Alexander.

She stood in front of the floor-length mirror in the "bridal" room, her stomach doing flip flops. Her mother and aunt had kindly given her space and left her alone with Norah, who always had a way of calming Shelby down.

"My God, is he gorgeous," Norah was saying, peeking out past the opaque curtain on the arched window on the door. "He's in his Sunday best."

"Really?" Shelby asked, coming over to the door to look through.

She sucked in a breath at the sight of Liam, so incredibly handsome and sexy in a dark blue suit and tie. Shane and Alexander were in their carriers, and if Shelby wasn't mistaken, they were wearing sleepers that looked like tuxedos.

"Those babies are too adorable," Norah said. "God, you're lucky. You're getting a gorgeous, rich husband and two babies. I know last weekend was rough, Shelby, but God, did it turn around."

"It's not exactly fun and games to marry a man for any reason other than love and wanting to spend the rest of your life with him," Shelby reminded her dreamy-eyed younger sister.

"I know. But if you need to marry a guy, you couldn't do better than Liam Mercer."

Shelby took one last look at her groom, hardly able to drag her gaze away from him.

"Okay, let me see you," Norah said, inspecting her from every angle. "Dress, perfect. Makeup almost non-existent but the bride insisted. Grandma's earrings—stunning. Ancient off-white sling backs from the back of your closet, passable. All in all, Shelby Ingalls, you look absolutely beautiful."

Shelby looked in the mirror. The dress might not be lace or beaded or have a train, but it was just right for her noontime wedding. She wouldn't have expectations in this outfit, in these old shoes; and her grandmother's earrings, worn by her mom at her own wedding, would serve as a blessing from generations past. Shelby liked that.

There was a tap at the door. "If you're ready," Annie, the elderly officiant, said. "Oh, and Shelby, you look absolutely lovely."

Shelby smiled at Annie, who poked her head back out and shut the door. "Am I ready?" she asked her sister. "To marry someone I didn't know last Thursday?"

"You're ready to marry Shane's father. You're ready to be Alexander's mother. Right?"

"Absolutely."

"Then you're ready," Norah said, opening the door.

There was no bridal march, but there was a red carpet creating an aisle to her groom. And there were three Ingallses on the left and five Mercers on the right, all in the same row.

Shelby focused on the babies in their tuxedo-printed sleepers and they looked so cute and sweet that she couldn't help the smile bursting from inside her. But when she glanced at her groom, waiting by the mayor's side, her smile faded. From nerves.

She was marrying this man. He would be her husband. Not in every sense of the word, but he would be hers.

As she stood inches across from Liam, facing him, she forced the cotton from her ears and the strange sensation from her head to focus on the mayor's words.

"Do you, Shelby Rae Ingalls, take Liam West Mercer as your lawfully wedded husband?" Annie asked.

She looked at Liam, who was looking directly in her

eyes, not a hint of worry or concern. *Because he's getting exactly what he wants and needs.* The family unit. A mother for Alexander. His biological child, Shane. An agreement: no love, no romance, no passion.

She glanced at the babies in their tuxedo sleepers. *You're doing this for them. And for you. So you can have them both without worry.*

And you're doing it for Liam, whom you've come to care deeply about.

Because he's a good man.

A thoughtful man.

A kind man.

"I do," she said.

Liam repeated his vows, and rings were slid on their fingers, hers fitting so perfectly that she knew her new husband must have involved her sister for her ring size.

Some plain gold band. The ring was beautiful, gold and studded with diamonds. It twinkled on her finger.

"You may now kiss the bride," Abe said, and Liam reached over and gave her a quick peck on the lips.

"Congratulations, Mr. and Mrs. Mercer!" Annie and her husband, Abe, shouted.

The audience stood and clapped.

Shelby noticed that Liam's father took a minute to get himself up, as though he barely thought it necessary. The man was angry and upset in a place deep inside, Shelby could tell. Liam's mother looked a bit confused, as though she didn't understand how she'd gotten here, at her son's wedding to a woman she'd never heard of before last weekend. Liam's brother, who'd announced that he was the best man in spirit if not practice, clapped Liam on the back and shook his hand then hugged Shelby and welcomed her to the family.

"It's not like this is a real marriage," Harrington Mercer said. "You two only got married because of the situation you found yourselves in."

"If real and legal are synonyms when it comes to weddings, then this is real," Liam said, a slight growl in his voice.

His father turned away, and Larissa Mercer frowned in commiseration with her son and new daughter-in-law and said, "We'll see you at the Pie Diner."

Liam's cousin Clara and Shelby's family jumped in front of the newlyweds with their phones, snapping photos, so there was no time for Liam to react to his father's dismissal.

"Guys, pick up the babies," Norah said. "We need a few shots of you holding your children."

That was what this was all about, Shelby thought, scooping up Alexander while Liam picked up Shane.

She gasped. "This is the first time I associated the words *your children* with Alexander," she said, tears coming to her eyes. "Normally I'd go for Shane. But I went straight for Alexander." She snuggled him against her chest. "You're my son and you always will be. Just like Shane."

Liam kissed Shane's forehead. "Switch for more pictures?"

They switched. The familiarity of Shane in her arms was comforting. Now she'd have all the time in the world for Alexander to feel as familiar. She held him close, taking in every bit of his sweet little face, the tiny dimple in his right cheek, his inquisitive blue eyes and quirking bow mouth.

"What a shot," Aunt Cheyenne said, showing her

phone to her sister and niece. "I'm going to have this one printed out and framed for you, Shel."

Her family must have taken a hundred shots of them in the boring old room and more outside. Some folks passing by gawked—the gossip mill would be running once word got out that the second-hand shop owner had married a mighty Mercer.

"Oh, Shelby and Liam," Annie said, her blue eyes misty with tears as she linked her arm around Abe's. "I'm so happy for both of you! And just think, the Wedlock Creek legend has already come true for you!"

Shelby glanced at her brand-new husband. "Um, Annie, I'm not pregnant. With one, two, or three babies."

"Yeah, but you have twins now, don't you?" Abe said, straightening his blue bow tie. "Those little fellas are exactly the same age, born the same day at practically the same time. They're as close to twins as you get without being blood related."

Shelby gasped.

Liam raised an eyebrow.

"Well, we definitely have multiples," Shelby said, looking down at Shane and Alexander. "There are indeed two of them."

Liam tilted his head. "Huh. Multiples." He smiled and gave each baby a gentle caress on the head. "I did get married in the chapel and I do have multiples." He looked at Annie. "How does that legend go? Multiples in some, way, shape or form?"

"Yup," Annie said. "I can add another notch to the wall of couples for whom the legend came true."

While Shelby tried not to think about the legend coming three-quarters true and what that might mean, they all made their way to the Pie Diner, which Shelby's family had decorated with Congratulations banner and balloons and streamers.

The Mercers, including Harrington, were warm and friendly and everyone enjoyed the pie sampling, coffee and iced tea. But when Harrington asked to hold Shane and made a special point to bond with the little boy, Shelby couldn't help but notice Liam watching his father. Watching his father *not* hold Alexander—even once. Watching his father not look Alexander's way.

All the other Mercers treated Alexander as the adored grandson he'd always been and they fussed over Shane as the new addition to the family. But Harrington never veered from his focus on Shane.

God. The man clearly didn't know he'd been adopted. Because if he did know, DNA couldn't possibly mean so much to him. He'd know that family was a word built on love and commitment and taking responsibility and caring.

As Shelby listened to Clara Mercer rave to Norah about how amazing the chocolate chip peanut butter pie was, she glanced over at Liam, who was staring at his father, eyes narrowed, as Harrington Mercer held Shane and pointed out the window at a little red bird on a tree.

Shelby knew her new husband enough by now to know that he was steaming mad and that there was going to be a showdown. Maybe not today—not on their wedding day, however practicality-focused it was. But a showdown was coming. And truth be told, Shelby had a feeling Liam would learn a thing or two about how love really worked, too. Because you couldn't pick and choose whom you loved. If you were capable of the emotion, and Liam clearly was, you couldn't just decide you weren't going to love the woman you had to marry. Just like his father couldn't decide he suddenly didn't love his six-month-old grandson because he wasn't a "real Mercer."

If Liam couldn't love her it was because chemistry and the mysterious properties of love just worked that way. But to decide you weren't going to love? Nope, didn't work that way.

And Shelby knew both men were going to find that out the hard way.

Because Liam felt something more than just friendship. That was one of the few things she was absolutely sure of. She looked down at her beautiful wedding ring sparkling on her left hand. Yes, she was sure.

There were surprises waiting for Shelby at her new home. She knew she'd be moving in after the wedding and had packed two suitcases to start, but Liam had not only moved all the babies' things into the nursery at the ranch, he'd also added another fancy crib for Shane and had his name painted on the wall above with the U of Wyoming Cowboys' logo beside it.

Liam had been right when he'd said Shelby would love the guest room his cousin Clara had decorated. The moment she stepped in she felt like she was at the beach, in a bungalow designed just for her, with the most soothing of pale blues and yellows and white, a hint of pink here and there. There was a glider chair by the window by a bin of baby paraphernalia, everything she could need to soothe a fussy little one in the middle of the night.

There were red roses in a vase on her bedside table.

A plush white robe and matching slippers on the edge of the bed.

And a big wrapped gift on the bed itself.

"What's this?" she asked, suddenly feeling a little too aware of the bed in the room. On her wedding night. Well, wedding late afternoon. But still. A bed. A wedding ring. A husband and wife. And nothing was going to happen.

"A gift for you," he said.

Shelby smiled at the huge gift. It was rectangular and she had no idea what it could be. She took off the giant silver bow, then ripped open the wrapping paper.

"Oh, Liam," she said, staring at it. "This is absolutely beautiful."

It was a treasure chest, a hope chest, antique white with her name stenciled across the top in gold. She had a few hope chests for sale in her shop and they always went quickly, but she'd never found one that she wanted herself—until now. She loved it.

"I've always wanted one. Thank you, Liam."

"I have a big desk drawer where I keep all Alexander's keepsakes. I figured a hope chest would be nicer. More room as the boys grow up."

She bit her lip, a little too verklempt to speak. "It's perfect. I have something for you, too."

She dug in her tote bag on her shoulder for the wrapped box and then handed it to him.

He unwrapped it and smiled. It was a photo of Alexander and Shane in their bouncers, and Shelby had caught a moment when Shane was reaching toward Alexander's little cowboy hat. Shelby put it in a pretty antique frame she'd found at an estate sale.

"That little cowboy hat makes me very sad now, unfortunately," he said.

Oh, darn. She hadn't even thought of that when she'd

wrapped the gift this morning. She thought it so well represented who Alexander was, who Liam was.

He stared at the picture. "Well, if my father is really the baby in that letter you found in the music box, we know one thing for sure. He doesn't know he was adopted. Or he'd never turn his back on Alexander just because they're not blood relations."

"I was thinking the same thing at the Pie Diner. I'm so sorry, Liam."

"How do you just stop loving a six-month-old baby? It's insane."

She nodded. "There's no way he stopped loving Alexander. He's just put a wall up. That's all. And walls can be blasted through."

"Walls are strong, though. And my father is stubborn."

"Talk to him. Tell him how you feel. Tell him how painful this is—not just for you but for Alexander. He might be little now, but to be rejected by his own grandfather?"

"The hell he will reject him!" Liam shouted. "I won't stand for it. I'll give him a couple of weeks to come around. After that, if he doesn't, well, there won't be any more Mercer family Fridays."

"You can't cut him out of your life."

"Why not? If he cuts Alexander from his?"

"God, this is complicated."

"No, it's not, Shelby. Love and family aren't complicated when it comes right down to it. Take us, for example. We went into this knowing exactly what's what, right? It's not like I was madly in love with you and then upended the status quo or changed the rules midway because of this or that."

"But you're so sure you can't change your mind about love, Liam."

Had she said that aloud? She felt her cheeks burn a bit, hating that she'd exposed herself. But maybe she had to. For both their sakes. If he was going to help his father, maybe she had to help him see how stubborn *he* was being.

"Not *can't*. The way I feel about romantic love is a decision. To opt out."

"And what if you fall madly in love with me, Liam? How are you going to opt out?"

"I'm not going to fall in love with you. Because I've made a decision not to."

She smiled. "Right. Because that's how romantic love works. Liam, please. Romantic love conks you over the head."

"I can choose not to—that's all I'm saying. And I do choose that. Because I've experienced the devastation firsthand—twice. And I'm not going through that again. Now I have everything I want and need. My two sons. A mother who loves them both. And nothing will come between us—because we're not romantically involved. We're a partnership."

She took a deep breath. "Liam, your dad is choosing not to love Alexander right now. That's not okay with you."

He sat down on the edge of the bed. "I'm not so sure it's a choice. I mean, I don't think he woke up and decided that Alexander isn't his grandson. It's a feeling that came over him very strongly out of…fear, I guess."

"Choice, not a choice. We can go around and around trying to figure all this out. Your father will come around. I believe that."

"You have more faith than I do."

"I know," she said. "Believe me."

He stared at her then, and his blue eyes narrowed, but he didn't ask what she meant—or what she was really talking about. Because he probably didn't want to delve too deeply into his own feelings about love and romance and marriage.

She had a good seventeen and a half years ahead of her to help Liam Mercer open his heart to her. She wondered what would happen after the boys' high school graduations. When they turned eighteen and were legal adults. Would Liam say, "Well, we did our jobs and now we can go our separate ways?"

She had no idea. The subject had never come up and was so far in the future there was no point. Shelby wasn't so sure she could see a month into the future, what it was going to feel like to wake up every day as this man's wife. But not his *real* wife in the true sense of the word.

Suddenly, real and not real were more complicated than she expected.

"So," he said. "This is a special occasion. How about I make us two great steaks and we have some wine?"

That sounded kind of romantic. And like a good start, even if he didn't intend it that way.

Chapter 11

Liam woke up the day after his wedding, the photograph of Alexander and Shane on his bedside table the first thing he saw.

The second thing: his wedding band.

Liam had taken the rest of the week off to research what they needed to do about adopting the boys, to investigate the letter in the music box and most important, to bond individually with the switched baby and to spend time together as a family.

Liam had made breakfast for everyone, blueberry pancakes for him and Shelby, and boy, had she been surprised that he cooked—and pretty well, too. Then they packed up and headed to the Wedlock Creek park. April in Wyoming wasn't exactly short sleeves weather but the sun was bright and they walked the path along the river and showed the babies the beauty of Wyoming wilderness.

A visit to the courthouse in the county seat informed them that the magistrate had no idea about the legalities and ins and outs of their situation but would make calls. Shelby and Liam let the man know they'd like to formally petition to adopt both boys so that there was no question as to their legal status as the boys' parents.

That taken care of, they had a picnic lunch on the town green, thankful that a taco truck had taken up residence in the center of Wedlock Creek. Otherwise, there was only a coffee shop, an Italian restaurant where everyone celebrated special occasions and a saloon-like steakhouse with amazing mashed potatoes and creamed spinach.

After sort of crawling on the big picnic blanket for a little while, both babies managed to tucker themselves out and were now fast asleep in their carriers. Liam held up his soda can. "A toast to our first full day as a family unit. Went great, I'd say."

She clinked colas with him. "I agree. This marriage may be a practical partnership, but today felt truly special, Liam. Thank you."

And then she leaned close and kissed his cheek. A sweet kiss. A thank-you. Nothing more.

But desire and instinct had taken over and before he could stop himself, he put both hands on either side of her face and kissed her full on the lips.

He pulled back and blinked. Why had he done that? "Whoa. Swept away by the moment. Sorry about that."

"I'm not, Liam. Swept away is a good thing. It's natural. It's—"

"It's not going to happen again. Don't you worry."

He'd make sure of it. For the sake of the two little guys napping inches away, he couldn't fall in love with their mother. Because falling in love led to eventual discord and disappointment and broken hearts. Right now things were close to perfect. They were becoming true friends, real friends. Last night, over steak and his garlic mashed potatoes and wine, they'd sat on the couch in the living room, talking about everything from the time Shelby climbed a tree in her front yard and couldn't get down and the fire department from two towns over had to come get her out, to when Liam was named President of Mercer Industries, what he'd thought was the happiest day of his life.

Until Alexander was placed in his arms by a doctor at the clinic, the same doctor who'd had him sit down for the news about Liza.

He couldn't quite call that the happiest day; not with losing Liza, with Alexander never having the chance to know his lovely mother. But it had been the most special, the most moving—the first time he held his son, his child. The first time he felt the fierce love of parenthood.

They'd talked for hours, moving between serious memories to lighthearted ones. And they talked about the babies—Shelby had filled him in on everything he'd missed in Shane's six months on earth. The ear infection from hell. The first time she heard him laugh. The way she could have the worst day of her life and then look at Shane, needing everything she didn't have left to give, but finding it because she loved him so much.

He knew exactly what she meant.

And then she'd reached for her wineglass and her sweater lifted enough for him to see an expanse of creamy soft skin at her waist and between that and the curve of her breasts and her beautiful profile and sexy hair, he was overcome with lust.

More than lust. Last night he hadn't just wanted to have sex with Shelby. He'd wanted to make love to her. Slowly and lovingly and for hours.

And so he'd retreated, missing her the moment they'd said their good-nights and their bedroom doors closed.

He had to be careful. And it wasn't just now. Kissing her like that, being spontaneous, doing what he felt like doing instead of being his usual guarded self.

Being spontaneous and doing what he felt like sure felt better than holding back all the time.

"Penny for your thoughts," she said. "A dime for inflation."

"I'm just glad we're in this together," he said. Again—spontaneously. Couldn't he have told her he wanted another turkey sandwich?

"Me, too," she said, squeezing his hand.

And he didn't want to let go.

The next morning, as Shelby turned the sign on the door of Treasures to Open, one of her favorite customers, Charlotte Linden, came in, a small cardboard box in her arms.

"Charlotte, let me help you," Shelby said, rushing over.

"Oh, please," Charlotte said. "I might be seventy-eight but guess who just came from hot yoga? And I kept up with the millennials, too."

Shelby smiled. "No doubt." Charlotte was glowing with good health. "Just trying to be a doting proprietor. What do you have for me?"

Charlotte opened the box. "I inherited these from my

great-aunt years ago and to be honest, I think they're the ugliest things I've seen. I don't like frogs, though. Some people do."

Shelby laughed. Two matching miniature lamps with a bronze frog inlaid on the base. "You know who loves frogs? Callie Minnow. I'll bet she'll grab them the moment I put them on display. I'll give you fifteen for the pair."

"Twenty and we have a deal."

She'd list them for twenty-five and break even at twenty when Callie, as expected, would fall in love with them this Friday.

"Oh, my goodness!" Charlotte exclaimed suddenly, her mouth hanging open. "Is that what I think it is?"

Charlotte was staring at the ring on Shelby's left hand. Shelby had just started getting used to the feel of it. But every time the beautiful, sparkling diamonds caught her eye she would stop and wonder: Where did this come from? I'm married? When did that happen? She was always taken by surprise. Maybe that would go away in time. When being married—and to Liam—felt like… real life.

"Sure is. I got married yesterday. To Liam Mercer."

Charlotte's eyes widened. "Liam Mercer? You're kidding. You gonna sell this place?"

"Now, why would I do that? I love Treasures. I love when someone just like you comes in with frog lamps to sell and I know just who will want to buy them."

"You're a millionaire now. You don't have to work."

A millionaire. Shelby Ingalls? She almost laughed. Then realized it was sort of true. Liam had told her he would not ask her to sign a prenuptial agreement because no matter what, their relationship would be forever. "Regardless of my new husband's net worth, Treasures is my heart, Charlotte. You know that."

"Those Mercers like things their way. Trust me, I know that family going way back. You'll have to stand your ground. I hope you will."

The hairs rose on the back of Shelby's neck—and not because Charlotte sounded at all mildly foreboding. The part about "knowing the family from way back" meant she might have information about Wilton and Alexandra Mercer. "Oh, I will. I don't think Liam would have it any other way." *Ask her about the Mercer family*, she told herself. *This is your opening.* "So, Charlotte, you knew Liam's grandparents? Wilton and Alexandra?"

"Well, of course I knew them. Knew of them, really. Like everyone in Wedlock Creek in some fashion or another. They had glittering parties every weekend at their fancy ranch. If you were invited, you knew you'd arrived." She smirked. "I was never invited, of course. Oh, the beautiful dresses and coats Alexandra Mercer used to wear—even to the park and to pick up milk at the store. She was so glamorous. She was really the first businesswoman many of us in town ever knew of. Some say she was the serious brains behind Mercer Industries. I admired her, I must say."

Shelby smiled. "Did she keep working while she was pregnant?" Shelby practically held her breath, waiting for what information Charlotte might have.

"Hmm, I really don't know. Like I said, I only really knew of her and saw her around town sometimes. But I did see her once when she was heavily pregnant. She looked so happy. I remember thinking, now there's a baby who'll have everything he or she ever dreamed of."

Heavily pregnant. So Liam's father wasn't adopted?

Then what was the letter in the music box about? Based on the year the letter was dated, Harrington Mercer was the baby in question.

"Must be nice to be so rich," Charlotte said. "And now you know, too, my dear." Before Shelby could tell Charlotte that she had no intention of living her life any differently than she always had, Charlotte added, "My friend Pearl used to work for the Mercers as a maid and was responsible for caring for the jewelry. She told me the first time she saw the collection she almost fainted from shock."

As a maid. The words echoed in Shelby's mind. Maids had a way of seeing and hearing things because they were often considered invisible. Maybe Pearl could share some of her memories of Alexandra and Wilton—and the pregnancy.

"I'd love to meet Pearl and hear about those old times," Shelby said. "Liam was young when Alexandra died, and he said his parents don't talk much about themselves or the family."

Charlotte smiled. "Of course you're interested! Because you appreciate the past and all its history and stories. It's no wonder you own a secondhand shop. You know that big old farmhouse off the service road? That's Pearl's. She has a dog rescue. You'll hear the dogs barking and you'll know you're close."

"Thanks, Charlotte. I'll stop by tomorrow."

Shelby couldn't wait to tell Liam about the lead. And she had a feeling they were about to uncover a big Mercer family mystery.

On Saturday morning, with Norah filling in for Shelby at Treasures for the morning and her mother and aunt Cheyenne babysitting "the multiples" as Norah had taken to calling them, Shelby and Liam headed to Pearl's farmhouse. Just as Charlotte had said, they heard the dogs barking and a curve in the road led right to the house. Six dogs, all sweet mutts, ran up to the car, excited to see who'd come to visit.

"Let the poor folks have a path, for goodness' sake," a woman said as she came down the porch steps from the house. She appeared to be in her early eighties. She was tall and looked strong and robust, a long, silver braid tossed over one shoulder, green mud boots on her feet. "Are you here to adopt six dogs? They're yours." She smiled and laughed, and Shelby could hear the affection in her voice for the dogs.

"Actually, with two babies and a skittish cat, we're not looking for a dog," Shelby said. "A friend, Charlotte Linden, told me you worked as a maid for the Mercer family years ago. I was hoping you could tell us about your time with the family."

"Interesting timing," Pearl said, eyeing Liam.

"Meaning?" he asked, glancing at Shelby.

"You're Liam Mercer, right?" Pearl looked him over from head to toe and back up again.

"I am," Liam said. "Interesting timing because our visit is either a total coincidence or you left the music box on my parents' porch?"

Shelby almost held her breath. Had she?

Pearl lifted her chin. "I'm sure it's no coincidence. I did leave the music box on their porch. But I'm surprised Harrington Mercer isn't here himself to ask questions. I suppose he sent you to try to find the person who wrote the letter."

Shelby and Liam stared at each other for a moment.

Thank you, Charlotte! The woman and her frog lamps had led them right to the very woman who'd left the jewelry box for Liam's father. "Actually, Harrington never saw the letter," Shelby said. "His wife found the package on the doorstep, thought the box was lovely, but said their house was overflowing with stuff and she donated it to my shop, Treasures. I found the letter under the lining while examining the box."

"Ah. So Harrington never saw the letter," Pearl said, and it was hard for Shelby to tell how the woman felt about it. She seemed to be thinking about it, considering it. But her expression gave nothing away.

Liam shook his head. "Not yet, anyway." He stared at Pearl. "Charlotte told Shelby that she recalled seeing my grandmother, Alexandra, when she was heavily pregnant. So we're confused. If Alexandra was pregnant and gave birth to my father, then…"

"She wasn't pregnant," Pearl said. "She didn't give birth to your father."

What? "But—"

"I'll get to that," Pearl said. "It's quite a story. Anyway, anyone can look pregnant with the right device or pillow strategically placed. Actresses wear that kind of stuff for movies all the time."

Liam stared at Pearl, taking that bit in. "Are you my father's birth mother?"

"Goodness, no," Pearl said. "But I know who was. I was her friend."

Was, Shelby thought, tucking that away for now.

"So it's true," Liam said, surprise and wonder in his voice. "My father was adopted by Alexandra and Wilton Mercer?"

Pearl nodded. "Yes. At birth." She glanced at Liam

and bit her lip. "Why don't I make some coffee and we'll talk."

Liam nodded. "Thank you," he added, strain in his voice.

"Well, come on in, then," Pearl said. "Make yourselves comfortable," she added, leading the way into the living room and gesturing at the couch and love seat and overstuffed chairs.

As Pearl disappeared into another room, Shelby squeezed Liam's hand and sat down beside a cocker spaniel napping on the couch. The dog eyed Shelby, gave her a sniff, then went back to sleep. Liam finally sat down beside her, hands on his hips as if bracing himself for what was to come.

"I didn't doubt the letter," he whispered. "But to hear it said so plainly…to learn something so fundamental about my father all these years later…" He shook his head.

"Something he likely doesn't know about himself," Shelby said.

Liam nodded and turned away. They'd had their share of major surprises concerning close relatives—that was for sure.

Pearl returned with a tray holding a silver coffeepot and three cups and cream and sugar. She sat down on the love seat across from them and poured three cups.

Liam fixed his and then sat back. "What was it like working for my grandparents?"

"They treated me well," Pearl said. "I even got myself promoted to head maid. They were good to me."

"Pearl," Liam said, taking a sip of his coffee. "How did you come into possession of the letter to my father?"

Pearl took a sip of her own coffee. The cocker spaniel jumped off the couch and jumped up next to Pearl, curled next to her and went back to sleep. "I had a good friend named Jeannie. She wasn't in the best of health and it was hard for her to work, but she was all alone in the world and had to earn a living, so I got her a job on the housekeeping staff at the Mercer mansion. Your grandmother employed a housekeeper who had three maids reporting to her."

A housekeeper and three maids—one being the head maid. Shelby couldn't imagine. At that point, Alexandra and Wilton were childless, too.

"Well, poor Jeannie put her hopes in the wrong man who turned out to be a cad. He got her pregnant and that was the last she ever saw of him. Jeannie could barely take care of herself and was so scared about her future—her child's future."

Shelby's heart squeezed. Shelby had done the same—trusted the wrong guy. But at least she'd had family support. She'd never been on her own, not really.

"I feel so sorry for her," Liam said. "To be all alone like that."

Pearl nodded. "We were all struggling, but Jeannie's poor health added to her problems. Well, one day she had terrible morning sickness and had to sit down and chose to sit right on Alexandra Mercer's new divan the moment Mrs. Mercer was coming down the stairs. Your grandmother did not look pleased. But by then, Jeannie was beginning to show and your grandmother's expression changed. Mrs. Mercer took Jeannie into another room."

"Now things are beginning to make sense," Liam said.

Shelby nodded. "Did Jeannie tell you what was discussed?"

"It took some prodding but she finally did. She swore me to secrecy because Mrs. Mercer swore her to secrecy. Jeannie told me that Mrs. Mercer asked if she was in trouble, and when Jeannie told her she was, that the baby's father had abandoned her, that she was sickly, and had no idea what to do, Mrs. Mercer offered to adopt the baby and give Jeannie enough money to convalesce out of town. Far away from Wedlock Creek. Jeannie said that Mrs. Mercer promised to raise the baby with all the love in her heart and that the little one would want for nothing."

"What a position to be in," Liam said, shaking his head.

Pearl nodded. "Jeannie was both relieved and heart-broken. She knew letting her boss adopt her child was the best thing for the baby. And so she followed Mrs. Mercer's instructions to the letter. Mrs. Mercer rented her a small home a few towns over, paid for her prenatal care, and when the baby came, took the newborn son home to Mercer mansion. No one knew the child had been adopted. It was all a big secret."

"And no one was the wiser because my grandmother wore a prosthetic of some kind," Liam noted.

"Exactly," Pearl said. "One that grew as needed with the passing months. No one knew. I'm sure her husband did, of course. But no one else. Your grandmother didn't like the ruse, though, so she kept a very low profile for almost the entirety pregnancy."

"Wow," Liam said, seemingly speechless.

Shelby leaned forward. "Pearl, what happened to Jeannie?"

"She died a few months after the baby was born. Complications from a flu strain or something like that, the doctor had said. In the weeks before she died, she gave me the music box, the one thing she'd never sold for money, and said she'd tucked a letter under the lining for her baby boy, that maybe one day, if the time was ever right, it would find its way to him. I wasn't sure I wanted the responsibility of deciding when the right time was."

"I can understand that," Shelby said.

"A closed adoption, a secret adoption at that," Liam said. "Sharing that letter would affect many lives."

"Right," Pearl said. "Which was why I held on to it for almost sixty years. But now that I'm in my eighties… I don't know. It just seemed wrong to hold something so…vital, a truth that does matter, that does mean something. It felt wrong to take it to my grave."

"So you put it in a bag with Harrington's name on it and left it on his porch," Liam said.

Pearl nodded. "I figured one of two things would happen. It would be brought to Harrington Mercer and he would take a look, notice the bumpy lining and see what was tucked under and find the letter. Or, a maid or his wife would find the package, mention it to him, get dismissed and toss the box in the garbage or the attic. I just wanted to try—to do something that might get the letter to him, exactly as it had been given to me. I admit, I hadn't considered the music box might end up in Treasures, a secondhand shop where someone else might find the letter. In fact, I figured no one ever would."

Shelby took a sip of her coffee. "But someone did. And not just someone—Harrington Mercer's son's new wife."

Pearl seemed to notice Shelby's ring for the first time. She gasped. "Congratulations!" she exclaimed. "Isn't that something? I thought by leaving that box on the porch that whatever would be would be. But perhaps it ended up in just the right hands after all."

"Why is that?" Liam asked.

"Because you're family," Pearl said gently. "You'll know whether you should reveal the secret or burn the letter."

Liam let out a breath. "God, I don't want that responsibility."

"I know just how you feel," Pearl said. "Sorry."

Shelby took the last sip of her coffee. "Pearl, do you think it's possible that Harrington Mercer knows he was adopted?"

Pearl shook her head. "I can't see how. Alexandra went as far as to fake her pregnancy. She swore Jeannie to secrecy."

"Do you think I should tell my father?" Liam asked Pearl.

"That's for you to decide," Pearl said. "It all comes down to whether or not you think he would benefit in any way from the information, whether it would change his life in a positive way. If it would only hurt, then no, maybe not. I'm just not sure, dear. Truth is important, but then ignorance is bliss. Right?"

Shelby thought about Shane and Alexander. She'd been living in ignorant bliss for six months while the baby she'd given birth to was being raised by someone else, also living in ignorant bliss.

"I really don't know," Liam said. "Not anymore."

And with that, they thanked Pearl for everything they'd shared, said goodbye to the dogs who'd come to see them off, and then left, both of them quiet on the ride home.

Her new husband had quite a decision to make.

Chapter 12

Liam sure was glad to be back home at the ranch and not at Shelby's tiny apartment. He'd walked the fields for over an hour, Shane against his chest in a sling. Shelby had taken Alexander to work with her, wanting to show him the shop and point out all her favorite pieces.

And Liam had pointed out all his favorite spots on the ranch to Shane. Starting with the outdoor play yard his father had ordered as a surprise for Alexander to celebrate his one month on earth. There was a big cedar playground with swings and slide and a jungle gym for when he was a bit older, and a toddler area with pint-size climbers and hidey spots.

"You and Alexander will play here together as brothers," Liam said, one hand against the protective sling at Shane's back, the other on the wood fence surrounding the play yard.

Shane looked at him with those beautiful blue eyes.

"One day, when the time is right, Shane, I'll tell you about your birth mother. Liza was a wonderful person. And I know she's looking out for you and always will be watching over you."

Shane's little bow mouth quirked. Liam caressed his soft cheek, so in love with this precious boy that he felt like his heart would burst. "I lost the first six months of your life but I want you to know I'll always be here for you. No matter what," he added. "You're my son. Same as Alexander."

If only his dad could see it that way. That Alexander was Liam's son same as Shane. How could the man who'd raised him have such a different way of looking at things? How could they have such different values?

"DNA alone doesn't make you family," Liam said, watching a bird land on a post. "Family is about love and taking responsibility and commitment."

How could his father not understand that?

And because Harrington Mercer didn't understand that, how could Liam show him the letter Shelby had found in that music box?

But how could Liam *not*?

"I've been walking around that question for over an hour, Shane," Liam said, heading back toward the house. "And I'm no closer to knowing what I'm going to do than I was when your mother and I left Pearl's house."

"Ba-la!" Shane babbled, reaching out a hand.

Liam smiled and shook Shane's tiny hand. "What should I do, wise one?"

"Ba-wa!" Shane said with a huge smile.

Unfortunately, Liam could take that to mean anything: tell him or don't tell him.

Maybe Shelby would have some advice. "Let's go home and wait for your mother. If I know Shelby Ingalls—Shelby *Mercer*," he corrected, "she'll have been thinking about it all day at work. It's good to surround yourself with smart women, Shane. Remember that."

On the way to the house, he'd decided he should share the letter with his father.

But by the time he opened the door, he'd changed his mind.

That went on for a good hour more until Shelby finally came home with Alexander. The sight of them made him forget all about the questions buzzing at his brain. Shelby, as usual, looked so beautiful, her blond hair loose around her shoulders, her V-neck sweater bringing out the green in her eyes.

"Make any decisions today?" Shelby asked, shifting Alexander in her arms.

He slapped a hand against his forehead. "I just put it out of my mind a second ago after killing myself all afternoon."

She smiled. "Sorry. We don't have to talk about it. You don't have to decide anything right away."

"Except it feels awful, knowing a secret about someone—and not just someone, my father."

"Let's put these two to bed and then I'll make us comfort food for dinner and we'll talk it out."

"Sounds like a plan," Liam said.

Comfort food. Smart woman talking him through this. Just what the doctor ordered. They headed upstairs to the nursery bathroom, took care of baths, fresh pajamas, two stories, three songs and many kisses goodnight. Both boys stirred and fussed a bit before finally falling asleep, but finally, Liam heard nothing but Shelby's cat, which had taken up residence at his ranch, meowing for her dinner.

"How about you feed Lulu while I take care of dinner," Shelby said with a smile.

Liam knew he had the easier job and gave the cat her can of ocean fish in gravy. "Can I help?" he asked Shelby.

"You can take this and yourself into the living room and relax," she said, handing him a beer.

"You're good to me," he said.

"You're good to me."

The marriage was a success. Plain and simple. Granted, they'd been married since Tuesday, but it was working. They *were* good to each other. Good for each other. And good for Alexander and Shane.

Liam sat down on the couch, put his feet up on the coffee table, and enjoyed his beer, trying to not think too much about whether or not he was going to tell his father about the letter. Every time he thought he made the right choice, he'd change his mind.

"Dinner is served," Shelby said, coming in with a tray that she set on the coffee table. "My favorite comfort food. And I'm going to admit that I didn't make it. It's Norah's special tonight at the Pie Diner. Beef pot pie."

"It smells amazing," he said, sniffing the air. His mouth was already watering for it.

She cut him a big slice, succulent beef stew, soft chunks of potatoes, carrots and who knew what else making for a great-smelling dinner. He took a bite—delicious. "Please tell Norah this is the best pot pie I've ever had."

She smiled. "I will."

"What do you think I should do?" he asked. "About the letter?"

"What I think is that you know your father best. I did agree with what Pearl said, that sharing the letter with him may be the right choice if it would benefit him. But I was thinking about how everyone involved has passed on," she pointed out. "His parents. Jeannie. He'd have Pearl for information, but the three people he'd really want to talk to about it are gone."

He hadn't considered that. "That's a good point."

Shelby took a bite of her pot pie. "What she said about Jeannie really touched me. How alone she was. It made me think about how lucky I am to have my family. I can always count on them. And for your father, he has a loving family, too. He has your mother, you, your brother. So if you did decide to share the letter, he wouldn't be alone. He may not be able to turn to his parents or Jeannie for answers or clarification, but he'd have you guys."

"Another good point."

She smiled. "Not very helpful, I know."

Liam sipped his beer. "I've been trying to think about how telling him would help him see that DNA isn't the be all and end all. That not having Mercer DNA doesn't make him less of a Mercer. I'm still a Mercer, right? If I am, then Alexander is. Same as Shane. None of us is more Mercer than another. Especially given the new information we have about my father."

"Except he feels how he feels. The news might devastate him."

"Except it shouldn't. He's still the same person he was. That's what he needs to understand. Which makes me think I should tell him."

"You'll do the right thing," she said. "That's all I really know for sure."

"I appreciate your faith in me. Believe me. Sometimes I have zero in myself."

She reached over and kissed him on the cheek and again, he took her face in his hands and kissed her.

But this time, she kissed him back.

Which made pulling away impossible.

He couldn't if he wanted to. And he didn't want to. He wanted Shelby in his arms. His hands were suddenly everywhere, in her hair and under her sweater, moving to her waist and rib cage and her breasts, hidden by something lacy. He kissed her hard, leaning her back on the couch, and she wrapped her arms around him, her husky breaths and little moans pushing him toward the edge.

She shifted slightly. "Liam, not to be a cliché, but I don't want to do anything you're going to regret."

"What?" he asked, kissing her neck.

"Right now you're caught up in the moment. You're turned on. You're not thinking. And when you do start thinking, like after we've had sex, when we're spooned together and you're suddenly itchy and uncomfortable and realizing you messed up your perfect vision of our family unit partnership. You'll pull away, I'll get hurt and guess what—the discord you were afraid of from the start."

He reached up a hand to her face, to her soft cheek in a gesture of thanks. *She cares about me, for real*, he realized.

And that was scary enough to make him sit up.

"You're absolutely right," he said. "Thank God one of us is always on their toes."

She moved a few inches away on the couch, clasping her hands in her lap. "I need to be careful with you, Liam. Very careful."

"Meaning?"

"Meaning we're obviously physically attracted to each other. We're married. We share a home, a family, a crazy situation that brought us very close. If I give in to how I'm feeling, my inhibitions loosened with a glass of wine, I could end up losing everything that matters to me. You know, I used to think you were being too cautious. But now, who knows what would happen if we hated each other's guts? If we were fighting for custody. And for whom?"

His stomach churned. *But I want you so bad*, he thought. *You're one hundred percent right, yet how am I going to keep my hands off you? You're all I think about now.*

"Let's eat," she said. "And watch the news. That's always good for killing the mood."

As she pointed the remote at the big-screen TV, Liam sighed inwardly and picked up his plate. Hadn't he told Shane how important it was to surround yourself with smart women? Shelby was being smart. A hell of a lot smarter than Liam had acted a minute ago.

But he wasn't supposed to want her with this kind of ferocity. He wasn't supposed to fall in love with her.

His own wife.

Fool, Shelby chastised herself as she tossed and turned in bed—alone. Yes, she believed every word of what she'd said to stop him, to stop *them*, from getting into trouble, from doing anything that could jeopardize their very good arrangement. Their *marriage*.

Sometimes when Shelby thought about the way

they were both keeping one giant step back from each other—emotionally, physically—the whole idea seemed so dopey. *Just kiss and make love and go from there, idiots!* she wanted to yell at them sometimes. And if it turned out that Liam was hot for her physically but thought she was a snooze otherwise? Then what? They'd be "friends with benefits" but married? Or what if they made love and she realized she just didn't feel "that way" about him? He'd be hurt and suddenly there would be cold shoulders and distance and who would pay? Two six-month-olds, that was who.

Not worth the cost. Being with Liam, truly being with him, was priceless. But losing her babies? She wouldn't jeopardize having both of them in her life every day, living with them as a family. She couldn't.

So great. She and Liam were on the same page. To cold showers and wishing things could be different.

She flipped onto her stomach. Then on her back. Then to her side. Her other side. Dammit! She couldn't get comfortable. She wasn't comfortable.

Because she already loved her husband. And was just not acting on that love. She knew Liam cared about her, but she wouldn't say he *loved* her. Wanted her, maybe. Okay, definitely. He'd proved that tonight. But a man as passionate as Liam Mercer wouldn't be able to control himself to the degree he had so far if he loved her. Hadn't he said over and over that what he wanted most was for the four of them to be a family unit? He was a red-blooded male, he was attracted to her and he'd acted on that a time or two. Didn't mean he was in love.

So get your head out of the clouds, Shelby.

And get out of bed, she told herself. She might as well go check on the babies.

She put on the fancy spa bathrobe that Liam had provided her in her en-suite bath, then padded down the hall. A soft light glowed from the nursery. The night-lights?

She pushed open the door. Liam was fast asleep in the glider by the window, *Moo Baa, La, La, La* open on his lap. Once again, he was shirtless. In sweatpants. Barefoot. And so sexy she could hardly take it.

Sexy because he was hot, hot, hot.

Sexy because he was kind.

Sexy because he was a great father.

Sexy because he was a good husband.

How much longer could they really go on this way? Both afraid of getting hurt. Both afraid of destroying the family? Both afraid of losing Shane and Alexander. Was this what they wanted to teach their children? To avoid real life and real emotion and how messy the heart could get?

Shelby sighed and headed back to her room. Tomorrow, Liam would tell his father about the letter—or not. She had a feeling that doing so, or not doing so, would change *him* forever.

But in what way?

Chapter 13

In the morning, with ten minutes to go until open-ing time, Shelby held Alexander against her chest and showed him the new collection of paintings that had been donated to the shop from a regular customer who'd inherited them from her grandmother and hated them all. Shelby liked quite a few of them and knew they'd sell, and the drearier still lifes might appeal to someone.

"What do you think, Alexander? I love the way the artist used a hint of pink to brighten up the gray sea in the background. And do you see the rowboat? I'd love to take you and Shane out on a rowboat when you're older and—"

A wheeze suddenly came out of Alexander's tiny body, a raspy cough that froze Shelby. And was it her imagination or was Alexander's face suddenly flushed—and mottled? He fussed and squirmed, and she put her hand to his forehead. Hot. Very hot. He coughed, wheezed again and Shelby's heartbeat sped up.

"Oh, no. You definitely have a high fever." She dashed upstairs to her apartment, where the nursery was still intact. She took Alexander's temperature. Scarily high. Grabbing her cell phone, she called the pediatrician, the same one she used for Shane, and was told to take him to the clinic right away and that he'd meet her there. She called Liam and explained the situation.

"Wheezing?" Liam repeated. "Like a cough from a cold? A high fever? That'll go down with some baby Tylenol, right? I mean, it's nothing, right?"

"Well, a fever that high can be alarming in babies, so Dr. Lewis just wants to examine him, make sure he doesn't need fluids—just double-check everything is okay."

"I'll meet you at the clinic in ten minutes. Shane's in the day care, well taken care of."

"Perfect," she said. "See you soon."

In less than ten minutes, Shelby was at the clinic. Dr. Lewis arrived quickly after and led the way into an examining room. Just as his stethoscope was going into his ears, a nurse led Liam into the room. He looked very worried.

He reached for her hand and held it, and again Shelby was struck by how real a couple they seemed, acted like—were, except for that one major area. Regardless, she sure was glad he was here.

"Well," Dr. Lewis said, "from the fever, wheezing and listening to his chest, it's clear he has RSV—respiratory syncytial virus—a common childhood illness that often first strikes before two years of age."

"Is it serious?" Liam asked.

"It's serious, not life-threatening—no worries there. He has a touch of bronchiolitis, which means we'll need to watch his airways. He'll need to stay at the clinic for a few days so we can monitor him around the clock and also because he'll be contagious for at least a week."

"A week? But Alexander and Shane share a nursery at the ranch. There's a guest room we can move Alexander into when he's discharged."

"I don't think the two babies should share a home for at least a week," Dr. Lewis said. "Just to be safe. RSV is highly contagious."

"I'll keep Alexander at the apartment," Shelby suggested. "Shane can stay at the ranch with you. That way we can be sure Alexander will be fully cured before he comes back to the ranch. Shane will have less chance of catching RSV that way."

"I think that's the way to go," Dr. Lewis said.

Separated.

Just like they didn't want.

"It's just for a week," Liam said, his hand on Shelby's arm. "A week is nothing. We're in this for a lifetime."

She nodded and actually did feel better. In the grand scheme of things, a week was nothing. But every hour of every day would crawl by. She was glad to see Alexander through his illness, but she hated the idea of being away from Shane for so long. And Liam.

"I'll call my family and let them know what's going on. Expect pie deliveries," she said, mustering a smile.

"Pie always helps."

"Call your dad," she said. "One word about Alexander being sick and stuck in the clinic for days and he'll rush over with a life-size stuffed bull."

Liam frowned. "Bull being the key word, unfortunately. I'm sure he won't. Alexander isn't his *real* grandson, remember?"

"Liam, a baby in the hospital has a way of knocking through very stubborn walls. Call him."

"I'll call," he said. "But I'm not expecting his feelings to suddenly change."

Shelby sure hoped she was right about his dad. If she wasn't, it was the Mercer family that might never recover.

Liam delegated the afternoon's work to his cousin Clara, who promised to visit Alexander in the clinic when she left the office, and then he headed over to his parents' house with Shane. Shelby was right. She had to be right. His father would have a complete meltdown over his beloved Alexander being so sick and in the clinic for a few days. Liam figured he should tell his parents in person so that he and his father could begin mending their relationship right away. He didn't need problems with his father to burn in his gut when he was worried sick over his son.

His mother wasn't home, but his father was in his home office, having a glass of scotch and reading dossiers on companies that Mercer Industries might look into acquiring.

"There he is, my young man," Harrington Mercer said, his gaze on Shane in Liam's arms. He stood up and came around his deck, smiling at the baby. "Let me have my grandson."

Liam froze. The split second was long enough for his father to pluck Shane out of his grip and hoist him high in the air.

"Aren't you a magnificent young man," Harrington

said. "We have a lot of catching up to do. I was just look-ing at companies that MI might buy. Here, come see."

He took Shane back around his desk and sat down, the baby gurgling happily on his lap. "Winston Tech had a terrible quarter. And honestly, I don't think their products are top-notch. Let's move on to Branston Man-ufacturing—"

"Dad," Liam said. "There's something you should know. Alexander is sick. He has RSV and it grew into bronchiolitis. He'll be at the Wedlock Creek Clinic for around three days, and then he'll stay with Shelby at her apartment while I keep Shane at the ranch to make sure Shane doesn't catch it."

"Well, that's smart," Harrington said. "Trust me, Shane, you don't want to catch some nasty virus. You'd miss a ton. Every day you soak up countless bits of knowledge and—"

Liam frowned. He waited a beat. His father contin-ued chatting to Shane about osmosis and paying atten-tion and how when he was three and started preschool, Harrington would add a home-school business segment to his curriculum. "Are you going to ask if Alexander is going to be okay?" Liam practically growled.

"I'm sure he is," Harrington said.

"He's going to be at the clinic for *days*, Dad."

"And he'll be fine when he's released."

A hot burst of anger, bordering on rage, bubbled in Liam's chest. "Jesus, you really don't care, do you?"

"Liam, for God's sake, stop overreacting. Alexan-der is no longer my grandson and you know it. He's an Ingalls. His people run the Pie Diner. This," he said, hoisting up Shane again, "is my grandson. And I need to focus on getting to know him."

Liam stormed around the desk and grabbed Shane away from his father. Shane stared at him, his little face crumpling. He rocked the baby a bit and patted his back. "Sorry, little guy. It's okay. Everything is okay."

But it wasn't. Not by a longshot.

"Goodbye, then," Liam said. "You don't know the meaning of family." He turned to leave, prepared to estrange himself from his father until the man woke up, which might never happen.

His father stood up. "Liam."

He turned, his stomach twisting. Harrington's expression was one Liam didn't often see. It looked to him like resignation.

"DNA matters," his father said. "Whether you like it or not."

He should just come out with it, tell his father what he'd learned about his own DNA, show him the letter, introduce him to Pearl. But to what end? To hurt him because Liam was hurt?

Tell him if there'll be some benefit, Pearl had said.

Would there be? If DNA mattered that much to his father, the truth about himself would destroy him. That wasn't what Liam wanted, either.

He might not like his father right now. Might not agree with him. Might not share his values.

But he loved his father and always would.

"I should know," Harrington said, his voice cracking. "Trust me. I *do* know."

Liam stared at his father, taking a step toward him. "Dad?"

Harrington walked to the wall of windows, his arms around himself protectively. He stood there looking out, inhaling, exhaling. "I know because I was adopted as a baby." He turned toward Liam and looked at him, then away. "Because I'm not a real Mercer."

Holy hell. He knew. He knew he was adopted.

"I can tell from your expression that you're shocked," Harrington said. "Of course, I couldn't tell you because then you might not think you were a real Mercer. I kept the secret to protect you."

Oh, Dad. Liam closed his eyes for a moment, letting this all sink in.

"I overheard an argument between my parents when I was nine," Harrington said. "I'd left for school but forgot a book and had come back. My parents were in the living room, their voices raised. I hid behind the wall and listened. My father said it was getting ridiculous that I didn't know, that he wasn't going to put up with it a day longer, but my mother pleaded with him to let it go, to just make it go away. At first I had no idea what they were talking about. But then I understood. I'd been adopted as a baby. My mother wanted my father to pretend that wasn't the case. That I was my parents' child, end of story."

Liam tried to picture his father, tall, strong, imposing Harrington Mercer, hiding in the kitchen and eavesdropping on an unbearable argument between his parents only to discover he'd been adopted. That a secret had been kept, a secret about him. Liam recalled photos of his father while looking for pictures of Alexandra Mercer during her pregnancy. He'd been a solemn-faced kid, with serious blue eyes. Liam could hardly bear imagining that boy standing there in shock, confused, hurt.

"My father kept saying that the truth was the truth and it was wrong to keep something so important from me, that I should know for many reasons. But then my mother said something I'll never forget. She said, 'It's too late. If he'd grown up knowing that would be different. But it's too late. It'll break his heart to know he's not a real Mercer.'"

"Oh, God. Dad." Tears pricked the backs of Liam's eyes and he blinked them away.

"I turned and ran then. I don't know what else was said. But I do know they never did tell me. Long after my mother died, when my father was in hospice and I'd visit him, he would hold my hand and tell me to never forget that I was a Mercer, that it would carry me through."

Liam's heart clenched. There was so much he didn't know about his dad. There was so much the people closest to you didn't reveal. Incidents and memories and trauma that seeped their way inside their bones, changing them this way or that.

"I never let on that I knew. I didn't want to break his heart at the end. And I know it would hurt him deeply to know that I'd known the truth for decades." He turned back to the windows, his chin lifted, the strain in his jawline evident. "But do you want to know what kept going through my mind as my father drifted in and out of consciousness? That I *wasn't* a real Mercer. That a lie *wouldn't* carry me through. To fill my father's shoes at Mercer Industries, I'd have to work very hard, make my life the business and try to become a Mercer in all the ways I knew how. I think I passed just fine. But I never felt like I truly belonged, that the name wasn't really mine."

Liam tried to process everything he'd just heard, but the words echoed in his head. *The name wasn't really mine.* "Given all you just said, how could you say that Alexander isn't a real Mercer, then? How could you turn your back? Your parents brought you up to be their son. That made you a Mercer. Not your DNA, Dad."

"Because the truth was unbearable, Liam. And Alexander is going to grow up knowing the truth. He's not a Mercer. He's an Ingalls. And I'm not going to lie and pretend he's something he's not. He's not my grandson. Shane is."

"So you're not a Mercer. That means I'm not. And guess what—that means Shane isn't, either. So it looks like you don't have *any* grandsons."

His father stared at him then, hard, then looked away.

"When does it end, Dad? Who gets to be a Mercer in this branch of the family?"

His father walked over to the bar and topped off his scotch. He didn't say anything.

"I have something for you, Dad. It's in the car. I'll be right back."

Liam's legs—and heart—felt so heavy as he walked out of the room. Part of him didn't want to leave his father alone with his thoughts, with the admission hanging in the air like that. But he wanted to give his father the music box and letter. The time had presented itself.

Liam returned to the room with the box, his father still standing by the windows. "Dad, do you remember Mom showing this to you? She found it in a brown paper bag with your name on it, left anonymously on the porch last week."

Harrington shrugged. "Your mother shows me a lot of things."

"Well, Mom gave it to Shelby for her secondhand shop, Treasures. But when Shelby saw the box, she fell in love with it and decided to keep it instead of offering it for sale. She was examining it and found a letter hidden away under the velvet inside lining."

"And?" his father asked, bored and impatient. He sipped his scotch and sat down in the club chair by the fireplace.

"Here," Liam said, handing him the box. "The letter is inside. You need to read it."

Harrington rolled his eyes but took the box. He opened it and unfolded the letter, his expression changing a second later as he read the date.

"That's my birthday. The day and year I was born," Harrington said, looking up for a moment and then returning his gaze to the letter.

Liam sat down on the chair across from his father, looking down, wanting to give the man some privacy.

He heard his father gasp and looked up. Liam knew exactly where he was in the letter. The first time "Mrs. Mercer" was mentioned.

Harrington sat still as a post, staring at the letter. He appeared to be rereading it, then again. His hands flew up to cover his eyes, his shoulders trembling.

His father was crying.

Liam got up and walked over to his father and put his hand on his shoulder. Harrington stood and wrapped his arms around Liam, sobbing, and Liam held him tightly, saying nothing, just letting him cry it out. It was the third time he'd seen his father cry; the first time had been when Liam was just a kid, when his father's mother was dying, the second time at the funeral.

Harrington pulled back, wiping at his eyes. "Good God, this almost ended up in some stranger's house on the mantel."

Liam smiled. "But it didn't. It ended up in your

daughter-in-law's hands. Shelby. Shelby *Mercer*. She's a Mercer because she married me. I'm a Mercer because you're my father. Alexander is a Mercer because I'm *his* father. And you're a Mercer because you're Wilton and Alexandra Mercer's son."

Tears glistened in Harrington's eyes. "I'm also this woman's son. Whoever she was."

"Yes. Also. Just like Shane is *also* my son. Even though I didn't raise him for the past six months. Even though someone else did. In that case, DNA says so. In Alexander's it's because I love him. *Love*, Dad. That's what matters. Your birth mother clearly loved you. Your adoptive parents clearly loved you. Love makes you family. Period."

Harrington stood up and moved to the windows again. Not saying a word.

"Shelby and I did a little investigating. It led us to a woman named Pearl who runs a dog rescue out of her home on the outskirts of town. Pearl is the one who left the letter. Your birth mother was her friend. She can tell you the story, if you want to hear it."

"I'm not sure," Harrington said, taking a sip of his drink.

"When you're ready, then," Liam said. "If you're ready." He walked over to his father and put his arm around him, then kissed his cheek, ignoring the way Harrington stiffened. *Tough nuggies*, Dad. In the doorway, he paused and turned around. "Oh, and Dad, I'll be at Alexander's bedside at the clinic till five and then I'll go pick up Shane and take him back to the ranch. Just to keep you in the loop."

His father nodded and again didn't say anything.

Liam had no idea where things would go from here.

He just knew he was desperate to see Alexander and hear that he was improving, even though Shelby had told him exactly that an hour ago. But first he'd have to stop at the office and take care of some pressing business, then pick up Shane and drop him off at the Pie Diner with the Ingallses for the couple of hours he'd be at the clinic for visiting hours.

Liam wished he could just head over there right now. If he didn't see Shelby's face soon, hear her voice, feel her in his arms for a bracing hug, he would spontaneously combust.

"It's so hard to see a baby in the hospital," Norah said, barely able to hold the stuffed monkey, the five board books and the blanket with the chew ends she'd bought for Alexander. She glanced down at the little guy asleep in the bassinet.

"You're a sweetheart for bringing him all these presents," Shelby said. "Between you, Aunt Cheyenne, Mom, Liam's brother, mother and his cousin bringing heaps of gifts, we could open a big-box store."

Norah smiled. "Alexander's color looks pretty good."

Shelby nodded. "The doctor said he responded well to treatment. He may only have to stay here for two days."

One day less without Shane and Liam, the four of them together as a family. That was good. And so was the news that Alexander was already on the mend with antibiotics for the bronchiolitis and fluids.

Norah had to get back to the Pie Diner for the after-dinner rush, but just as she was leaving, Liam arrived. He hugged his sister-in-law, thanked her for all the pie she'd had delivered to his home and office, told her how her beef pot pie was the best he ever had and then turned to look at the stacks of gifts for Alexander.

"Wow. Alexander sure is loved."

And lucky. Like his cousin had said the morning Liam's entire life had turned upside down. Lucky because he was cherished.

"My parents came with the huge stuffed dolphin?" he asked, eyeing it in the corner.

"Actually, that was your brother's doing. The dolphin, the Harry Potter and Narnia collections on the windowsill and an iPod preprogrammed with lullabies by his favorite artists."

Liam smiled. "That's Drake, all right."

"And your mother brought that," she said, pointing to the giant play mat with all kinds of pop-up fun for a six-month-old. "She was very concerned about Alexander and said she'd call later to see how he was doing."

Liam frowned. "My father wasn't with her?"

Shelby shook her head. "He hasn't been here."

"How did my mother seem when she was here?"

"Uncomfortable. Upset."

"No doubt." Liam filled Shelby in on everything that had happened during his talk with his father.

"He's known he was adopted since he was nine years old," Shelby repeated, shaking her head. "That must have been so hard to process."

"What *isn't* hard to process? Loving a six-month-old baby. You don't get to pick and choose which baby to love."

Shelby reached out for Liam's hand. He was spitting mad, his cheeks flushed, his blue eyes flashing. She'd never seen him so angry.

"He should have been here. Two hours have passed

since I left him. How could he not have rushed over here to see his grandson? How the hell can he act like this?" His voice was raised and he expelled a breath, looking in Alexander's bassinet to make sure he hadn't woken him. He closed his eyes for a moment and turned away, his arms crossed over his chest.

"Liam—"

He paced the room. "Just goes to show you how family can cut you to the quick. How you can't really let yourself count on anyone. What we're doing, Shelby, this arranged marriage with our list of dos and don'ts—that's how you set up a family. That way, no one gets hurt."

No, no, no, Shelby thought, her heart pleading. *We're supposed to move past this. The way we feel about each other is supposed to blast through this ridiculous arrangement and make our marriage real in every sense of the word.*

"Like I said," he continued, "you were right to stop things last night. Thank God you did. Because all it would lead to is heartache. And I've had enough."

"No, Liam. I wasn't right."

He stared at her, waiting.

She stepped closer. "I was scared! Just like you are. But avoiding real love, a real marriage, because of fear— Liam, *that's* wrong."

He turned away and ran a hand through his hair. He was clearly frustrated and she could tell he was thinking she just didn't get it, didn't understand.

No, it's you who doesn't understand! Think about what you can have!

Yes, just explain that, she told herself. What was waiting for them if only he'd open that locked-up heart, guarded by bitter old trolls.

"Liam, every minute of our lives is going to be filled with risk. Alexander got sick. It could have been worse. It wasn't. Shane will fall out of a tree when he's five. Alexander will take a hard fall off a bike when he's eight. There will be accidents and mishaps and heartache and who knows what else. That's life. And we have to deal with it."

"Yes, stuff happens, Shelby. Believe me, I know. So do you. So let's not add to it by messing up a platonic marriage that's working just fine."

"You call this argument *fine*? You call going to bed every night alone *fine*? You call wishing we were truly together *fine*?" She paused, wondering if she was going too far. Maybe it was only she who felt this way. Her heart clenched as she realized Liam might not have the same depth of feeling for her. But everything inside her told her he did. "And what about the boys? Do you really want them to grow up thinking that a marriage is based on nothing more than practicality and friendship?"

He turned away again, let out a heavy sigh and faced her. "Nothing wrong with practicality and friendship. I'd say there are worse things to build a marriage on. Like nothing more than passion."

But we have it all! We have the friendship. We have the practicality. And we definitely have the passion!

She opened her mouth to say so, but he shook his head. "There's nothing more to say, Shelby. I'm going to pick up Shane and bring him home to the ranch. A few days apart will probably serve us well, anyway. Let you bond more with Alexander and me with Shane. And give us some time to forget last night ever happened and start fresh."

I don't want to start fresh. I love you! I want my husband in every sense of the word.

But now wasn't the time to make her case for that whopper. Liam was hurt and angry and lashing out. Maybe a little time to themselves was in order.

Maybe he'd come to his senses.

Except what if he didn't? Like father, like son?

A chill ran up Shelby's spine.

Liam stood by Alexander's crib and touched a kiss to his forehead, then left the room, taking Shelby's heart with him.

Chapter 14

Alexander had been discharged the next afternoon, and Shelby brought him back to the apartment above her shop. Liam had called at least ten times for updates.

And to ask if his father had stopped by the clinic to see Alexander before he was sent home.

The answer was no, and the silence on the end of the phone made it clear that Liam hadn't made peace with his father's rejection overnight. As if that was possible, anyway.

Shelby had stayed at the clinic last night, watching Alexander's chest rising and falling with every breath, her love for him keeping her awake. She hadn't wanted to miss a moment. Not when she'd missed so much already. She must have fallen asleep eventually on the uncomfortable built-in "parent" cot, grooves in the side of her face, her hair a disaster and her back all wonky.

Her mother had come by the clinic with sesame-seed bagels and cream cheese and orange juice and coffee and given Shelby a wonderful massage, and it had taken all Shelby's doing not to let loose with everything that had happened.

She usually would, but this was her husband's family business and it didn't feel right to blab about it just so she could feel better.

Except that was what family was for.

By the time Shelby was back home and Norah arrived a half hour before she had to open Treasures and take over as proprietor for the day, Shelby had let it all out.

"Oh, Shelby," Norah said, pouring them both coffee at the table in the kitchen. "He'll come around. The man loves you. The man is *in* love with you. He can't put the kibosh on that no matter how hard he tries."

Shelby felt her shoulder slump and dumped a tea-spoon of sugar in her coffee. "His father did it."

"Baloney. His father is processing. The man was handed two big kicks upside the head—first that his grandson was switched at birth. Then that his birth mother left him a letter. He had a minute to process that letter yesterday when Liam expected him at the clinic. Give him a little time."

"That's a good point. Liam worries he's a lost cause."

Norah took a sip of her coffee, frowning at the pink-red lip gloss stain she left on the mug. "Look, I don't know Harrington Mercer. I barely talked to the man at your pie-diner wedding reception other than about his favorite kinds of pie. But I know people. And the man has heart."

Norah was awfully good at reading people. She always had been.

"You think so?" Shelby asked, feeling herself brighten a bit.

"I do. Oh, by the way—the lawyer and I broke up."

"Oh, no," Shelby said. David Dirk had been very good to Shelby during one of the most difficult days of her life. "You okay? Here I've been hogging the conversation and you have your own big news."

"Big schmig. And it's not big at all. I'm totally fine. He told me he met the woman of his dreams at the Wedlock Creek Bar and Grill. She was shooting darts and almost hit him in the chest. Bull's-eye to the heart and that was that. We weren't a love match, anyway and only made out a few times—and badly. Zero chemistry. Oh, well."

"What about Liam's brother, Drake? He's gorgeous."

Norah nodded. "He is, but he's got it bad for someone."

"What? Liam never said a word! Who?"

Norah took another sip of coffee. "Oh, I'm not a hundred percent sure, but I've seen the way he looks at a certain someone. Mark my words, there's something brewing. Anyway, like I said, I've seen the way Liam looks at you. The man loves you. No doubt. Am I ever wrong? About anything? Wait—don't answer that. Just trust me."

"I love you," Shelby said, reaching to hug her younger sister.

"Ditto." She popped up from her chair, taking her coffee with her. "Time to open up Treasures. Can't keep the Minnow sisters waiting."

Shelby smiled. Suddenly, a fussy wail came from the nursery. "Thank you for everything, Norah. I'll see you later." She saw her sister out, then headed to get Alexander. He looked a hundred percent better, his color great and he was clearly hungry.

At least she had one third of her heart right here with her.

Shane had just finished his applesauce, half of which seemed to end up on the baby's chin, when the doorbell rang.

Please be Shelby, he thought. He hated the way they'd left things. Hated the way he'd hurt her when that was the last thing he wanted to do—in fact, the very thing their marriage was supposed to protect them from.

But of course it wouldn't be Shelby. She had Alexander, freshly discharged from the clinic, and wasn't supposed to bring him over for a few days. At least the doctor had amended it from a week. And as Liam had said, he could use a few days apart from her, though it killed him to be separated from Alexander for even a day. He needed the time away from Shelby to reinforce his original plan for their marriage. Once he had all that as solid and settled in his head as it had been when he'd first proposed to her, he'd be good to go. Onward for the future for the good of their family.

It was looking at her that started problems.

Seeing her when she first woke up with those sleepy eyes and her sexy bed head and the way her long T-shirts and yoga pants clung to her curves.

Watching her scoop up the babies and smother them in morning kisses, her love for them shining in her eyes and in her every gesture.

And catching the way she'd look at him sometimes when she wasn't guarding herself.

Except he wasn't supposed to want her to look at him like that.

He shook his head to clear it, as if that ever worked, then plopped Shane in the playpen in the living room and headed to the door, sure it was yet another delicious delivery from the Pie Diner. The Ingalls women had stocked his fridge full of quiche, pot pies and fruit pies.

But it was his mother standing on the doorstep. "Just thought I'd pop by to see how you are. Lovely evening." She seemed to be trying to muster a smile but couldn't make it happen.

Larissa Mercer was a very private person and hid her emotions well, but Liam could plainly see she was a nervous wreck.

"You okay, Mom?" Liam held the door open wide, and his mother stepped inside, her heels clicking on the tile.

"Dad told me about your conversation," she said, taking off her jacket and folding it over her arm. She sat down on a tall-backed chair facing the fireplace. "I don't think I've ever seen him so emotional and lost for words at the same time."

Hmm. That was unexpected. Liam sat down across from her. "Did you know he was adopted?"

Larissa waited a beat. Talking about family secrets, talking about anything other than the weather or last night's dinner or their feelings in the most superficial manner, wasn't the Mercer way and he knew this had to be hard for his mom. "I've known since the day he proposed marriage to me. He broke down about it a couple of hours after I said yes. He told me he couldn't accept my hand in marriage unless I knew the whole truth about him—which was that he 'wasn't a real Mercer.'"

Once again, Liam was struck by the image of his father as a younger man, a man on one knee, proposing to the woman he loved—and refusing to lie to her. Refusing to go forward in life when she didn't know something he deemed fundamental about him.

That was character. And it gave him hope for his dad.

"I told him he absolutely was a real Mercer," his mother continued, "and that I'd love him the same no matter to whom he was born. I'll never forget his expression   he was so touched. But once I knew and he felt comfortable moving forward, he put the whole thing out of his mind. He never brought it up again."

His parents had been married for thirty-one years. They'd never talked about it again? Jeez. Talk about repression.

"That's no way to live," Liam said. "Blocking out the truth, pretending something isn't so."

Like his feelings for Shelby. How much he wanted her.

How much he loved her.

There it was. What he'd refused to admit to himself. He loved Shelby. So much. His love for her had come bursting out of every cell of his body without his control. Because like Shelby said, that was how love worked. You couldn't control it.

But you could control yourself. You could pretend. You could deny.

Like his father had.

Like Liam had to. To make sure all he cared about was protected.

Arrrgh! Why was this so hard? He'd had it all figured out. And then *wham*, blast to the center of his theory and the practice.

"No, it's no way to live," his mother said. "But it's

what he needed to do. It was his business, so I never pressed him to talk about it. Maybe I should have."

"I understand why you didn't bring it up. He wanted it forgotten. And Dad can be difficult to talk to sometimes."

"No kidding," she said, finally smiling.

"I'm not sure I can forgive him for not visiting Alexander in the clinic. He was really sick. And Dad didn't come. That was the true test of his feelings for his grandson and he failed miserably."

"I know. And trust me, your father was tormented about it and still is. Right now your father is very wrapped up in how he *feels*, how he thinks things have to be. But there are consequences to his actions and we'll just have to see what happens."

How he thinks things have to be. Like Liam and his insistence that he and Shelby have a platonic marriage?

Consequences. Like losing Shelby, anyway?

He felt his heart sink along with his stomach. Arrgh again! *Focus on your dad and not yourself.*

"I'm not sure I want to watch," Liam said. "Family train wreck coming up next. Stay tuned."

"Well, whatever happens with your father, know that you and Shelby and Alexander and Shane have my full support. They are my grandsons. Both of them. They're my treasures. I've just known one a bit longer than the other."

Treasures. Like the name of Shelby's shop. Like Shelby. Pure treasure.

His mother stood and went over to say hello to Shane, scooping up the baby and giving him a cuddle. "I can't wait to get to know you more and more." She kissed his cheek, then put him back down. "I'll see you soon, Liam."

He walked his mother to the door, so damned twisted up about his marriage. How it was supposed to work. How it was supposed to last. Shouldn't he keep up the emotional and physical distance from his wife?

If so, why did that sound so incredibly stupid and impossible to his own ears?

Liam walked over to the wall of windows, looking out at the dark night, the woods dimly illuminated by the yard lights. A chill ran up the nape of his neck as a terrible thought came over him.

Maybe the answer was *no* marriage instead of a farce. All this time he'd thought they had to be married, legally wed, to have what they needed and wanted—both babies. But maybe it was better to live separate lives and share custody. Splitting the week. Splitting the babies. Not that that sounded like a good idea.

He didn't want Shane only half the week. He didn't want to give up Alexander half the time. He wanted them to grow up as brothers.

Which brought him back to being married to Shelby. Their mother.

Except living a lie was no longer acceptable. His father had proven that. Harrington Mercer could live with his head stuck in the sand all he wanted. But Liam wouldn't. He and Shelby weren't a real husband and wife. And pretending to be a family under a lie like that was wrong. But living together as a real husband and wife in every sense of the word? No. Liam knew that led to nothing but heartache down the road, and would pit him and Shelby against each other. Love didn't last.

As least for him. And two little boys' lives would be affected. Again.

He needed to sit down with Shelby and talk this through, how they were going to deal with the situation.

Because he couldn't live like this.

Liam dropped off Shane with the Ingallses, who doted over him and tried to push more pie on Liam. At this rate, he'd be a thousand pounds in a month. He thanked them for watching Shane for an hour or two—however long it would take him and Shelby to reach some kind of new arrangement—and headed over to her apartment.

He rang the bell and when he heard her footsteps coming down the stairs, his heart sped up.

He couldn't wait for her to open the door. He couldn't wait to see her face. He couldn't wait to pull her in his arms.

Because he loved her. So damned much he felt it in his blood and veins and every beat of his heart.

What the hell? He'd come over here determined to change things between them, to live truthfully.

And the truth is that you love Shelby Ingalls Mercer, your wife.

That is the truth, the whole truth, so help you, God.

The door opened.

Shelby stood there, looking beautiful as always in her faded jeans and long-sleeved T-shirt, her wedding ring sparkling in the dim lighting of the vestibule on Alexander's back as she held him.

"Liam, is everything okay? Is Shane okay?"

"Shane is fine. I left him with your family for a bit. To come see you."

Her expression went from worried to alarmed.

Because she loves you, too, moron. It hit him like a ton of the old bricks. That was what she'd been trying to say earlier. She loved him. And always had.

He reached for her hands. "You were right about everything, Shelby."

"I was?" she said tentatively, putting her hands in his.

"About how love works. You can't control it. Try and you'll only end up with an ulcer."

She smiled. "I know. I've been popping antacids left and right."

"If we love each other, and it's clear as day that we do, we need to have a real marriage. Full of love and passion and give and take. Support. Loving, honoring, cherishing. In sickness and in health. For richer and for poorer, for as long as we both shall live."

"Oh, God, Liam. I do. I do!"

He laughed and pulled her into a hug. "And if we argue, and I'm sure we will, if we stomp off all angry at each other, we're strong enough to withstand it."

"You're right," said a deep voice from behind him. "Because we're Mercers. And that's what Mercers do."

Liam whirled around. His father stood inches away on the sidewalk.

"I'd like to see my grandson, if that's all right," Harrington said. He was holding a small bag in his hands. "I have something for him."

My grandson. Finally.

"Sure," Shelby said. "Come on up."

Liam walked up the stairs to Shelby's apartment and realized the usual hundred-pound weight was gone from each shoulder.

The moment his father entered the apartment he rushed toward Alexander in his playpen and lifted him up, tears in his eyes. "My grandson. My precious grandson. I'll never let you down again. I promise you that. I have something for you. Something that's yours." He reached into the bag and pulled the little brown cowboy hat he'd given Alexander the Friday that all their lives had changed.

"I've been looking all over for that," Liam said. "Glad you found it."

Harrington looked away for a moment, then square at Liam. He kissed Alexander on the cheek and then put him back down in the playpen. "I didn't find it. I took it back. The night you and Shelby told us about Alexander and Shane and the baby switch."

Oh, God. Dad.

"After you left the other day I sat looking at that tiny Stetson for hours," Harrington said. "Your mother tried to talk sense into me but I wouldn't listen. And finally I just kept thinking about lines from the letter. From my mother, Alexandra. From my father, Wilton. And from what Pearl said."

Shelby practically gasped. "You went to see Pearl?"

"Damned right, I did. I adopted two of her dogs, too."

Shelby laughed. "Really?"

Harrington nodded. "I named one Clint. Your mother gets naming rights for the second one. Young German shepherds mixed with God knows what."

"Good for you, Dad. You always wanted a dog. Now you'll have two."

"Two sons, two grandsons, two dogs," Harrington said. He looked from Liam to Shelby and back to Liam. "Son, I'm sorry I couldn't see my way through this until now. It took some serious soul-searching, I'll tell you that. But no matter how I feel about myself, Alexander is my grandson. I love the stuffing out of him."

"I know you do, Dad. It must have hurt like hell to withdraw from him."

"It did. And it'll never happen again."

Shelby hugged Harrington and he hugged her back tight.

"We're Mercers," Harrington said. "And we're Ingallses. And we're McCords."

"McCords?" Liam repeated.

"My birth mother," Harrington said. "Her name was Jeannie McCord."

Shelby smiled. "Well, hopefully we'll be blessed with more children. I want five, did I mention that, Liam?" She grinned at her husband then turned to Harrington. "How about we give our next born McCord as a middle name. In Jeannie's honor."

Tears shone in Harrington's eyes. "I'd like that."

"Me, too," Liam said, holding his wife's hand.

That night, Shelby lay in bed, Liam spooned against her back, his arms wrapped around her. A breeze fluttered through the bedroom windows and ruffled the sheet covering them, goose bumps covering Shelby's very naked body.

Making love with Liam was everything she'd dreamed it would be, everything she'd fantasized about.

She hadn't felt this happy since she'd held Shane for the first time in the Wedlock Creek Clinic. Since she'd held Alexander for the first time and felt in her heart—long before her head caught up—that she was his mother, too.

Liam stirred, his hand moving up to her hair, then down to her shoulder. "I could get used to this," he murmured.

"Oh, me, too," she said, turning over.

"I love you, Shelby Mercer."

"I love you back, Liam Mercer."

"And I love our family." He sat up and reached for the glass of champagne they'd had to celebrate their new status as a "real" husband and wife, every wonderful, messy moment life had to offer. He held the glass up. "To us and our family."

She sat up and clinked her glass with his. "To us and our family. Forever."

"Forever," she repeated and kissed him.

They put down their glasses and lay facing each other, Liam caressing her hair, Shelby trailing a finger across his sexy chest.

"Waaah!" came a little cry from the direction of the nursery.

"Waah!" came another. "Waah!"

"I think the first was the multiple known as Shane," Liam said.

"And the second was the multiple known as Alexander."

"Waaah!" the cry came louder. One of those *come get me this minute* kind of cries.

"I've got it," Shelby said, getting out of bed.

"*We've* got it," he said, scooping her up in his arms and carrying her to the nursery, kissing her along the way.

Epilogue

Some months later Liam, Shelby, Alexander and Shane sat in the county courthouse, listening to the family court judge talk about how nicely this whole baby switch thing had turned out. A family had been brought together.

Shelby heard sniffles behind her and turned around. The entire Ingalls crew was dabbing tissues under their eyes, Norah full out ugly-crying.

Shelby grinned at her very emotional younger sister. Norah was half-crying tears of joy and half-crying from being very hormonal.

Her single sister had just discovered she was pregnant…with triplets. According to Aunt Cheyenne, maybe just stepping foot into the Wedlock Creek Chapel could bring multiples into your life.

Shelby's attention was taken by Harrington Mercer,

who sat in the row across the aisle from the Ingallses, a giant stuffed kangaroo, complete with a baby kangaroo in its pouch, on the seat next to him. His wife and son and his cousin Clara sat on the other side of Harrington.

Finally, Shelby and Liam stood, each holding a baby, Alexander and Shane in matching little brown Stetsons.

"It's official," Liam said. "We're all Mercers."

"Real Mercers," Harrington whispered.

Liam smiled and squeezed Shelby's hand. She knew what that squeeze meant. That everything about their family—the Mercers, the Ingallses and Liam and Shelby's marriage—had been real from the get-go. It had just taken them a little while to realize it, to catch up to it. Head and heart, heart and head. Now they were in sync.

And they were off to the Ingalls-Mercer wedding reception 2.0, this time at the Mercer mansion, which Larissa had gone way overboard on preparing for the ceremony and reception. *Lavish* was her mother-in-law's favorite word. Fine with Shelby. This might be a very real marriage, but it felt like a dream to Shelby. A dream—and a legend—come true.

* * * * *